Benedict O'Boyle

BenedictsCraft Publishing
Calle Comercio, 1
Niguelas, 18657
Granada, Spain
Benedictscraft@gmail.com

ISBN 978-84-09-61956-6

Acknowledgements

Thank you to the 65 first-readers club, especially Steven for the excellent and encouraging feedback and others who picked up on various errors that my brain had refused to see.

Thank you to all my family, friends and teachers for the love, support and lessons and to Tom O´Boyle Designs for the awesome cover artwork.

Special thanks to my *sand-pit friend* Elizabeth, who has always been there in life and literacy and encouraged me to start working on this novel with the words,

"You are already a writer, go and write"

Benedict O'Boyle

Dedication

This book is dedicated to my parents and my daughter, who taught me the most important lesson in life, how to be a father. Love you always.

Enjoy the adventure, I loved writing it.

Solution 65

Nobel Sacrifice

by Benedict O´Boyle

1

There wasn't a cloud in the brightening pale blue sky. As the threatened to crest the buildings and cast out the cold shadov night, a fresh breeze drifted low along the cobbled high stree disturbed yesterday's papers and the gentleman sleeping underneath. Opening an eye he couldn't help but read from propaganda blanket.

CELEBRATE TOGETHER IN UNITY, JOIN UP T

The Solution Celebrations are upon us!

"Eighteen years have passed since our bold nation v one, to give opportunity and equal freedom to all. When c mighty government introduced their radical new idea, So Sixty-five. There was a moment of childish panic and out some more closed minds, but the collective wisdom of ou and courage to embrace change won through.

Our acceptance of individual sacrifice for the gooc and a motivated public ready for the opportunity to flou the foundations for real change in our country and then more across Europe and the World."

That promise to financially reward the uptake of an optional end of life management plan; the Solution became supported by the majority of the country as we grew together. In an un-United Kingdom - post pandemics and recessions - overwhelmed by poverty, homelessness and unemployment, something radical had o change. The steady flow of climate change refugees and those leeing wars over remaining fossil fuels and freshwater aquifers in he Middle East and Africa was too much for the fragile conomies and societies of Europe.

"A splintered country, failed health service, broken banking stem and a weak government all needed change. How far we ive come with a little sacrifice. The economic burden of a owing elderly population is no more, gone is the torturous wait r death of the terminally ill. No wasted years, being kept alive nger by pharmaceuticals, clinging to an unnatural life and in ing so, costing the state and their families money until destitute. longer do we need to leave the future generations with our bts, instead of inheritance, just to die "in dignitas" at in-human es."

When the solution was tabled initially, the predictions of a lic outcry that would halt it in its infancy had overlooked the erty stricken, overworked and desperate souls who needed e of another life or at least one for their children.

Solution sixty-five had started as an optional euthanasia plan, reby any citizen who opted to voluntarily end their life aged y-five (or before, should they wish) thus unburdening the state society as a whole, would receive sixty-five thousand pounds ompensation. Walk-in euthanasia clinics opened in every city,

with immediate transfer to a chosen account. Initially they were overwhelmed, suicide rates dropped to zero, the pressure on the health service from the terminally ill was instantly relieved. Those with treatable illnesses found a financial solution to their medical bills. The population began to decline to a more sustainable level. Statistics across the board showed a happier, healthier, more productive society. The economy began to boom. Inheritance was received and spent. Small businesses bloomed as young and old adults alike signed up to Solution sixty-five and received their personal injection of capital.

When they started signing up prisoners in exchange for early release and offering Solution Sixty-five as an alternative to prison sentences, crime dropped and the police, courts and prison services all experienced a much needed relief and reversal of mounting pressure.

"We should be proud of our progress as a nation and its great leadership. We must not waiver in our goal of a global solution as more countries adopt our model, our solution for a better future for all. When cancers, lung and heart disease, diabetes, environmental change and increased global violence threaten our old age anyway... why not be part of the solution to decrease the population and increase quality of life now.

With the flow of displaced humans from around the world. We need to do more to help our community, society, country and planet. We need to make brave choices for our lives now and our next generations. Do it for your children and yourself. Live life now. Sign up to Solution Sixty-five this weekend for an anniversary that will make a difference.

Our beautiful islands are blossoming, our strong leadership strengthening our borders and protecting it from pandemics and those that carry them. The more temperate weather with blue skies and hot summer months, the heavy raining season ideal for farming and water collection and the surrounding ocean allowing for desalination at most coastal cities. Our United Kingdom, is now a safe haven for any disease-free, able-bodied, English speaking refugees of oppressive nations, with their antiquated thinking and selfish refusal to unite for humanity. We stand against those countries like Portugal, Andorra and Cyprus who actively challenge our brave new world with their treacherous protection of criminals and cowards who choose to run from their responsibilities and debt to society."

The United Kingdom still has problems, growing unemployment in sections of the community burdens the hardworking, paying for those ineligible for the Solution due to existing illnesses that already weigh heavy on the taxpayers. Personal health and contribution to the community is our social responsibility, if your life expectancy is less than sixty-five, you cannot contribute or benefit.

Improve your health now, get a scan and sign-up

We must convince the "lifers" who refuse to improve their situation, that they are letting their children and community down with their stubborn refusal to enrich their time on earth and our time as a whole. Their selfish attitude is not that of the Great British people as a whole. The flourishing "livers" are climbing the class ladder and owning their own homes and businesses, creating economic growth and fueling progress. They travel the world and get the most from life before letting go. Their children are gifted, not only the chance to say goodbye, but with opportunities afforded to them as their parents hard earned money is not wasted on end of life treatment in a miserable care home. They live life now, fast and bright.

With the bonus of free health insurance for you and your children up to age sixteen, we are protected against the worst and together are building the well-being and immunity that keep our islands safe. It is our duty to show the next generations that we care about them and our future on this planet, they should give their responsibilities at sixteen careful scrutiny and do the right thing for their community.

The environmental battle hasn't gone away and climate change is a spiraling sycamore seed, that will eventually crash to the ground. Live life while you are young.

For our younger readers... Sixteen year old citizens who sign up this weekend will get free driving lesson vouchers with Gov-Drive. Learn to drive and keep the nation moving.

With our combined efforts and those of our sister nations we are slowing climate change. Using their new capital, people are able to be creative in business leading to a growth of start-ups including many Eco-companies, whose sole mission is to invest their money and time on our planet to try and save her using green technology and sustainable agricultural development for our future generations. Mother Earth will be fine, it's us we need to save and Solution Sixty-five is working for our Great Britain as we lead the way with our innovation and integrity..."

Mike Higgins stopped reading and put the paper on top of the others, it was the same bullshit rhetoric from the very system that had profited from '65. The rich got ever richer, as the newly affluent consumed more crap they didn't need. Mike liked reading but there wasn't much variety for him now the public libraries had all closed down.

Keep 'em dumb, unhealthy and busy and you keep control, he said to himself.

Some people got the step up they needed, but many blew it and ended up right back where they started or worse. It was all the usual vices for Mike, drugs, alcohol and gambling. He didn't need The Solution to make his mistakes or learn from them.

"No point sitting here sulking about the system, least it's not raining." Mike muttered. He yawned, stretched his big arms, exhaled and waited. Nothing. That was six days now without the hint of a cough and five months without a cigarette. He was feeling pretty good.

"Good work lad." He said aloud, acknowledging he still needed affirmation.

Mike was talking to himself more these days, but solitude will do that and sometimes the only way to get a sensible conversation, is to talk to oneself. It wasn't like he had a lot people to talk to. Only one.

Mike stood and stretched again, letting the reams of his newspaper blanket fall to the floor as his bear-like frame filled the doorway. He was getting too old for this shit, he'd enjoyed some of the driftin' and always liked seeing new places, even with the Army, but park benches and doorways were a young man's game and he was tired, every inch of his broad 6'8" frame ached. There were less of his friends around now, the guys who had served in the Forces and were on the streets, people who understood his peculiarities. Most homeless guys died a decade younger than they would have, so he'd lost a few of the older guys over the years, it was easy to get sick out here with the pandemics around. A cashless society and the outlawing of begging added to the consequences of "the life". Mike had stayed in the abandoned high-rise towers for a few years, with others who wouldn't or couldn't sign up and as a result quickly couldn't afford to keep up. Once the water and power was cut it went from a delicately balanced community to a dystopian nightmare. Gangs and the resistance groups vying for control. Mike moved into the woods.

Most homeless guys, if healthy enough signed up to the solution straight away and others caved and got chipped-up eventually. Filling their pockets with silver, giving up freedom and believing the new whispers of a system that had never had their backs. Everything quickly got really expensive as inflation bit, pretty soon they were scraping by in crappy flats barely better than the towers.

Mike collected the newspapers before the breeze could take their pages, leaving them folded and neatly piled in the corner of the doorway. He picked up his heavy rucksack and slung it easily over his shoulder slipping the other arm through the strap.

The sun warmed his face as he wandered down the pavement, easing his bones. None of the worker bees were out yet, so he'd have to wait for the generosity of a coffee or croissant for a bit, but he didn't care; he loved this time of the day, when the sun has risen just enough to touch the streets and bring them out of their frigid slumber. He jogged through the park to warm his cold body, along past the lake. Happy in solitude. When he ran here during the day, there would be slow joggers to avoid, clutching their energy drinks, or the 'bloody' cyclists whizzing along with their 'idiot plugs' in and mums with prams, three-abreast, and dog-walkers always stopping to pick-up mess, eager to avoid fines should a police drone spot them while surveilling the park.

Sometimes Mike ran on the grass, making his way through the lines of kids hanging out in small groups, two metres apart. Many looked at screens, while stuffing that tasteless, high-sugar excuse for chocolate into their mouths. Smoking that shit government taxed weed and drinking that cheap government energy drink. Mike wanted to scream at them,

"*Wake up guys, don't trust the system! They want you fucking loaded on their crap!*"

They weren't all bad though, some would say hi, or give a nod; some

would offer water or food on his cool-downs, after stretching he enjoyed sitting in the shade of the Oak, lying out in the sun, or sheltering from the rain under a tarp, no such thing as bad weather. Occasionally someone would throw food or spit verbal abuse at him, but he usually had a suitable answer to their ignorance, that or a fierce glare.

Sometimes the youngsters would treat him like Rocky, cheering him on or racing him as he put the final sprint effort in, back to his tree. He was a modest guy, but he liked that. Not as much as he liked the inquisitive kids who wanted to talk; he always waited to be asked any questions, like why he was on the streets, what it was like, he was honest in his answers. Unfiltered.

Mike prepared his breathing, pushing the diaphragm down, lungs opening. A fresh spring morning, glistening green of the dewy grass, insects buzzing in the trees and birdsong in the air, his gentle footfall breaking the silence. He sped up into a run and kept going, feeling like he could run forever. His black hiking boots had molded nicely to his feet now and although his pack was moving up and down without all the straps done up, he wasn't uncomfortable.

Today was going to be a good day, he could feel it. That sense of something you can't quite see yet, but intuitively know is coming. Mike, wasn't superstitious or religious, but he believed in a universal energy that if he was open to hearing, could help guide him. Mike had come to this conclusion the hard way having not listened to the universe, not seen the signs or worse still seen them and not paid attention. Some might call it intuition, but Mike felt it was more than that. Happier now he had left the vices behind and opened himself up to a more mindful approach, life was on his terms. He listened to the energy and was enjoying living freely, accepting the generosity of strangers and trusting that things would work out fine. They always seemed to in the long run.

It was a half hour jog to the community kitchen for breakfast. A volunteer opened by 7am to make porridge or maybe eggs. Aches in Mikes spine had eased with the run and the warmth of the morning sun, he slowed to a walk and turned the corner into the cold shadow of the big new hospital. It had been there a decade at least but was still new in his mind. Huge, with all the modern medical equipment required to keep those wealthy enough to have healthcare alive and healthy. The day reminded him that it was still young with a chill breeze and he lifted the hood of his jumper. His mind turned to coffee as the smell of fresh ground beans teased from the little maroon van that did a great trade with the stressed staff and visitors. This was part of his daily morning routine and often, if he hung about for a bit, a generous customer would shout him a hot drink. This morning he decided it was too cold to stand in the shade, he would wait for coffee at the shelter. It was cheap instant stuff, but it was warm and caffeinated, which would suffice. His eyes drifted back to the maroon van.

2

Mike saw the guy too late to get out the way, but just in time to drop a shoulder and protect himself from the impact. The man had flown through the entrance doors of the hospital and hadn't seen Mike at all, landing heavily on top of him.

"Motherfucker!" The expletive slipped out as they tumbled to the ground, the offender grabbing him with both arms as they went down and rolling on his back to absorb most the impact.

Mike was lying face up, with the rucksack in the guy's lap and him turtled on top. It wasn't an aggressive "*motherfucker*" just a statement of surprise, Mike wasn't a "whoops-a-daisy" kind of guy. Mike noticed the offending chap was almost as big as him and apologized with real meaning in his voice, as they helped each other up with a mutual grin.

"No, sorry fella! Totally my fault." the big guy said, slightly winded. "I was looking at my phone, sorry, I'm having one of those days..." He tailed off.

He was about 6'6 and athletic, maybe late thirties, clearly younger than Mike. Wearing smart khaki trousers and a crisp white T-shirt that enhanced his natural tan and muscular torso. With cropped blonde hair and a neat beard. Mike knew instantly he was ex-military, probably still active in some capacity, from the looks of the expensive smart phone he was distracted by when they collided. *Probably doing private work now, if he's smart.*

"Don't worry mate, no harm done." Mike shrugged.

They stood awkwardly for a moment, before the guy remembered his phone and started scanning the floor.

"Over there." Mike nodded to the chunky black mobile, near the edge of the pavement. The guy pocketed it and turned to go, brushing his khakis off.

"Cheers, sorry again."

"No problem man, hope your day gets better." The guy stopped and turned back.

"D'you want a coffee or something? Tell Jerry to put it on Hawk's tab." He waved an arm and gave a nod of the head at the van and then turned and broke into a jog down the road.

Mike headed back to the van and stood back from the counter until a lady had been given her drink. As she turned and saw Mike, the flash of disgust and judgement involuntarily crossed her face, before she composed herself and scuttled away. He had seen that look many times, he didn't care, he probably could do with a shower and some clean clothes, but his scruffy jeans and grey hoodie had life in them yet, the black "She Drew the Gun" T-shirt underneath could do with finally going in the bin. New socks would be good too.

***

"Jerry?" Mike looked for some sign of recognition.

"Yes, boss, what can I get you?"

"Hawk said, to put a coffee or something on his tab." Mike waited for a reaction.

"Cool guy, Hawk. One of my regulars, no problem my man. What can I get you, pastry, tea?"

The big affable guy in the van smiled a big wide smile that would have put anyone at ease. He had maroon overalls with Jerry stitched neatly in silver and black threads, his long dreadlocks, fell to his shoulders. Robert Johnson was playing softly in the background on the radio.

"Just a black coffee please." Jerry looked like he was going to say something, but just nodded instead.

Mike didn't want to take the piss out of Hawk's generosity, besides there would be breakfast at the shelter and a quality coffee for the walk was a gift from the universe, he didn't want to be greedy and spoil what was definitely going to be a good day.

"Could you put a splash of cold in it please?"

"No, worries man." Jerry replied. "Hawk would want you to have a pastry too man, he's a good guy..." Jerry said with a meaningful look. "Know what, I'll chuck in a pastry. If you want one."

Mike wanted one for sure. Never turn down free food.

"Cheers fella, that's very generous of you, I'd love a chocolate croissant."

Mike loved his chocolate as a treat, but tried to keep a healthier diet. He liked running around the park to keep fit and used the free exercise equipment. Not many people were in the habit of using them now after the pandemics. Mike was pretty healthy though. The shelter had fruit and vegetables from the allotment and food donated for those struggling by some generous "livers" who despite newfound wealth remembered where they came from and the struggles of others under this system. There were also donations from "pro-choicers" who just wanted everyone to have freedom and fought the growing control of the surveillance state.

Some "lifers" who passionately opposed the oppressive nature of the system clearly saw Solution sixty-five as designed to cull certain portions of the population and clear the nursing homes and ghettos. They still took the money for their own personal reasons and just moaned about the system later. It was a cull and it worked. But, despite the majority swimming with the current, Sixty-five wasn't for everyone.

"We all got to take care of each other man." Jerry said, handing over the coffee and two chocolate croissants. "What's your name?"

"Thanks man." Mike took the coffee. "My friends call me Bear."

"No worries Bear, stay safe." Jerry replied.

3

Arriving at the community kitchen Mike threw his empty coffee cup in the recycling bin and walked round to the front door. A mouth-watering smell of eggs and chorizo filled the entrance. It meant one thing. Tom Kind was back, he always made a little extra effort.

A damn good day.

***

"Bear! How are things? How's the cough?" Tom called out from the kitchen. Mike enjoyed his easy company, he was one of the good guys.

"Ghosted." He replied, shooting two big fingers at the door.

"I won't be a moment."

They couldn't be more different. Tom was forty-one years young, a carpenter of some skill. Good looking, with glasses that probably made him look smarter and an energy that could calm a wild animal. He was only 5'7" but was in good shape from cycling and running. Mike was turning fifty soon and having spent the last fifteen years mostly on the streets and in damp squats, he had not always been healthy, but his intermittent chesty cough had gone and his fitness was almost as good as ever since he'd stopped smoking, the one vice he'd allowed himself after casting others aside.

"Finally all better; thanks for the support mate. Had a jog over this morning, lungs feel great. That smells bloody marvellous." Mike said, as he lowered himself into a chair at the table nearest the serving hatch.

"We'll have to run soon. You hungry? Just finishing a batch now, 'Eggs Benedict' of course, ready in a jiffy." Tom said, middle-class and accent-free, as he poked his head forward through the hatch. He wasn't posh, his parents had been teachers, so as well as being able to read and write before he started school, correct pronunciation had been drilled into him.

The rush was usually around 8.30am for breakfast and most of the visitors were gone again by 10am. It was still quiet when Tom brought the plate out to Mike.

"Get yourself around these, chap." Tom plonked himself down opposite Mike.

"The chives are a nice touch. The effort is appreciated man." Bear said, as he enjoyed the flavors of perfectly light Hollandaise sauce sprinkled with chopped chives and scrambled eggs with spicy sausage.

"You're too kind." Tom wasn't a chef, but had learned how to cook pretty well over the past few years and had a talent for it. Mike was his biggest fan and the feeling was mutual.

"So, where you been?" Mike asked.

"You'd know where I've been if you were online." Tom said.

"Fuck that. Screens are poison man, Kryptonite to the free-mind. My phone stays at the bottom of my bag, it's been switched off for months."

Tom rolled his eyes, a little dig at Bear's conspiracy theories or "truth and lies" as Tom Kind preferred to call it.

"I know where you were brother; you were in Calais volunteering - building shelters, then in your studio writing or making something in your shed. Right, right...right?" Mike teased with a wry smile. "Don't need BookFace for that mate."

Tom replied with a couple of mock jabs to the body. Bear was a smart ass ...but that's how you knew he loved you, he was kind, gentle and respectful to everyone else, if he gave you some shit, you knew you were family.

"So? What you working on?"

"I'm making a walnut desk... and working on a Calais journal to spread the truth." Tom returned to his coffee. Despite his talents, he always felt uncomfortable discussing his work and taking compliments. "There's a tear in the back of your sweater, lots of donations in." Tom noticed the details.

Tom was smart, he learned fast, had strong opinions and to some people would have come across as arrogant. But Mike wasn't some people, he knew Tom was rightly confident. Bear had taught him backgammon and chess in no time, he had a green thumb and his cooking was better every meal. But, above all he was a man of integrity and Bear respected that.

"The chives are from the allotment. It's looking great mate, lots coming through now." Tom returned from the kitchen, placed a coffee next to him and let Bear enjoy the meal.

"I'll be there a few days this week if you fancy it, still lots to do." Bear offered. He enjoyed spending time growing food at the council allotment plots they had.

"You want some more? There's plenty left, there's loads of eggs..." Tom asked, standing up.

"...Bare eggs." Mike affected the local youth dialect, patting his stomach in refusal.

"Very good old chap!" Tom beamed as he headed back into the kitchen to get ready for the rush.

"You sticking around, fancy a game?" His head poked out the hatch again.

"Business meetings all day Tom, but I'm sure I can squeeze a couple of games of backgammon in." Bear tried the coffee, it was better than normal. "Good coffee?"

"Bought it in from home for us to use. couldn't have you drinking crap coffee when you're celebrating five months without a smoke mate. I'm proud, I hope you are." Mike smiled to himself. Tom cared.

Reading the paper Tom had left for him, Mike kept to himself as people came in and out, as he always did. He looked in the donations store and collected some fresh fruit. Grabbed a couple of pairs of black socks from the array in the big sock tub and a couple of "She Drew the Gun" black t-shirts from a shrinking stack of identical black shirts that had been delivered by a company with an excess stock of XXXL shirts; someone at a computer screen had pressed an extra X. Fortunately for Mike, he was about the only person they fit so they had lasted him well. Especially as he could wash clothes at the shelter while he had a shower and use the dry set in the locker that Tom had sorted alongside his own in the staff room.

If the weather was bad, Mike would occasionally crash there. Kind would take the floor and Bear the sofa and they'd talk for hours. Tom would invite him over, but people need their space, Bear especially. He didn't even like staying in the shelter unless it was really cold. Preferring the outdoors, a couple of tree branches for his hammock and the stars as a roof. By association Mike was trusted and a blind eye to the odd staff-room sleepover was accepted by a nice lady in management "*as long as it didn't become a regular thing.*" It didn't. *Don't take the piss* was a rule he stuck to.

After getting them both another coffee, today from a fancy looking French press, Bear collected his board from his locker with the key around his neck and placed it on the pine table with Jerry's pastries. Tom picked one up and ate it absently while staring into his coffee.

Sometimes they played in silence and other games they had long animated conversations about life, love or politics. There was no talk of TV shows or films, celebrities or popular culture. They were both disconnected in that respect.

Breakfast had been served and people had drifted on, Tom took the bins out and made a phone call, then returned after a short, quiet conversation. After shutting the doors and finishing the washing-up he joined Mike at the pine table and pulled up a red plastic chair.

They threw the dice to see who would go first. Tom lost.

"My lucky day." Mike played well, having often taken a small board along when he first served. Ready for moments of boredom, of which there were many in the Army, those were the ones he preferred to remember.

Mike was whites, he threw a five and a two, *perfect start.* Picking up one white counter from the five in the top left corner and leaving it safely on another of his rows seven moves away. Tom threw a five and a four, Mike grimaced for him, no way to leave a nine safe.

Tom paused for a moment, then moved a piece, forced to leave it alone and vulnerable to attack. Mike threw a three and a one and considered his options. Run one of the three home and cover it up safely, or he could go on the attack and hit Tom's isolated brown that was so close to its home.

"Sorry mate." He offered with a sheepish grin and a shrug.

"All's fair in love and backgammon." Tom said, rubbing his shaved chin and running a hand through his short hair, with an absent mind.

Mike picked up one of his pair of whites and snapped it down with his finger. Tom's counter was placed on the bar between the brass hinges. It occurred to Mike that they had seen better days, with greenish corrosion showing on the plates and a rusty colour to the heads of screws, a little job for later. Using the remaining one he'd thrown, from a stack of two he slid a counter one place forward leaving them both exposed. No danger just yet, Tom still had to throw a double to get back on the board.

Tom threw a double five, removing his piece from the centre and sending Bear to the bar.

"Back to the start for you."

Mike never tried to will the dice, some guys he played would say things like, "*Come on the sixes*." Mike preferred to respond to the result of the dice. It was pure chance what they would be and your choice of move would come thereafter. He knew the thirty-six possible combinations of the dice, the possible combinations to keep counters protected and the numbers that he didn't want. The probability of getting a seven was one in six, with six possible ways to get a seven with two die. Tom shouldn't have left himself vulnerable to a seven.

The game was shaping up nicely for Bear; Tom looked concerned, unusual considering it was only just starting and he rarely won against Mike or lost to anyone else, it was just for fun.

"Only a game, early days yet."

Tom looked at him dead in the eye for a moment and then opened his mouth to speak. He exhaled and paused, before giving himself a little nod and said,

"We've been friends a long while now Bear. I know I can trust you not to say anything, but I'm really in the shit."

This was a worry, this was going to be a day they talked about something real, as they often did when they spoke, but this was clearly bigger, much bigger. Tom was scared.

"You know I got you Tom, did you sleep with Kiri, the lady you were telling me about?"

"I wish." Tom replied as he took a swig of coffee and a deep breath.

"So mate, what's going on?" The backgammon had stopped and Tom Kind was searching for the words.

"I was in the Jungle..."

He regularly went over to the "Calais Jungle" with donations and helped the community of hard-working volunteers and displaced people there with anything he could. From running the wood-yard and fixing machines for firewood production to being on the ground, building and fixing shelters, helping wherever he was needed. Together they had almost succeeded in getting every one of the ten thousand refugees, men, women and children, living on a muddy, disused rubbish-dump in freezing Northern France - out of tents and into safe, secure, shelters.

"Jungle..." Bear prompted. Tom nodded and continued.

"The car was all loaded up, tools and my bag, ready to come back. I'm giving a lift back to these twins, Maia and Lawrence. They're fantastic, they do loads in the Jungle, shelter allocation and locations, children's centre, journalism, cool people..." Tom paused. "Anyway, the car is loaded, plenty of space for them when they arrive. Last coffee before we leave. I'm chatting to Rosie; incredible woman who takes care of many of the unaccompanied minors of there."

"Kiri's friend? Rosie that helps keep the kids under some level of control, gives them people they can rely on so they can begin to trust someone again?" Bear remembered the stories.

"Exactly. I'm talking to Rosie, about one of the kids, Mo. Mo's twelve, he had a shitty time getting there from Iran, lost family members back home and doesn't know if any of his family are still alive. He's run from violence in his homeland and survived untold suffering on his journey, only to find himself shin deep in mud and faeces in an illegal French refugee camp. The only thing he wants is to come to the UK and he keeps taking more and more risks with lorries, trains and more to get there. The kid is desperate."

Bear leaned in, fully engaged, fearing what he thought he would hear next.

4

It was a few weeks previous to their backgammon game when Tom had last been volunteering. There was little wind for a change on the sunny morning in Calais. The car was loaded, ready for the thirty minute "chunnel" train back to Dover. Leaving France at midday, he would arrive at eleven-thirty local time and turn his watch back, feeling like he had just travelled through a time portal and arrived before he left.

Tom appreciated the strong French coffee in the bright sun outside the volunteer base. Marie had made it as always, nobody would step on her toes when it came to the enormous morning brew, the volunteers all needed. Marie, was efficiency itself and didn't tolerate "helpful boys" in her kitchen, shooing any would-be assistants away.

On dry mornings it was pleasant to stand around in little groups and have a natter about the days' jobs ahead. It was later now and most of the volunteers were in the Jungle busy fixing doors damaged by attempted break-ins or mending roofs damaged by wind. Teams scurried around organizing food or clothing donations. Tom could hear the buzz of three chop-saws cutting up timber for fires, which meant they were all still working since he repaired them. The rhythmic sound of an axe splitting logs told him Paul was "in therapy". Wood was the main fuel supply for cooking and warmth in the refugee camp. There was never enough.

Tom enjoyed a little smoke, a habit he allowed only when not at home in England. Sitting on a white plastic chair he watched Mo, bowling a tennis ball at a sauce bottle on a box. He was getting closer every time. Mo, was wearing filthy, damp trainers, no socks, a dirty, once grey joggers and a navy t-shirt that said, "Just do it." Mo hadn't washed for days, probably weeks and he smelled like it, he didn't give a shit about that, or anything in fact, other than getting to the mystical UK.

***

First crossing paths in the Jungle, Kind has been stapling plastic sheeting to the pine baton frame of the shelters, when Mo had approached.

"English, give me." A young lad pointed at the staple gun. Tom had finished using it.

"Please?"

There were a limited number of staples, so when empty it would be useless, so it wasn't like he'd nick it. Kind had a unique policy of lending out his tools to refugees and they usually came back, even if they didn't they got passed around and used. Work happened faster if you let people help themselves, many had the skills but lacked the equipment. Other volunteers never lent tools as they couldn't afford to replace them, but some had adopted Tom's policy of - *a hammer in the Jungle is worth five in the workshop*.

"Please, give me, I need for house. One minute." Kind checked it for staples, there were plenty there.

"What's your name?"

"Mohammed." Of course it was, everyone's name was Mohammed.

"I use this to help many people Mo. What do you need to do? I'll help."

"Mo shelter, plastic, tck tck tck. Mo can do, Mo the man." His youthful defiance and independence was impressive. Tom gave the young character his staple gun.

"I'm Tom. You find me, bring back to me soon. I'm here, working." Mo nodded and headed off to his shelter to do repairs.

Later, Tom spotted his friend Marcus and waved him over. Early forties, six foot plus with long dreadlocks and an easy energy.

"Easy brother, what you on today man?"

"Just finishing up some shelters for the Kurds, three left after these, it's been a good day, teams are working well and some of the residents have been pretty helpful. You?"

"Couple of roof repairs and door latch fixes from break ins. The usual. You want a hand with these then lunch?"

"Always. Perfect timing, get yourself on roof duties big man, we'll need your aerial assistance for some of the shorter ladies...and me."

"You got any staples Kind?"

"Yeah, loads, you out?"

"Yeah, I gave a load to this kid, Mohammed."

"Shit man, I just lent him my stapler."

Marcus roared with laughter.

"You ain't seeing that again. He'll be running around charging a euro to fix peoples plastic, then he'll buy himself more staples and keep going. He's a little grifter that one."

"You say that like it's a bad thing. Good for him, smart kid. I hope my twenty-euro stapler makes him a hundred euros."

"You're something else brother."

"Shut up, you're awesome." Tom laughed.

"No, you're awesome."

This sarcastic encouragement was an ironic solution volunteers had found to the saviour complex that could develop while doing good. Marcus headed off with some staples and a broad grin, a Sudanese guy greeting him in passing with a high-five,

"Bob Marley, yeah Rastaman. Cool guy."

The volunteers continued building in the Kurdish area, just inside the new perimeter, now overlooked by the road. In the empty scrub were various caravans for families, the usual tents and self-builds. Some finished the insulation or roofs of nearly completed shelters, others prepped the mud foundations for the next floor. Picking up large rocks, old socks and nappies with a gloved hand and kicking and scraping the ground level as best they could. Materials were ferried to the site from the van and Tom directed where he wanted the three sets of components to go for an efficient build, each team's door, plastic, pallet floors and eleven lengths of timber, might as well be as close to them as possible while being out of the way for the other teams.

Tom helped the beautiful Kiri with a shelter, she was a Jungle pro. Marcus returned and floated around, helping anyone who needed it. The sun was out and there was little wind, it was a good day to be building.

The children from the caravan were bored and a four-year old boy insisted on helping Tom screw the base together. Using the electric screwdriver is probably the most fun he'd had for a while. Kind took his time. They built the floor together and jumped up and down on it to make sure it was solid. With a handshake on a job well done, he re-joined his friends.

"You're cute with kids." Kiri smiled, as Kind's cheeks reddened. The boy returned with his friends, but Kind couldn't let them all help and explained it wouldn't be safe. The children threw dirt on the shelter floor in disgust before Marcus, the "Rastaman" roared with an underlying smile that saw them scatter, laughing as they ran. A Mother scolded them and smiled at the group, they smiled back. That was enough.

They had the baton framework nearly done when Marcus was asked to go and fix a caravan window.

"You got this? One minute?"

"Go for it, I was about to take a smoke break anyway." Kind replied.

Kiri and Tom enjoyed a short respite from the physical labour. A very short break; as twenty-plus Kurdish men were heading in their direction holding crow-bars, hammers and other makeshift weapons, intended to intimidate. Kind whistled and gave Marcus a look, he was up a ladder fixing a caravan skylight, but could see there might be trouble.

Tom Kind moved towards the approaching group, away from Kiri and the others and attempted a smile. Now labeled as the boss, they surrounded him and they were not happy. Two of them had good English, one spoke as fluently as a British native. Tom didn't speak any Kurdish.

"We want you to stop building and leave. Right now, I want you to stop building, take your tools and leave here."

"Salam brother, I am Tom. What seems to be the problem?" Kind held out a hand. It was accepted somewhat begrudgingly.

"I am Raf."

"I'm sorry you are angry my friend, what can I do to help?" Tom put a hand lightly on Raf's shoulder and guided him away from the other men and volunteers, until they were alone.

"You do not build enough for us, you build for everyone else, many for the Afghans who makes trouble, we are angry. We Kurds are a peaceful people but we can make trouble if our people need it." Tom believed him.

"I'm sorry you are angry, we are trying, there are many people. Young children and women. We will build more for you. Can we please finish these? Your brothers and sisters have worked hard building and are hoping to have somewhere to sleep tonight." Kind tried.

"No. We will finish. You come here to build, you are slow, no organisation, shelters are not fair. It makes many problems. Who is your boss?"

"There isn't a boss really, we all just try and work together."

"See, no organisation. Who pays you to come and build, UK government?"

Tom laughed.

"We don't get paid. We volunteer; we all pay ourselves for the boat to come here, pay for hotels to stay here. Raise donations for the materials for the shelters. We are just here to help. No government, no money." Tom held his empty palms out, he was amazed that it had been assumed they were paid workers. Raf was more surprised to learn the truth.

"We decided we want you to stop, but I will speak with them and see if maybe you finish." Raf offered, his mood softening.

"Thank you Raf, I appreciate your help." They returned to their groups. Raf and the Kurdish men huddled and discussed options. Tom called a halt.

"Stop building, team meeting." Everyone who wasn't already outside and watching came out of the shelters and he explained the situation.

Tom phoned Lawrence, who spoke to Maia, who would be fifteen minutes, as she was on the other side of The Jungle. They packed their tools and prepared to leave. Insulation rolls were placed inside the shelters, in case it rained. He left a hammer, Stanley knife and nails in the centre of each floor. Everything someone needed to finish the build.

A young volunteer asked about keeping a hammer or crowbar handy, just in case. Tom couldn't blame him; it had crossed his mind for a moment.

"I don't want to see a single tool in hand. There won't be any trouble"

He sat on the toolboxes and had another smoke with Kiri. She was a little shaken by the experience, Kind put an arm around her and gave her a squeeze.

While waiting for Maia Strong - chief of shelter allocations and resolver of disputes, the Kurds were returning with greater numbers.

Tom asked Kiri if she wanted to leave. She did. He told her to go with the others and went to talk to Raf. Kiri didn't leave, but stayed along with the other volunteers, all unsure of what was going to happen next.

Marcus had returned and stood with Tom as they went to parlay with Raf and his friend with some English.

"We have talked. We want to build with you. We will help." After they had scared the shit out of the volunteers, Kind wasn't sure.

"No Raf, you have everything you need to finish, many men, many hammers. You have scared people who are here to help you and there are others who need our help." Raf looked down and with a hint of apology in his voice said,

"My friend, please, we can build together."

Tom understood he was in a difficult position, trying to manage and take care of his people, with a hundred angry opinions, trapped in this hell-hole. It was a reasonable compromise. Checking for a few nods from the volunteers, Marcus and Kiri smiled as Kind announced loudly,

"Okay. Together we build."

The other shelters were appointed Kurdish helpers and they got back to work. With the extra hands they even managed to free up people for another build.

Maia arrived with padlocks and keys, which Kind gave to Raf and Raf gave to the new tenants.

"Bit of drama then Kind? Sorry it took me so long. Jungle time."

"No worries Maia, I handled it."

"Obviously." She said with a smile over her shoulder as she walked away leaving him blushing once again.

"Awesome work brother, you should be a politician." Marcus gave him one of his big hugs with a grin.

"Fuck you man, that's harsh."

5

Tom Kind had parked the car outside the warehouse and kitchen, got a coffee and had a look around for any jobs that needed doing. He cared about the volunteers and the refugees, he cared about the homeless and the environment. His ex-wife had said Tom cared too much. Can you care too much? He had been called over-sensitive, a champagne socialist, do-gooder and a hypocrite, but not by anyone who really knew Tom and not by those whose lives he'd touched. Most of the people who knew him here, just referred to him by his surname, "Kind". It just seemed to fit.

Kind approached Mo, still practising bowling at sauce bottles.

"Salam Mo, how's it going man?"

"Shit! No go UK. Fuck you Kind." Mo replied with venom in some of his best English as he missed the bottle with the ball by a centimetre.

"Nice to see you too Mo." Tom checked to see who else was about. Rosie came driving around the corner in her seven-tonne, four wheel drive truck at the same time and slammed on her brakes, fag in the mouth nearly falling out. She kicked the door open and jumped down.

"Everywhere, I bloody go, there you are getting in my way Kind, what's your excuse today? Or, have you just followed me here so you can block me in with your fancy car again?" Rosie approached gruffly.

"It was only a minute Rosie."

"A Jungle minute, Kind." Everything took longer in the Jungle and someone else always said, "*One minute, one minute, you fix...*" It was never one minute, sometimes it was hours.

Rosie gave him a big-mamma squeeze, full of love and strength despite her slender figure. Rosie had wild, brown hair, streaked with grey, kept controlled under a headscarf. Her face was blessed with the lines of life, earned over many years of laughing, loving, crying and always helping others. Rosie was Tom's hero, in his eyes she ought to be sainted. She was good through and through.

"Giv' us yer fuckin' coffee then." Rosie reached, as they stood in the fresh air, under a blue sky.

"There you go, you hard-working, old woman."

"Come on then, let's see if Marie has got any pastries." Rosie said, turning to go.

"Are you going to leave that, parked there?" Tom nodded at the monster vehicle, blocking two vans and most of the track to the workshop around back.

"One minute, one minute. I'm around an' it ain't gonna fit in my handbag is it? C'mon coffee, breakfast." She strode away in her warm, woollen poncho, brightly coloured over her black trousers and boots, hidden bum-bag round her waist.

"Smash."

"Yeeeah!"

"Mo! F'fucksake, what you doing now you little bugger? Bloody carnage and chaos, wherever you go!" Rosie chided, with affection, looking at a small pile of broken bottles in a messy puddle of glass and red sauce on the floor.

"Why Mo? Clean this up. Trouble, trouble. You trouble, me trouble. Behave." Rosie seemed tired.

"No trouble Rose. Herc say, food no good, practice good. Practice. Practice, Clean."

"Herc... Interesting, okay."

"Herc good guy, get Mo more balls, more practice. Maybe *Herc* take Mo go UK."

Mo scowled at Tom as he put an out of date jar of tomato sauce on the crate.

They left him to it and went to see Marie. Tom noticed a brush and pan and bucket of water next to where Mo was bowling from, ready to tidy up afterwards. A good kid really. A tough, hurt kid. Just a kid.

"So how's it going Rosie?" Tom knew it was shit, it was always shit, even when things were going better than expected. With over a dozen nationalities sharing the Jungle, ancient dislikes and new disagreements lead to incidents of violence and posturing. Iranians, Iraqis, Pakistanis, Syrians, Afghans, Palestinians, Egyptians, Eritreans, Sudanese and more. All crammed together in shelters and tents, with pitiful water and sanitation. Braving the harsh winds and rain of repeated winters in Northern France, waiting in the mud to get to family or friends "in UK". Some with job opportunities waiting, qualifications from good colleges in the Middle East; graduates, teachers, doctors, engineers, professors, designers, tradesmen, tailors, people with the skills, money and education to get out when they could and get to a supposed safe haven. Along with those who have nothing, they have left everything, lost everything and paid heavy prices. They wait in their thousands, men women and young children, even a new Jungle-born baby. Thirty miles from their sanctuary from disease and mud and squalor, away from the violence of the CRS border agents and their teargas, rubber bullets and batons.

"It's shit, Kind. You know that."

"Yeah, but shit, shit, or really shit?"

"It's fucked, I'm really worried. You know what happened last time they cleared a section."

Tom, remembered when they were so close to having everyone out of tents and in shelters, the CRS closed half the Jungle, bulldozing the church and mosque to create a clear zone in front of the motorway for their teargas and rubber bullets. Volunteers had arrived en masse to literally pick up shelters and carry them across the Jungle through camps, past and over tents and shelters and rebuild where they could. They had done it despite the odds and it was credit to the collective spirit of those volunteers and residents. Tragically, over one hundred and twenty children had gone missing during that stressful and uncertain time. Choosing to trust the intentions of strangers offering security and hope. Tom hoped at least some had found that.

"Mo's out every night, trying to jump onto trains or lorries, hanging on the underside of trucks. He's obsessed. Mo go UK, Mo go UK. He doesn't know the UK is as fucked as anywhere, with or without their moat. He thinks if he gets there, it's all easy from then on. If he doesn't die tryin'. He walks miles back, covered in bruises, no shoes from where the CRS have caught him. He's fucking twelve for Christ's sake. He's just a bloody child. He's going to die here; I'm just waiting for the call."

Tom could tell Rosie meant it, as she forced back tears, she loved Mo fiercely and all the other unaccompanied kids she looked after. They had lost kids before, too many. Mo needed the extra care, but Tom could see she was exhausted, she had been here years and worked harder than anyone to keep the women and children looked after and the male leaders communicating through meetings. Everyone respected Rosie.

Tom went and checked the car and moved some bits into the back seat where Maia would be sitting, making space in the boot for any muddy bags or kit. Lawrence and Maia should be there soon and would be joining him for the trip back to save on their volunteering costs. Twins in their early twenties from Kent, they were always working hard to do their part. Lawrence was handy at most things from film-making to building and Maia had been key in assigning shelters to the most vulnerable first. For a young, beautiful, blonde woman, with an angel's face and the kindest temperament, it was an incredibly tough job that she handled incredibly well. The screaming men, demanding they get a shelter next, the young scared boy who wasn't at the top of the list yet, she held her composure. Tom respected her greatly.

As Tom Kind walked back towards Rosie, he could have sworn he heard a voice.

"*Do it, you know it's right.*" There was nobody there. "*You know it's right.*"

Tom knew it was the universe quietly speaking. He had heard it before and both listened and been grateful and at times, ignored it to his demise. As simple as the voice that tells you to take your ID to work, when the gate-man knows you. On arrival there's a new guy, because the usual one is ill. That shit. The universe speaks to us all, you just have to be open to listen. The universe speaks. Kind tried to listen. It wasn't always a voice, sometimes it was a sign or a feeling. This time it was as clear as a bell and there was no ignoring it.

"*He's just a kid.*" Mo was the same age as Lucy, his niece. What would he do if it was her stuck here taking these risks? This was a human child, who had been through hell. It was illegal, but fuck the law. If the law allows this, then the law is an ass. Legal routes hadn't worked, even when it was declared that unaccompanied minors could come to the UK, the doors were never actually opened. Tom worked through the consequences. A hefty fine for starters. Money versus a life. Easy choice. Prison? Kind knew he wouldn't do well in prison.

"I'd be someone's bitch by brunch." Tom had once observed, before a friend enlightened him to the fact, brunch was unlikely served in prison.

No brunch and high risk of sexual assault...tough call. Tom had another smoke, on his own.

"*Integrity. Do it. It's right.*" The universe spoke again. Tom stubbed out his cigarette and walked over to Rosie.

"I'm going to the car, I go UK." Tom told Rosie as he passed. "I'm going to leave the boot unlocked and get another coffee."

Kind looked at Rosie then looked over to Mo, now cleaning up the broken glass and sauce.

"We need to talk. Come with me Kind." Rosie dragged him around the corner and spoke in hushed tones.

"Have you really thought about this. I mean really. It's seriously risky." Rosie pressed.

"I know that. I've had the van searched every time I go back. I'm in the fancy car though, I've had a shower, got clean clothes on, I look like a tourist."

"You know what happens if you get caught?"

"I know, I know. It's fucking insane. Do you honestly think he'll end up getting himself killed?" Rosie didn't need to answer that, her face said it all.

"I'll go to my car and then get a coffee." Tom Kind resolved, feeling sick.

"If you get caught, he'll say he snuck in. Stick to the story, he's a good kid, he won't snitch."

In the sun, Tom drank another coffee and wondered how many cups that was today and what prison might be like, the coffee was almost certainly terrible. He spotted Maia and Lawrence as they came through the gates with their bags and gave them a wave.

"Maia, Lawrence, bonjour."

"Hey Tom, is the car open?" Maia's eyes smiled at Tom.

"It should be open, but the boot's full, so chuck stuff in the back."

They said their goodbyes and made the usual promise that it wouldn't be too many weeks before they were recharged and back to help.

"Let Aunt-Rose know you got back safe." Rosie said as she gave Tom a big squeeze.

"You know I will."

"Where's Mo today, Rosie?" Lawrence asked.

"He's around somewhere, probably getting into trouble... Safe journey." Rosie walked away.

6

In the boot, quarters were cramped and Mo was already struggling to breathe normally. He tried to wiggle himself some space, but he was wedged knees to chest, with bags around and on top of him and a hard box pressing against his shins.

***

The trio in the car talked about progress in the camp and plans for the future. The youngsters had energy and passion. For now, Tom's jug was empty and he needed time to refill, before he could continue to fill the cups of others. It was emotionally and physically exhausting to be there, and to leave. Turning away from the terrified parents, struggling to stay positive, with the smiling children, reading their books and learning in a damp, cold hell. Coughs gradually getting worse. Leaving the long term volunteers there to steer the ship and friends like Naseer and Arif in the "Hamas" who used his generator to charge Tom's drill batteries and gave him free showers and haircuts as reward for his hard work. There were so many good people, but he needed a break, it was time to pass the baton and do good at home, find somewhere where the odds weren't so stacked. This was like fighting a tsunami with a teaspoon, every time they made progress, giving displaced humans the safety and security of a shelter, more were destroyed by the authorities desperate to keep the refugees a defensible distance from the road should the lorries start to queue and become targeted. It wasn't a Palestinian or Yemeni scale atrocity, watched on screens by the masses through apathetic, if sad eyes. It was two governments ignoring the plight of innocent humans, two countries and their people not doing enough to help these victims of circumstance, each pointing at the other and saying - not our problem.

"Can I turn it up?" Lawrence asked, having taken the passenger seat. Partly as he was the eldest twin and partly to keep his sister from making eyes at Kind. He was a great guy, but as he told her, way too old for his sister. She was free to make her own choices, but Lawrence reckoned it was trouble.

"Yeah, crank it!" The tunes went up, Tom put his foot down, the car surged forwards with a low growl and Kind did his best to act normal.

***

On arrival at the port they followed the signs and wound their way to the back of the queue for the train under the channel. At the bottom of a ramp it opened up to passport control, Kind chose a lane, took a breath, counted to three and centred himself.

They had to pass through UK customs,where many vehicles were checked thoroughly, from numerous previous searches, Tom knew if that happened it was immediately over. All vehicles had to drive through an X-ray machine as well as the random spot checks, less random if you were in a dirty van and they thought you had connections with the Jungle.

The French were the first authorities to pass, but usually they just waved you through, the UK's problem. If you made it past the

UK authorities and on board you were pretty much safe. With no checks in Dover, once the train pulled out, they would be home free.

"I'm going to tell them we were on holiday visiting a Uni friend in La Madeline, Lille, hopefully we can fly straight though without any Jungle bullshit." Tom suggested. Kings of Leon played as they queued.

They passed through the big X-ray machines, the French customs officer glanced at the passports and then the screen in front. Tom focused his breathing and tried to look nonchalant. It could have been that a man pointing at a blurry screen is a cheaper deterrent than an X-ray machine that works or that the tools and items shoved in the back stopped a clear image of the boy crammed in the boot; but there were no alarms or lights. The officer waved them through, too hot to work hard today. They moved on.

"*I wanna beeee somebodaay*." They sounded pretty good together, pulling up to the UK customs window, lowering the music and window so the uniform in the office could ask for passports. Tom lifted his prescription driving glasses so he could make eye contact.

"Business or pleasure, sir?" The uniform checked the chaps ID's, peered at the back window and looked again at Maia's passport.

"Pleasure, visiting a Uni friend in Lille."

"Could you lower the back window sir." Kind pressed the button once and the window slid down. "Very nice, I've got a friend in Lille, where about?"

"La Madeline." Maia said through the open back window with an elfish smile.

"Lovely." The uniform replied with a smile. Looking at Maia once more for luck, before handing the passports back. "Thank you. Safe journey, sir. Straight on to the train follow the signs. You can turn the music up again now, classic album."

The dial was turned up with a grin and a thumbs up, Kind pulled away. Driving past the currently-full vehicle spot-check area, to join the back of the queue in the waiting area. As soon other cars joined the wait and vehicles boxed him in behind and lined up either side, he felt safer. Anonymous. They were just another car in a row of queues, waiting to join the hundreds of vehicles snaking onto the train.

Kind got out and lit a cigarette. The man in the high-visibility jacket with clipboard was four lines of cars away, he had some time. Inhaling deeply he enjoyed a last smoke in France and at the same time looked forward to giving his lungs a break. Finishing the cigarette he decided to take a gamble.

***

It was tight in the boot and after forty minutes, Mo couldn't feel his left foot where it was wedged, or the left arm he was lying on, his legs were cramping and he was thirsty and sweating. It was getting harder to breath and hotter too, with no light or ventilation and crushed by tools, bags and boots, he felt trapped. Controlling his breathing the way Rose had shown him, he kept calm. They would let him out, he would go UK this time. "*It's okay, Mo, it's been worse, you tough Persian, no fear.*"

They moved and stopped, noises and voices, any moment expecting the trunk to open and angry hands to grab him and start beating him, again. They went up and down, around tight bends and eventually came to a stop. Mo felt faint, he stank and could barely breathe in there, he would rather die here than get caught though. Wouldn't he? The engine was turned off. More voices... Any second now, he would be caught for certain...

The boot opened and all he could see was light, fresh air hit him like a wave and he breathed in as Kind lifted a toolbox and blanket out and said,

"You go UK." The boot shut again.

In case anyone was watching, Kind took a spanner from the toolbox, pretended to fiddle with a nut on the seat-belt and put the spanner away and the tool box in the back with Maia and their bags. Maia looked confused.

After a short wait they drove onto the train, Tom had kept it tight to departure, wanting an excuse for the boarder forces not to hold him up at customs. They sat and talked, engine off. The lady came round with the wheel chocks and checked handbrakes. After what felt like an eternity, the train pulled away and headed under the English Channel - Kind could breathe again.

"Sorry about the toolbox. I was making space in the boot, not a lot of breathing space in there." It took a minute, but they twinned and turned together.

"Who?"

"Mo."

"Mo! No, fucking way, you serious? Mo!!! Amazing... the balls. I had no idea, how the fuck did you pull that off?"

“I couldn’t say anything Lawrence, I needed you guys to be as natural as possible. You were both perfect.”

“Lille, Kings of Leon, customs, shit man, you were ice... wow Kind, just wow.” Maia folded forward the back seat next to her as much as she could with the bags and leaned in.

***

A light appeared above Mo’s face. His cramping legs and breathing were better without the toolbox, but it was still hot and stuffy. He pushed his face towards the opening.

“Mo?” Oxygen flowed in to the boot and he sucked it in, squinting through the gap.

“Maia, is you Maia?

“Mo! Yes, its Maia. Mo... you go UK.”

“Mo, go UK...”

7

The call was made and they parked up near a small church, down a quiet lane. Maia jumped out and ran round to the back of the car letting Mo out of his claustrophobic coffin of clutter. He fell down to the ground, his dead legs not yet awake. Lawrence helped him up as he stretched out the cramp, limping around. Blinking in the March sun, they hobbled over towards a little graveyard in front of the church and took a perch on the stone wall.

As they waited, over-looking a wide, untidy, dry, riverbed with abandoned warehouses on the other side, Tom wondered what the kid made of it all. Kind smoked a cigarette, despite his UK rule. Lighting up with Mo, sitting on a wall in silence, nothing needed to be said. They went for a wander, hours to kill. Mo walked around the old stone church, looked at the names and dates on the gravestones, the flowers in the graveyard, the yew, oak and elm trees at the back and the birds in the hedges. He didn't see the shopping trolley in the riverbed or the broken windows of the warehouses, Mo saw hope, beauty, safety and an end to his suffering.

The collection was done. Hugs with a tearful Rosie, handshakes and final words of advice given before Mo continued the first steps of his new life. Kind handed the rest of his cigarettes to Mo,

"I quit. You should too. Only so much luck."

"Thank you Kind, you good good guy. Mo go UK."

"It was an honour my friend, be good Mo, big chance now, please be good."

"Mo be good. I see you Kind?"

"Inshallah, Mo, Inshallah."

"Inshallah." Mo nodded in reply, future uncertain.

"Mo..."

"Yes, Kind."

"You owe me a stapler, tck tck tck."

"Fuck you Kind." Mo slid the van door shut with a huge smile and stuck his middle finger up. *This kid would be fine.*

The trio had a group hug and reloaded the boot, which now had a noticeable, 'teenage boy with rotten feet' smell about it that might never leave. Tom drove them to the train station and they said their goodbyes, he wondered when he'd see them again, for now he was certain, that was enough, he was out. Enough time, emotional energy, physical labour and personal risk, it was time to recharge and do some self-care.

***

A glass or two of red wine were on Tom's mind as he turned into the cul-de-sac and up the hill on which he had his two-bed terrace house.

Parking on his drive, he unlocked the front door and put the contents of the car in the hallway ready for washing or the workshop. Giving it a sniff, he decided the smelly boot could wait for tomorrow, it would be dark soon. Tom closed the boot and looked down the road, a strange feeling coming over him.

Probably just adrenaline. He saw Ms Charlotte his elderly neighbour coming up the hill with her shopping bags and made his way down.

"How are you Ms Charlotte?" he asked taking the shopping bags from her, long passed were times of proud protest.

"Thank you lovely, the arthritis is still bad but I'm still getting about. Use it or lose it son, I'm not a quitter."

"That's for sure."

"I see you've been away, you helping those migrants in France again? The TV said they're all men and some are terrorists. Are you sure it's safe?"

"Well the refugee children I read with and the mothers I spoke with weren't either Ms Charlotte. The men are looking for a safe life for themselves and their families, they all want to work hard and create a better life, nobody wants to be there. It might not be safe, but I wouldn't believe everything you see on TV, that's why I first went, to find out the truth."

"You're a good boy Tom, you're probably right, it's hard to know what to believe anymore, if the government had their way, I wouldn't even be here."

Kind put the bags just inside the porch and Ms Charlotte said her usual,

"I can manage from here, got to work my muscles a bit. Thank you Tom, you really are a lovely young man."

Tom's smile faded before he got to the end of her garden path as the police car pulled up, lights flashing. Ms Charlotte wondered if maybe she had been wrong about that good young man.

“It could be for a neighbour.” Tom said aloud, trying to convince the sinking sick feeling in his stomach and the tightness in his chest.

An officer exited the car and stood at the end of Ms Charlotte’s path.

“Mr Thomas Kind?” Kind nodded. *Shit. This was bad.* “Sir, immigration need to have a chat.” The officer looked down the road and back at Kind. No threat perceived, this guy wasn’t going to hop the fence and run.

An unmarked car pulled up behind the squad car and two men in plain clothes got out.

“Shall we take this to the station Mr Kind?”

“I’ll get my jacket and lock the house.” The uniformed officer followed.

Tom Kind got into the back seat and tried to smile at the bewildered Ms Charlotte watching from her porch as they pulled away to turn at the top of the road. She was still stood there watching as the two cars passed back down the hill, with that nice young man inside.

8

Tom rolled the dice and moved some pieces.

"So? What happened with the police?" Bear exasperated.

"Arrested, station, cold cell, plastic mattress for the night, early morning interrogation."

"How did they know?"

"X-ray machines in France picked him up. A more detailed scan is delayed, but they spotted him and they alerted the UK authorities of the number plate - they drove to my house and picked me up."

"Fuuuck man." Bear rolled and moved.

"Fuck man indeed."

"What's your lawyer say?"

"Very slim chance that I get off with unknown transportation - slap on the wrist. If I'm found guilty, I will get at least ten years prison or the option of signing up to Solution sixty-five and a three-year sentence. There's no proof I knew he was there or let him out, but you know what the Home Office and department of Justice are like these days. They could use satellite images of the hand-over to fuck me. Worst case my lawyer reckons they could rule that I was endangering the national health with illegal human trafficking of an un-vaccinated migrant - I could get twenty years with the Solution. Bail cost me a fortune and I had to give up my

International Travel and Vaccination cards so I can't run.... and they gave me this." Kind held out his arm and beneath the skin a faint blue light shone.

"Shit, they got you man. Can't you run? If you stay, your options are the solution and between three and twenty years of wearing lipstick. I don't see you have much choice."

"Okay, you know about staying off the radar and getting by. Say I run. What do I do?" Tom was well out his depth.

"Go home and pack light, get as much cash together as you can and leave. Don't withdraw everything, if all your cash leaves your account they'll know you're running and will send a private firm to collect their bounty. They don't fuck about. Dead or alive shit." Tom looked nervous.

"Leave where Bear. I can hardly hide in the park with this tracker." Tom rattled the dice into the box. They had continued to play automatically and the game was pretty tight until Tom threw a double-four allowing him to pass Mike's barricade and make for home.

"Hmm." Mike realised with that throw, he had almost certainly lost. He smiled and rolled.

"Calais." Bear announced.

Tom thought about it. Friends, potential transport, if he got there maybe he could disappear and get to Spain and away to a safe country like Portugal.

Kind edged ahead, taking counters from the board, in silence but for the die as they rolled and removed, waiting to see if a double-six might save the day for Bear. It never came, Tom won that game and Bear put the counters away and closed the box. Despite the rare win, Tom wasn't elated.

"Lucky day?" Bear asked with a sympathetic smile. "I'll put the coffee on."

While Bear made the brew he had had time to formulate a plan.

"Okay man, firstly - do you want to run?"

"Yes, I'm going to have to man, hell I want to get out of this oppressive, grey country and even with some luck, I'm looking at serious time."

"Right. Prep, go home, pack a rucksack, sleeping bag, food, water-bottle, clothes, money, useful equipment, knife etc. We'll be running and camping, pack light."

"Okay. Wait, we?"

"I need a holiday, like you said, it will be nice to miss the rain. I might as well hang out with my best mate." Bear put a hand on Tom's shoulder. "I've got you man." Tom had never felt so relieved. "Next, we get financed, you got any rich friends who could buy your house cheap for cash, do it."

"I couldn't sell the house that fast but I've got some furniture I could offer to clients at a good cash price."

"We get ready, then come back here. We cut out your chip and we head for France. Nobody is looking for people getting smuggled out of the UK, so it should be easy. They'll pick up your car reg' at Dover and give chase from London, that's all the head start we have. We need to get to the Jungle, hide the car and swap it for something inconspicuous like a van."

Thus far, Tom liked the plan, the cutting the chip out didn't sound fun, but at least he wasn't going to be on the run alone.

"Then what, keep running?"

"No, that's what the hunter will expect, we wait in the Jungle a couple of days, lay-low, volunteer. Blend in. Hopefully our pursuer will shoot straight by Calais."

"What if we got someone to drive my car towards Belgium, as if we're heading for sanctuary in Scandinavia?" Tom suggested.

"Perfect, if you know someone who's willing to be bait, like I said some of these guys shoot first and ask questions later."

"I know some people, but maybe that's not a great idea, I don't want anyone getting hurt because of me. Where are we heading?"

"Cyprus, Morocco or Portugal I guess, changing direction regularly and using any contacts we have to help us along the way, I might know a guy near Malaga, if he's still alive. Then into the Mediterranean and away from the European Solution agreement."

"When?" Tom asked, dreading the answer.

"Early tomorrow morning. I've got things to sort. You know what to do. We meet here at o'two hundred and we go. I'll book tickets."

Bear went back to the store room and apart from some oranges, removed the fresh produce from his bag and swapped it for tins. He grabbed some more clothes and an extra Sigg water bottle and nodded for Tom to do likewise. There were suitable bags in the donations and everything from sleeping bags to hammocks were there as required. Bear placed the backgammon board back on the shelf, someone else would have to clean those hinges.

"Okay, be subtle, meet here at two a.m. to cut the chip out and then we run."

"I'll see you then." He paused. "Thanks Bear."

"De nada brother, de nada."

9

Bear left his backpack at the shelter and jogged back through the streets and the park. The spring day had warmed up and there were groups of people, habitually spread evenly across the social distance grid, marked out with white chalk like a sports pitch. Some with masks on, others eating, drinking and smoking or in family or social bubbles, masks discarded next to them or on their forearms.

The usual bikes, runners and mums were out, kids and kites. Dogs and Yogis. A circle of teens all in black, looking morose, with ear pods in all staring at their phones like zombies. The pretty girls by the flowers, sat on the bench over-looking the lake, all made up for the park, taking model shots of each other for social media, or swiping left and right, only pausing to show each other their potential engagements.

A large group of jocks were drinking tall cans of GovBeer and snorting "rage" the new supercharged cocaine produced in Dutch labs. The usual young, testosterone filled obnoxious morons, with all their solution money but not the sense to use it wisely.

"Get a fucking job you parasite." One yelled, as Mike jogged by.

"Get fucking euthanized. For the planet and the kids." Another joined in, throwing an empty can, but not getting close. Mike ignored them and continued his jog down the channel between human clusters and towards the Oak at the end of the park.

***

"Bear!" He turned and saw Peter waving, sat with his friends in a social group, he weaved his way through the grid.

"Hey Peter, how's the cross-country going? You still on for a scholarship?"

"On track Bear, working hard in the classroom and on the running, promise."

Peter was a good lad and a gifted runner, as Bear had once discovered when Peter's friends had dared him to steal Bear's backpack while the giant slept in his hammock.

***

Peter crept closer and stretched out a hand.

"I wouldn't if I were you...I'm quicker than I look." A deep voice said from the hammock that hadn't moved. Peter decided that it was too late to back out now, grabbed the rucksack and ran. Despite its weight, he made a good start. He was tall for fourteen and strong.

Bear was out the hammock in a flash and with a roar, tore after the boy. Gaining fast. Fear and youth gave Peter an extra boost and quickly the larger, older man slowed. He never stopped, just slowed, like a predator, following. The smoking didn't help. Eventually, Peter got enough distance from the stalking Bear to buy two ice-creams and two bottles of water and walked towards Bear with a grin and the peace offering.

"You're pretty quick lad, do you train?" Bear wheezed.

"No, I just like running."

"You have talent and I'm out of shape. Maybe we should both start training. Thanks for the session kid."

They laughed and talked with their refreshments, then sat with Peter's friends. They were a nice bunch and gave Mike a glimmer of hope for the future. Peter and Bear remained acquaintances and occasionally joined each other on a run when their paths crossed.

***

Distracting himself from the night ahead, Bear chatted with the kids for the afternoon, enjoying early spring in the park, the company and the moment. Some having a drink, others a smoke. Talking about online exams, their infuriating cyber-teacher, the government and media, the system, consumerism, free-speech and free-thought. The solution always came up and lots of these kids were coming of age. Many of them had parents who had signed up; found success and a comfortable life, but a few of their parents were already in their fifties and the reality of the ticking clock, brought its own stresses.

Peter had already rejected the idea, his parents had managed with their jobs in nursing and accounting. He was doing well at school and should have no trouble securing employment and making his way in life with hard work. Others had bigger dreams or fewer choices; from poorer backgrounds, less academic, or without health insurance. They would likely be resigned to monotonous manual labour in a GovFactory or a GovLabour organisation with little hope of climbing up far from there. With that injection of capital, at an age when you can have some of your most brilliant ideas and feel most passionately about projects, it can be the springboard you need to make a comfortable life.

John, Peter's friend was a talented mechanic, but wasn't academic - without qualifications, money or insurance, he would struggle to find training and employment outside the GovVehicle network. John had created a business plan with his father to set up an small independent mechanics' shop, allowing him to be an "Autonomo" and work independently from the ever encompassing GovSystem - with fees and at a higher tax rate of course.

Bear never judged or offered a direct opinion, these kids had to work out for themselves what would be best, for them. He would probe and ask how others in the group felt about their friend's options, they would talk about their own choices and feelings and the fragility and unpredictable nature of the world, the human life span and what living really means. These kids were deep; even the ones who weren't stoned, they had grown up in this insanity. Bear appreciated the conversation and the shared picnic and they stayed until dusk and a cool evening breeze began to cut across the open grass.

"I might not be around for a bit, Peter." Bear confided as they said goodbye. "Can't say much more, but take care of yourself lad and keep at it."

"Thanks Bear, I will. Good luck, wherever you're going. You've got my contact details, keep in touch, and Bear... keep running."

***

The silhouetted Oak at the end of the park stood out against the fast darkening sky. While there was still natural light, Mike Higgins gathered what he'd come for. Around the back of the Oak, a shoulder-height bough had been removed. The tight circular rings showing the age of the ancient tree at its amputation. Using his Leatherman, he pushed the closed nose of pliers into a small knot in the centre of the disc and opening the jaws, he pulled the tool towards him. The round plug of wood, freed from the branch, revealed a hole. Reaching his long arm into the hollow trunk of the huge tree, with an armpit full of bark, his fingers identified a string, he unhooked it and fished up a small canvas sack. From inside he removed the large, "Bowie" knife in its leather sheath. A tightly rolled wad of notes in a beeswax cotton wrap and a small, heavy wooden box, smaller than a ream of paper. He shoved the wooden disc back into the hole, said good bye to the old Oak and headed for the shelter of a doorway. The knife shoved in his belted waistband at the front and the heavy box tucked in the small of his back. Out of the breeze of the open park, the early night was mild. Bear lay down cardboard and spread the neat pile of newspapers over himself and shut his eyes, early start and a big day tomorrow. He could sleep fast and never needed an alarm. Four hours should do it.

10

Whether it was the laughing or the wet that woke him he was unsure, but he was awake fast. Mike took in the situation; a howling, drunk idiot pissing on him. Not for the first time. Egged on by a couple of pissed-up jocks, with another hanging back. He recognised his aggressor from the park.

"What the fuck. You fuckin' animal." The papers fell as he grew to his full height in front of them, shoving the guy back with the palm of his hand. Grabbing the fallen broadsheets, he wiped himself down. The asshole finished and put it away, grinning. He was athletic and looked like a rugby player.

"You're the fucking animal fella, living in the gutter. Taking off people who work and pay their way."

"Yeah, sign up and stop being a burden on society you bum."

"Or, get a fucking job you lazy cunt." The third joined in. The fourth said nothing and looked uncomfortable.

"I done my bit for this... society." Mike growled and then paused. "I choose to live a simple life, away from control and consumerism . Without money or possessions. I've got everything I need and I don't take anything that's not freely offered. Where's the harm?" Mike held his temper. They weren't worth it.

"You're a dirty fucking tramp mate. You lot should be rounded up and euthanized, with the disableds and mentals." As

Mike walked away, towards the shelter for a shower and change of clothes. The drunk shoved him in the back. He staggered forwards, but didn't fall. He turned.

"I'd just leave it if I were you son. You're lucky you're not on your back already."

"Fuck you, Hobo. What you going to do about it?" His friends, moved closer.

"I'd walk away if I were you lads. I don't want anyone to get hurt. Just walk away." Bear tried.

The main prick moved towards him, his pair of testicles either side. Bears big hands were up, not in fists, but flat, palms out defensively. Piss boy, shoved him again, harder in the chest with both hands, Mike went over backwards, rolled to his feet and assessed his situation.

"He's a massive pussy."

Mike got to his feet slowly, breathing, watching. Hands up, palms out.

"That's enough. Last warning."

The asshole wound up a haymaker that Bear saw coming before the kid had balled his fist. It was blocked easily with a left forearm and he shoved the kid one-handed off his feet. The other two rugby tackled him to the ground and started flailing with irritating blows to the head. Protecting his face with his hands, he kicked one attacker hard in the knee and heard the crack of splintering bone as the joint folded and he collapsed screaming. The other attacker paused long enough at the scream for Bear to sit up and viciously chop him in the throat with the back edge of his huge hand, leaving him choking for air. Bear looked right just in time to receive a stamp to the face from Piss Boy.

The world span, dots of grey and white flashed across darkness and he felt himself fall back down and a boot land in his stomach making him feel sick. Bear could take a shoeing and had been through worse. He shook it off and grabbed a swinging leg, overturning its owner. Easing himself to his feet, he saw that there was only Pissy left. The observing friend had gone, probably to get the police. Tweedle-dum was doing his best to call an ambulance for Tweedle-dee and Piss boy was squaring up to him full of rage.

Bear needed to leave, if the authorities were coming this would not go well for someone carrying weapons with no fixed abode, against the word of these preppy college kids. There was no choice though, the guy came again, full of false confidence, ignorance and hate, arms swinging. Mike parried the blows easily and walked backwards defending himself, the kid threw a left jab that slipped his guard and caught Bear in the eye, a right upper-cut followed. It wasn't great technique, but he felt it hit his chin, the shock-wave absorbed as he set his jaw and took the punch with his thick neck. Instinct or training kicked in and seconds later it was over, a shove from Bear and a lighting right hand and the kid was falling back and hitting his head on the floor before Mike processed that he'd thrown the punch. Taking in the carnage around him, he checked the kids pulse, there but weak. Blood was coming from his head, but not too much, he'd live. Bear looked up at the building on the corner and saw what he expected to, a camera was pointed right at him. Despite the moans of the guy with the broken knee he could hear the sound as the camera zoomed in and he imagined his face, large on a screen at GovSurveillance. The clock had started ticking early. It was go time.

11

By the time Tom Kind arrived with his rucksack; Mike had already showered and
changed. His bag resting heavy on a chair by their table, knife and box carefully stashed and the wad of cash on the table.

"Shit Bear, what happened to your face?" After a quick explanation of the night's events, Kind took in the situation. "So, how are you going to smuggle me to France if you need to be smuggled out too? We're fucked."

"Not necessarily, we just need a friend. Know anyone going to Calais? We've got funds."

The wad of notes on the table must have been around twenty thousand pounds. Tom put his funds next to it. It was significantly bigger. Tom looked at Bear.

"Well...I sold the house to a shady solicitor acquaintance at the golf club, less than half value, but it was as much as he had in cash. Where did you get the money, rob a bank?"

"I've had the money for years. Services pay out. I keep it for emergencies. I choose my way of life man, I've always said that."

"I know, but I didn't think you meant it quite so literally." Tom divided the notes roughly in half and handed Bear a wad. "In this together now, might as well split the funds."

“We need an escape, fast brother, we got plenty of cash. Time to ditch that chip and get over the channel, who do you know?”

Tom took out his phone and put it on speaker as they waited for the ringing to cut.

“Kind, how are you man?” A deep, warm northern accent came over the speaker. “Are the Jungle drums playing true brother, did you do what I heard?”

“Yes, I did, but... Marcus. Are you in the city? I’m in the shit, I need some help getting out the country. It’s big, but I can pay.”

“Fuck they got you man... Anything brother and just cover costs, I’ve been meaning to go back to Calais for a while, I need out of here.”

Kind proceeded to update him on the course of events and their plan, as Marcus jumped in his van and headed through the city, phone on speaker.

“You still in Marcus. This could be dangerous.” There was a pause.

“I got you Kind, Cherry and I are on the way.”

After he hung up Tom looked at his friend, Bear gave a sympathetic shrug as he rose. They left their bags by the door, cash now safety secreted between them and headed for the kitchen.

“I guess now we wait.” Tom groaned.

The call came within forty minutes. Tom looked nervous as he hung up.

“It’s time.”

First-aid kit ready, Bear took his small Leatherman tool from his pocket and unfolded it. Mike heated the knife and the pliers over the gas hob in the kitchen and assessed the faint blue glow in Tom's arm.

"Try and keep quiet mate, this will hurt." Bear, rested the hot, sharp point of the blade next to the small blue lump in his friend's forearm and with a flick of the wrist, opened a slice that quickly produced blood. The chip was removed efficiently with the needle-nose pliers, Kind's eyes wide as he held his breath. Bear quickly dressed and bandaged the wound. There wasn't a sound, until the sigh of relief that it was over and the noise of an engine pulling up outside. They looked at the bloody chip, now flashing red in gory mess on the table. Bear clapped Tom Kind on the back as they grabbed their bags and walked out the door.

***

Marcus had arrived in Cherry, his red Volkswagen van.

"You sure about this man?" Kind knew what this favour could mean for Marcus.

"After what you did man, forget about it. We all need to take care of each other, besides I'm done with this country for a while, get in." They climbed into the storage compartment underneath the truck bed. Lying next to each other, Marcus shoved sleeping bags, boxes of shoes and bin liners full of donations (headed for the Jungle) either side of them until they were no longer visible.

It was an uneventful journey, save for their unusual location. It was reasonably comfortable and warm, over the rumble of tyres on tarmac they could hear Leonard Cohen, Nick Drake and Tom Waits playing loudly in the cab, Marcus knew what Kind liked.

Tom focused on the music and slowed his racing pulse. After the stop start and murmur of voices at Dover, it went quiet and from the rocking motion they knew they were on the train. Ironic Kind thought, when he considered his last trip on the channel tunnel crossing, how quickly one can become a refugee.

12

In the back of a camper van tea was poured by Mary, she kissed his cheek as she popped a sugar cube in his mug and handed him thc biscuits with a smile. Martin was an ex-professional skier. Medium height, with barely an ounce of fat, he was in exceptional shape for almost sixty-five. According to him it was mix of luck, exercise, diet and a nap at every possible opportunity. When awake he was always busy, reading or training, keen to live every last second of his life. A University professor once his skiing days were done, he spoke French, courtesy of his mother and Spanish from a period ski coaching in the Sierra Nevada. That was when he was young, before he met and instantly fell in love with Mary.

They enjoyed the tea, and the moment of peace, possibly their last.

Supplies loaded in their Hymer camper, they held hands as they walked through the car park, shoulders touching. They passed over the zebra-crossing and up the quaint village high street to a little drinking establishment on the hill. It was nearly Martin's birthday and he had met his love here almost thirty years ago to the day.

***

A young thirty-five at heart, full of confidence, but still reeling from the end of an exciting downhill ski career, his knees had finally shown their age and damage. The door swung open as he made an entrance into his local, already half-cut from the previous pub or two. Scruffy jeans and a black Sea Shepard hoodie.

"Good evening all, lovely to see you."

"Bolt... good to see you." There was real warmth, the collective showing of affection caught Mary's attention. Shaking various hands and heading to the bar, Martin was already aware of the new barmaid, like he'd notice if the beers had been changed or furniture moved. He also knew someone called Mary had been interviewed yesterday, an athlete needing extra income.

"Put that on my tab love." A cool looking guy in his fifties wearing a leather jacket nodded at the newcomer.

"Cheers Bart, appreciated fella." Martin winked.

Despite the outer cheer Mary could see a sadness and something familiar in his tired face. This guy was hurting. Not interested in damaged, handsome guys, she liked being independent. No need or want of a man. Mary was still empathetic.

"You must be Mary, welcome to the Reading Rooms. I'm Martin, I think you'll like it here." He smiled and held eye contact. Mary tried not to swim in their bright, blue pools.

"Thanks Martin. Have we met before, you seem familiar? You remind me of someone I went on a date years ago."

"Impossible I'm afraid, if we'd gone on a date years ago we'd still be together now." Martin grinned as the other barmaid rolled her eyes and Mary blushed. "So, what brings you here Mary?"

"I love the books, I love reading. I need the money. So, Martin, not Bolt?" This time there was a look from Martin that was almost bashful.

"You can call me whatever you like, Mary. If you pour me a pint of Pale." The eyes flashed at her again. They held each other's gaze and smiled, Mary blushed again and handed him the pint.

"So, Bolt?"

Martin, reached up to one of the many shelves of books and removed a book, next to a few more like it. Inside the cover he wrote his phone number and a short message.

For Mary,

"Live fast, try not to die!"

Love Bolt (Martin)

Mary raised an eyebrow, looked it over and realised who he was. Marty Bolt, the ex-Great Britain skier.

"You wrote this? I've always wanted to write a book. You're ..."

"Well, yeah. I was a skier, not a writer." The brightness in the eyes slipped away for a moment.

"It looks like you're a writer to me." Mary held the book up. Martin joined the end of the long table nearest her with a grin and was welcomed with pats on the back. Everyone listened to him speak like he was the only one in the room. Mary couldn't stop looking at him, he was charming, funny and engaging, everybody loved him... but Mary could sense more as he steadily put away the beers. This one was troubled.

The eye contact and flirting continued, between his numerous trips to the bar and bathroom. He was energetic and exciting but Mary had her career to focus on besides he must be ten years older than her at least.

"So, someone as lovely as you must have interests outside the dispensation of alcoholic beverages to the somewhat inebriated. What do you do for fun?" Martin asked, as Mary closed-up, an old hand at bar work. He finished the free beer she'd poured him after he offered to walk her to her car and the other barmaid had given her the thumbs-up.

"He's lovely, likes a drink. He's in most evenings and stays till close. Heart of gold, just lonely." She confided.

"I don't have a lot of spare time." There was an element of warning to the statement. "I'm actually trying to be a professional athlete too. I'm training for the Olympics, but it's tough. You know." Martin did know, training while working, limited funding and sponsorship. The diet, sleep. It was tough.

"What event?"

"Modern pentathlon is my focus, but I also do cross-country skiing and rifle shooting." The smile came to his face too fast to disguise. A fellow skier and a beautiful one.

"When are you working next Mary? We should talk."

"You know I'm working tomorrow; I saw you peek at the rota."

Martin grinned in admission.

***

At Mary's car she held his gaze for a moment too long and was helpless in the azure as he brushed a hair out of her eyes and leaned in. It was an incredible kiss, gentle yet passionate, Mary's walls came down and she kissed him back hard, her hands in his hair.

"See you tomorrow Mary."

"What colour are my eyes Bolt?" Mary called, as he walked away into the dark. He stopped.

"I've been unable to stop looking at you all night. They're hazel, but they turn green when you talk to me." The arrogance was unbelievable. He grinned at her, he was right they were hazel.

"And I know, you know, mine are blue. See you tomorrow, gorgeous."

Martin disappeared into the night. Mary got in her car, turned the keys and flicked on the light to the mirror. Her eyes were really green tonight, shit, he was infuriatingly lovely. *No. No. No.*

***

The following night, Martin had walked in wearing smart jeans, leather boots, a blue shirt and an All Saints leather jacket that had fortuitously arrived that morning from eBay.

"Bolt!" The collective greeting.

"You look nice mate, going out?" Bart asked.

"No mate, just for you. Pint of Pale and whatever Bart's having please Mary. I'd offer you a drink, but I'm sure you're not poisoning yourself."

"Thank you Martin, I'm training hard so won't, but feel free to tip well." Bart returned Mary's wink with a grin. Martin, handed a tenner over with a cheeky smile.

"Keep the change bar wench."

"Thank you, kind sir." Mary adopted a Dickensian accent and curtsied. "I enjoyed your book..."

"You've read it already?" There was a small nod of affirmation. Martin was clearly impressed and somewhat honoured.

"You write beautifully; it came from the heart, it really touched me. I'm sorry you had to stop what you loved." There was a wavering in her voice and she disappeared upstairs with a tray full of glasses before he could reply.

"Think you're in trouble there son."

"That's okay Bart, I like a bit of trouble from time to time." Martin gave him a gentle elbow and sat next to him at the bar.

"So, Mary... I googled you. Impressive, especially the shooting, I won't piss you off." Mary looked flustered as she concentrated on putting clean glasses away.

"Thanks, I guess."

"I've spoken to some sponsors and a friend at GB and if you would be interested in splitting your training between Pentathlon in summer and Biathlon in winter, he may be able to get you funding from the Winter Olympics committee..."

"Wait, I've been slogging for years and getting little support and you make one call and now they want to help me." Mary was indignant, but secretly excited and impressed.

"That's the game. Besides, it was seventeen calls."

Mary had told herself on the way home last night and the drive in today, that she wasn't going to start seeing Bolt, she needed to focus on her sport. Then she read his book; he was so sweet and honest and he understood the lifestyle. Mary walked round the bar and green eyes met blue as she kissed him on the lips.

"Thank you Martin."

"Call me Bolt, everyone does."

"I'm not everyone Martin." Bart shot him a look that said, I told you so son.

They talked about reading, writing, politics and sports and plans for the upcoming holiday period. They even got around to age, Mary being twenty-five and Marty being a decade older.

"I'm seeing family at Christmas, but this New Year I'm going to Amsterdam." He was clearly exited at the prospect of the city with the world renowned reputation for drugs and debauchery.

"Cool, I've never been, you going with friends?" Mary pretended she wasn't curious while thinking about what he would be getting up to there.

"No, flying solo. I thought fuck it, adventure."

"That's actually pretty cool."

"What about you? Training? Family?"

"Family and healthy Christmas with heavy training and then a bit of rest over New Years. Might just sleep, or work."

"You should come to Amsterdam, have a break." The words left his mouth before he knew they were said.

"I'd love to." They weren't the words Mary had meant to say, but they were the ones that came out.

Amsterdam was incredible and they had been living, loving, travelling and working together each other ever since. Mary had even helped Martin stop drinking and quit the mild coke habit he had been unsuccessfully hiding. Having given him an ultimatum early on, it was her or the drugs, he chose in a heartbeat and hadn't touched anything since.

***

A few days from his sixty-fifth birthday, Martin swung open the door of the bar and stepped in.

"Bolt... Mary, welcome back!" The collective beamed. The romantic older couple were still well known and well liked, despite less frequent visits than in the past. Mary looked at the shelves and spotted a copy of Martin's book "Black Ice" looking well read, a tired looking copy of her own autobiography, "Shooting in the snow" nestled alongside.

"Cider for me please and... Martin?"

"Pale, please."

Mary, paused and nodded. Bolt rarely drank these days.

"It's a special occasion and I know I'll need a drink for this one."

After their pints, Mary had a rum, Martin a whiskey. They said goodbye and took one last look at the place they had met, before holding hands and walking back to the camper in silence. Before climbing in Mary pulled Martin towards her with an arm around the waist, looking into his eyes, she kissed him passionately.

"All these years later, you're still as beautiful as the day I met you my love. Are you sure you want to run away with this old man?"

"Well, the camper's packed now, so I might as well. Besides if you hadn't signed up to sixty-five when I got cancer you wouldn't be running anywhere and I'd already be dead. So, in for penny in for a pound, sexy old-man. Let's cut these chips out and go have an adventure."

"I like it when you've had a rum." He laughed, as he slapped her bum affectionately and they climbed aboard, heading straight for the bed. Before they hit the starting gate and the clock started ticking - their story taking on a new chapter filled with urgency and danger - they enjoyed each other, mindfully appreciating every inch, as skin touched skin and they melted into one.

Showered and dressed, Mary got out the first aid kit and removed two scalpels from their sealed plastic bags. After recovering from her treatment, she had immediately signed up to the solution. Ten years without Martin was a very long time, decades ahead waiting for a natural death would be torture. They had agreed years ago to keep her solution money and prepare for this day, training, planning, they even had fake travel documents from a Chilean ski contact of Bolt's. They would not be separated from life or each other by death, not without a fight. They would run and live and love and laugh and both keep going for as long as they could to whatever grisly end. They had lived hard and fast and loved each other the same way, anything more was a gift.

Aiding and abetting a traitor to the government was a serious crime against society. Those who had signed, taken and reaped from their contract were expected to honour their agreement, almost all did. Few wanted the legacy of dishonoring family by running and being shot down like a dog. Preferring to drift off in peace surrounded by the ones you love, thanking you for your selfless death after weeks celebrating your fully-lived life. Being hunted, was not many peoples first choice. You would run alone. The sentence for helping a runner was death, shoot on sight orders. There was little point in running; the hunters were the highest trained of European elite ex-forces and following agreements at the summit, most of Europe had agreed to allow the operation of hunter operatives in their countries, even France and Spain who refused to allow Solution sixty-five to become part of their nations identity accepted that repatriation of runners dead or alive was legally just. Only Cyprus, Andorra, Portugal and a few others refused and obstinately remained a destination of peace and freedom should runners make it to their protection. Cyprus, the friendly isle of Aphrodite was economically penalised in trade deals, but it's flexible banking laws and the influx of money from wealthy runners replaced the old tourism industry that pandemics had crippled years earlier. Cyprus was coming out of its lean times, unemployment was at its lowest in history and having a decade earlier followed the success of Portugal's decriminalisation of all drugs, it now had the fastest growing economy in the European Union and high rates of illegal immigration that was welcomed. Those who had amounted wealth using their pay-outs and could somehow buy or make their way to the sandy shores, could live out their days in comfort and safety in paradise. The true numbers of runners who made it to safety was not public information but was reported to be less than one point one percent.

Drying his hair with a towel, Martin came into the kitchen area and sat down smiling at his lover and best friend despite the gravity of the situation.

"You ready? Once these come out..." Mary put the scalpel to her arm.

"Wait, I thought we'd do each other, I'm not sure I can cut into myself." Martin looked pale.

"Come on tough guy, let's do this." Mary, stuck the blade into her own arm, red trickling down onto the towel on the table. With a grimace and a deft movement of the hand the chip fell onto the towel, blue LED flashed red and it was done. "See, easy."

There was no response, Martin had fainted. Which made the removal of his chip much easier. Awaking at the first cut, by the time he knew what was happening, he was taping a piece of gauze to his arm and watching Mary drive carefully out of the car park, away from their discarded chips; sipping a cup of coffee as if she'd just made a sandwich rather than performed surgery. What a woman; he must have done something good in a past life.

13

Returning from a job in the Lake District, after cleaning up and filing a report at HQ. Andrew Hawkins first stop, as always, was the hospital.

Passing the desk of the children's ward, he nodded to the tired looking nurse - Anna was nearing the end of her night shift. They shared a sympathetic smile. The staff were used to Mr Hawkins coming at all hours, his job kept him busy. His easy going nature and relentless positive attitude made him a popular visitor with the nurses and his good looks didn't do any harm either. But, there was always pity in their eyes, he had no time for pity. A waste of time and energy in Hawks opinion, Hawk preferred solutions.

Sitting at her bedside, he held his daughters hand and let her sleep. Tired, he finished his coffee from Jerry's. Sarah's long-term illness had started a year or so into his new job. His work ethic - to fund treatment and avoid the situation at home, had been too much for his isolated wife, when not in a hospital ward she was at home alone.

One day Hawk returned from a job to be told by his employer that his wife had taken an early solution option and the money was in his account. It was cold, but life was brutal and it had been dealt with in an emotionally efficient way by the husband left behind to be sole carer. The woman he had fallen in love with had gone long before, lost in a mother's grief. It had been just two of them, living separately together for almost seven years. Even with the expensive treatment, it may not be enough to keep the inevitable at bay and doctors reservedly gave her three years at best, she probably wouldn't make fourteen.

Andrew loved Sarah more than anything in the world, she was his only focus and refused to give up. There was always a way and with enough money and the right doctors and treatments, he believed there was hope and he would do anything for even a glimmer. Problem, reaction, solution.

Anna walked past the ward and could see Mr Hawkins, head bowed, resting his eyes, holding his little girls hand.

14

The young man was wanted for ditching his chip after being convicted on a rape charge. Hawk didn't hate these missions as much as others. A job was a job, but some were easier than others. Thinking he could disappear into the wilds of the Lake District with a tent, Gary Smith was sadly mistaken. HQ had the quarry easily tracked. First picked up by street cameras, then followed with plate recognition leaving in his brothers vehicle with an unconfirmed but assumed driver. All carefully watched in an office, on a screen, with camera footage from near the targets home where the chip was removed, the motorway journey and then later by satellite to Thirlmere, drones were on standby if requested.

Cruising north with a confirmed location Hawk enjoyed the change in scenery and appreciated a domestic job.

Hawkins walked high into the hills from the Traveller's Rest car park in Glenridding, where he had parked the black Sprinter van with its tinted windows. Jogging up most of Swirrel Edge he reached the top quickly, with an excellent scope of the lake below, he headed along the ridge. A flat slab of granite made the perfect spot, getting comfortable and using his telescope he located the purple Vango tent tucked under the trees. In the valley he could see Smith stooped over a gas cooker, making food a kilometre away. Sausage and egg rolls by the looks of it. There was a guy with him, from the file it looked like it could be the brother.

Hawk checked the file and confirmed it was Kevin Smith, brother of target, Gary.

Hawk settled his breathing after the climb and let the brothers eat a last meal together. Gary picked up the plates and moved towards a bowl of water. Dinner finished there was no reason for him to endure the washing-up. Hawk exhaled slowly and held his breath, feeling his pulse in his chest. On his next heartbeat Hawk, squeezed.

One thousand yards away, the plates fell from Gary's hands into the bowl with a splash and Kevin froze like a seated statue. Gary wouldn't have even heard the crack of the rifle before his head disintegrated into a bloody mess. It was clean.

By rights Hawk should collect the reward for the brother for aiding and abetting an enemy of the state. Leaving him to grieve over the headless corpse, he packed away his rifle and drank some water. Updating headquarters with a body location for the clean-up crew, Hawk headed back to the van via Striding edge. With some fast scrambling and running where possible, he was down before dusk. Hopefully the brother would be smart and just go home.

***

Job done, Hawk enjoyed a pint of ale and a roast dinner with beef, potatoes and vegetables all swimming in a pool of gravy in a huge Yorkshire pudding. Choosing thoughts of Sarah and her inevitable hospital bill, rather than the exploding head of rapist Gary Smith, the weeping brother and shamed family left behind.

15

The phone in his pocket buzzed, Hawk awoke at the hospital bed and looked at the screen. An image of a Hymer Camper with registration and accompanying mugshots of a couple filled the screen. The brief below stated the facts:

24/03/2042
L9:5657 Hawkins, Andrew. Codename: "Hawk"
Targets:
MARTIN BELL (65) - retired athlete, solution 65 traitor to the state. Sentence: Death
MARY BELL (55) – retired athlete, aid and abet traitor to the state. Sentence: Death
Client: Solution65
Location: Unknown. False documents used to reach mainland Europe.
Last confirmed visual: Calais, France. January 7th 2042.
Last reported sighting: Tignes, France, March 23rd 2042.
Notes:
Targets: Physically and mentally strong. Skilled in use of firearms.
Assist Hunter code name Viper.

This was a interesting one.

They'd been running a while and evaded Viper. He was a decent operative. Level six, clinical and a wealth of experience, he was old school. Not Hawk's kind of ethical approach, but brutally efficient and with some of the highest numbers in the company. If he hadn't been an asshole he could have made level seven years ago. He wasn't liked by many, but Hawk was a professional.

The hunter paused as a Father, held his daughters hand a few moments longer and considered waking her despite it being so early. The targets were in the wind and a few minutes more would make no difference.

Hawk decided to let Sarah rest and spoke to Nurse Anna. There was no significant change, he hadn't expected any. Yesterday had been a good day; she had been awake, sitting up and talking, but was very tired by the afternoon and had slept since. Accounting had left a note requesting payment for the next round of new treatment, one more job and that would be covered. A double-hunt would cover some inevitable future expenses too. Returning to her ward, Hawk hovered over his daughter, hoping she might stir before he had to leave. The mobile device in his pocket chimed again.

Agent Viper has potential vehicle location. Liase in Tignes.
Mission urgent.
Agent Hawk progress - static.

They knew where he was, they didn't care about Sarah, they had other priorities. Hawk kissed his daughter's warm soft forehead, catching the scent of her hair and noticing the peace in her face. There was work to do, the medical staff were doing all they could to keep her alive and he must do the same. Nodding goodbye as he passed the desk, he took the stairs at a jog, reaching the lobby faster than the elevator. As he crossed the lobby and exited the hospital, his mind wasn't on the job. Despite the pain of seeing her suffer, he hated leaving Sarah, but he was a practical man and focus would return quickly. The mobile in his pocket alerted him to its presence again and he checked his latest update.

Channel tunnel - London to Calais 9.30am departure.

Just enough time to make it, they were in a hurry. Hawk didn't see the person, but he felt them. As he dashed into the morning light and looked up from the phone, something large blocked out the bright sun. He felt a shoulder in his chest and instantly knew he was going down and taking this unsuspecting victim with him. Turning them as they fell, Hawk wrapped the obstacle in his arms and took their impact as he crashed into the ground and what appeared to be a big guy with a large pack landed in his lap, both looked like they had seen service.

"Motherfucker!" It didn't sound angry, more surprised.

As they helped each other to their feet, there was a moment of mutual recognition. Not the kind that comes from knowing each other as a previous acquaintance, but one of knowing. They were obviously both ex-military and clearly in the ninety-fifth percentile when it came to physical presence. More than that; it was the natural instinct that a top predator feels when it encounters a rare beast that could potentially cause harm. An innate yet rarely felt sense for both, not fear but respect or wariness.

Hawk ignored the slight winding and apologised, the guy was cool about it. Nice even, pointing out where his phone had slid off to.

Hawk could see he was a rough-sleeper and told him to put breakfast on his tab with Jerry, before he rushed off to his van ready to point it south towards the English Channel. Despite his experience, the nature of his work meant he always had butterflies at the start of a mission. There was a reason the pay was so good, you never knew where it might lead, only how it would end, one way or another, with death. The hunt was on.

16

A train rolled into Calais from Dover. Wedged in the storage space in Marcus' van, with no room to move and little air, Tom Kind was less than comfortable. His back was aching and he wished he could stretch his legs out just an inch or two to relieve the cramp working its way up his hamstrings. The warmth of the motor and donations around them made it stifling and he pondered two questions. Had it been like this for Mo? He could only assume it had. Also, how the fuck was Bear asleep? The snoring stopped with the sound of the engine starting up.

"How you doing mate, cozy?" Bear yawned, big spooning Kind.

"I'm looking forward to getting out of this sardine tin and breathing fresh air, but I guess it won't be long now. How the hell you sleeping man?"

"Warm, safe, it's not so bad. My right arm has gone to sleep though."

"If we both move around a little bit, maybe we can create some space."

"Give it a go."

As Marcus wound Cherry out of the port, with Bob Marley's "Exodus" playing loudly on the stereo; nobody was wise to the fact that underneath the flat bed of the VW doka, surrounded by bags of clothes donations, spooned together - Bear and Kind were doing the salmon dance, with fruition as it compressed their surroundings and allowed a little space to move and blood to flow.

In the cab the music wasn't distracting him. Marcus was sweating. *What the hell had he got involved in.* Before he had known what he was doing, he said yes. Next thing he knew he was in Cherry crossing the city, now he was on the run. Maybe he could just hide out in the Jungle for a bit then return. But, if his van was connected with the disappearance of Kind, he would also be a target. They took no prisoners.

***

Cherry rested in an open warehouse, tucked away on an industrial site. Around her were a vast array of clothing donations, most organised on rails or shelves into items and sizes. Large bins for each size of carefully paired shoes. Some clothes in a giant pile ready to sort and another giant mountain of unsuitable donations that would be recycled. It would be a hub of activity in a few hours but for now it was quiet.

The cool night air rushed in as Marcus opened up the flap doors and pulled the donations out, slinging them into the sorting area.

"Kind, you go Calais." Grinning, Marcus pulled him out and gave him a steadying arm as his legs got used to standing again and he leaned on the van.

"Cheers man, can't thank you enough for this."

"Don't worry about it brother, I needed an adventure." Gripping Bear's forearm, he helped him out the tight space and onto his feet. "Hope it wasn't too tight in there big fella."

"Thanks. We managed." Was all the big guy said as he shook off his massive frame, Marcus could have sworn he saw them both blush.

They jumped into the cab and pulled face-masks over their mouth and nose. Heading away from the yard, they needed to hide the van and make a plan, everything had happened so fast. They all agreed the first thing they needed was coffee and breakfast, nothing much would be open for a while so they had limited options.

They could visit Naseer in the Jungle; Tom's friend would not mind being disturbed to make the sweet milky tea that took a long time to prepare, but Kind detested its flavour and only drank it out of politeness and necessity on long cold days, breakfast would be biscuits. Sometimes a sweet, milky tea was bearable after building a few shelters, but right now they needed proper fuel to think.

McDonalds was considered, but they all agreed they'd rather go hungry and didn't like the risk of being seen together somewhere so public. Marcus and Kind shared a look and both said,

"*Family Pub.*"

"What the hell sort of pub is open at this time of day?"

"They won't be open, but I'll call Xaxu and see what he can do." Marcus made the call.

***

Marcus parked Cherry on the narrow street behind the Family Pub on Calais high street. They walked around the block to the front entrance. There were a few lamps on inside dimly lighting the bar and as they approached a figure looked up from the coffee machine with a grin and rushed to the door.

“Mon ami, comment ca va?” The slim, energetic Frenchman hugged and kissed Marcus and Tom on both cheeks. “Qui est-ce beau geant?”

“Je suis Bear, plaisir.” They shook hands and kissed once. “Merci pour votre aide ami.”

“My pleasure brother, we choose a side and do what we do. Now, enough of your terrible French gentlemen; come, drink good coffee and we speak English. Tell me ze shit you are in boys. Maybe Xaxu can help.”

17

Hawk was just resting his eyes; seat tilted back in the static van, enjoying the low hum and gentle rock as the train shot through the tunnel to France and an onward rendezvous in the Alps. Hawk loved the mountains.

"Ping." Eyes open in an instant, immediately aware, he reached for his phone.

24/03/2042
L9:5657 Hawkins, Andrew. Codename: "Hawk"
URGENT UPDATE -
New targets:
THOMAS KIND (41) – Human trafficking, traitor to the state.
Sentence: Death. File attached.
MARCUS DRUMMOND (41) – Human trafficking, traitor to the state.
Sentence: Death. File attached.
UNKNOWN MALE . Aggravated assault, traitor to the state.
Sentence: Death. Information to follow.
Location: Calais. Drummond used cell phone at 9.50am. CCTV visual: Rue Royale, Calais, France. 10.05am

The usual company bullshit, trying to save a few quid on travel by chucking en route jobs his way. What was interesting, was that one of the accomplices was unknown, a known unknown was almost unknown.

Neutralise targets in Calais and continue to intercept targets: MARTIN and MARY BELL

Hawk opened up the files on Thomas Kind and Marcus Drummond and started reading. By the time he had finished, not only did he not consider human trafficking to be a little harsh, he already knew this would be one of the jobs that he hated. If he hadn't been so close they would have probably paired this job up with someone like Gorilla, he gave zero fucks. This was the job. He needed the money and should see it as a gift. Get it done. He refocused, pushing the Bell's to the back of his mind to concentrate on a humanitarian runaway and his friends. He opened a grainy image sent from the French authorities, legally were required to help, but they didn't exactly pull out all the stops. The UK/French boarder had always been a sieve and the French didn't seem too bothered who moved where as long as it looked like they were doing something. All Hawk could tell for sure about the mystery accomplice, was he was big, really big and there was something familiar about him. The tech guys in London would clean up the image, find some background information and use time and location to find their own recorded satellite data. Either way these guys were his new targets, so they were as good as dead already. Thirteen minutes to Calais, Hawk shut his eyes and slept.

18

Xaxu placed another plate of croissants in front of Bear, as if he knew this was a man that was always hungry but would never ask. As Bear ate his third, the others went over the plan.

"We take Cherry to the Jungle and hide her there, plenty of friends and tarpaulin to disappear among and no cameras or drones." Kind stated. "Tonight you collect us from the Jungle at 20.00 just after sunset and we will go to your friend for the respray. Cherry will become Vanilla and we change the plates and disappear into the French country roads. It's perfect Xaxu."

"Perfect? It's tragic, a travesty, I knew there would be sacrifices, but bro, white?" Marcus and Cherry had been adventure companions for a decade and the deep red bodywork of the 1986 VW transporter was her identity.

"Sorry bro, white will blend in more. The canvas back is enough of a feature to still catch attention. We may have to ditch her and change vehicles at some point."

"He means store man, we'd never ditch Cherry." Bear offered. Marcus was gutted, despite his easy going nature, the reality of what he had got himself into was beginning to dawn. On the run he had assumed he'd at least have his faithful lady with him. He forced a smile and gently punched Bear on the shoulder.

"Cheers man. I can't store her, she needs to be free, I'd rather give her away or go down in a blaze of glory together." Marcus put on a brave face.

"Let's avoid any blazes of glory for now." Kind suggested.

"Okay, my crazy English friends, I will see you later. Now get outta here before you get me in trouble... I'm supposed to be making croissants and café for my wife, the kids are with my mother." Xaxu winked. They laughed, got to their feet and headed to the door, watered, fed and buoyant with their plan.

Xaxu locked up and returned to his apartment upstairs and a somewhat nettled wife, who was ready for breakfast in bed.

19

Marcus drove the familiar route through the industrial estate, giant chimneys belching out billowing fumes, a toxic plastic taste catching the back of the throat. Under a motorway bridge, past the various "refugees welcome" graffiti, including the remains of a very faded Banksy, protected with tired looking perspex, depicting tech giant and son of a Syrian refugee, Steve Jobs.

Currently quiet, the motorway led to the port. When lorries were nose to tail, the refugees would cross the empty no-mans-land en masse, through tear gas fog and rubber bullets fired by the CRS agents protecting the boarder. If they could navigate the steep bank and climb or cut through the high fences between the highway and the camp, they would attempt to sneak into, onto or under the trucks queuing there. Cutting through the plastic with small blades and climbing into the back, before repairing the hole with secreted duct tape and offering prayers, praise and blessings to Allah. Marcus and Kind knew a lot about the methods and mayhem of the Jungle, after all, refugees had to get their cutters, blades and duct tape from somewhere.

They drove past the CRS agents on duty. Dressed in black riot gear they looked menacing; volunteer or refugee, if you found yourself on the wrong side of their baton, they wouldn't hesitate to be violent. Marcus wound down the window, waved and smiled, with the usual cheery,

"Bonjour messieurs..."

Sometimes, he'd get a nod, today it was too early to make the pretence of politeness and they just ignored him and continued smoking their cigarettes.

They crossed the barren space between the fence and shelters of the camp, a few boys were sleepily kicking a football around in the early morning sun, trying to get warm. As they drove into the camp, the familiar smell of human waste hit their nostrils. There were never enough of the portable facilities and it was pungent. Bear winced as the stench made his nose sting and took him back to times in foreign lands that he'd rather forget. To Kind and Marcus, it smelt like work and ten thousand humans in need of help.

Cherry crawled past the water taps and away from the toilets. A queue of people already patiently stood in a snaking line following the available sunlight, just slicing over the low huts. Chatting, waiting for a cold morning wash and drinking water; they watched as the red van passed, some waving and smiling, recognising Cherry and its volunteer helpers. A tall, very dark-skinned Sudanese man passed, singing and smiling. The small shops were opening up and smell of breads cooking wafted from the restaurant shacks, as over the sea of plastic tarpaulins and tents, thin wisps of smoke rose in the still morning from hundreds of campfires betraying the massive scale of the community.

All around, life was awakening in the Jungle, children running, mothers scolding, fathers worrying. Despite the squalor, there was laughter and the human spirit burned brightly enough to inspire all but the coldest hearts.

Beyond the Afghan area, past the Eritreans and Sudanese, they came to the Kurdish area. They had history here and having overcome initial problems had built many shelters here. They now knew the community well and had been openly told when with the Kurds; they were, *untouchable.* It also offered access to the back exit of the Jungle in case they needed to move fast. Kind, jumped out and spoke to an elderly man at his caravan and was back in moments.

"Well, what did Hamed say?"

"The community hall is empty, we can park in there, oh, and you need to fix the skylight on his caravan - it's leaking."

Marcus drove Cherry around behind a row of shelters and caravans, into a small marquee the size of a double garage. Hardly a community hall it was a heavy duty gazebo with walls, but it was ideal for hiding their van for the day.

"Okay, we're here, we've got a dozen hours to kill, lets blend, who can we help?" Bear was keen to do something, the scale of the community in need here was heart-breaking.

Marcus smiled. "I knew I liked you, I'll fix this skylight for Hamed. Then we can take a walk, we won't get far before someone asks for help." Marcus handed Bear a heavy drill box and locked the van.

"Good luck chaps. I've got a few people to see; I want to say goodbye to Kiri, Amir and Naseer. Meet at the Afghan Flag at 11am?"

Kind said hello to Raf as he emerged from his caravan nearby and then disappeared into the plastic forest.

***

Marcus and Bear went to a shelter and spoke to Mehram, a beautiful, softly spoken Iranian man in his fifties. His shelter was wonderfully decorated with Persian rugs and cushions. Before he had to flee his homeland, Mehram had been a successful interior designer and his new location had not extinguished his flame; his tiny hut was decorated with ornate metalwork and colourful fabrics he had carried from home. After hugs and handshakes, he bustled them in and they took off their shoes.

Marcus, grabbed a mastic gun and tube of silicone from his tool bag under Mehram's bed.

"You will stay for tea?"

It wasn't a question. Marcus promised to return after fixing the skylight but told Bear to stay. It was a one-minute job; he'd be back before the tea was ready.

"One minute, one minute, Jungle time my friend. I will make tea for you."

"I'll be back, five minutes max." Marcus, slipped his shoes back on and shut the door behind him.

Mehram directed Bear to the most comfortable cushion and turned on a small gas burner, poured milk into a pan and threw in some teabags and some water.

"He always working, busy busy. He build shelter for me. We do together, this year. Before, I was in tent for long time. Many boys need shelter first. In winter it was very bad. Marcus and Kind, they see my friend. He is old. He was in very bad tent, very wet, very mud, very bad. My friend is scared he get sick and die. The boys get shelter, old mans need too. Kind and Marcus, they see my friend tent and in one hour we are building shelter for Ahmed. He says they save his life and are sent by Allah. Good people. They build many, many shelter, help many people from all places. I see it is hard for them here, is hard for all people here. They are sent by Allah and will be blessed."

"They are amazing guys, but I'm not sure that's how they see it."

"Not important." Mehram waved a hand dismissively.

"You have made your home here beautiful, but it must be very hard, I can't imagine what it was like in winter."

"I think maybe you can." Mehram looked at Mike Higgins weathered face, his bright green-blue Persian eyes met Mikes with a knowing sadness of shared suffering. He added what must have been four tablespoons of sugar and continued to stir the teabags in the warming milk and told Bear of life before the Jungle. His shop in Tehran, where he and his friend lived and worked. For years it was very good, until his friend was taken and executed and his shop was burned down. Mehram was at his parents in Qom when he was told by a friend, what had happened to Jawed and their shop, he should not come back as the authorities were looking for him on charges on homosexuality. He packed everything he could into two large bags, said good-bye to his family and caught a flight to Turkey. Leaving behind a confused and crying mother and carrying the unexpected blessing of his father's handshake, pressing money into his hand as he left.

"We speak on the phone. I can never go back; they are safe if I am here."

Mehram poured the tea. It was sweet and sickly but Bear sipped it anyway at least it was hot and wet. Listening to his host talk of family and home, he remembered his time in that part of the world and as more tea was offered, he realised his cup was empty and actually, he did want some more.

Marcus returned and left his shoes on the mat, replaced the tools and settled into a brightly coloured cushion with silver embroidery.

"Skylight sorted in a Jungle-minute?" Bear asked.

"All fixed! Time for a quick tea, thanks Mehram."

"Anytime brother you always welcome in our house. So you see the football?"

20

Tom Kind, threaded his way past shelters, tents, campfires and rubbish piles. Nodding to residents who were used to passers-by. Ducking under a washing line, he headed through the Ethiopian area navigating some human excrement on the pathway and making his way towards the Women's and children's area. The big red bus was easy to spot, a welcome addition to the growing arsenal of support and organisation required by the ladies who worked tirelessly to protect the most vulnerable in the Jungle.

This was generally a male free zone, but if you were building and respectful, you were welcome during the day, or at night if you were willing to do security detail, a sad but necessary precaution against uninvited male intruders. Kind was a recognised face.

As he bounded up the steps of the bus, hoping the wonderful Kiri would be there he was surprised to see the beaming face of Rosie instead.

"Fucking Tom, fucking Kind, come here you nutcase!" Rosie grabbed him and squeezed with all her wiry strength.

"Rosie! What are you doing here I thought you were in the UK with Mo."

"Admin, you know this place falls apart without me. But they'll have to learn, I've got responsibilities in England now thanks to you."

Kiri pushed past her friend, her beautiful tanned face glowing with an impish smile and eyes that burned with an inherited mix of strength and mischief. Her arms wrapped around Tom and she kissed him hard on the lips looking into his eyes.

"You, are my hero."

Tom Kind blushed and felt guilty for the attention. Helping people wasn't supposed to be about how you felt or what people thought of you. It was just about helping people. Kiri looked him in the eyes and kissed him again, Kind decided maybe it was okay this time to take the acknowledgment and despite his uncertain future, kissed her back.

Rosie rolled her eyes.

"Gerroff my mate, she's got work to do. So, what you doing here? I told you to lay low."

"Lots to talk about, not here though. Afghan eggs at the flag at ten?"

"We will see you there." Kiri beamed as Kind kissed her on the cheek and floated down the bus steps and into the labyrinth, picking his way through the sea of plastic in the direction of the Good Hope theatre dome and his Pakistani friend Naseer.

***

Kind had met Naseer in his first moments, on his first day in the Jungle. After only a few hours in the workshop making shelter frames, a build team needing another man and possibly more importantly a van convinced him to join them assembling shelters in the Jungle. Kind was nervous as he pulled up at the entrance of the camp parking near some bins. Refugees milling around.

"The van will be fine here. Plenty of people to keep an eye on it." Tom was unsure despite the volunteers experience.

Naseer had good English and a kind face and offered to help carry tools as soon as Kind opened the back. At ease with the friendly interaction Tom, maybe naively had chosen to trust this stranger and that trust had been returned with a fierce and lasting loyalty. The following day Kind had helped fix the roof of his shack, a structure ingeniously hobbled together in the woods, the pair had been friends ever since. Naseer lived in a group of ten, Noor was the eldest, a professor in his past life. Naseer had been one of his students and they had journeyed together. Noor had gradually found himself joined by more young, intelligent and sensitive Pakistani men who sensed his scholarly and fatherly nature. They were like a family and everyone played a part.

***

Since the destruction of part of the Jungle for the barren no-mans-land zone, Tom, some friends and the Pakistanis had moved them from the woods and they now had four shelters. Between them they had fixed tarpaulins to create covered areas, one kitchen section had been designed so it could be opened to vent the smoke from fire. There was an area for shoes so the inside of the accommodation would be as clean as possible, with nails for hanging wet jackets. In another section, were soap and buckets and on washing lines hung clean, hand-washed clothes, in this muddy hell-hole, it was all very impressive.

Crouched over the small fire, tentatively feeding it sticks was Naseer. Wearing his usual flowing cream Shalwar Kameez, somehow always immaculately clean. He had insisted that Kind would have one tailor-made when Naseer made it to the UK, pale blue would be a good colour for Kind he promised.

"Salaam Naseer my friend."

Naseer jumped to his feet and ran to hug Tom despite his old injuries from a Taliban bomb.

"Brother, you are here again. It is good to see you."

"The place looks great, very clean."

"Yes, we work hard. You like our finish extension?"

"Very good Naseer, you remembered. Extension."

"Of course, you told me, extension, so I remember. Fire is ready, you want coffee?"

"Coffee, Naseer you spoil me, coffee is expensive, tea is fine."

"You don't like tea. You make the face when you drink. I buy coffee for you. I don't like, I make the face when I drink. I make coffee."

They both drank coffee and Naseer made a face. It was instant, but it was better than the tea and Kind knew it would have cost more than Nass should be spending. Naseer opened biscuits before he could stop him and Tom quickly updated him, Naseer's eyes grew wider and then sad.

"You are refugee now Kind, I am so sorry my friend... Kind, why you no take me to UK brother?"

"I´m sorry Naseer, it wasn't planned, it just happened, inshallah, he was just a boy. You are a man Naseer, you can get to the UK, you must try. Don't give up here. I won't give up either."

"But, my legs. I cannot run to catch lorries and if CRS beat my legs it will be very bad for me."

Kind drained his coffee and Naseer copied with a wince.

"Three years Nas, it's no life. You can't stay here forever brother; you have to try. I have to go now. I don't think I will see you again. Promise you won't give up." Kind pressed some euros into his hand and Naseer made the usual pretence that they didn't need it. Tom insisted it was from donations and for the whole group for food, as usual their dance of politeness and pride eventually ended and it was gratefully accepted.

"I promise, I will try." Naseer had tears in his eyes as he thanked Kind for all his help and wished him the blessings of Allah on his onward journey.

Months later, Naseer would arrive in the UK dirty and exhausted from clinging to the underside of a lorry. He would hand himself in to Acton police station and begin his justified and successful claim for asylum and begin a new life. Tom Kind now a refugee, sadly would never know of this happiness; see his friend in the UK or shop for the tailor-made, pale blue shalwar kameez with Naseer.

***

It was close to 10am as Tom went into the steamy Hammam and barbers. Before his eyes could adjust, the giant frame of Amir wrapped him in his strong embrace. Amir raised his voice over the hum of the generator. A plumber in Iran Amir spoke seven languages and was considered neutral by all of the communities, his baths a place of peace. Something he had to literally fight for shortly after he arrived in Calais.

"Mr Tom, you want a haircut or you need your tools? Your batteries are charged, I check every few days."

"Not this time Amir, I've come to say good-bye my friend. I want you to keep my tools and let people you trust use them to help. I'm in trouble and I have to run, I don't know where but I wanted to say good-bye. You have been a good friend to me and a good leader, helping people and keeping peace here. I will miss my shaves and our talks brother. Thank you for everything Amir."

"My friend I am very sad to hear this. I will miss you. Thank you for your work here, you made a difference to many people in the Jungle. I wish you luck on your journey in this godless world." He whispered the last bit and looked around, giving Tom a wink and said aloud.

"In this life or the next brother."

Kind gave him a big hug.

"I hope you get to the UK and your family join you again soon my friend."

"Inshallah."

They hugged again, Amir kissed him on both cheeks and watched from his doorway as his English friend made his way down the dirt road to the Afghan flag and disappeared. The Jungle would miss Tom Kind.

***

Marcus and Bear, left the cosy home of Mehram. The sun was up properly and the Calais Jungle was warming as a fresh spring morning turned into a warm day. Marcus had heard there was a build going on near the Sudanese area. It was three shelters for eight Iraqi boys. The Sudanese, were often more open to having neighbors from other groups, especially if they were in need and offered no threat.

The tall man who had been singing that morning was cooking food and some of the youngest Iraqi boys were already sat on their haunches eating by his kitchen. A couple of other Sudanese men were helping some taller boys with their tarpaulin roof. One of the shelters was still only a pine frame, two metres by two metres, made from two inch square lengths of timber, used sparingly, with braces at forty-five degrees in the corners. A simple door, hinged and wrapped in tarpaulin with a latch ready for a padlock.

The walls of the third shelter were already wrapped in plastic and on the roof was a blonde haired, teenage girl working efficiently with a staple gun while giving clear and concise instructions to an Iraqi boy who was pulling the plastic tight and folding the corners like origami to ensure water ran off and the wind didn't tear it free.

Marcus and Bear were impressed; she was young even for a volunteer in Calais. They politely refused food but returned fist bumps with Manny the chef and pointed at the shelter. Manny nodded and they headed over.

"Hello, are you in charge here?" Marcus grinned his big grin up at the girl.

"Not really. Pull that corner down and fold it over with your arm in a straight line while Jamil staples it." She said, chucking the stapler at Jamil who caught it deftly and grinned as she nodded.

Marcus knew shelter building and did what he was told, as did Jamil. The girl looked down and assessed them, she was very pretty, maybe sixteen. Slim and athletic looking and clearly light and nimble enough to move carefully on a two inch timber roof.

"Thank you..." She waited.

"You're welcome. I'm Marcus, this is Bear."

"Thank you Marcus, bonjour "Bear?".

"No one is in charge here, it's chaos. But, if you want to help you're just in time. I'm Chance, she moved carefully to the corner, having built a number of these shelters now, she had worked out the parts that were structurally strong enough to support her and allow her to fit a roof tarpaulin without the help of a man or carrying a ladder round the Jungle. Despite this independence, she paused, assessing the two tall men while standing at the corner of the roof; with barely a nod to Bear, she leapt without a word, into the air. His quick reflexes caught her easily and he lowered her to the floor as if she were a feather. Chance laughed loudly and the faux tough exterior melted as the two men towered over her and this elf-like child smiled with her bright blue eyes.

"You're alright Bear, we're going to be friends. Help me finish this roof, you can reach the rest. Marcus, we'll see how good you are at fitting insulation and maybe we can be friends too." She laughed again.

"I've insulated a few shelters, what we using blankets and hammer and nails?"

"Where you been man? We've got foil bubble-wrap stuff now. Stanley knife and staple, it's warmer, it reflects the light and... it makes it look like a spaceship, it's awesome. Hercules is inside, he's probably messing it up if you want to help him. Jamil and Bear can help me and the others with wrapping the other shelters. *Hercules*!"

A broad-shouldered man emerged from the shelter, almost as tall as Bear. With long blonde hair and beard and the same bright blue eyes he looked like a beautiful Viking. Despite the size difference, there was a clear resemblance.

"I'm doing a great job on the insulation and I've told you, stop jumping off the roofs... and call me Dad." She rolled her eyes.

"Sure thing Herc, this is Marcus, he is going to help with the insulation."

He let it go, he liked her cheekiness at the right time and she was usually on point. *Besides, teenagers - what you going to do?*

"Don't wander off anywhere."

She rolled her eyes again and said to Bear,

"He thinks I'm a child, I *can* take care of myself."

The men shook hands, Chance mocked them shaking Jamil's hand, chest puffed out in a mock masculine way. Jamil bent over laughing.

Hercules and Marcus squeezed into the shelter, already chatting about their Jungle experiences. Marcus wondering if he needed a nickname. Both men got started immediately, keen to make progress before the day got too hot. Warm is good at night but, with barely enough space for makeshift beds and a few possessions, during the day most people preferred to be outside their stuffy shelters, doors locked.

With her experience and Bears height, they worked quickly, manoeuvring the long plastic sheets around the walls for Jamil to staple. They had neatly folded and fixed the first corner of the roof with staples and hammer and nails when the other boys called Jamil to play cricket. He was the oldest and told them to play, he had to finish their house.

"Go and play cricket, we've got the roof, right Bear?"

"We do silver blanket?"

"Go play cricket, bring the boys back later to do silver blanket. I'll leave the knife and stapler here. If they don't come back, they will be cold tonight."

Jamil smiled and ran after the boys, accepting some food forced on him from Manny as he passed. They got back to work and finished the roof before sitting down with Manny for sweet tea and a little food that could only be accepted with grace.

"Know what, you're alright Chance, I think we will be friends."

"So, Bear...you show me yours?" She waited, he looked confused and uncomfortable, she laughed at him squirm for a second before putting out a hand.

"I'm Layla Chance, it's nice to meet you. So, what you doing here?"

"Mike Higgins, nice to meet you Layla, it's a lovely name. But, I kinda like Chance, it suits you."

"I like Bear, it suits you too. But, don't change the subject, what you guys doing here. That Marcus guy was playing it cool, but he's scared about something."

"What about me, do I seem scared?"

"You don't seem like anything would scare you."

"We all get scared Chance, it's part of caring. Sometimes fear doesn't help and we have to be brave and focus."

"Fuck, you sound like my Dad. He's gonna love you. What you doing for lunch? We've been here since six am. We're going for food soon, she finished the tea and examined the grainy sugar sludge in the bottom with a grimace."

"We're going to somewhere called the Afghan flag for Afghan eggs."

Layla laughed.

"Alright new boy, flag for eggs, it's a date, I'll have to bring my chaperone he's always hungry." she winked at him with a laugh.

"So, how come you guys are here in the Calais Jungle, shouldn't you be in school?"

"Long version, it's just me and Hercules. He hates the system and was outspoken enough in the past about his views at times to make life difficult. He couldn't stay in a country that allows and encourages its people to die and do nothing. So we're on an aimless mid-life crisis quest for paradise. We've been all over, helping refugees, staying at hippie camps and meditating, we were on a farm for a while, I liked that and where we are staying now is okay, but we always keep moving. Current stop Calais - to ease his conscience, to spit in the eye of the system and probably to teach me a lesson about humility or gratitude or some shit, like I don't get it already."

"That's the long version, what's the short version?"

"Dad's a knob." They both laughed.

"So this journey of personal growth and spiritual development, is it working?" He smiled at the short silence.

"For me or him... Yeah, alright, fuck you. Yes, even the hippies, but don't tell him he's right, its unbearable." She grinned.

"Our secret. So how long you been here?"

"A month today. We're actually moving on after lunch. Dad has a friend he wants to surprise, they have a horse ranch in the countryside. I can't wait."

"So, back to the subject...what are you doing here Bear?"

"I'm not sure I can say, we're passing through, but it might not be okay to say more."

"Well that's far too intriguing to ignore. I'm going for a wee. But, when I get back, I want to know more Bear."

Chance headed off, Bear sat a moment looking into the small fire and then remembered where he was and that her father had asked her not to wander. Piss off his new independent friend in this dangerous environment, or risk upsetting a man who's hand he shook after hearing his words. Bear stood up and followed Layla Chance.

***

Weaving in and out of shelters at a light jog, Chance knew where she was going and Bear had to be quick not to lose her. As she passed a group of boys she didn't appear to notice them stop talking and then also start tailing her. Bear quickened his pace.

As she went into the stinking portaloo Chance allowed herself an unperceived glance back. Just as she thought, there were only three of them. Careful to touch nothing, Chance held her breath, hovered and took a tissue from the packet in her pocket.

When Layla emerged into the sunlight, the boy in the middle held a small but deadly looking curved dagger, flashing by his side. Bear watched from the side of a nearby portaloo, close enough, but out of sight.

"Money, phone." There was menace in the voice but Layla didn't seem bothered. She looked relaxed, made eye contact with him and his knife a metre or so in front of her.

"That's pathetic. I haven't got any money and if you try and take my phone I'm going to stick that in your shoulder."

The arm holding the knife went limp and she could tell he was unsure what to do next. One of his friends said something angrily to him and he stiffened up again.

"Money, phone." He hissed.

Chance, twisted round to reach her back pocket and Bear made to move from the shadows. Before he could break cover, Layla Chance surprised everyone but herself, as she span perfectly balanced and roundhouse kicked the boy in the face. He dropped like a stone, knife falling from his hand. Before his almost unconscious body had hit the deck, Chance had already thrown a mean right hook into the face of the angry friend. Nose exploding in blood, tears in his eyes, he ran, his unscathed friend following.

"Pricks." Layla Chance walked over to the knife and picked it up, standing over the now groaning boy on the ground. "I told you what would happen if you tried to take a little girls phone. You were very rude." She pointed the knife at his shoulder.

"I sorry. Please, I sorry."

Layla stood up as the adolescent on the floor scrabbled backwards.

"Go on then, fuck off."

"My knife, please, is a gift my father."

"I keep this. Is mine now."

The boy looked ready to cry, Layla sighed and threw the knife on the ground at his feet. The boy gathered it and quickly retreated into the Jungle.

"Well you made your point, lesson learned." Bear waited.

"Probably not, but it is what it is." She turned and wandered off as if nothing had happened. Bear jogged after her as she walked slowly enough to let him catch her.

"That was..."

"Stupid, rash, dangerous...yeah yeah, I've heard it."

"I was going to say impressive. You can handle yourself kid...sorry I mean, Chance. That kick was fierce."

"Thank you, I've done some... ballet."

"Yeah, you can dance."

"I did feel braver knowing you were there, I wanted to see if you would interfere like some knight in shining armour."

"You knew I was following you?"

Layla laughed.

"Before I knew they were following me, you're hardly incon-fucking-spicuios Bear. Dad told me not to wander. You followed because you're a decent guy but held back because you didn't want to piss me off."

"You're pretty perceptive Chance. So, tell me was I supposed to be a knight or not?"

"You were supposed to wait, if it had gone differently and I'd needed a knight I'm sure I'd have been very grateful. You're alright Bear."

"Man, complex. You're a question mark wrapped in an enigma. I don't envy your Dad."

"Who we won't be speaking of this incident to..." Layla raised an eyebrow.

"You can handle yourself, nothing he needs to know. You can trust me Chance."

Layla looked him dead in the eye.

"I believe you Bear...you can trust me too."

"I believe you too Chance."

"Excellent. So, what are you doing here Bear?"

Checkmate. Well played, she was good. Bear took a deep breath and then the strong, silent man started to open up about their situation to a sixteen-year-old girl he barely knew and like the most natural therapist in the world, she listened to the fears of this fugitive without a word.

***

Hercules and Marcus had put the world to rights and made the inside of the shelter NASA like with tightly stretched foil bubble wrap insulation, stapled to the batons. It was warm in there and they were glad to get into the fresh air. Like Bear, Marcus had probably shared to much. The guy was easy to talk to.

"Well Hercules, it was an absolute pleasure man. Good luck with the adventure and I have to say your daughter is awesome, great job man. How long is your drive going to be?"

"Should be about a fifteen-minute drive back to Marie's and the horses and dog. Ought to put some fuel in her car on the way back too, she's been amazing. Then on towards Limoges. My friends ranch is a good twelve hours with the animals, so will stop on the way. But, like I said man, if you guys are heading that way you're more than welcome to catch up, you got my number and address."

"Thanks Hercules, like I said I'm not sure where we're going, I'm kind of a passenger, chauffer, swept along with these guys, but I've got the address and your number, I'll talk to Kind, he's the plan man. Like I said, it could be dangerous."

"Life's dangerous these days. I'm looking forward to meeting this Kind guy, I'd like to shake his hand. Let's go get some eggs, I'm hungry."

"You're always hungry." Said a voice behind them. Layla smiled at her Dad and allowed the rare affection of a one-armed, teenage daughter squeeze as they led the way.

"Let's eat, to the Flag. By the way Dad, I've invited Bear and his friends to join us at the ranch." Hercules considered saying this was presumptuous, but then thought better of his hypocrisy.

"Cool, I did mention it to Marcus but he said..."

"Need to talk to Kind." Layla laughed. "I want to meet this guy, they love him. You hear what he did?"

"No, but there's certainly a lot of respect there."

"There's more to it Dad, a lot more, but it's not my story to tell."

Hercules nodded respectfully. Nothing more was said.

***

Behind, Marcus and Bear updated each other, Bear left out the incident at the toilets.

"I don't think we should get them involved." Bear wanted to spend more time with them and a ranch would be a good hide-out. But, it was too risky and he'd already told her too much.

"We need to head somewhere and he has a plan to get the fuck away from the reaches of the UK through the countryside to friends. What plan do we have except for defacing my van? Where do we go when we leave Calais? Left, right?
Bear could hear the panic in his voice.

"West, we head for Portugal or Gibraltar, then Africa or Cyprus, we have options. We'll all be okay man. Trust us Marcus. We have the funds. Kind has his game head on and I'll look out for you brother, you got us out, stick with us, we're family now. Everything will be okay."

21

The Afghan flag comprised of bench seating and long tables situated along the walls of a large timber frame and corrugated metal shack with cheap round tables and plastic chairs in the middle of the room. Layla saw some familiar faces and joined a long table, the others followed.

Sweet tea was always ready and immediately served in plastic cups. The huge woks of tomatoes and garlic bubbling away in an unhealthy amount of oil. They ordered bread, beans and other sides to go with their eggs. Chance shot her father a look when he asked for the deep fried bread. He caught it and shrugged, giving her the "gun-show" she rolled her eyes and placed her fist on her chest, opening closing it in a beating motion. He assumed this meant she loved him. Then she exploded her fingers apart, mouthing "boom" with wide eyes. Head back, laughing. Hercules, quietly changed his order.

"Bear, Marcus, I want you to meet Kit and Geoff." They shook hands. "Geoff is the digger-man!" They felt like this should mean something and Chance gave Kit and some others a look as Geoff hung his head.

"Geoff, Geoff the digger-man, he works his digger, whenever he can.

Geoff, Geoff the digger-man, works his digger, never sleeps in his van.
Geoff, Geoff the digger-man, he works all day, he works all night..."
The table chorused.

"...because no one fights like the digger-man fights. Digger-man!
Geoff, he's the digger-man...Digggeeer-maaaan!"

Geoff looked embarrassed, but rose a fist and smiled tiredly through his long beard,

"Fuck the system."

"Geoff literally sleeps in his digger and works through the night clearing areas for new refugees and shelters." Chance sounded impressed. Bear was impressed too, her father was right, these are good humans for a teenager to be around.

"What about you Kit, what you been doing?"
Kit hesitated and looked at Geoff, who burst into laughter.

"Tell her."

"I was strimming the brush to make space for tents, but kept hitting hidden obstacles."

"Like what?"

"Oh, you know, nappies, curdled cartons of milk. It was pretty rank. I hit a carton of milk and it just exploded, all fetid and disgusting, it covered my face mask so I had to take it off and clean it. I had a spliff break and then carried on. I could smell poo nearby and guessed there was some sort of makeshift Jungle-toilet, so for half an hour I was trying to strim away and find the location of the shit so we could clear it with the digger. I couldn't find it anywhere but the smell was still there... Eventually I worked out I had put my face-mask down in human poo and that's why the smell was following me."

Chance mock gagged and Kit and the others laughed.

"Jungle life. It is what it is."

"It is what it is." The table chorused.

Tom Kind walked into the Afghan flag and held the door open for Rosie and Kiri as they arrived from the other direction.

"Such a gentleman." Rosie mocked affectionately.

"I think you're lovely." Kiri said as she walked in.

"Open your own doors girl." Rosie laughed as they joined the table.

"We've been invited to stay on a ranch, with Herc and Chance." Marcus updated Kind quietly, handing him an address. Kind looked at the father and daughter and just shook his head. Bear nodded.

A text from Xaxu alerted them to the opportunity to get the van sprayed early, they could leave shortly and be done and on the way by nightfall.

Kit got to his feet, pushed his long mullet back over his shoulders and raised his plastic cup of tea to Kind.

"We heard on the Jungle vine brother, good for you man. I can't believe you got away with it. Mo needed to get to the UK more than most. One love man."

Kind was about to speak when the food arrived. The eggs had gone into the tomatoes and were cooked beautifully, whites swimming in the thick tomato sauce, with yolks bright and runny.

The bread was on the table and they all tucked in hungrily using it as scoops. Kind introduced himself to Hercules as the owner came to the table and said the food was on him as a thank you to Mr Kind.

"I hear what you do for Mo, my friend, Allah be with you."

"Okay, enough. What did you do man?" Hercules looked around the table and Rosie looked at Kind who nodded.

"Let me tell you about this guy." Rosie licked her lips and wiped her fingers as if preparing for a storytelling. Kind rolled his eyes and then blushed as Kiri squeezed his leg and dipped her bread in the egg closest to him with a smile.

The exodus story of Mo told. Hercules sat back, replete.

"That's some pretty ballsy stuff man. I'm impressed. Lucky you got away with it." there was a pause.

"I didn't." The table fell silent. "We're here because when I got home the police were there. I was facing a long prison sentence or Solution sixty-five. Bear agreed to run with me and then had some trouble of his own. Marcus agreed to get us here and essentially go on the run with us. We're fugitives, hunted. We are leaving today as soon as possible and disappearing into Europe and won't be able to return. This is good-bye my friends."

Rosie was silent for the first time in memory. Kiri had tears leaving wet tracks down her cheeks. The rest of the table were trying to take it in. They all knew deep down that this was an almost certain death sentence. Without Marcus' sacrifice they wouldn't have even got out of the UK and once they surfaced, the agents hunting them would almost certainly be successful as always. Layla Chance was the first to speak.

"Don't be so negative, you're in France, it's massive, the countryside is not far. You can do this. I believe in you. If you can get to the ranch..."

"Woah, hold your horses there. I'm sorry guys, but I have to rescind my invitation. I can't get Layla or my friends mixed up in this sort of trouble."

"Dad, I already knew when I invited them, Bear told me everything."

Kind raised his eyebrows at Bear, who shrugged.

"Dad, they did the right thing it was just illegal. They need our help. This is exactly the sort of shit you're always talking about. Affirmative action, doing the right thing even when it's hard. Standing together for what's right against oppression. Protecting those who can't protect themselves."

"But, I have to protect you."

"I don't need protecting!"

"We can look after ourselves Chance, your Dad is right." Bear offered.

Hercules looked at the men with a sadness, like he was looking at three ghosts. Dead men walking. Hercules took a deep breath.

"I'm sorry to be so blunt gentlemen; Chance, these guys are probably going to get caught and... have their sentences carried out. I'm really sorry, you don't deserve this guys, you're all good people, but I can't put my child in the firing line. It really was an honour to meet you all, Mo is a lucky kid. But, I'm truly sorry for what you have sacrificed. We have to leave Chance. Now. I'll walk and get the car, be ready to leave in ten minutes. Finish your eggs and say... meet me outside."

Chance had furious tears in her eyes. She knew her father wouldn't move on this, once he had made a risk-assessment and a decision there were no emotional elements considered. It made her so angry. It was her life, she should be allowed to choose the risks she took and the path of integrity she wanted. He got to drag her on this stupid mid-life crisis.

"You're such a fucking hypocrite. I bet if you were on your own you'd help them."

"Your Dad is right Chance, it's way too dangerous. We'll be fine, I'll look after them." Bear forced a smile.

Hercules shook hands with everyone and wished them the very best of luck and more apologies.

"Don't apologise. It's far too dangerous. We need to get away from everyone as soon as possible." Kind agreed.

Hercules left the Afghan flag, an attempted word with his daughter only received "the hand" he assured himself she would calm down later. You can't pray for a strong, smart, empathetic and independent daughter and then be surprised when she is everything you hoped for. Especially when she was right. Right or wrong, he had one priority now and that was his daughter, her safety and the opportunity for a different life away from a selfish society and its constant decline into the swamp. His daughter would live with nature, in peace, in freedom, not on the run... but at what cost?

How can you teach integrity through a veil of hypocrisy? One of Layla's favourite digs, she knew it stung. But, every decision he ever made had started and ended with his child.

Rosie, Kiri and Kind volunteered to walk and fetch Cherry and at this point Marcus past caring, got another tea and threw the keys to Kind, slumping on the bench and staring into the tea as he considered his mortality. Bear and Chance ordered another tea too and sat to one side as she vented her frustrations at her father to Bear, whose turn it was now to just listen.

After a short time, a high pitched horn sounded outside the Flag.

"You know. It's only because he loves you Chance, from what I can see he's done a pretty awesome job, I've never met anyone quite like you."

"I know, it doesn't make it any easier though, I have no control."

"Doesn't it? You'll have plenty of time for decision making, for now trust your dad."

Layla pondered on that, as with an atmosphere of palpable sadness they stood and hugged. Offering each other good luck in their next chapters they made their way out into the late morning sun.

22

Hawk sensed the train slowing and meditated on what happened next. His equipment was ready in the back of his black Transit, as ever. Mentally it was time to move head space. Targets pictured in his head he visualised taking the shot. The breathing, the control, the stillness. The train halted and after an age the lady in the maillot jaune removed the chocks from his wheels and the partition in front of him rose. The last sighting was Rue Royale in Calais, according to the file there was a known volunteer friendly bar on that road, The Family Pub. Not a great place to hide, but a good place to start looking for leads. It was 11.30h local time as his tyres touched French tarmac.

***

Xaxu had made up for the delayed breakfast in bed and was back downstairs in the bar preparing for the midday rush when a figure filled his door. At first he thought it was a CRS agent. Dressed in black fatigues, gun in holster at his side. But this wasn't a French agency uniform, it was more menacing with no insignia and the man in the uniform didn't make him feel any easier.

"A quelle heure ouvrez-vous pour le dejueuner". Hawk asked through the glass door barely audible in passable French. Xaxu opened the door.

"Pardon, lunch?"

The words had barely been spoken before Xaxu found himself physically lifted from the floor by a powerful arm and run backwards into his bar. His feet still off the floor, he dared to open his eyes and found himself face to face with the barrel of a gun, behind the weapon was a face that gave him no doubt as to the seriousness of the predicament he was in.

"You speak English." It wasn't a question. "You know why I'm here. You know my jurisdiction and powers of investigation that go with that. I'm going to make this really simple Xaxu. You can answer my questions honestly and do what I ask. Then I will leave and you can serve lunch and see your wife. Or, you can lie to me just once and Xaxu, I will know and I will shoot you in the face as an accomplice, make myself a coffee, shoot your wife and then go and find them anyway."

Xaxu didn't say anything, what was there to say.

"Where are they?" The cold barrel of the silenced pistol touched Xaxu gently on the bridge of the nose.

"Jungle."

"The refugee camp?"

"Oui."

"What is the plan, the whole plan please Xaxu."

"Tonight my cousin will spray the red van white, they will change plates, go into the countryside and run. I don't know where, I swear that is all I know." Tears ran down his face.

"I believe you Xaxu. I have one more thing to ask and then I will leave you here. Whether you are alive is still up to you. I need you to unlock your phone and send a message."

It was only fifteen minutes later when the first of Xaxu's legitimate lunch customers arrived to find him tied-up behind the counter, crying and demanding to be untied fast. As soon as he was released he ran to his office behind the bar and searched manically in drawers for his phone book.

***

It wasn't a long drive to the refugee camp and the motorway bridge was the perfect vantage point. Thc van, with blacked out windows, parked on the hard shoulder of a motorway by a refugee camp caught the immediate attention of the CRS agents and four made the walk up the bank and through the heavy metal gate in the fence, before one spotted the plates and spoke to the others, they shrugged, turned and walked back. The CRS thugs wanting nothing to do with what was about to happen and the paperwork that could potentially be involved if they were present.

Inside the back of the van, Hawk checked for updates, still no confirmation on the third target, he opened two small windows in front of tripods and looked through his Zeiss telescope at the sea of plastic and human movement in front of him and started scanning the small streets between shops, shelters and restaurants. Looking for a sign of his quarry.

23

Hercules drove Marie's little white Fiat carefully through the Jungle´s bumpy tracks from the dome where he had parked it, no hurry with people all over the track. Besides a long slow drive with an angry Chance lay ahead. He pulled up outside the Afghan Flag pointing towards the back entrance and the direction of Marie's campsite and stables not far away. Hopefully seeing the horses and dog would help. Herc opened the back door, hiking boots and clean socks ready for Layla to change out of her dirty work-boots into, he assumed she wouldn't want to sit up front and chat.

Hercules got back in the car, engine running, window down and beeped the horn, he wasn't going to be drawn into a debate or long goodbyes.

Marcus drained his tea and stepped off the veranda into the sunlight and opened the passenger door, leaning in to shake Hercules hand.

***

On the bridge, Hawk had followed the movement of a small white car that had come from the North of the Jungle, it turned East away from him and stopped a short way along the main street, the restaurant area of the camp. A figure moved into vision towards the car, it was target two. Marcus Drummond. Sentence death.

Hawk moved behind a second tripod and found his shot. Was he about to get into a vehicle which may well contain other targets, were they about to get out, were they nearby. Too many questions, he focused his breathing and waited.

***

Marcus leaned into the car.

"Hey man, good luck I hope she's not too mad at you. It's the right thing man, we got to get the fuck outta here. The others don't seem worried man, but I'm shitting it. I just want to get going. I don't feel safe here. Maybe I'll never feel safe again."

"I hope you guys beat the odds brother, you're good people. If it was just me, you know..."

Hercules broke off as the burble of Cherry's 2.0l engine and throaty exhaust announced her imminent presence. As she rounded the corner in front of them, Marcus couldn't help but smile, she was such a great van. Rosie was smiling as she drove towards them with Fuck the system, by System of a down, playing loud. Despite the sadness of the farewell, having just finally connected, they were trying to be positive.

***

"Who knows where we will find our paths taking us and whose paths they will cross. Goodbyes are not forever; we could meet again." Kiri didn't know if Kind was trying to convince her or himself, but she felt a little better when he gave her the address Marcus had given him. "I think it's a bad idea, but we're desperate and that kid might convince Hercules, even if it's just a night, while we figure out the next move."

Rosie had seen enough shit; this was just another Doc Martin to the groin in a bastard world. *Fuck the system*, she pulled up on the other side of the road, tight to a shelter wall ten metres behind the Fiat so people could still pass easily.

"She's lovely Marcus." She left the engine running, climbed down and gave Marcus a fist bump. Tom gave Rosie a hug and then slid towards the driver's door as the phone in his back pocket pinged.

A still angry Chance stepped into the sunshine and out on the street, eyes red. Bears massive arm around her shoulders as they walked towards the little Fiat and she climbed in the back door, determined not to speak to HIM.

***

In the van, climate control was keeping it cool despite the warm spring day. Hawk took a sip of water from his Sigg bottle. The target vehicle was approaching from the East, Hawk waited. Target Two, had moved back from the passenger door and didn't look like his intention was to enter. He was now between the two vehicles. He put his cross-hairs between the targets eyes and then moved to the red van as a female exited, it was the vehicle from the file and it looked like the primary target was in the vehicle but he couldn't confirm as the sun was reflecting off the windscreen. He waited. More movement from the building as a young girl with blonde hair stepped into the street with an enormous man next to her. The build gave him away as the third but unconfirmed target, Hawk scanned the face and recognised him instantly, the huge rucksack was a giveaway. The homeless guy from the hospital. Motherfucker! He couldn't take the shot with the civilian so close and no official identification, meant no confirmed kill order, who was this ghost? His phone pinged.

Confirmation Order Clear to Kill:
Michael "Bear" Higgins
Sentence: Death
Client: British State
Location: Calais
File: Currently classified. Information to follow.

Hawk panned back to Drummond, Higgins, then the van and waited.

***

Kind hopped down from the van; fished his phone out his pocket and read the new message. A look of horror took his features and drained the colour from his face. It was from Xaxu, it was short.

I AM SORRY. RUN NOW!

***

Hawk had waited long enough, three targets confirmed. Time to engage.

"Bear, Marcus, we have to go now!" Bear could tell from his face and the phone in his hand that he was still looking at. This was serious, Bear automatically scanned the surroundings, immediately noticing the van, now obvious on the bridge in the distance. Marcus followed Bears gaze, as Kiri ran towards Kind, eyes wet, but he was now looking past her towards the Jungle entrance.

"What is it?"

***

On the bridge, Hawk breathed out slowly and paused. It was an unmissable distance, he squeezed the trigger.

"*Crack*!"

24

In the French Alps, Martin and Mary Bell were enjoying their freedom, skiing in the late March sunshine, high on a glacier. They were skiing fast down a double-diamond black run, heading back towards the main pistes. Their legs looked like pistons, knees moving up and down to absorb the moguls as the younger Mary, pushed the stubborn Martin at well over 100km/h. To the uninitiated their off-piste pace would have looked like insanity, but they were in complete control, in matching white racing cut ski-suits, they made quite the pair as they joined the run and sliced through the slower patrons.

They schussed to a smart stop at a bar, not far from the main gondola. Removed their skis and sat on the large deck in the warm sun. Bolt nodded to the barman and a bottle of champagne arrived at the table. Bolt handed some notes over. Even without the shades, you'd struggle to age either. Their tans and laughter lines deep from years of love and adventures. They were "Livers" through and through and had been before they had taken the money or it was a label.

They raised their glasses in their own toast, "Amsterdam" where they had shared their first bottle of champagne so many years ago and cemented their romance. What followed was a whirlwind of passion and connection. Mary had helped Martin clean up his drinking habits, something that he found surprisingly easy, enveloped in the fierce love of such a woman. Martin had helped with Mary's professional career, speaking to sponsors and securing funding. In time Mary's skiing and shooting abilities had rocketed her career and her natural charm and beauty had made her a well known and loved sports personality. Eventually working in winter sports journalism and commentary. Mary's professional earnings and later book sales had dwarfed Bolts somewhat failed career from an earlier era. But, nobody could have been more genuinely pleased about this deserved success than her husband.

"King's cross?" Bolt asked. Playing their game.

"We had given up drinking, we went into London for a comedy show and mocktails. There was a busker and sober as judges, in front of everyone going home you danced with me in the tunnels as the busker played louder and louder and passers-by stopped and joined in."

Mary smiled fondly, she had invented their game, "moments" and truly believed the mindful reminisces of their love was part of a healthy relationship. One of her many tools for a happy marriage. They truly appreciated each other and what they had. Not everyone is so lucky.

"It's still one of my favorites, my love." He said. "I didn't care about anything but you, in the busiest city in the world, I felt as if it was just us."

"And Neil Diamond and Sweet Caroline of course."

"I'm pretty sure the buskers name was Alan, but he was pretty good."

They touched glasses, took a sip and appreciated the mountain view in front of them. White against blue sky, it was a bluebird day. Mary looked at Bolt and raised an eyebrow in that way she did. Martin already knew the conversation was coming. Since leaving the UK they had been drinking most days. Despite their planning, fake documents and success in reaching the mountains, there was still an underlying fear lying heavy in the pit of their stomachs and a glass of wine here and there had helped settle the nerves. But as ever, Bolt had been drinking fast and ordering another. It was time for another break.

"We're not on holiday, we have to be smart." Mary offered.

"I know my love, it's time. We should move on again too. As much as I love hopping from resort to resort in the Alps and skiing and drinking. We have disappeared, maybe we should make our run to Andorra or Spain."

It made sense, they agreed that they would head down to the van after some lunch and then head off the next morning on the long drive towards Spain and then hopefully cross the Mediterranean to Morocco. Once on the water surely they would be safe and the fear would lift.

"So, lunch?" Mary asked.

"Woah, wait a second. You have to choose a moment."

"Of course my love." Eyes closed a smile came across her face. "Guess."

"I'm not sure that's allowed in the rules."

"I'll check with the inventor...yes, its fine."

"Do I get a clue?"

"It was cold, but I have never found you more romantic." Mary smiled and sat back in her chair, sun on her face, enjoying the memory.

"The Reading tree?" Bolt grinned as Mary nodded.

***

It had been a December country walk in a Hertfordshire woodland. They came across a giant squat Oak, branches outstretched and low, offering easy steps for all the adults and children who had climbed the tree over the decades, many had carved their initials into the great Oak's trunk.

They had climbed the tree and found a branch for two. In the cold they had wrapped each other up in their arms and Bolt had taken a tired looking paperback from his back pocket and proceeded to read to Mary in his warm voice. He could have made a great sports commentator, if his reputation hadn't made him too unreliable and unstable to employ, once they had repaired his image, he had only wanted to support his wife's blossoming career, preferring the background and academic work.

***

"Do you remember what I was reading?" Bolt knew, it was one of his favourites and a book that Mary had stolen from a book café a few days before their walk in one of her rare and wild moments of moral abandon.

"Man and Superman, by George Bernard Shaw of course." Mary blushed, remembering how he had come to have the book. "You are my Superman and Shaw is one of my favourite writers, I had to do it." They both laughed.

Martin stood up from the table, took her hand, kissed it and they touched glasses again and drank. Martin looked deep into Mary's eyes and they held each other's gaze, suddenly Martin pulled Mary to her feet and kissed her lips as the familiar sound of a rifle shot rang clear in the mountains and blood ran down Mary's face.

25

Marcus saw the van and Bear's face, realised maybe this was it and regretted he hadn't had more adventures. Kind looked at Kiri and smiled, he didn't have time for thoughts of regret. There was a loud *crack* and then everything happened fast.

***

Kiri felt like she'd been sprayed, a warm sticky liquid peppered her face and when she smeared it from her eyes, Kind was in front of her, a hole in his forehead. Tom stood frozen, eyes and mouth open, he looked at her in surprise, before collapsing to the floor on his face, a gaping hole in the mess that was the back of his skull. Kiri fell to dirt next to him in shock.

***

Seeing the van, Bear had moved fast, first shoving Layla into the Fiat, he then ran towards Cherry, he didn't want Chance hit by accident. Before he had taken three steps, only metres from him, he watched powerless at the shock in eyes of his best friend Tom Kind. The crack of a rifle was accompanied by the snapping back of his head as the bullet entered his brain and left again taking the back of his head with it, his body spasmed with the impact. The puff of pink and lifeless body dropping to it's knees and rocking forward to the ground left no doubt. Kind was dead. Bear turned and ran.

***

On the bridge, Primary kill confirmed; instead of taking a second shot, Hawk checked on the female who had moved towards the target, she was physically unharmed. He panned right just too late to find Drummond or Higgins. They had both been moving away from the white vehicle towards the red VW. He scanned the area and waited as the white car with the kid in it got the hell out of there driving North deeper into the Jungle camp.

The red van with its canvas cover also roared forward and tore towards him across the wasteland towards the tunnel bridge and Jungle exit. The driver was a female, she could just be running from danger, but the other targets could be in the back. Hawk scanned again, no sign of the targets. He slid into the driver's seat and called in an update and information request. By the time he had his seat belt on and pulled onto the motorway he already had a tech guy satellite tracking the red van. There was no hurry in this business, one at a time, in priority order was perfectly acceptable. The hunt is a marathon, not a sprint.

***

"Kiri, get in the fucking van now!" Rosie screamed.
Kiri staggered backwards from Tom Kinds body, half-blind, swayed to the van and fell in. Rosie floored it, they weren't necessarily targets, but she wanted them away from flying bullets wherever they were coming from.

***

As his friends body fell; Bear stopped, turning back he ran and bundled Marcus towards the Fiat's passenger door. Bear jumped in the back headfirst and Hercules stamped on the accelerator the doors swinging shut as they sped forward into the Jungle. Heading for the back entrance, Hercules called Marie.

"Marie, listen. I need you to load the horses and get Rumi in the van. I've already loaded the bags. We'll be leaving fast, sorry, no time to explain. Merci Marie."

Hercules threw the burner out the window, pulled out of the Calais Jungle and turned East, heading for the country roads and a small farmhouse on the edges of Marck.

***

Barking orders. Hercules parked on the edge of a woodland and they jogged through the woods and climbed over a back fence and through a field, over another fence and across a lawn to a stone farmhouse. The three figures following were barely more than zombies on autopilot, obeying his commands.

On a large gravel driveway around the front of the house, next to the stables the Horse-van was running. Marie looking down the road for them, she turned as she heard the crunch of boots on gravel.

"No time to explain, everyone in. Au revoir Marie, Fiat is around the back, merci." Hercules kissed her cheeks as he ran past to the driver's door and the others bundled in the side door to the living space between the horses and cab.

"Wait!" Marie called. "The dog, she is not here, she was in the field and wouldn't come."

"Dad, Rumi, wait." Hercules, put the van into gear and gave his daughter a look she may never forgive and said.

"You've trained her. Call her."

Layla tried to get out, but with Bear and Marcus between her and the door, there was no exit as Hercules pulled away. The horses stamping and whinnying in the back. As he drove down the long gravel exit, Layla clambered across and opened the sliding side door and with everything she had, screamed.

"RUMI! RUMI COME! RUMI COME NOW!" She put her fingers in her mouth and whistled harder than she had whistled before. Tears streaming down her face, she called and whistled. Marcus and Bear joining in as they picked up speed and drove away down the road. Layla kept calling out the door, until after a few minutes, breathless, she collapsed back in the seat and wept. Bear went to close the door, but Chance put her hand on his.

"Wait. Give her a chance, she's a good girl. Give her a chance. *Rumi come!*" She called again and whistled loud and long. "Please Rumi, come, everything is going wrong, I need you girl."

Bear, leaned out of the door and waited. As he looked back down the road, a small brown shape crested a rise in the distance, it was gaining on them down the hill.

"Chance, keep calling." He banged on the side of the van and pointed at the wing mirror and signalled to slow down. Hercules eased off the accelerator and the brown shaped got closer. Chance leaned out the door, Bears long arm around her waist.

"Come on girl, good girl, come on."

A beautiful Hungarian Vizsla sprinted alongside and leapt into the van, knocking Chance backwards and licking her face like they just played the best game in the world. Layla collapsed into tears on the floor hugging her dog. Bear shut the door and took a seat. One hand on Chance's shoulder, still sobbing after the days events, her dog nuzzled her neck and sat in her lap. Bear put his other arm around Marcus, together in silence they sat, cried and later slept. Exhausted with fear and grief.

Hercules drove through the night, keeping to smaller roads, only stopped for fuel in little country towns, he payed with cash, Bear had already forced a large wad of notes into his hand. The horses would have had to suffer the long drive; they wouldn’t stop until they were safe at the ranch of his old friend, where they could rest and organise the means to defend themselves or escape. They had bought some time, but this was far from over.

26

Viper had been closing in on the Bell's movements since the bar manager in Tignes had done his extra-curricular job. Confirming that the targets had been drinking champagne on his terrace the day before.

It had been many weeks and seven resorts, every time he thought he was close, he'd find they had moved on and have to get the tech guys to do what they could, but it was slow. They were sticking to cash and avoiding hotels with their camper. Mountains and forests were not good for satellite tracking and there were a lot of campers out there, so Viper was forced to do a bit of old school tracking and reached out to every contact he had. Viper never failed, he would do what needed to be done, bring in mercenaries, pay off snitches, reward hackers or torture witnesses.

He didn't understand these guys who worked for the company but were squeamish about doing their job and using the full extent of their substantial powers. He was a hunter, he was a killer and he was good at it. If you were on his list you were there for a reason, he only browsed files, getting the details needed to find and execute his orders. Whether they were a nurse, a nun or a ninja was irrelevant. Viper would kill them, knowing details would only make them human. They weren't human, they were targets, prey, they were his next pay-check and besides all that, these two had started to piss him off. In the cold fucking mountains, chasing some middle-class twats while they go skiing, a level three agent could handle this cat and mouse bullshit. So far they had been lucky, but not today.

A morning of scouring hacked camera footage run through facial recognition technology had finally been fruitful. They were spotted at the bottom of the gondola, tracked to the far side of the glacier and then tracked back across towards the resort. Viper had picked up his Samsonite case and headed straight up the mountain, they were trapped. At this time of year there was one lift down from the glacier, the only ski run down ran out of snow half way, five kilometres or so from the resort, turning to mud and then pistes of green grass. They would have to take the lift, it was a cleaner shot in the mountains, less risk of a civilian spoiling his line of shot.

He took the gondola up and then a short six-man chair lift, rifle case next to him on the seat. At the top, next to the small stone lift house he had a perfect vantage of the gondola station and restaurant terrace next door. It was a longer shot than he'd like, but if he hiked down closer he would lose the shelter from the wind. It was a comfortable wait here in the sun and out the wind, besides, they might get past him while he found a position, this would do for picking off a couple of pensioners.

The lift operator at the top pretended not to see him as he settled in for a few hours of lying in the snow rifle pointed down the hill.

There was little movement below him on the mountain and Viper scanned the panorama, looking for white ski suits and a face he would recognise. The sun helped, if everyone had been in goggles and face masks this would likely be near impossible. Working his way through the lift queues and restaurants it wasn't long before he spotted two white suits ski gracefully to the corner of the restaurant opposite the gondola, prop their skis against a wall and hang their poles on the tips. They took a seat at a nearby table in the sun, smiling as his waiter brought champagne almost immediately and greeted them with a familiar smile.

This was almost too easy; with any luck he could be off this mountain in thirty minutes and eating lunch. He did some final wind and distance measurements allowing them one last glass of champagne.

Martin Bell was moving around the table. Viper waited. The woman Mary Bell, seated was the easier target to take first. The second target would likely not run for cover, in his experience the shock froze most people, allowing an easy concluding shot. Controlling his breath, he drew a bead, rifle cross-hairs on the back of her blonde locks. Viper squeezed the trigger.

***

The crack of the rifle shot, rang through the snowy mountains as Bolt pulled Mary towards his embrace. The champagne bottle on the table exploded and a heavy glass shard, sliced through Mary's beautiful cheek as bright, red blood stained the white snow at her feet.

The adrenaline and the internal fear they had carried for weeks, manifested itself in an immediate flight response. Grabbing each other and sprinting to their skis, taking cover between the two buildings, they ducked low as they ran. Another shot kicked up snow at Bolts heels as he ran, skis and poles under one arm, the other hand pushing Mary in front of him towards safety. They took cover behind the stone gondola building. Entrance to the cable car and ski runs now covered by a sharpshooter above them, the piste down to the van - incomplete, they were trapped. Cornered, their instincts took over.

They needed to get out of immediate danger and considering their skill set, the only option was to ski down as far as they could and then make their way on foot to the van before their escape was cut off. They couldn't get to the start of the piste without breaking cover, but there was another possibility. Underneath the cables of the gondola, as with most cable cars, was a cliff face, dropping almost vertically thirty metres before its gradient eased a little. The drop wasn't a problem, as long as they hit snow not rock their impact would be absorbed by the deep powder, but the momentum would propel you towards the many rocky outcrops below that you would have to avoid almost immediately, before threading your way through a narrow crevice with no space to turn. They should in theory then pop out joining on the ski run below and be able to make their way down until the snow ran out. It was not a route that many would have taken previously, it looked impossible, but Bolt had pointed it out from the lift, they'd both agreed it was ski-able, theoretically, with younger legs and heads.

***

"Shit, the bitch moved!" Viper couldn't believe it, he hated missing shots. They recorded ammunition and it went on your statistics sheet. They loved a single head shot at HQ. Frustration and surprise lead to his rushed second shot missing the now moving target too. Shit like this didn't happen, lucky, lucky bastards. They were trapped now though, they would have to either make the run to the gondola entrance or the piste down, giving him a shot as soon as they broke cover from the West corner. One thing was certain - he wouldn't miss again. Viper waited patiently.

Skis on, their boots cranked up tight; the pair in white, Mary now decorated with red streaks down one side, stood at the top of a cliff face.

"How's the face darling?"

"I'll be fine love, lets get off this mountain... Age before beauty." The fear still clear on her stained face but the adrenaline flooding her bloodstream.

Pressing snow against her wound, Martin kissed Mary hard on the lips before he took a breath and pushed off the edge of the mountain and into the void. Eyes on his landing, arms forward he dropped through the air, weight perfectly balanced he landed in deep snow, absorbing the impact with well experienced legs. Still on his feet, he burst through a cloud of powder and narrowly missed a group of large black rocks in his path, a few neat turns to slow and the narrow crevice appeared in front of him.

Mary watched him disappear and then reappear, knee-deep in powder, safely navigating the rocks. Despite the danger of the moment and the fact he was now sixty-five, Mary realised, she had never fancied that sexy old man more and couldn't wait to spend every minute of whatever time they had left together. As Bolt approached the crevice, Mary dropped in.

Falling through the air after what seemed like an age she spotted the landing between her skis. It was bloody steep. Another safe landing, a less obscuring puff of snow exploded as she landed in Bolts tracks, this allowed her to see the rocks and calmly take measures to avoid them, but carrying more speed, it took everything she had in her knees and hips not to crash, squatting deep and carrying her pace through the rocks she raced towards the narrow passage. Arms and poles tucked in, skis together; Mary Bell rocketed through the crevice, stone walls blurred past inches away from her elbows, she negotiated a fallen rock on the right, grazing a ski edge, sparks flying before the yawning exit opened and Mary burst into the sunshine, just as the ground in front of her disappeared. The drop this time was smaller only five metres, but it was a surprise. Finding herself unbalanced and in mid-air, Mary's arms wheeled wildly, before she landed on the piste below on her left ski, the other in the air, she held the landing and got the other ski to the snow before controlling her speed and coming to a stop she looked for Bolt. Bolt was a little way down the slope and as she skied down, he clipped a ski back on and brushed snow from his hair and sunglasses.

"Did we have a little trouble dear?" Mary called as she skied past.

"Last bit caught me by surprise." Martin followed.

Picking up speed as they snaked down the mountain, they tucked low, knees bent, skis apart, hips thrown into each turn as they transferred their weight from ski edge to edge. The aerodynamic racing crouch allowed them to gain speed fast and within minutes the snow was softening between their feet. As mud and grass slopes appeared below. Bolt loved his skis and hated to do this too them, but he tucked lower and aimed for the iciest part of the mud, rock and grass piste below. At over a hundred kilometres an hour, the difference between surfaces was like throwing an anchor out, the skis slowed and the momentum pushed Bolt forward, sitting back as much as he could, ski tips in the air, he held his balance and found himself skidding over the icy stretch, into slush and then on to the grass, still moving fast on the steep slope. Mary followed his lead.

Friction beat speed and they ground to a halt after a hundred and fifty metres. Un-clipping the skis and loosening his boots, Martin hoisted his skis onto his shoulder as Mary shot him a look.

"I'm not leaving these, come on, let's go." Mary didn't argue, but loosened her boots, left her skis on the muddy grass and using her poles, started a steady jog, checking her speed as they made their way heavily down the steep grass slope before them to the village below.

***

Lying still in the snow, sun beating down on him, Viper waited. Cross-hairs on the western corner of the building waiting for a glimpse. They had to move.

The sound of the cables and wheels of the chair lift hummed over the sound of a tinny radio, playing French rap on the radio. The occasional waft of cannabis or conversation floated over from chair-lift passengers as they reached the top. A loud American voice, eclipsed the other sounds.

“Crazy motherfuckers, I can’t believe they made that drop, I thought they were dead for sure man.”

“Awesome bro, but... Fuck that insane shit, I’ll stick to the pistes.”

“Yeah bro, but he was like a Grandpa or something and she wasn’t young, she just followed him over. Crazy old fuckers.”

Viper knew immediately that he had made an error of judgement somewhere. They had escaped somehow. Before the American voices had faded, he was on his knees and packing away his rifle, cursing again. These two were really starting to piss him off.

The lift operative didn’t ignore him as he got back on the chair with his long black case,
“*Malchance*” was delivered with the sneered disgust only achievable by being French. He had heard the Americans conversation and was clearly pleased that this snake had failed to strike. Scowling Viper made his way down to the gondola station and his continued pursuit.

The gondola down gave him the time to check his phone and read the files properly. The information on the vehicle had finally been sent from the tech geeks and he had a location on the Bell’s van. As he passed over the last of the snow and to grassy lower slopes, he allowed himself a smile. This day wasn’t over by a long shot.

It was hot. Away from the snowy glacier, the late March sun was unrelenting. Mary had stopped and abandoned her jacket and was moving fast despite the cumbersome loosened ski boots, blood dried in a wind-blown mask, running down and then streaking back across her face. It was a slog either way, so she kept putting left in front of right using her poles to keep a rhythm. Bolt wasn't enjoying the yomp either, ski bindings jolting into his clavicle, having refused to leave his skis he was determined not to put them down. But, Mary was leaving him behind. He swallowed his pride, ditched the jacket and his super- stiff racing skis and took after his wife using his poles to propel himself forward.

"Bit more comfortable now my love? Sorry you had to lose them."

"Just skis darling. This is about survival now, we need a plan."

"About that." Mary's green eyes flashed, looking warrior-like with the red blood painting her face. I have an idea, but you won't like it."

"How do you know?"

"Because... I don't like it."

They never argued, but an intense debate was not unheard of and they argued the strengths of their individual plans for escape. Martin wanted to run as soon as they got to the van, pedal to the metal, just get out of the Alps and France. Mary's plan was a little more finessed.

***

Viper had done the math; even skiing fast (as the file suggested they would) and being able to make their way on foot at a good pace, they had a distance to cover. By his reckoning, he should be able to descend and make the four minute run from the gondola base to a flat area of grass on the edge of some trees before they escaped. It was the perfect spot just above the open car park with the Bell's camper-van parked in it. He would be in place for an easy shot when they arrived tired and panicked from their exertions. Re-energised from his ride down, on which he ate a protein bar and took a go-pill from his pack with a swig of water. Straps over his shoulder, the rifle case was high and tight on his back. Viper was coiled and as the doors slid open he left the gondola taking the walkway at a sprint, dodging a few snowboarders before flying down metal staircases and out onto the quiet street. Sprinting down the road to avoid obstacles, Viper over took a slowing bus and raced around a wide corner. Spotting a gap between two cars, he accelerated across the small roundabout and down the hills. The assassin was at his firing spot in three and a half minutes. This time there wouldn't any mistakes, it was less than a two hundred metre shot, their heads would be the size of a tractor wheel in his scope, he couldn't miss; after running him through the cold-ass mountains for weeks, it was pay day.

Viper removed his rifle and lay on the grass in a perfect firing position and waited, any minute now they should appear from the village main street. Carefully checking every face that entered the car-park he waited. They had been slower than he thought, he'd given them more respect than deserved. "*Well, they are old...*"
"*CRACK!*"

"*They are old...*" was the last thought that entered Viper's head, before a bullet went through the back of it. His face collapsed into a bloody pulp in the grass as his body went limp.

Viper had it coming. The only person that really liked Viper, was Viper. Not that it would matter to Mary, but he really wouldn't be missed by anyone but his employer.

***

Two hundred and forty metres away, beyond a small woodland behind Viper. Mary packed away her rifle and wiping away a tear made her way down to the car park where Martin emerged from behind a large lorry and hugged his wife tight and held her.

"Amazing job, you were right. Great plan, are you okay my love?"

"I'm fine. Let's get out of here."

"I should have ditched the skis earlier, we could have been too slow, I saw him arrive thirty seconds after you made the tree line. You're incredible darling."

They had known this may be a step they had to take to survive, but it hadn't been a path they had wanted to walk.

"I'm not amazing or incredible... I'm a murderer." Mary climbed quietly into the back of the camper, put the rifle case under the bed and started cleaning her face, before giving up and laying down on the bed. Martin climbed up and stepped through into the front cab, settled into the captain's chair and started the engine, swinging out the car park and away down the mountain, he open a packet of Hobnobs and grabbed a biscuit from the packet. *Just one.*

27

Hawk didn't have to track the Cherry red van for long. Once it went screaming out of the Jungle it took a few wild turns and stopped on a back road behind a large blue skip. Hawk pulled up, approached the van from behind and listened. Inside the cab he could hear crying, but there wasn't a breath, or sign of movement coming from inside the canvas back. Gun drawn, he released the clips holding the canvas and unzipped the back... *empty*.

Arms around her inconsolable friend, Rosie looked up at the tap on the window to find herself looking at a gun. It wasn't the first time, but that wasn't much comfort, as she slowly wound down the window.

"We were just trying to get out of there, we're not involved."

"Involved in what?" Hawk paused. "Rosie, you're driving a target vehicle and there's a photo and note in my file that suggests you and Mr Kind were involved in the movement of an illegal person into the UK."

"No human is illegal." Rosie replied.

"I am sorry for your loss, I don't disagree with you or have a problem with the actions of the late Mr Kind. It's not personal."

"You bastard." Kiri said with venom.

"Ladies, I have a job to do. I have a few questions and if you answer them. You can drive away and never see me again. You could go back to Mo in the UK. But, so you know you can trust my word, I'll give you some free advice. If there is any proof you were involved, don't go back to the UK yet, the file on you is growing."

"Fuck your questions." Kiri spat.

Hawk sighed and pointed the gun at Kiri's head.

Why did they always have to make it hard?

"*Wait!* What do you want to know?" Rosie had seen enough blood for one day. This guy wasn't fucking around, his polite tone and calmness made her feel uneasy, as if shooting people in the head didn't bother him at all.

"Where are they going? Who was driving the small white Fiat, why did they head deeper into the Jungle, where would they hide?"

"Cyprus." Rosie answered. "They're heading for Cyprus." It wasn't surprise or particularly useful information, there were a hundred routes to get there. But, it gave him a direction.

"The driver."

"Hercules."

"Rosie, please, don't test me."

"I swear, that's what everyone called him; he's big guy, long hair, looks like a fucking Spartan or some shit."

"Please answer one last question Rosie, then you and your friend can leave. Where would they hide out in the Jungle?"

Rosie hesitated.

"I don't know, there's a thousand tents or shelters to hide in, people everywhere, hundreds of buildings that could fit a small vehicle, I guess you have to start looking."

"Sorry, don't buy it Rosie, you just lied to me." He pointed the gun back at Kiri's head with a sad look. "Sorry kid."

"Okay, okay, wait. They're not in the camp, there's no reason for you to tear up the Jungle looking for them."

"Rose, no!" Kiri looked at Rosie, who looked away and addressed the man with the gun.

"There's a small back entrance that is sometimes closed, they would have headed for that gate."

"It's not in my file." Hawk was annoyed at the bad intelligence.

"They put it in when the Jungle was reduced, it allowed police to enter from both sides and better access for the refuse collectors. I swear."

"I believe you. Bon Voyage Rosie, don't go home... and get your tyre pressures checked, I think the back ones might both be low." He walked away, pausing to have a look at the tyres on each side.

After a few minutes, Rosie spoke.

"Well at least Mo is safe in the UK with friends from the Jungle. Looks like we won't be going back for a while. What was the address for that ranch, I saw Kind give you that piece of paper on the way to the van, just before... was he going to try and convince Hercules."

"They just needed somewhere for a night." Kiri reached into her pocket and took out the crumpled piece of paper and burst into tears.

"Come on girl, let's go get you cleaned up. It will be okay." Rosie pulled away.

***

Down the road, Hawk had put in an update to central, the tech guys would already be at work on tracking the Fiat. Hawk in the meantime, was watching a small blue dot move across a map of Calais. As the magnetic tracker he had put inside Cherry's wheel arch stopped at a service station, he was finally able to take a break. Hawk called into a Patisserie ordered a croissant and coffee and sat heavy in a plastic chair. Feeling a little bad about his slight exaggeration. While Rosie was in his file, she was currently only a suspect, there was no evidence of her involvement in the trafficking. Only that she had booked a ticket and left Calais moments after a call from Tom Kind in Dover. She was free to return to the UK and to Mo, instead Hawk had pushed her and her friend towards danger. It had to be done he told himself as he sipped his coffee and made a call to the hospital for an update on his daughter.

28

Following the strobing white lines on autopilot, the road stretched ahead of him through a forest, after driving through the night Hercules was tired, tired and scared. What had he been thinking? He should have driven away with Layla as soon as the first shot was fired. After years of moving around, they were finally off the radar. Now he had assisted Marcus and Bear in escaping a hunter, he would be investigated and once that happened, he knew he would be a target once more. Which meant Layla was in danger. It also meant soon they would have to have a conversation he had been avoiding for too long. They would have to talk about Layla's mother, how she really died and why they were now in serious trouble.

***

Hercules remembered holding Layla that first day, sixteen years ago, so small she almost fitted in his palm. Sofia, exhausted from the labour and her mystery illness throughout most the pregnancy, slept almost immediately after kissing her daughter. Holding their baby to her glistening breast as it rose and fell, recovering from her exertion, tears running down her face. Hercules was so proud of her, as strong and brave as in any of their many missions working together.

Hercules didn't sleep that first night, he just sat at her bedside, his daughter in his arms, watching them sleep. Listening to rain fall outside the window of the hospital he had come to know well. Lost in the flood of emotions, the reality of the tiny human resting in his embrace, his heart more full of love than he could have ever dreamed possible and his head swimming in fears for his love and for the future of this innocent child and the world she was joining.

Sofia was getting worse and Hercules was terrified he was going to lose her and be on this ultimate mission alone. Living on their savings, professional bridges burnt; was this baby even safe from the company? Who knows what effect the scientific tests Sofia had undergone voluntarily could have had on the fetus she hadn't known she was carrying. They knew Sofia was faster, stronger and cognitively superior now she had undergone the gene modification and stem cell treatments. But, they couldn't diagnose her current illness or confirm it had anything to do with the groundbreaking experiments performed on her.

The company didn't care about the health of mother or child and the legal department had tried to force the continuance of the research and even suggested termination of the pregnancy. That was the final straw. Hercules handed in his notice with immediate effect and eventually convinced his lover and team leader, Sofia, to quit the company. Despite initial offers of raises and promotions, it turned nasty fast with threats of court proceedings for breach of contract. The whispers filled the halls of HQ and the resulting political fall-out from the division created in the company had created in-house chaos. They had walked away, their third team member and a few other employees joining them on principle. It had been a shit storm.

***

Everyone but Hercules and the weary horses had drifted into a long exhausted sleep. As dawn lit the van they left their unconscious comfort, the warm blessing of those first sweet seconds of ignorance and confusion upon waking passing; the memories of the previous day hitting like an icy wave. They stirred with the heavy stone of grief in their stomachs, it was a silent morning in the back of the van.

29

It was early morning when the wheels of the horsebox crunched onto the gravel driveway of a picturesque ranch. Green paddocks, enclosed with white fences edged the track, inquisitive horses watched the van make its way to the large stone farmhouse. Hercules turned into a large courtyard in front of the house, encircled by outbuildings. Their haven was nestled in rolling pastures and mountainous forests on the outskirts of Foix, near Toulouse; it was the perfect place to rest and plan their next move.

Hercules parked next to a well-used Toyota pick-up. Their approached easily heard, a lady looked up from the beautiful grey horse she was grooming with affection. Brushing long blonde hair from her eyes, a broad smile came across her face as Hercules climbed down from the driver's seat, face wracked with exhaustion and stress.

"Cornelius Chance, perfect timing as always. I've finished cleaning Storm, just going to put her out in the paddock."

"Alex, I'm sorry..."

"Unless it's for waiting so long to visit, stop right there, you know you don't need an invite. Rory's in the bottom fields feeding the sheep, he won't be long. Tea, breakfast?"

***

Chance gave Bear's big hand a squeeze. She had no words for her new friend. Bear squeezed her hand and stood defiantly taking a big breath and following her out the van. Layla, Marcus and Bear stepped out, stretching. Rumi jumped out and ran around sniffing everything and peeing, excited to be finally free, but staying close to Layla.

"This must be Layla, it's been so long, I doubt you remember me...and who is this?" Alex smiled at the dog.

"I like Chance now, this is Rumi... and our friends Marcus and Bear." The two big chaps nodded uncomfortably and tried to smile.

"Hi Chance, gents, I'm Alex; you got horses with you too?"

"Yes, two, do you have a stable or paddock I can put them in? They've been couped up for hours and they could do with breakfast."

"Don't worry Aaron will get them, he should be done with the chickens, you all look exhausted. I'll put the kettle on and you can tell me what trouble you've got yourself in over breakfast. Come on."

Layla didn't know who Aaron was, but she could kiss him; she was ready for breakfast not mucking out the van. She got Rumi's food and water bowls and left her having breakfast outside. Rumi happily ate and enjoyed the new surroundings, Layla joined the group in the house. Introductions and instructions had been given when she arrived in the kitchen.

"Thank you daarrling." Alex said as a tall, attractive blond boy in a red checked shirt was walking towards Layla out the kitchen. Sleeves rolled up with muscular arms, jeans and socks.

"No problem Mum." Aaron smiled at Layla as she kicked off her shoes by the front door.

"That's what I thought sweetie." His mother replied, as he pulled on his boots.

Cute boy alert. "Need any help?" Layla asked. He seemed familiar.

"No worries, I've got this, have some eggs." Aaron smiled, shut the door and stood outside a moment. *Idiot, you could have hung out with the hot girl.*

Layla looked at the closed door behind him - *Boys are dumb, but eggs sound good.*

In the kitchen they sat around a big pine refectory table, Alex making eggs, bacon and tea as Hercules briefly explained the situation. Afterwards, he was about to say sorry again, when Alex gave him a look and interrupted.

"What do you need? You've known since the wild days, you're family."

"Oh, I remember your wild days." Hercules smiled for the first time in what seemed like a week. Layla looked at her Dad - *he was being weird.*

"We need supplies; food, weapons and equipment, somewhere to hide today while we plan the next move."

"Sounds like you need to speak to the quartermaster. First let's eat." Alex put the food on the table and they ate in silence.

A quad bike pulled up outside and the door banged open. A man with a bushy greying beard, flat cap and gilet bounded in, Aaron following behind.

"Got your message. Visitors?" The man had a slight Irish lilt, Bear placed it as Northern, east coast, somewhere south of Belfast. Old habits.

"Jesus, it's not, bloody hell man, Cornelius! You bastard, what you doing to me, trying to give an old friend a heart attack or here to steal my wife finally?"

The two friends embraced, kissing each other fiercely on the cheek and smiling, remembering their fun college days when they'd competed for Alex's affections. After nineteen years it had clearly been a good choice and Hercules had been honoured to be their best man, close friend to both and a witness to their love for each other.

The smiles didn't last long as Hercules explained the gravity of the situation.

"So fella, what's the plan? Rory took a bite of his sandwich, a little yolk running into his beard, Alex was already handing him a napkin.

30

After placing the tracker on the red van carrying Rosie and Kiri, Hawk had time to eat and rest. This wasn't a sprint. He reported in and received an updated order:

25/03/2042
L9:5657 Hawkins, Andrew. Codename "Hawk"
UPDATE –
Target: Tom Kind - Kill confirmed. Clean-up en route.

Updated Primary targets:
MARCUS DRUMMOND - Human trafficking, traitor to the state.
Sentence: Death.
Location: Locating
File attached. Civilian. Activist. Low threat.

MICHAEL "Bear" HIGGINS - traitor to the state.
Sentence: Death
Location: Locating
File: Classified. Military - highly trained, consider dangerous.
Further information to follow.

CORNELIUS "Hercules" CHANCE - traitor to the state.

Sentence: Death
Location: Locating
File attached. Activist, low threat. Further information to follow.

LAYLA CHANCE – Dependant : PENDING
Location: Locating
Additional note: Targets Martin and Mary Bell neutralised Viper in the Alps. Additional agents in play. Terminate current targets and await further orders.
Personal note: Sarah is doing well. (Steve).

Hawk finished a coffee and re-read each targets files again, including an addendum report on Vipers elimination. This was getting interesting; it was time to hit the road again, he'd rather stay ahead of the additional agents, it could get messy. Hawk didn't want them getting in his way, or riding his coat-tails and then sharing his bounty. The big bucks always went to the trigger-man whether they had done the lions share of the hunting or not.

31

"I think we should split up." Hercules held up a hand. "Hear me out. The horse box is slow and conspicuous and moving as a group is a risk. They are looking for three males and a young female. We can't get far together. I need to go to Barcelona and see a friend who I hope can help us with a boat I know he has on the coast. If I can leave the horses and van here and borrow your pick-up,

"Sure thing man, you paying the doctor a visit?"

"I am. I'll go to Barcelona. I want you guys to go on foot, they can't track you easily on foot. The safest country near us is Andorra, just on the other side of the Pyrenees mountains. I'll return for the the horses and meet you there, from Andorra we can get away into the Mediterranean and be in the wind or head overland to Portugal."

"I've got questions." Layla, didn't look thrilled. "How far is Andorra and Rumi comes with me right?"

"Yes, Rumi goes with you guys. It's about an hundred kilometer hike from here, Rory and I did it years ago, there's a path, it's a tough slog, killer height gain. Layla didn't like the idea of splitting up, but she knew he was right, a big city was a risk with cameras and police drones. One person was safer.

"Guess we're hiking." Layla forced a grin, this wasn't going to be a walk in the hills.

"Fancy some company?" Aaron spoke. "Okay. I know this situation is dangerous but..."

"Everyone has a voice here." Chance said. Alex raised an eyebrow. Aaron continued.

"Okay, with the technology at their disposal you will be tracked here eventually. This place should be a ghost town when they get here. What about if we all go? Mum, Dad, we know the route well, even at night. We could take the horses through the forests, up to Les Cabennes along the river path, then they can continue up the Randonnee Etand de Riete track to Cabane de Senard and we can take the horses to Sally's and wait out for a few days. Hercules can come back for the van and then pick up the horses from there."

Nobody seemed to have an argument. Rory spoke,

"The lad's right, we shouldn't hang around here. Let's get the gear ready; Alex food, Aaron equipment, the usual and pack some ropes, extra first aid... just in case. Cornelius, come with me to the barn, I assume the young lady is perfectly capable of driving the horse box in."

Hercules and Rory headed to open the big barn doors and Layla shut the back of the now clean horsebox. Impressive work from Aaron considering their long journey. Maybe this wasn't the end of the world, yet. Smart, good with horses, fit, if Rumi liked him he could be in with a *Chance*. Layla allowed herself a tired smile as she drove into the barn. Then she remembered Tom Kind and felt guilty for any levity she felt. Bear was hurting; he'd barely said a word. Layla got out the van.

"Layla, go-bag." Hercules called. Layla went immediately to the back of the van and pulled her 30 litre backpack from under the bed, clothes and some dried fruit and nut rations. She gathered a few important items; her archery equipment, knife, a hairbrush and handful of hairbands and a hard drive with music and some photos stored on it. Finally shoving some extra socks in for after the hike ahead, Chance was out of the van in less than a minute, it was a "go-bag" but she was human and a teenager, life's always a bit messy.

From under a mezzanine floor, with a solid pine ladder leading up to hay bales, Rory put his head round the steel door of a room in the corner of the barn and yelled.

"*Chance the younger, come see Uncle Rory.*"

Hercules left the room, head down and walked towards her. Now with various weapons sticking out of holsters at his hips and back - looking different to any time Layla could remember; she had seen him angry, furious on occasion and even scared once or twice, but this was different, she had never seen him scary. He looked like a bad guy. As he got closer and saw his daughter, he transformed, smiling with his eyes, he kissed his daughter on the head as he passed and went to get his own go-bag.

***

The room was unlike anything Layla had seen before. Chance was not a fan of guns. They were either used for violence against fellow humans, or to gain an unfair advantage against an animal. But, this was impressive, this guy must be a Virgo. Clean and well lit, there was a large workbench in the middle, on the walls in neat lines, carefully organised were racks and racks of weapons and ammunition, twenty pistols, thirty rifles, automatic shotguns, some things that said “Claymore” on them, even a dozen hand grenades - boxed in sixes as if they were eggs. As a centre piece in a rack were a pair of carefully crafted shotguns, stunning wood stocks, with rich Walnut grain and beautiful leaf engraving on the shiny metal.

“They’re amazing!” Layla knew the right things to say and they were a work of art.

“Thanks kiddo, I made them myself. I am rather proud of them.”

“Rory... How’d you know my Dad?” Her dad seemed to know some interesting people.

“I stole his girl at University, because your old man is just too damn nice for his own good. We became friends, later worked together for a little while after we got our degrees. It was well paid but we both decided that we wanted a different path in life. To be honest I think us pair of old softies both just fell in love, we wanted families, life changed... the world changed.” Rory paused, then continued,

“Anyway, to current things. I doubt you remember me, it’s been some time and you were wee. But, if anything ever happens to your old man, know we are family girl. We are always here, no matter what. Your Dad knew that when he brought the shit-storm, we’re practically brothers and I’m your legal godfather. Now your parents and me weren’t really into all that religion thing, but you needed a name and a celebration day, so... what, I’m trying to say

Layla, is by my reckoning I owe you quite a few birthday and Christmas gifts."

Layla laughed, she didn't remember him, but she liked Rory, he was funny, she could see why her Dad was friends with him.

"I always knew your old man's rebellious streak would get him in trouble. Told him to buy land, keep his head down and wait it out... But you know him. People need help, systems need fighting and he wanted you to see the real world. Anyway young Chance, *gifts* - I been waiting for a long time to give you this and your Dad says it's the right time, and you know how he feels about these things."

Rory went to a drawer and took out a small wooden box, around the size of a laptop, but thicker. With an air of expectation, he presented the box to Layla. It was a simple pine box but very heavy. Layla put the box on the table and opened the lid. Inside as she expected in this room, were guns. What Layla wasn't prepared for was the beauty. Purple silk lined the box, along with some boxes of rounds, inset, pointing towards each other were two small pistols. Walnut grips. Nickel plating shining brightly, the intricate carving on the handles showed trees growing into a deer with large antlers. Chance picked one up and turned it over, acknowledging the workmanship depicting a river flowing from a mountain waterfall. The ivy leaves engraved on the metal work was delicate and done with skill and patience. Layla couldn't remember ever receiving such a gift, made with such time and care. Let alone from someone she didn't know.

"They´re heavier than I expected."

"Yes, guns always weigh heavy in your hand and your heart, don´t spend your life with one in your hand, they never get any lighter."

"Did you make these?"

"Yes, for you. I told you we're family."

"Thank you Rory, they are truly beautiful."

"Promise me, only if you absolutely need to use them. Last resort. Your dad will show you how to use a pistol. One of the best shots I've ever seen."

Layla nodded and let the last comment pass as if unnoticed and hugged Rory tightly.

"Thank you, they are a work of art and thank you for being my Dad's friend, for helping us, for everything." Layla was feeling overwhelmed it had been a tough day.

"What are godfathers for? Besides I wasn't just your old man's friend, Alex and I loved your mum too, she was a special woman. But that's for another time. Come on, let's make sure they're getting things sorted and get some more tea before we leave."

Layla put the box in her go-bag and they headed to the house, heaving the heavy doors closed, shutting the horsebox in the barn.

***

Within an half an hour they were fully packed. Layla, Aaron and Alex had tacked-up the horses in the sunshine, it was warm, late summer in France, blue skies and barely a cloud. Hercules threw his waterproof go-bag in the back of the pick-up. Bear had his big green rucksack on and was sizing up the large cob that was going to carry him. It had been a while and then only as a last resort. Layla could see his doubts.

"Don't worry Bear, I can help you. You got this." Bear grimaced and nodded.

Marcus had been given some of Aaron's clean clothes. Everything lost in Calais. Marcus hadn't ever ridden before and to be honest, wasn't looking forward to what it was going to do to his soft areas. Aaron had winced when he'd mentioned it was his first time. Marcus made a choice.

"Hercules... want some company in Barcelona? I don't think anyone should be on their own. We need to watch each other's backs."

Hercules hesitated, but saw Layla's face light-up at the suggestion. Hercules shrugged and gestured to the back of the pick-up.

"Jump in Marcus, let's hit the road."

They said their goodbyes. Rory and Bear shook Hercules hand firmly and gave him a look that he knew meant - Layla is safe... *Safer than with him right now.*

"Look after him Marcus, when he took me to Barcelona we walked for hours and found nothing but museums and old buildings, I swear he was lost. It took us all day to find The Chocolate Factory." Layla made everyone smile and gave Hercules a big hug. "Be careful Dad. I love you."

"I love you too." They climbed into the truck. "I'll see you soon. Trust your instincts, follow your gut." Hercules forced a confident smile and wave as they drove away.

After a quiet moment, Alex broke the silence.

"Cup of tea, or shall we get moving?"

"Let's get out of here." Layla wanted to keep moving, she didn't feel safe yet. Rory nodded and Aaron hopped-up gracefully onto his horse. It was still early morning when the five riders left the yard. Rumi happily followed Layla and her horse Coco, excited to be off on another adventure. Bear bumping along behind on Herc's horse, Royal.

32

They hadn't spoken much, but Kiri was glad to have Rosie next to her. French radio played some rap in the background as they cruised south on the motorway. They were going as fast as Cherry's thermostat would allow. Rosie had owned many vans over the years, overheating was one of the various reasons she had got rid of her old VW bus, hip as they are. They were making reasonable progress at 100km/hr. But, eventually the red light flashed and with hills on the horizon, it was time for them all to take a break. They pulled off the motorway into a small town just past Limoges and parked.

Finding a restaurant, they ate in almost silence and then went to sleep in the back of the van. Rosie fell asleep immediately. Kiri lay thinking about Kind, his rucksack lying next to her in the dark, eventually sobbing herself to sleep. Exhausted.

***

Hawk had a good night's sleep in the van. Parked in a lay-by a few miles before the location of the stopped target vehicle. There had been no notification of movement, but there was a morning debrief request. Hawk called in to control and went through the security protocol before being put on hold.

"Hawk, what the bloody hell is going on?" It was Steve, his superior technically, but a friend if Hawk had one. "I've lost an agent in the Alps, you're making slow progress in France and they've sent two more agents to join the hunt. Upstairs are going nuts, it's all numbers with them. In the meantime, you're the closest to various targets - so be prepared to be flexible."

"Affirmative."

A military source has given me a little bit of unofficial information on the classified file of Michael "Bear" Higgins. I have nothing to send. But, my guy reckons this "Bear" was like a Special Forces ghost. A guy sent in alone to do things that had to be deniable and quiet. Survived what seemed like suicide missions. Eventually, he was injured in the line of duty and had to drag himself back. Half-dead by the time a patrol found him in a ditch by the side of the road. When he eventually got out of hospital he wasn't the same - no longer a useful weapon so they canned him, he disappeared, until now. What you got for me?"

"I've got a tracker on a vehicle that is going to our targets, but it's not exactly a race car so I'm being patient. I read the report on Viper. The Bell couple are formidable, intelligent and skilled."

"I agree, but Viper got over confident too. Keep playing it smart. I will support your strategy upstairs, but you know what it's like when they lose an asset. They want results."

"Remind them this asset is one of their most valuable. Once I've caught up with this group I'll clear up the Viper mess. But, slowly, slowly catchy monkey."

"Speaking of which..."

"Oh no, Gorilla, really? Who's the other agent?"

"They're sending the Wolf."

"Wolf and Gorilla, bet they're not happy are they? I take it they are not working together."

"Ha ha! Doubt it's got that bad yet. They're considering sending Fox Team over, but they are hoping that won't be necessary."

"I hope not, we need clinical, not a bloodbath. They've not got any finesse, it's all machine gun fire and explosions with those ladies."

"Update soon, I've got one of the tech's looking into this activist, protester guy Cornelius Chance. Bit of mystery, not much information, arrived from Cyprus aged sixteen, University then nothing. Re-surfaced on hospital records, not as a patient but as a bill payer. Weird thing is he's not Armed Forces, but most of his file is currently classified on our system. I'm trying to go through the patient route, but hitting walls. It's like someone here doesn't want people to know who he is. He could just be some politicians son, a hippie activist causing unwanted embarrassment, but it has me intrigued. I may have to go upstairs; I'll need weight from the Director behind a few calls to Government departments. Someone knows who these ghosts are. Keep me updated, I'll do the same."

"Affirmative, and Steve thanks for the update on Sarah."

This was getting more and more curious. Two targets with classified files. The tracker notification alerted him that the VW was on the move. He'd give them a head start, get a coffee and catch up. They weren't racing off anywhere.

***

Rosie had bought some coolant from a local shop and topped up the low fluid, must be a leak. She should be able to get up more speed without it over heating for a while now. Tired and always worried about Mo, her immediate worry was now money. She was running out of the cash she happened to have on her and daren't use a card for food or fuel. Kiri had already given her what she had.

Kiri having slept was feeling much more like herself, she was still sad and prone to unprovoked bouts of tears, but felt more in control and was sorting through the bags in the back. In Marcus' bag she had already found a big warm hoodie to borrow. The clothes were all too baggy, but with a pair of joggers and some clean woolly socks, she felt almost human. Clean clothes were great, but a shower would be wonderful. For now, she'd kill for a coffee and a spliff. The universe answered immediately as she found Marcus' stash box in his rucksack. She checked inside the wooden box and found everything she needed. She knew Marcus wouldn't mind in the circumstances, they'd already stolen his van... she might as well have a smoke.

"Come on let's get moving, I want a coffee and a poo. No bloody cafes around here. Find anything useful?" Rosie had zero filter around her bestie.

"There was a cafe in a village a little way back, I saw it last night. I'd love a coffee and bathroom, I found clothes and toiletries...and this." Kiri presented the box. The aroma of marijuana wafting from it as she lifted the lid.

"Lovely, we deserve a bit of luck my love. Let's roll."

"I'll roll one in a sec. There's fresh clothes in Marcus bag, but Tom's might be a better fit."

"I could do with a jacket if he has one."

Kiri opened up Kind's bag, inside, right on top was a blue North Face puffer jacket. Kiri pulled it out and passed it to Rosie, a thick brown envelope fell to the ground, hundred euro notes spilling out of it.

"Fuck my life, there's got to be a hundred grand in here!" Rosie shoved the errant notes back inside. "Expenses covered, lets go for breakfast."

***

Hawk watched the red dot move out of the small town, but instead of continuing in their previous direct, they were going the opposite way towards a little village. They were coming right towards him. He'd be spotted here, sat on the lay-by, only a few trees for cover. He turned the van on and drove out of the parking area, heading towards the village, only a few minutes ahead of the target vehicle, he parked the blacked-out vehicle in a residential street and waited for them to pass by.

***

Kiri had rolled a joint by the time they reached the village and was rolling down the window.

"After coffee, no?" Rosie shot her friend a look.

"I guess... and pastries?"

"Why not, we've got some driving to do."

Kiri rolled the window up and looked out at the passing morning, families, old ladies on their way to buy bread, old men on the way to have a coffee and brandy.

They found the small cafe, over the road was a patisserie, they parked, split up and met back at the van. Kiri with a big bag of French pastries. Rosie with two black coffees and a bottle of water.

"There's a bathroom at the cafe, let's clean up first." Rosie suggested.

They left the coffees to cool in the van and went to freshen up.

Kiri removed smudged make-up and splattered blood from her face and tore a comb through her tangled locks. Rosie used the facilities and splashed cold water on her face, taking a moment to look at herself in the mirror take a deep breath and ask - *What the actual fuck*?

Both returned to the van feeling more human. They ate the sweet pastries and drank the strong french coffee, slowly conjugating the events and options as sugar and caffeine worked their magic.

***

Parked on the residential road he watched the red dot as it turned onto the highway towards Toulouse. Hawk, continued his hunt.

33

Mary and Martin Bell were in their camper; using back roads and moving through forested areas whenever possible, they had managed to evade being located for a long while as they headed south through France. They spent the first weeks driving in random directions, heading south though the Alps and staying at rural campsites, away from cameras, drones and detection. Since their escape from Tignes and the death of their pursuer, they had only stopped for fuel and to switch drivers. Their destination was Andorra. Unknown to them, the agency had tech wizards, trying to follow them via satellite. But, the time lost dealing and assessing the Viper situation, and losing and re-finding them through the many wooded areas, meant that they had been able to evade their trackers temporarily. For now, the Bell's were safe.

34

The horses and riders headed off into the French countryside, some more comfortably than others. Layla rode alongside Bear as he found his rhythm, in silence at first. Aaron, Rory and Alex lead the way. Both groups needed to talk.

Layla reigned Coco in closer to Royal and the two horses gave each other a nuzzle, they were good friends.

"Sooo, how you doing Bear?"

There was an understandable moment of contemplation, the horses breathing, hooves and singing birds the only sounds. Bear had only ever had one real friend, he was a really good guy. He had done something that was good, but illegal. Now he was gone before Bear could comprehend his passing. He had lost comrades in his early Forces days, but never a true friend.

"I'm not really sure Chance. It's all happened so fast, days ago we were playing backgammon and sharing conversation. Now, we'll never speak again... I just can't believe he's gone. Forever. I need to pull myself together and deal with the current situation, that's what I do. But, I was an orphan, I generally worked alone. Tom was the only friend I ever had. I've never lost anyone... I loved, before." Bear, took a deep breath and stroked his horses neck.

"You ride well for a big guy. Royal likes you, I think you're going to be okay cowboy. I'm really sorry about your friend Bear. Tom seemed like a special guy, it doesn't mean much while it hurts so bad, but trust me, it gets easier and even though he is gone, you're not alone. We're in this together now, we're now connected in this crazy world. We're family, or as close as we'll get. Tom was an amazing person, I'm glad I met him despite the shit show we're all in now, but he won't be your last friend Bear. Maybe he was just the first of many. Love and loss are two sides of the same coin. Don't shut people out just because you're hurting. I know about that... but that's for another time."

Layla hugged her horses neck and unseen wiped a tear on her mane. It wasn't about her right now.

"You can talk to me too Chance, I'm sorry, I'm supposed to be the adult. I told your Dad that I'd look after you, and you're taking care of me. How did you get so smart?"

"Don't worry about Dad, I'm glad of the break, I just hope Marcus is up to the babysitting job." Bear and Layla both laughed and for the first time in twenty four hours, both believed that some how, at some point, it might all work out.

"Right, change the subject big man, apart from why you're on the run, what's your backstory orphan? I'm allowed to be brutal, I've got a dead Mum."

Bear still wasn't quite used to the super-charged directness of a teenager who seemed quite possibly, way smarter than him.

"Good idea, change of subject. So... Aaron seems nice..." Layla almost visibly blushed, subconsciously wanting to trot away, Coco sensed it and pushed on, Layla reigned-in delicately.

"Well as we're sharing Bear... he's cute. Smart, brave and he knows horses. I like him, it's weird, I don't know if it's because I haven't been around many guys my age or if I actually like him. But, I feel like there's a connection there. Like, I know him, not who he is, but his energy...does that sound super-weird? It does to me."

"I haven't known you long Chance, but I think you can trust your instincts. Your Dad does know you, he has faith in you to see it through without him, following your gut and doing what it takes. Trust yourself."

"Yeah, trust. Hey Bear, what do you think Rory and Dad did when they worked together? Something is going on there; Dad's always hated guns and now he's kitted out like a commando, I intend to find out the truth."

"No idea, he knows his way around a pressure situation and seems very comfortable with weaponry. I'm sure you'll create a way to squeeze that information from somewhere."

***

Further ahead, the family were having the discussion you would expect. How deep do you go, where was the point of no return, when do you go from potential contacts to conspirators. Aaron was steadfast. It was plain and simple, in this brave new world, the rules didn't apply. There was right and wrong and you had to take a stand, it was about integrity. While Rory was fiercely proud of his sons position he not only knew what they were up against, he knew it wasn't his moment to speak.

"That's all well and good Aaron, until the moment I have to watch you get murdered by those bastards. Or they poison us all.

Ask your father. You don't understand the sort of people who are after them. I love Hercules and Layla, but you are my priority and this is getting dangerous. I know you like her, she's amazing. Considering her parents, I'm not surprised. But, we decided a long time ago we wouldn't lose you kids or each other to the company and their insanity. I know you like her, but I'm not about to lose you to a crush. Not even this one. We're not going on with them, just to the trail. After that I vote we take a long holiday somewhere, away from the farm and from everything. François will look after the animals for us." Alex looked at the towering mountains ahead.

"It may be too late for that my love, this didn't happen to us today at breakfast, it started over sixteen years ago when we made choices that had consequences, we knew this might catch up with us eventually. When we played with our babies together and you held Layla in our kitchen while Hercules cried for his wife. We decided then to run and hide, our situation is the result of our choices, not the actions of Hercules, Layla or their friend in Calais. This day was always coming one way or another."

"What do you guys mean? What am I not getting?" Aaron looked confused. Alex trotted on, she knew the story and they had already agreed with recent developments, it was time.

Rory took a deep breath and nudged his horse closer to Aaron's.

"You know we met Layla's dad way back at college. He and I worked together for a good while after University, making great money. In time we didn't like the work, both fell in love and our partners got pregnant around the same time, we wanted a new life for our families. The company we worked for considered us valuable assets and didn't want us to quit, made threats. We ignored them and Cornelius and Layla paid the price - we believe they poisoned her mother. Layla was only a baby when she died."

"Whoa, who the fuck are these guys Dad? Who did you work for?"

"I'm not proud of it son, but we were recruited and trained to be in the first generation of hunters for Solution sixty-five. We were young, had been in the Scouts and Army cadet program, but we still should have known better. The money was too good to be true and it was legal. We felt like James Bond at first. You wouldn't remember and they kept it quiet. But, it was bad back then. The amount of people who tried to run on the first wave, we were busy, the agency was a monster. They wanted us to create a situation where running was worse than suicide. Encouraging torture before execution, that wasn't us. We were professionals. I already wanted to get out when your Mum told me she was pregnant. When Hercules told me two weeks later they were pregnant, we knew we had to find a new life. Sonia was our team leader and agency superstar, she was against leaving at first, looking for compromise, but she came round eventually. We left despite their threats, we were their top agents. It created quite a stir at the time, quitting on moral grounds. They changed policy and didn't continue down the torture route, too many other agents spoke up. Instead they increased the tech, science and marketing budget and created a reputation for near perfect kill rate and a social belief that to run was an act of cowardly theft. They turned it round with the media lies as they do. Making it seem like a selfless sacrifice for humanity. It's all about population control and money. Billionaire private backers. Keeping economies moving and creating inflation until they're ready to collapse the whole house of cards.

"I don't understand."

"They give everyone money, people create businesses. They invest money and time and knowledge into creating. But all this money creates price rises, inflation, in time the money runs out, or more accurately up. Eventually the market crashes and there's a recession. During the difficult times, the billionaires buy up more resources and businesses and gain more wealth and control. They are whales, they have the wealth to weather any great storm. The rest of us are gulls, hiding in nests or tossed in the wind."

"So... What happened to Layla's mum?"

"A month or so after we left the company, Sonia suddenly got sick. It was a difficult pregnancy, in and out of hospital, but it was more than that; they kept her in after the birth for testing and treatments, but she steadily declined and never left the hospital. One day when you and Layla were little we were in our garden, Cornelius took a call and we knew Sonia was gone. It was like part of him had died, a light went out."

"So... they poisoned Layla's Mum, to punish you guys. She was innocent."

"Innocent? She was dangerous. The reason they allowed her to live to give birth to Layla, was out of respect, she was and always will be the greatest agent the Company ever had. Layla's mother wasn't a helpless victim; they took her out because she was too lethal to allow to live as a potential threat, with the training and scientific developments, Sonia was a weapon and they felt they owned her. When she agreed we should leave we all knew the risks, but with three of us together and by disappearing, we hoped we could have a live and let live situation. The board felt it would be safer for the company to eliminate our leader as a precaution and a warning. I wanted to burn HQ to the ground.

Layla's father brought her to our house, sat you both on his knees and told me he'd shoulder the pain on this one. Let you kids have a different life. It broke my heart, I knew how angry and hurt he was. But, he looked at that baby girl and left any thoughts of vengeance behind. If he could walk away, then so could I. Until now we've stayed out of the UK, kept our heads down and not been harassed. I don't know how much Layla knows, so this is between us, but your Mother has been through this before and lost a friend in Sonia; she's on board, she's just scared - she knows what we're up against. If we do change from guides to targets, don't hesitate to do what I've taught you do son, this is what the training was for. If we're not in the spotlight already it won't be long. These are interesting times. I love you and I'm proud of you son, you're a good man."

Aaron, just took it all in. He had almost as many questions as he'd had answers. He'd always known his Dad was different, the guns, the training, the politics. It should have surprised him, he should have been scared, or pissed off that he didn't know until now. But, he wasn't. There wasn't even a conscious choice of what the next step was for him. The only thing he could think about was Layla. He felt slightly sick, she was so smart and beautiful, had survived all this shit and was still awesome and funny, but the pain she must have gone through. She had lost her Mother as punishment, so that they... so that he could live. So his parents could have love while her father and Layla were left alone. *She didn't even know.*

"What was Layla's Mum like?"

"Amazing woman. Brave, beautiful and dangerous. Skilled with weapons and hand to hand, but it was her tactics and decision making in the field, that made her special. Russian training, she was ice cold and had a very logical mind. Bossy too - there was no question who was in charge. I could see why Cornelius liked her, but she was always a bit distant for me, high walls. I respected the hell out of her though."

"Badass. I know Mum is scared but I'm in one hundred Dad. We owe them that."

"I know son, your Mum understands, I can't promise she'll leave the horses, she doesn't like guns and she'd feel like a burden. I have to see this out Aaron. They're family and I have a responsibility to help."

"I can help too Dad. Sometimes you have to take a stand."

"You sound like Layla's Dad."

35

When Rosie and Kiri arrived after a very long drive, they found the horse ranch empty. Kiri held the stained, crumpled paper with the neatly written address, it was the right place. The others had left, they were alone, exiled.

***

On a hill less than a mile away Hawk could see the situation. The targets had moved on before his quarry had reached them. He would pass it on to the tech guys to track onwards. These guys were good; he would need to step it up, most people stop, rest, sleep, feel safe. But, it was as if these guys knew the playbook and were breaking the rules. He wasn't worried, but it was time to take these guys seriously. Hawk called it in to Steve on the sat-phone and waited for the response.

"Well, I won't pass this on to upstairs just yet. I'll get the tech guys on it. If it doesn't pan out, you'll have to drop the goose chase and head towards Toulouse, Viper's couple were last spotted there. Intel thinks they're aiming for Andorra, we have a pattern on the Bell's, the mountain is their environment, they feel safer there, the next mountain range on their projected route is Andorra, see if you can get them in the cross-hairs we need some good news here."

"Affirmative, I'm on it, trust the method."

"Just be careful Hawk. There's all sorts of weird myths of ghosts and legends in the hallways. People are uneasy on every floor, from media to the top, this seems big. Even Wolf seems rattled."

"Affirmative, cheers fella, something does feel off, get me as much info on all parties as you can dig up, this is no cake walk. I need to know what I'm dealing with."

"Affirmative, over and out."

36

In a Toyota pick-up bound for Barcelona, Hercules and Marcus had been travelling in relative silence.

"So, Barcelona, what's the plan, who's this friend?"

"Doc and I worked together a long time ago, he was in what we called, *Logistics and Ballistics*. Getting people in and out of places and ensuring any required equipment was available."

"Like Q?" There was a silence. "Which would make you like..."

"Not exactly Marcus, I can't talk to you or anyone about it, sorry."

"Man, this is literally - *I could tell you, but I'd have to kill you* - shit isn't it!"

"Worse than that... I haven't told Layla everything yet. There are things she doesn't know about me and her Mum - Sonia. Things I wish I didn't have to tell her. Things I'm not proud of, which I guess is why I've avoided talking about it. But, she's getting old enough and curious enough, it's now only a matter of time. She's already lost one parent, when I tell her everything she might not want the one she has left."

"Shit man, I don't know what you were into; but you're a great parent and a good guy. We all have a past, we've all done stupid shit we're not proud of. It's what we've done since and do now that matters. That kid adores you, considering she's a teenager, that's pretty good going brother. It might be rocky for a bit, but that's the game isn't it? You've done a great job and whatever happened before you were a parent, it's the past. You're a great Dad, she might be the coolest kid I've ever met man."

"She's special alright. She gets that from her Mum." Hercules smiled. "So, the plan is to drive to the outskirts of Barcelona, somewhere with plenty of tourists. More people the longer the facial recognition software takes. We'll wear sunglasses, hats, face-masks and if we get lucky, we may even be undetected. Unlikely though so we want an in and out and ideally a vehicle change. Doc lives in the centre of the city, he has a ground floor apartment on the corner of a big old building, he bought half the basement. Nobody else renting in the building knows it's there, I guess they assume it's just private parking. But, he's got quite the set-up and he owes me a favour. Doc will be able to source a boat and get it prepared. Once we are set with a time and day, we gather the troops and we hit our window fast. They will be waiting for a move, hopefully we can get away and make it to Morocco, where it gets a whole lot more complex for them and easier for us. It's still a different world there. No masks, no controls, no Solution sixty-five or government jurisdiction. They can apply for permission to detain a foreign national, but they are likely to be refused. They may even cut their losses."

"Morocco it is, so where we headed now?"

Marcus felt lighter, it had been a hell of a week and he had been beginning to lose hope. Running endlessly until a high velocity bullet eventually caught up with him wasn't his idea of fun and to have what sounded like an achievable goal was what he needed.

Hercules on the other hand knew exactly how few people get away once the hunt is on and the closer you get to safety, the more danger you were in. They couldn't just let them get away, there was too much at stake.

"You heard of Gaudi?"

"The architect guy, of course, Barcelona's most famous son. I've been to La Sagrada Famila it's incredible. Porque?"

"We're heading to Park Guell on the outskirts of the city, plenty of tourists and there are shops in the area so we can buy hats and face-masks, from there we get the metro in. How's your Spanish?"

"Bueno pero no perfecto."

"Suficiente, blend in with the morning commuters. We go into the metro separately, buy a day pass, once we're there, there will be cameras. Keep your head down. It's a busy multi-cultural city, thousands of people rushing to jobs, to work with people they can't stand, to make money for a boss they've never met. Just act like you're on the way to work and you hate your life, you'll blend right in. I'll follow you. I'll always be close even if you can't see me. When we arrive at La Famila Sagrada, give your day-ticket to someone on your way out. If they ping us on camera in the metro, they will follow the digital path of the tickets initially, it's quicker than following camera footage in a city. If we can throw them off and buy some time we may be gone before they can locate us."

"Where should I go when I get out the station?"

"Find a gelato stand, buy one and sit down with it somewhere, head down the whole time. I'll make sure we're not being followed. After I walk past and ask you for the time, you wait ten seconds and follow me to Doc's. Sound good?"

"You had me at gelato man."

37

Bear wasn't going to say anything, but when in early afternoon Rory pulled up his horse and declared it was time to rest, he could have kissed him. His inner thighs ached and every time the others trotted, his horse followed suit and the saddle resumed tormenting his testicles. It had been a beautiful ride along sun-dappled paths, the river bubbling away through the forest, insects and birds flitting from water to tree. Glimpses of rising mountains ahead, wide countryside behind. Despite the peaceful location, the heavy stone of grief in his chest made levity hard and he was aching in places he didn't know he had. Layla had been quiet, it could be the perilous situation, separation from her Father, or the Aaron thing, but Bear felt like there was more. She was pissed off about something. He sat under a tree feeding a fire and rubbing behind Rumi's velvety ears; she must have travelled twice as far as the rest, running back and forth to chase scents and explore the woods and river. Apparently, they were getting near Les Cabennes, having followed the river trail.

***

Aaron and Layla fed and watered the horses. They had earned their oats and quickly ignored the grass at their feet in favour of the high energy feed. Once finished they returned to the group. After they endured an awkward silence, Layla asked Aaron,

"What do you think Bear's story is?"

"No idea, probably an interesting one though."

Rory was frying sausages and onions on the fire while Alex prepared a salad. Her logic was at least while they had the horses she could ensure they eat reasonably well.

As she passed, Layla said to Alex and Rory,

"Aaron seems lovely, he's great with the horses. Has he always been such an angel?" They looked up and smiled. *Has anyone*?

Layla sat on a log next to Bear's tree, Rumi between them enjoying Bears attention. Aaron sat on the log next to Layla and passed a thermos of tea and some dented and chipped enamel cups. In no time they were enjoying hot-dogs around the fire - Rumi without bun or accompanying salad. Once replete, there was some chit chat about their future itinerary, before Layla suggested they play a game.

"Right..." said Layla, with an edge that Bear sensed meant trouble. "We're on a perilous adventure together, agree?" There were wary nods. "Then in the spirit of trust and teamwork... I think we should have a truth circle." Before, Rory, Aaron or Bear could intervene, Alex gave her support.

"What an excellent idea, it's always good to have honest and open communication. Shall I go first?"

Bear breathed a sigh of relief. Rory and Aaron winced. Layla just smiled.

"Okaay, Layla... what do you think of my handsome boy?" Alex's eyes twinkled with mischief. Aaron's rolled as he looked at his Dad and received a helpless shrug in return. Layla barely hesitated and looking right at him said,

"I don't know him well, but he seems lovely. Smart, good-looking and great with animals, he seems brave too, I like him. We'll just have to see if he's brave enough to make a move."

"Watch this one son, she's a force." Rory roared with laughter and Alex beamed, as Aaron blushed crimson, wishing the fire would swallow him, while trying not to smile too much at the prospect. So far Layla's game was playing out well.

"I like this game, my turn." Rory's eyes settled on Aaron who prepared himself to take more embarrassment without getting upset.

"Okay, my angelic son... How did the digger really end up in the river the day you hurt your shoulder? Don't tell me you were avoiding a low-flying duck, I'm not buying it." Everyone leaned in curiously. Aaron, relieved to not be offering truth to questions his blushes had already answered, owned up.

"Pierre and I were clearing our stream to the river with the digger like you asked, we went for a swim to cool off...then someone decided, (I can't remember who) that I would hold onto the bucket and the Pierre would spin the digger round, flinging me into the water. We put the digger near the edge of the river by the reeds and silt we had cleared out the mouth of the stream. It was working perfectly, until Pierre built up momentum, I wasn't sure when to let go as I was spinning so fast. The water and mud from the dredging had made the edge of the bank slippery and with my weight and the centrifugal force, the digger slid into the river. I let go as it moved and ended up almost clearing the river, landing half in the water, dislocating my shoulder on the opposite bank. I got Pierre to help me put it back in and then we came up to get the ropes and Land Rover."

"Which was when I saw you looking green and we all spent the afternoon getting the digger out the river and a day getting her running again. Bloody idiot's. Well we all mess up sometimes son, at least nobody was seriously hurt. C'mon now, truth circle, who's idea was it?"

"It was Pierre's."

"Of course it was Pierre's, he only has daft ideas." Alex snorted. Aaron shrugged, parents aren't supposed to like all your friends. Aaron changed the subject.

"I think I should get to ask a question now, although I'm not sure I like this game. Bear, what did you used to do before all this crazy?"

Bear looked at Layla, unsure of what to say, for someone of his imposing stature, it was as if the idea of the truth turned him into a small boy.

"Go on Bear, no judgement here, circle of trust."

"For over a decade I was homeless in the UK - by choice. I didn't feel the need for luxuries or to be part of a system I didn't believe in. Tom was my best friend, when he got in trouble we decided to run. The night we were leaving, I got attacked by some brat-pack and think I really hurt one of them. Then Marcus, Calais, Tom and here. Not much to say really."

Nobody said anything for a moment, looking into the fire, until Layla broke the silence.

"Yeah, no, sorry. Love you, but you're not getting away with that Bear, c'mon. What did you do before, why did you decide to choose a different lifestyle outside the system?"

Rory agreed,

"Yeah, c'mon fella, we're all friends here, I know I have a past with things I'd like to forget, but sometimes it's good to talk about it."

Bear shrugged and nodded. They were going to rely on each other to survive, they deserved to know the truth.

"I was a soldier, a good one. I never knew my parents, I'm told my Mother died giving birth and my Father left. Foster care and school were okay, I was smart and big, kids generally left me alone. After school I was approached by recruiters and decided to join up and serve my country. I kept my head down and did the job, later I was given responsibilities, but I didn't want to lead and make choices over other soldier's lives. I learned you don't really get a lot of choice in the Army, so I used to find ways of reducing risk to life on missions, even if it meant extra yomping, or less kit in favour of speed and discretion, I would also take more risk's myself, I got a few medals, moved up through the ranks. Eventually, I was recruited from Special Forces by a Black-ops group to carry out surgical solo-operations. It was my ideal job, only relying on and risking myself, planning my own infiltration methods and extraction routes, eventually I was the first choice for more technically difficult or near impossible missions. I would get a brief on the target and neutralise them, whether that meant climbing cliffs from the sea, or a high-altitude, low-opening parachute jumps... I thought the world was down another dictator, drug-trafficker or worse. It was a job. I got suspicious of the increase in middle-eastern political and business related targets and made inquiries with my superiors. On my last mission I was left out there to die and barely survived. After that I was out.

While recovering, I found out with some hindsight and research into the targets; I was a pawn being used to clear the board to make way for oil deals, water source control, gas pipelines, technology purchases and more. The black-ops group had autonomy and had been using its resources to aid clients in the US and UK in achieving their business intentions. I had gone from soldier to mercenary. I emptied my bank accounts and went AWOL at the end of my next leave. I spent a few years in Wales living in a tent in the hills, before deciding I wanted to be around people, not speak to them, but just be around people living their lives. I moved back to the city and became... a bum. I guess that's my story." Bear looked at the fire.

"Thanks for sharing Bear." Layla asked. "So, you were a soldier, who did soldier things, like many young people you believed the rhetoric and signed up with best intentions and you left when you realised your mistake. You need to give yourself a break."

"I killed a lot of people Chance, many of whom didn't deserve to die. I decided after that I couldn't choose who lived and died, I couldn't pull the trigger again and until the night I left, I hadn't hurt a soul in years."

"Well, after that, I think Bear should ask a question." Alex said.

"Well, as Rory did say, it's good to talk about the past and be honest... where did you and Hercules work before the kids were born?" Bear decided to be bold, if he was being honest and trusting these people, being part of a team, he'd like to know who he was trusting and what unspoken truth was being protected.

"I don't know how much I can tell you, it's not just my story." Rory looked at Layla and then his wife.

"We're in an unusual situation here. I think she's old enough to know the truth and probably should have been told more a long time ago. But, that wasn't our call and there are things you should hear from your Father." Alex offered somewhat neutrally.

Layla looked at Rory.

"If someone else has neglected to share a truth, maybe that is their discrepancy. Maybe Godfather, this shouldn't have been your job, but it has been left to you in the circumstances."

Bear was impressed, he now realised Layla was a master at moving the chess pieces, he didn't know how she had done it but, four questions had been asked in this game, the answers to which, were all information she wanted. From Aaron's intentions and character, to Bear's past of which she had earlier inquired, now, in his absence, she was pushing for information on her Father's past, no wonder she had been quiet, she was creating a master plan. Layla Chance wanted answers, some to questions she had long waited to ask. Bear felt she deserved them. The genius was; she hadn't even asked her question yet.

"I'll tell you what I can, but as I said, this isn't just my story. Your Father an' I were recruited by Solution-sixty-five back in its early days as hunters, we were young and naive and for years followed the money over our morals. We listened to the talk of a better society for all, opportunities, fairness and sacrifice for the whole. We were greedy and idealistic and really, really good at our jobs. There was a lot of work back then and it was easy. But, we fell in love, wanted to start families and change our lives. We started to question the methods and ethics of Solution sixty-five and its boardroom. They started using new drugs to improve, strength, speed, stamina, decision making, they wanted to create super-soldiers, even experimenting with DNA manipulation. They were paid by government per signatory and were making a growing fortune, but only if the runners were successfully hunted. The company didn't want us to leave, didn't look good to the ranks or the numbers, we nearly caused a mutiny. They were terrified of bad press, if people thought there was dissent in the ranks, they would be more likely to run. If they'd realised that if enough of them ran, it would be impossible to stop the flood, Solution sixty-five would have collapsed. It needs the psychological pat on the back for your sacrifice and the fear of a painful or terrifying death being chased down like a hunted fox. Without both, the system collapses. But, it didn't collapse and we left. That's the truth of me and Hercules, neither of us are proud of it, but we are different men now. I think that's enough questions for today."

"Wait, that's not fair, I haven't asked my question yet. Everyone else got a question."

"That's true Dad, it's only fair."

The group looked at the fire and waited to see who Layla would interrogate. Bear leaned against the tree trunk, closed his eyes, smiled to himself and listened.

"Alex..." Layla started sweetly. "How does my Mum come into all this? I don't believe she just got sick and died. I've seen photos, she looked so strong and healthy. I don't know why, but I don't believe Dad, I can tell when he's not telling me the truth, it's rare, but I know. I'm old enough to make decisions about what I should and shouldn't know and be allowed to deal with the information as an adult. Alex, I want to know how my Mum died. Please."

Alex had tears in her eyes, they had hidden this truth from the kids for so long and while it wasn't her place to tell the story, they were in great danger and anything could happen, this young woman deserved to know what happen to her Mother, Alex's friend, Sonia. The fiercest woman she ever knew. Alex sighed and wiped a tear, watching the flames dance, she asked herself not what Hercules wanted, or even Layla, but what would Sonia want Layla to know as she set out on this potentially lethal journey. She would want her to know everything. Alex exhaled quietly.

Bear open his eyes and sat up a bit, *well played Chance, check-mate.*

"Okay lovely, I'll tell you about your Mum, she was an amazing woman and my friend as much as she could be. Your Dad and Rory worked together at Solution and were a brilliant pairing and with their leader, they were part of the most effective hunter squad at the time."

"Ever." Rory interjected.

"A tight squad of three members, led by your Mother, Sonia. Her call sign was Snow Spider, it suited her. From what I'm told, she was tactically brilliant, lethally efficient with almost any weapon and completely ruthless. Beautiful but a little cold. She'd never get angry, just go quiet and intense. She was careful and sparing with her words. But, if she loved you, she did it with everything she had. You always felt like she could handle anything, control any situation. I always felt safe with your mum around. It was as if she knew what was going to happen before it happened. She'd put a jack in the car before going to a picnic and then we'd get a puncture. We'd find someone on the road that needed a tow out of a ditch and your Mum would have a rope under the seat that your Dad swore wasn´t there before.

Your mum was originally Russian and was trained there. I don't know a lot about her past, she wasn't the sharing kind. When governments became more unified, she emigrated and immediately found work with Solution sixty-five. She could have ended up running the place if your Dad hadn't melted that heart. They were seeing each other for about a year - that we know of right Rory? We'd been together nearly three at that point. Everything changed when they discovered Sonia was pregnant after a holiday in Turkey. Rory and I were expecting Aaron and I wanted him to quit the company. Until your Dad brought it up, Rory wouldn't consider abandoning the team. Eventually your Mum agreed and said she was getting tired of the field, the medical tests and missions. Maybe the Universe was telling her it was time to make a change. She confided in me that she had never known her parents, but despite her cool exterior, she wanted to be a Mother and not to her squad."

"She never said that." Rory spluttered.

"Yes, she did. She once affectionately referred to you two as - *her boys*."

"Well, I guess she did save our asses on numerous occasions. It was that sixth-sense."

"Now, let me finish telling Layla about her Mum. As Rory said, when they tried to resign the company put enormous pressure on them to stay. It was a delicate time for numbers and the future of the company could be at stake. They tried financial incentives, bribes, threats, legal battles for breach of contract. Your Mum was a determined woman and replied with threats of her own if they didn't stand-down. Threats not taken lightly considering their source. Eventually, the Company agreed to let them go if they put a stop to the growing union of disgruntled employees. Sonia made ethical and tactical demands on behalf of the union and an agreement was reached about hunter conduct in the field. Extreme measures that had been employed recently by some and encouraged by those upstairs were stopped. Some were happy about this change, others were furious.

Before you were born your Mother fell sick, shortly after you birth she passed away. We always believed she'd been poisoned. Rory swore vengeance, but your Father said that it wasn't what Sonia would want. She was cool and calculating and would say that tactically, with inferior numbers and resources, we should retreat and take care of the children. We knew he was right. We moved to France and your Father took you roaming the world to keep you safe while on some personal mission to help people and undo the mistakes of the past. Losing your Mum hit him hard, but he had you and he held on to that."

"Yeah, a bit tightly sometimes." Layla wiped a tear away and leaned into Aaron, who had a welcome arm around Layla. Rumi put her head in Layla's lap.

"So the hunters become the hunted." Bear said. "Well, I'm sure of one thing, these hunters are going to find themselves a whole lot of trouble here and I'm way less worried about the guys in Barcelona now. You guys wanted to change things, you almost brought the company down once. Maybe we could do it. If we create enough trouble, escape and make it public somehow, people will follow. The dam will break."

"I think my Mum would like that." Layla smiled, eyes glistening fiercely. She was going to have some things to say to Hercules when he got back.

"So Dad, what was your call sign?"

"I was Raptor, Sonia was Snow Spider and Hercules was Cobra. We didn't choose our names, they were assigned by the Director. I never met him and I heard he was replaced after we stood down, but he certainly had a knack for call-signs. Right time to move. We've eaten and rested long enough, this is just the start."

38

Marcus left the Metro station and crossed the square in front of La Sagrada, wearing sunglasses, face-mask on and cap pulled low. Defiantly forcing his eyes downwards, while the tourists craned their necks and took photos as they marvelled at the intricately carved stone and brightly coloured architecture of the stunning Cathedral.

Pressing a few euros and his metro ticket into the hand of the lady asking for spare change, he pressed on and found a gelato vendor. Feeling rude as he focused on the array of ice-creams, he ordered a pistachio and chocolate cone without making eye contact and put five euros on the counter. Leaving the change, he found a bench on the Placa de Gaudi, removed his mask and ate his already melting gelato as he focused on his feet. All the sounds of the busy city, cars, families, salesmen, sirens; his senses, calling to his every natural instinct to absorb the world around visually, but he kept looking at his feet, finishing the last of his ice cream, which he had to admit, was pretty damn good.

"Perdona, que hora estas?"

"Son los dos y media." Marcus replied, head down looking at his watch.

"Gracias." The man walked away.

Marcus put the mask back on and watched Hercules walk out the square and cross the road, head down, cap low. Marcus followed, careful not to lose him, get too close, or look up. Hercules turned the corner and headed left onto Carrer de la Marina before taking a right on Valencia, crossing the road and using the glass windows of a bank to check for a tail, before rounding the corner past the Centre de Medic I Psicologic. Marcus slowed as Hercules checked the menu at a Spanish restaurant, Casa Rufio's and glaced back - Marcus did the same at a Turkish restaurant nearby, looking over from the menu just in time to see Hercules go through a green door between Rufio's and the neighbouring bar. Marcus followed to the door and tried the handle, it was locked...now what? There was a key code but, Marcus didn't know the passcode. Then he heard a click and tried the handle, the door opened and he stepped into a lowly lit, long hallway.

"You can take the sunglasses off now, you did great."

Marcus removed the paraphernalia and his eyes adjusted. They walked down the long hallway and into a large living space, with contemporary furniture and colourful abstract art on the walls.

"Doc?" Hercules had a look around and headed into the kitchen, put the kettle on and found some teabags.

"What do we do now?" Marcus asked, confused.

"Make yourself at home, bathroom through there. He's got a great record collection if you want to put something on."

Marcus used the facilities and sat on the sofa.

"So, we just wait and hope he's in town?"

“Give him five minutes, fresh groceries in the fridge, Doc already knows we’re here. Tea?”

“Porque no?”

“Sugar?”

“No thanks.”

Hercules made a pot of tea and put it on a tray with three cups, saucers and a jug of milk.

***

“Hello gentlemen; entering his castle and helping yourself to an Englishman’s tea! I’ve shot people for less.”

Marcus, turned to see a man of medium build, probably in his seventies, with messy grey hair and a pistol in his right hand. Marcus’ heart seemed to stop and his lungs no longer wanted to suck in oxygen, he was feeling dizzy...

“You old bastard, stop winding the kid up, he’s had a tough time. Where did you pop out from?”

“Sorry, lad couldn’t help myself.” Doc chuckled. “I finally put in the secret ladder down to the Doc-cave, I don’t have to take the stairs down to the garage now. I saw you come in on the security cameras, I was in the middle of some tricky work on a non-lethal concussion weapon.”

“I didn’t see any cameras.” Marcus queried.

“Well no lad, you wouldn’t, that’s the idea. I see you still remember how I like my tea Cornelius.” Hercules smiled as he poured tea from the pot over a dash of milk and handed the cup and saucer to Doc, who sat on an elegant Barcelona Chair and took a sip of tea.

"Lovely cuppa as always, now if you're making me tea, I know from experience you want a favour. So, Cobra, what you got into now and how can I help?"

39

Rosie and Kiri sat on a hay bale drinking tea and eating a bacon and egg sandwich. Rosie had jimmied a window and helped Kiri wriggle through, finding the fridge relatively stocked they decided to wait and see if anyone with information came home?

"So, how long we going to sit around here?" Kiri was exhausted and wanted to go home. To Calais or the UK.

"Well we've been in the van all day and it's not like we have anywhere to go. We have no idea where they are or if they came here. It's a wild goose chase, but we can't go home. We have to contact Mo and then move on somewhere."

"That's not strictly true." A voice came from behind them and they both whipped round in surprise. Hawk was standing a few yards away, hand next to a holstered pistol.

"How long have you been there?" Rosie hadn't heard a sound.

"Long enough to know you are of no further use to me. I'll pick up their tracks from here."

Kiri turned white, this was it, no more running, no more sadness or fear, it was over. She thought about seeing Tom, if this was the end, she hoped for that, but Kiri knew that despite the sorrow, she wanted to live.

Hawk approached, the right hand staying close enough to his holster in the unlikely event they were carrying a weapon.

"I've taken the tracker off the van. I lied to you in Calais, you are not on the system, there is no file on you Rosie, you are free to return to England or Calais. I needed you to follow my targets. As I said, you are no longer of use. You can go home. You might as well keep the van; its owner won't be needing it soon."

Rosie wanted to call him a cold bastard, but he hadn't had to tell them anything and now they had their lives back. Kiri felt differently.

"Fuck you, you murderous cunt. I hope you die."

"We all die." Hawk turned and walked away.

***

Hawk watched from a distance as they borrowed some supplies from the farmhouse and drove away. A loose-end tied up. He drove down to the farm and started a search. These guys were clearly dangerous and had chosen to run here. Hawk needed to know why.

The house didn't give any clues, he followed tyre tracks to the barn. The locked, heavy metal door he found in the barn gave him cause for concern, once he'd picked the lock, the interior told him everything. These guys were tooled up professionals with weapons and potentially skills that matched his and he was solo. It was time to make a call, he needed answers.

"Steve, I need information. I've just found an arsenal at the targets last suspected location."

"Hawk, I've just come back from upstairs and am sending files through now. We've used satellite tracking to confirm the white getaway car was switched for a horsebox which we tracked and have confirmed arrived at your location."

"It's parked in the barn, it was clean and half the paddocks here are empty. I think they may have all left on horseback." Confirmed Hawk. "So, who the hell am I dealing with here?"

"It's a shit storm Hawk. I went upstairs and the Director finally unlocked the files. It turns out Cornelius Chance is "Cobra". It was before our time but you know the whispers. The suits went crazy and I was taken upstairs. They're worried."

"So, I'm tracking one of the greatest hunters the company ever had." Hawk didn't feel scared, he was excited, it was a great challenge and he believed in his abilities. "So, who the hell does Cobra visit to get armed to the teeth?"

"We believe the property you tracked them to belongs to Raptor, obviously you've heard of him too. Wolf and Gorilla have been briefed by upstairs via sat-phone, they were both here in the old days. Hawk, there's lots of nervous people here, they want to clear the board on this one. If we don't take these guys out, it sets a dangerous precedent to people with training, they'll think they can get away and we all know if enough run, we can't catch them all. Like I said, nervous people upstairs demanding results. We can confirm a group of five riders left on horseback with a dog.

Targets, Cornelius Chance and Marcus Drummond have been tracked as far as Barcelona's Metro, no exact location yet. Wolf and Gorilla are in Barcelona and are following leads. Your orders are to follow Raptor, Higgins and their group and neutralise anyone assisting them."

"Affirmative. To confirm, the daughter Layla Chance is a kill order."

"Affirmative. All members of the group and anyone aiding them is a confirmed kill order."

"Acknowledged, I guess I better get moving then. Over. Oh, Steve, one other thing. Could you call the hospital and see if there's any news on my daughter, I didn't expect this to turn into such a long mission."

"Of course Andy, I spoke to them this morning, no change, she's sleeping a lot but the nurse, Anna, promised to tell her your job is going to take a little longer this time and you'll be back soon."

"Affirmative. Thank you Steve. Over and out."

Hawk, brought up a map on his device. They were smart to go off-road, it made it more difficult to track them by satellite and left him with the choice between leaving his kitted-out van and following their path, or predicting where they might come out and trying to get ahead of them. The path they'd taken followed the river towards the mountains and then eventually gave them various options of crossing into Spain or Andorra. Either way it was a hell of a trek with too many possible destinations. Hawk, would ideally go by road to Andorra, rather than ride a horse like a bounty hunter in a western. But, if he lost Raptors' group, tech' may not find them again in the vast mountain range. The board was full and there were dangerous players at the table.

Hawk grabbed his rifle and go-bag, with standard med-kit, rations and clothing inside and went to find a horse that looked friendly. The stables were empty, so he took a head collar from a hook and headed to the paddocks. As he passed one of the sheds near the stables, something caught his eye; a rubber wheel poked out from under a sheet; which upon removal made Hawks day. A black Honda motocross bike, Aaron's.

Hawk had the upper hand, old school tracking of horses and people, with the modern advantage of a motorbike. Before long he was ready, in black fatigues and boots, a lightweight bulletproof vest, supplied by the company, but optional. He checked the smart device for their last confirmed satellite sighting. There was enough fuel in a can to fill up the tank, it wouldn't last forever. With pistols at his sides, rifle strapped to his pack and Aaron's black helmet on, he looked formidable as he rode through the farm gates. Hawk opened up the throttle and gave chase.

40

Doc drained his tea.

"That's quite the pickle young man, you never could help but find trouble could you?"

"As I remember it, you were quite instrumental in the trouble I found in the old days."

"And, I appreciate you keeping me out of it. You lost a lot, but it did force some of the changes you and Sonia were fighting for. The medical tests, the DNA manipulation trials, the extreme methods used to extract information, it stopped after..."

"Like you said, I lost a lot. I'm not losing anymore. Can you help us out with a boat?"

"Of course, I've got a sailboat we can use, it's sat in Valencia, I obtained it on a private job many years ago."

"You always were good at collecting trophies; speaking of which, what have you got in the garage, we could do with a vehicle change."

"You take the Land Rover Discovery to Andorra; space for the other passengers and it will be ideal in the mountains should you need to off-road. I'll take the Mini to Valencia and arrange the boat, we leave in the next forty-eight hours. With the wasps nest you've poked I imagine you may be coming in hot, you still have your ring I see." Doc pointed at a blue stoned ring on Hercules hand.

"Never without it."

"Let me know when you're approaching the city, I'll find you. Marcus can join me if he likes, it's a secure place to hide and one less civilian on the ground for you to worry about."

Marcus at this point was beyond questions and decision making and just shrugged. Being on the ocean sounded like as good a plan as any.

"You're coming with us then old man?" Hercules smiled.

"Well I needed a change; I hardly use the boat and to be honest young man, I think you may have finally blown my cover. If the suits upstairs are gunning for you, they will find this place. We are out-numbered, out-gunned and at a financial and technological deficit; but we're not dead yet, we best get moving before that changes. Let's head down to the Doc-cave and load the vehicles, then I'll make us some dinner. It will be dark in a few hours, perfect time to move."

***

Doc grabbed a few bags and threw them in the back of a bright orange Mini.

"Subtle Doc." Hawk grinned and threw his waterproof holdall in the back of the black Discovery with heavily tinted windows.

"She's special, ready for my escape plan. Besides, I like orange. Both cars are clean, with your face being searched for I figured the Disco would suit you."

"Suits me perfectly, tints are ideal."

"It's bulletproof glass, can't say too much, I brought it back from Africa after..."

"A private job?" Hercules winked at Marcus.

Marcus forced a grin; this James Bond shit was way out of his league, he was a activist, supposed to be building shelters and schools for refugees, not going up against trained killers.

"Right lads, lets get you fed..."

A red light started flashing,

"Perimeter breach...perimeter breach...".

41

In a cafe across the street from Doc's apartment, a man watched the garage entrance through his sunglasses. He was of impressive build, in his early-sixties, drinking a cafe solo in the late afternoon sun, improving an already deep tan. His long black hair, highlighted with grey streaks reached his shoulders, held back by a plain black bandanna. Over the chair hung a leather jacket and on the seat next to him was a black motorbike helmet. As he lifted the comically small cup, large biceps and chiselled forearms flexed below his short-sleeved black cotton shirt. Even without knowing he had a Glock in his belt and a small arsenal in his bike, he simply looked dangerous. The man was known by his colleagues as 'Wolf'.

If Cobra and Raptor were back on the scene, there was only one place Wolf thought they would go, the Doc. In their earlier meeting the Director had agreed. Wolf, had known about Doc's place in Barcelona for years; he'd always had his suspicions that back in the day, Doc was working with Cobra and Raptor to fuck with his methods. He got results and they knew he'd be number one. They just couldn't let him have it.

With the Directors eventual approval and consequential equipment and budget available, keeping tabs on Doc was easy once he retired. He had very few visitors.

The two men that had entered were unknown to the waiter Wolf had on retainer at the cafe, nobody had left since. Wolf had arrived fast; they were still inside. Now all he had to do was wait for the ape to do his part and he could cross some debts off his list.

42

Gorilla was somewhere between chaos and peace. Calm and methodical as he quickly entered the door code and silently climbed the stairs. He was a professional, but inside, a small part of his mind was bouncing around like an elated child. He loved the kill, the hunt. The adrenaline. Out smarting and out shooting everyone else. It had been a long time in the killing game one way or another and he was still here. Never scared, always ready, at peace with the when or how. But not now, it was a lot of other peoples turns first. Today the traitors Doc and Cobra would get their dues. Today, Gorilla would get a handsome paycheck having convinced HQ he should breach.

He entered the code Wolf had been ordered to give him in their meeting with the Director. A green light confirmed they were good. Controlling his breathing, gun in hand he climbed the stairs and scanned the wide living area with fancy décor and large windows spanning two sides from a corner. The room was empty.

Where the fuck had they gone?

Outside tyres screeched, Gorilla got to the window just in time to see an orange Mini fly down the road. The Grandfather clock against the chimney breast chimed loudly.

***

From the cafe, Wolf saw the garage door opening and made it into the street in time to dodge the Mini, rolling clear as it sped out the garage and away with Doc and the civilian target in it. Weapon drawn, he entered the doorway and paused at the top of the short ramp, removing his sunglasses. *Where was Cobra?*

The smell of oil and rubber in his nostrils, he listened for any sign of his target. Not a scrape of a foot or sound of breathing, silence. He moved down the ramp and scanned the garage, his eyes adjusting to the light. Two bright headlights shone, blinding him as an engine roared to life and accelerated towards him. He fired twice hitting his target and dived to the right rolling away as the vehicle shot past and continued up the ramp towards daylight. Wolf took two more shots at the escaping car, but the bullets ricocheted off, he stopped firing. Getting to his feet he jogged up the ramp to the bright sunlight to get his motorbike, pausing before he emerged to put his sunglasses back on... just as the apartment above him exploded in a ball of fire, glass spraying across the streets, brick and concrete crashing down into the exit around Wolf.

***

"Guess Doc was right; this is a one-way journey."

Hercules put the trigger device on the passenger seat and drove the clean Land Rover towards Andorra, momentarily anonymous again. That was on a clock, having taken out the intruder in the apartment and the gunman in the garage, the company would be re-doubling their efforts, they didn't take kindly to having their assets neutralised.

43

Wolf stood up and dusted himself off, blood ran down his face from a large gash on the top of his head courtesy of flying debris. He had lost consciousness and could have done with a few stitches, but there was no time, he pulled the bandanna tighter. It hadn't gone to plan; but not a total loss, an orange Mini and a black Disco with bulletproof glass. His head hurt, but he was smiling as he cleared rubble and thought of Gorilla inside, one less thorn in his side. It didn't take long until there was enough space to squeeze out and back into the light.

Crunching across broken glass and collecting his helmet and jacket he left a generous tip at the cafe, passing its stunned onlookers he made his way to the bike and treated himself. Cleaning up the blood with his ruined shirt, he glued the wound on the top of his head together and threw the bandanna and shirt in a bin. The hunt was on. Donning a black long-sleeve base layer, the jacket and a clean bandanna, he took out his phone to update control, before he could call he felt the presence of someone behind him. He reached for the weapon in his belt, but not fast enough, as something heavy and hard hit him on the back of the head and Wolf's world went temporarily dark once more.

44

"You've had baths together."

Rory and Alex tried to keep the group entertained with stories of the old days, outside the job, happy times when the kids were small and Hercules would bring Layla to visit. The kids too young to remember.

Behind Layla grew quiet, possibly at the thought of saying goodbye to her ponies. Soon they would travel fast and light up the mountain pass.

In the middle of the group, Bear tried to enjoy the ride. There was still a long day in the saddle ahead of them. It was a beautiful afternoon in the woods as they rode their horses along the path that followed the river, the running water and birds sang as the dappled sun shone through the leafy canopy above, the smell of pine in the air. Despite the natural beauty, peace of the morning and his new found affection for his mount, Royal, Bear couldn't really enjoy it, he was saddle sore and his heart was heavy. Discomfort wasn't a new sensation and he didn't complain as he rode in the middle of the group and focused on the coming hike later, they were aiming for a route called Randonnee Etand de Riete. Bear couldn't wait, a good yomp was much more his cup of tea.

Rumi was still covering twice the distance of the others, exploring all the smells of the forest and running on ahead and disappearing, always returning from the vegetation within seconds when Layla gave a sharp whistle.

After the revelations at the campfire there was a quietness to some members of the troop, despite Aaron's parent's efforts to alleviate spirits. Layla and Aaron rode next to each other, holding the reins in one hand and each other's hands in the other. Rory and Alex took the lead ignoring the show of affection, holding hands themselves for a while. Trotting their horses on towards the mountains and quietly discussing their next challenge - convincing Aaron to leave with his mother and the horses.

Rory kept the pace up, he knew how resourceful the company could be and there was no guarantee they were safe. The house would have been compromised by now and the techies would be scouring the satellites looking for some clue as to which direction they had headed. There could hunters on their tail, maybe drones searching, Rumi would let them know. He hadn't exactly explained to Alex about what this could mean for their lives, but she had been through dangerous times before.

***

Hawk had ridden the motorbike until it ran out of fuel, the tracks from the horse's shoes were easy enough to follow, he ate then rested for an hour in the sun, he couldn't remember the last time he lay down and slept, he usually napped at Sarah's bedside... even hunters need to sleep.

An hour later, warmth still in the day, he secured his pack and rifle bag and walked on, leaving the bike behind, he left it visible, it was a nice bike, maybe some lucky person would find her some fuel.

Hawk settled into a steady jog, he needed to pace himself, the terrain was continually rising in front of him and from the sat phone he could tell he was headed for the mountain ranges ahead. Which route they would take was a mystery so he would have to be patient and keep tracking. They would tire. The horse manure trail was getting fresher, they couldn't be more than a few hours ahead.

To keep his mind occupied, he did what he often did in these moments and imagined all the things he would do with his daughter when she got better. Bike rides, horse rides, hiking, swimming, camping, climbing, skiing, beaches and mountains. Ice creams and barbecues. This life of chasing and killing would be over; despite his natural talent for it and years of training, he looked forward to that day every mission he had. Until then, he was just another person on the planet who had to do his job and pay his bills.

Today the job was simple - run. It was time to catch them. In a race, if you're in second place, you don't sprint to catch up, they'll see you coming and you'll arrive exhausted and ill-prepared for what comes next. You bring them back minute by minute, metre by metre, until you arrive unseen on their shoulder, unexpected and fresh and then... then you pull the trigger. Then you go home. This time tomorrow he could be at his daughter's bedside.

45

Wolf felt the sun on his face, his head was spinning, but he was pretty sure they were real birds singing, there was chatter and distant sirens. Forcing his eyes open, he blinked, the sun shining through the outstretched branches of an Oak, green leaves and then blue sky. It was beautiful. He had one thought...

"I've been knocked out again."

Wolf always quite liked the hazy coming around after a bout of unconsciousness. Closest thing he got to rest, as he had previously joked with his company enforced Psychologist. There was no time for a second thought as Gorillas furious mug came into view and slapped him hard in the face.

"You are one fuckin' cunt of a bastard. All these years we've competed and fucked each other over on jobs. The roofies in Amsterdam, the prostitute with the clap in Bruges, stealing each other's marks and screwing up each other's hunts... I never thought you would fucking kill me you cold bastard, there's a line. We're on the same team, it's a fuckin' game man. You had all the intel, you knew it would blow, you sent me in there to die!"

Wolf realised exactly where he was now, on a bench in the park behind the café. He didn't know how Gorilla had got out alive, Doc was a professional when it came to blowing shit up.

"How long have I been out you useless prick?"

"Fuck knows old man, a few minutes. You'll be out a lot longer soon if you don't agree to my terms."

"Okay. I have a couple of questions, then we can talk terms. I'm feeling agreeable. Firstly, I'm curious, how did you get out?"

"I heard the first car leave and realised you'd fucked me, Doc's place had to be rigged for final exodus scenario, there were no stairs down from the apartment, but I checked out the Grandfather clock and there was a ladder down the old chimney to the garage. Got there just in time, after the explosion I came down and saw you about to ride off into the sunset. That's when I decided to smash you round the head with a brick, it felt really fucking liberating, I've wanted to do that since I met you man. Now here we are... I'm a hunter too, some of the best numbers in the game. I have skills, but you always looked down on me, I do the job you do, killing, we're the same. What's your fuckin'problem?"

"We are not the same. You are an insane ape, an angry, damaged grunt, a psychopath, you like the hunt and the kill, you like the games and see it all as a fun journey into dealing death on your own route to destruction. You hunt and torture for enjoyment. I only inflict pain for information, you are an animal, I am an artist. The reason, I don't know or care is because Ape, you don't matter to me. You are an insignificant tool. I'm a professional, I clinically remove the problem of those who break their contracts. There is no pleasure in the task, only the pleasure in success and fulfilling my goal. I am the best. I have been doing this longer than anyone. I am better than you, I am a professional and will always be the best in the company. You are simply an incompetent bloodthirsty annoyance who thinks we are in some sort of competition. You're no better than those insane foxes."

"You uppity cunt, fuck you. You ain't no better than me, you'll find that out pretty fuckin' soon you prick."

"So my second question, before you teach me who's the big dog. Did you call in the vehicles that left the location? Every thirty seconds delay is an extra five-minute search in the initial tracking stages. You do realise how big this situation is for the company, if this goes south we'll all need new jobs."

"I know the techies bullshit handbook. But, I'm handling this my way today, my career is on the line and this time you tried to fucking kill me, I'm not playing games anymore. The deal is this Wolf; you stay the fuck out of my way. I'm going to request the contract for Vipers killers. I actually liked that asshole, he was an efficient agent and spoke his mind, since the old drama has come up people seem to have forgotten one of ours was taken out. On principle I'd even hunt down your killer. Viper was mean, but he was tough and one of us. You can have Cobra... you finish your business, I'll finish mine. No more fucking each other over, otherwise I won't use a brick, I will shoot you in the back of the head."

Wolf brushed back his hair, tidied up his jacket, stretched his neck, straightened his collar and bandanna and flexed his hands and shoulders. Gorilla had a point.

"This may surprise you Monkey, but I agree; I was tired of your games, that's why I let you find out if there was a final device. I'll call this in to control. You can fuck off now... if you ever change your mind, I will look forward to killing you and I'll look you in the eyes as I do it."

"Hope your head's alright." Gorilla walked away.

Wolf called the vehicle details into control. By his estimation it had been approximately ten minutes since their departure. Wolf pulled on his helmet and headed out of the city, covering ground while waiting for a confirmed target, intelligence suggested he would be re-joining the group in the mountains heading towards Andorra, one thing was for sure, they wouldn't be hanging around the city.

46

"*Aaron!*"

Both parents called at the same time. Aaron looked at Layla, shrugged and persuaded his mount onwards at a slow canter, there was clearly something to be discussed.

"Your mother and I have been talking son, we're in a fine mess here. But, it's my mess and we need to be smart. I'll guide the others on to the boarder, you will take the horses and meet Layla's father with you Mother. Maybe you guys will all join us, I have to take care of my Goddaughter. You need to look after your Mother. This isn't shooting targets or deer son; this is change your life stuff."

"But, we're the good guys right? I'm in, I want to help Layla and the others, I'm ready to do what it takes to see this through."

"Son, you say you're in this, but you have never taken a human life, I have. It changes you, I know what has to happen next, where I have to take my soul; but I don't want you to be like me, the memories, the ghosts, I don't want you to be a killer, even for the right reasons. Please, stay with your Mother, stay safe. You may be under the radar; you could still both be safe."

"Okay, I'll go with Mum and the horses and we'll catch you guys later, but I'm not thrilled about the plan. Dad... look after Layla, I really like her."

Aaron rode back to Layla.

***

"So what did you tell them?"

"Usual, exactly what they want to hear."

"Cool." Layla rode off as if pissed-off and joined Bear. As they rode, the tree trunks blocked the low evening sun and created a slow strobe-like effect. Bird-song filled the air and it could almost be considered idyllic.

"How's it going Bear? What you thinking?"

"Well, there's a question. We are in a colossal amount of shit. I'm riding a horse, which I'm actually starting to enjoy... still bloody uncomfortable. But, it's peaceful, listening to the water roll by, the breeze in the pines, the smell of the forest, the arguing birds and I feel like it's going to be okay. I've been in some situations before, but from what Rory told us, we have a serious challenge, these are professional hunters we're evading."

"I like challenges and I think together we can get through anything; more importantly, Captain Zen, what do you mean arguing birds. They're singing about the beautiful day."

"I wish they were, they are actually telling other birds to fuck-off out their territory, away from their food and potential mates. The males are feisty, but the females also make themselves heard."

"How disappointingly human. I'm worried, Bear. You know they must be catching up right? You were in the military, any plan?"

"There is only ever one plan when you're the under-dog on the run Chancer, evade then attack and repeat. We have some very skilled individuals and some surprises up our sleeves. Have faith, together we are a strong team."

***

An hour or so later the riders reached a stone section to the path that forked across two bridges. Rory dismounted and started breaking down the equipment. Clothing, rations, head torches, batteries and ropes. No tent or sleeping bags, they would be moving fast and resting short. Rory had some basic survival kit, a stove and lighters and enough emergency foil blankets for him, Bear and Layla should they get to rest. The weapons and munitions were heavy, but Rory and Bear were previously accustomed to heavy loads and long distances. The weight to equipment ratio was about as efficient as possible. Dried fruit and meat, nuts, protein, energy bars and a few teabags would have to see them through the nights journey. They would stay warm by exertion.

Rory kissed Alex and hugged his son, giving him a you better take care of your mother glare, Aaron returned the look almost equally. Layla and Aaron said their farewell; a tight hug, a kiss on the cheek and a whisper in the ear.

"Look after my horses."

"Look after my Da'."

Bear thanked Alex for her help, despite kind words, he could see that her protestations hid much fear for the future of her family, but as she said and the steeled look told - this was not her first rodeo.

The tired horses took a drink as they said their farewells and then Alex and Aaron took the left track to meet Hercules. The hikers and Rumi - who was having a fantastic day - turned right.

Bear was glad to be on his own feet again, his bag felt light, having taken the opportunity to unload bulky items like his sleeping bag and his old Brooks running trainers, he was sorry to see them go - they were tatty, but it was hard to find shoes that fit him. His big backpack was sitting high on his broad back, water bottle and pistol within reach.

Rory set a fast pace despite a pack heavy with the first aid, cooking and mountain equipment.

Rumi at her side, Layla was comfortable; with a light pack, clothing, rations and water. Her bow and arrows strapped to either side of the pack and the wooden box with the pistols Rory had given her heavy in the top pocket. Chance kept up easily, moving like a mountain goat, floating over the terrain. After four hours hiking steadily upwards through scattered woodlands, the evening passed to night, they didn't use head torches. A clear night ensured the moonlight was sufficient, they would save batteries for any harder sections later.

The trio took a quick water break and Layla slipped one of the pistols out of the box.

"So, here I am running for my life with two trained killers and all I know about guns is Dad's not a fan and they're really bloody heavy. So... who's going to give me my first theory lesson in firearms use and safety?"

"You're the godfather, over to you Raptor."

“Well, until you shoot one it’s hard to describe, but I’ll give you the basics...” Rory showed Layla how to place her feet, hips and shoulders. How to hold the gun in two hands, elbows bent, looking down the barrel through the sight. Aim at the torso and squeeze the trigger, don’t pull... and be ready for a kick.”

Bear nodded in agreement and added.

“That’s last resort, if bullets start flying you get behind us or run.”

47

Night was closing in, the sun had disappeared beyond the mountain range and it was already getting colder. Despite keeping hydrated and having eaten some of his protein rations, Hawk was beginning to feel the incessant run in his legs - he must be gaining. In all honesty, he was pondering how long he could keep chasing naturally, before needing an amphetamine boost to keep him charging. He didn't want to start too early, with only an hour of restless sleep at the hospital and after a drive through the night, he was slowing. A go-pill to speed up and shut this hunt down could definitely be an option soon. Not yet though, he wanted to keep his head clear before engaging in the final hunt. Hawk was ready for a water refill when he came to two stone bridges. There were horse tracks at the river, then two choices. His instinct told him he was heading for the mountains and boarder, but you never knew. He took the unlikely left and jogged on for a few hundred metres. Sure enough the horse prints continued. But, aside from the deeper tracks from the two lead horses, the others were now unladen. The group had split.

Hawk returned to the bridge and called in.

"Control, I'm sending you a location. The group has split, heading west to the mountains, requesting update and orders."

"Hey Andy, how's things?"

"What's going on Steve, you hardly ever call me Andy."

"It's a shit show here, everyone's tearing around the corridors, the brass are nervous. More importantly... I'm really sorry Andy, I've got bad news my friend. Sarah has taken a turn for the worse. Upstairs contacted me directly and told me they are personally ensuring she has the best medical care and drugs on the company and that you should trust them and complete the mission. I'm really sorry man, I can't imagine, I've been sick with the news for an hour waiting for you to check-in..."

There was silence.

"You there Hawk?"

It wasn't the first time Hawk had news like this on a mission.

"Yes, I'm here. The group has split again at my current location. I need a target update and I request a streamline manoeuvre."

"Why are you the only agent who ever makes that request? What are the details?"

"I believe primary targets Raptor and the Ghost "Bear" are continuing on foot Raptors wife and the kids have continued on horseback away from the fray. They are no longer a threat or an assistance, it could be argued they were coerced. It is my professional opinion as an experienced agent, they are no longer worthy of agency pursuit. I request we streamline our attention on primary targets and allow these loose ends to ride away."

"I don't know if it will get through this time, control is madness, but I'll put the paperwork in. The wife and two kids get a pass: we focus on the primaries. You followed protocol, made an example and burnt the farmhouse right Hawk?"

"Unfortunately there wasn't enough time during the pursuit to destroy that lovely old French farmhouse, I prioritised the hunt and left it. I'll let you word that how you see fit Steve."

"You are about the only human I deal with Hawk, I will happily do what I can, no promises. I'll speak to the nurses on my way home and see what I can find out."

"Are you sure there's no way I can come home, leave it to Wolf and Gorilla?"

"Sorry amigo, first thing I requested. Upstairs want you and the other two out there. Cobra created a mess in Barcelona; Wolf is in pursuit of target. Gorilla is being brought in to assist on the mountain. They're also sending in the Fox-team and alerting the freelancers to be ready for activation. Various high level-agents and priority targets seem to be congregating in Andorra, two lower level targets fled Barcelona in an orange Mini, they look coast bound, likely Valencia, they will be tracked and dealt with.

The Bell's, who took out Viper appear to be headed your way too. The group you are tracking are taking the scenic route. You have some serious mountain ahead of you, glad to see on your file you've been clocking in the required gym hours. Don't let Raptor and this phantom reach Andorra, our best chance is while they are separated from Cobra. Once in Andorra they have immunity until we can get the legal stuff started, it's a formality but it's still at least twelve hours from when they enter, don't let them get there."

"Understood, what's the situation with other agents in pursuit?" Hawk asked as he headed over the bridge and up the path at a steady jog.

"You mean the Fox team? You haven't worked with them before have you?"

"No, haven't had the pleasure, heard a lot about them."

"They operate mainly in Japan and Australia. Globally, as far as company statistics go, they are individually the top three hunters by a distance. The solo hunters don't even take their numbers into account when comparing stats in the bar. They don't send them to Europe unless there's a problem. They're en route and will be on the board tomorrow."

"Sounds interesting, no time for gossip I guess, let me know about the streamline request. I'm pursuing primaries anyway. Send me company profile details for the Fox team also more information on Raptor and Cobra. And Steve, please keep me updated on my daughter, I'm ending this now."

"Affirmative, I have information ready for you, sending now, over and out."

Hawk, took a moment to absorb the news, Sarah's condition had often fluctuated, but he felt uneasy and wanted to get back to her. Removing a small pill box from his med-kit he swallowed a yellow go-pill and jogged over the right-hand bridge and towards the looming mountains.

48

Wolf took a call on his headset. The Mini had moved towards the Valencia coast, the targets within considered less urgent than Cobra, his group on the trails and the killer couple, all of whom were Andorra bound. The Mini would be tracked and most likely picked up by freelancers.

The black 4x4 was heading towards Andorra as predicted. Having confirmed pursuit of the Land Rover with HQ he switched to sport mode and opened the throttle.

***

Since the Viper incident, the Bell's had made safe progress. Leaving the Alps through forested back-roads they doubled back and forth, eventually finding themselves on the coast near Marseilles. Changing up their modus operandus they stayed near the sea. Travelling from free campsite to free campsite, they continued to strangely enjoy life on the run. The death of their pursuer accepted if not forgotten. They played games in the evenings, read, talked. During the day they swam in the sea, Bolt fished, they foraged and stayed in nature, generally avoiding people other than to get fuel and groceries in small villages. Bolt had joked it was like a second honeymoon, Mary had corrected him that unlike the hotels of their honeymoon, it was more like a budget wellness retreat. Mary was happy and would not have it any other way. There were only basic amenities, but it was all they needed and importantly, it was always rural, there were no cameras and only a few other camper vans to blend in with. It was perfect. They had almost forgotten they were running.

They had passed Montpellier and eventually Perpignan, continuing into Spain and towards Lloret de Mar, before heading inland to avoid Barcelona and head back to high ground in Andorra. Bolt was driving and Mary was keeping him company, managing navigation, music selection and keeping him fueled with tea and biscuits.

49

With Doc at the wheel of the orange mini, they were out of the city in no time. Marcus was starting to relax and enjoy the drive as they headed anonymously towards Valencia, a boat and the open sea. Doc was quiet.

"Sorry your place got fucked Doc."

"Oh, these things happen, it's only stuff. When you rig a place to blow you have to accept everything within may be temporary. I have other properties; to be honest I'm surprised it took this long. It may surprise you young man but in my youth I made some enemies."

"So we're home free now?"

"Sadly not Marcus, the Mini is not on records so it was untraceable. Unfortunately; I saw an old adversary outside my place and with a description, last known location and time, they can find and track us in hours depending on our lead."

"Shit, so we're fucked again!"

"Come on lad, I know it's been tough, but you have to pick yourself up, we need positive energy now, I think you have a lot of that to give. You've made it this far. We just have to lose them."

"It sounds like you have a plan Doc. Okay, positive energy and optimism, whatever it is Doc, I'm in, let's disappear."

Doc took the turning for Tarragona and headed for the Roman Circus, stopping on the way for fuel and coolant at a service station, smiling at the cameras as he left. They pulled off the main road and wound though an endless maze of streets until they came to a small cemetery in a park looking over Roman ruins. Doc got out the car and lit a spliff in the evening air.

"You got weed. Awesome, mine is in Cherry, I need a smoke."

"While it will help calm you now. You need to relax Marcus and I'm not talking about a temporary high. Life has a way of working out, until it doesn't, at which time you're dead and it's no longer your problem. Trust the Universe young man, it has a plan and when it doesn't - Doc does. Now, give me a hand with this."

He offered the joint to Marcus.

Marcus got out and took the spliff, breathing in deeply, it had been a while...for him.

"I meant give me a hand with this."

Doc handed him some bolt cutters and started pulling ivy away from a gated crypt. They found the padlock and cut it, clearing more ivy as they inched it open. Doc drove the car in and pulled the gate to, Marcus pushed the ivy back to cover it and squeezed in through the gap, before pulling at more shrubbery through the bars and closing the gate.

"Brilliant, we've disappeared into a grave to hide, how long to we stay here?"

"We don't, get in."

Marcus jumped in and Doc hit the lights.

It wasn't a crypt; it was a tunnel. The city held ancient Roman tunnels open to the public, but Marcus had no idea there were secret tunnels. Doc drove on down into the tunnel, in the small car it was just passable and despite some bumpy terrain the walls flashed past inches from the untouched wing mirrors.

"I found out about this place years ago while doing some undercover work for the Spanish government, taking down some rather nasty Algerian traffickers - drugs and people mainly. They moved cargo in from the coast using various tunnels, the crypt was a back exit too narrow for their vehicles, but they used it to access a store of weapons, which I neglected to mention in the report. I came back for the artillery later of course - I know, *naughty Doc*. After the Operation, the Algerians were dead, so we might be some of the only people who know this entrance exists. Anyway enough chat... pit stop."

Doc pulled up as the tunnel widened and opened up into room with benches carved into the sides, big enough for carts to pass or people to rest. Marcus got out and Doc handed him a large cloth from the boot of the car as he proceeded to pour coolant over the Mini.

"Give it a wipe lad."

Marcus looked confused, but went ahead. As he rubbed in the coolant, the bright orange car with black detail, became white with black detail.

"Friction creates the heat, which catalyses the reaction between the dye they use in the coolant and the colour bleaching chemical I put in the paint. Brilliant hey!"

Doc was practically hopping from foot to foot. Marcus couldn't help but smile.

"It is genius Doc, you're a wonder."

"Thanks, one of many ideas the suits didn't continue funding, but I did some follow up experiments, first time I tried it on a full-sized vehicle...Keep rubbing."

***

Once the vehicle was no longer bright orange they had continued down the tunnel, with Doc turning left, then right while making noises that left Marcus wondering whether they were escaping or just getting lost in their own labyrinthine tomb. Eventually Doc pulled over and sighed.

"We lost?"

"No, we're here."

"Where?"

"Train tunnel near the coast. They brought the goods from the boats by van, then unloaded and carried them to here and reloaded into more vans using the tunnels to pop up in various safe places. This section wasn't feasible in a vehicle."

"What do you mean? We're in a vehicle."

"Do you trust me Marcus?"

"Yes."

"Good, there's a twelve percent chance this is about to go bad, but I think we'll be okay."

"What?"

Doc gunned the engine and the Mini shot out of its burrow at the side of a large train tunnel, covered by a trailing willow tree. The branches whipped the car as they emerged in the failing natural light, chunky tyres skidding across the heavy gravel. The light was fleeting as they shot quickly into a long, dark train tunnel. There was space away from the tracks for a rail-worker with a bag of tools or an Algerian with a bag of drugs to pass safely, but not a car. One wheel of the Mini was running between the rails and there was no end of the tunnel in sight. Doc floored it.

Marcus was white. Doc was grinning,

"Come on lad, where's that optimism? This is the plan, I just thought it was need to know on details, I prepped this baby for the perfect escape, have some faith."

"I'd like some details! How long is this tunnel and what happens if a train catches us?"

"Right, the tunnel is four kilometers long, hence the need for our current velocity and upgraded suspension and tyres. As far as trains, it's 7pm on a Sunday, trains are minimal, they only run every thirty minutes. With their speed they would spend approximately two and half minutes in this tunnel twice an hour, so if we move fast enough, we're looking at a good chance of being absolutely fine."

"So we could be caught by two trains in an hour?"

"No, that's impossible, we could only be hit by one train, in the next two and half minutes... and it wont catch us, we're heading towards the train."

"Wonderful."

It seemed like a lifetime before natural light highlighted the brick walls of the tunnel far ahead, the small bright circle eventually appeared in the distance ahead of them and grew bigger at a painfully slow rate. Leaning forward in his seat, Marcus willed it closer.

With less than a hundred metres remaining, ahead on the track beyond the tunnel, they saw bright headlights, moving towards them at a fast rate.

"Okay, it's now fifty-fifty." Doc and Marcus both held their breath and raced towards the light.

Marcus could tell that the train was travelling around their speed as it cornered the final bend toward the tunnel. They were equidistant from their escape; it was going to be close.

***

Simon was driving his freight train route as normal, it was always normal. He drove the same tracks every night, moving the same containers from here to there along the coast. Then he went home to his regular house, girlfriend and regular life. He was flicking through videos on his phone as he took the bend. He was going the right speed, everything was perfect, until he glanced up and saw the head-lights in the tunnel ahead. He put on the emergency break and held his breath as the train slowed and the lights came closer... they were going to hit.

In the white Mini, Marcus was shitting himself. Ahead he could see sparks from the trains brakes as it screeched towards them. The exit was nearing; he almost had hope.

"Doc?"

"You, son, are still not trusting in the Universe, or Doc. I know you're new to this, but Marcus...I got this." Doc flipped a panel on the dash revealing a red button that simply said,

"*Vrroom.*"

"Okay, you got this baby...Marcus, would you mind?" Doc gripped the wheel tightly.

Marcus hit the button and his world went warp-speed, pushing him back in his seat. Lights flew towards lights, machine towards machine, the train horn blared, brakes screamed as wheels ground on metal.

The white mini shot clear of the tunnel, just missing the train roaring in. Doc almost immediately swung a sharp left, smashing through a wooden barrier and up a gravel service road, braking hard he brought the car to a skidding halt.

Marcus finally released his breath and the colour returned to his face.

"Fuck me that was close!"

"Well yes, that was pretty exciting, just got to have a little faith Marcus."

"We were so lucky."

"Lucky? Technically, we were quite unlucky... statistically speaking. Yet here we are. Right, let's move, I need a wee and a cup of tea."

"Good wheels and an insane driver help too I guess. I'm not sure if I need some food after that, or to throw up."

Marcus wasn't sure at this point how he was still alive, but once again despite everything, he was okay. Maybe he should have more faith in the Universe.

***

What the hell were they doing? Simon picked his phone up off the floor of the train cab and put it in his pocket. No reason for anyone to know about his lapse in concentration.

50

Gorilla had checked in with HQ. Requesting permission to pursue Viper's killers. They were not friends; with money at stake, it was hard for hunters to trust each other, but previously mutual respect and potential gains, had found them exchanging information rather than sharing it with the other agents, they had on rare occasion shared a forced conversation over a coffee or beer that usually turned to work, often with ulterior motive. In this game you had to trust someone, sometimes. Not again though.

He sat in a service station outside Barcelona, his truck ready to roll as he enjoyed a menu del dia, made a few calls and waited for the techies to work their magic.

Gorilla's handler called back.

"That's a negative on the Bell contract. Tech are still working on a location. Orders are return to the Barcelona office immediately. Liaise with Fox team and chopper in to Andorra. Multiple targets. I'm sending you a file now."

"... Confirmed." No point arguing with control, Viper's killers could wait, multiple targets meant multiple payments. It would be interesting to meet the Foxes, he only knew them by terrifying reputation.

51

The Bell's were cruising towards Andorra, slowly rolling hills and farmland had turned to high, wooded mountains filling the vista ahead. The setting sun cast an orange, pink glow, reflecting from the towering stony peaks.

They weren't going slow as darkness set and they began to climb the winding mountain road, but there was no hurry either. The only moments of interest, beyond the stunning scenery and a change of biscuit brand; were a black Land Rover Discovery that flew past at an unnecessarily fast pace and when they were overtaken twenty minutes later by a suicidal biker who flashed past. Bolt just rolled his eyes and smiled at Mary. They weren't risk takers on the road.

52

As time passed, Hercules was less confident in his anonymity in the blacked out Disco. A satellite or drone could be on him already. His confidence waned further as he climbed the winding road, a single light at a distance, slowly gaining.

***

Wolf was cold, he ached all over and was done with the day. But he had a hunch and that can't be ignored. He could either let the techies track the snake, hoping they get a confirmed fix before he got to Andorra and the warrant bollocks, or he could try to intercept; kill that bastard and get a warm room for the night... he flexed his cold fingers and wriggled his toes - fuck this for a game of soldiers, he felt for the gun in his chest holster. With the head start Cobra had had, and the time and distance passed, he was almost certain it was the lights of his quarry ahead. Wolf put his head down and pressed on. Time to end this.

***

Hercules turned a long right hand bend, that then swept sharply to the left, a mile or so ahead of Wolf. Turning his lights off, he left the car in the road. He pulled a pistol from a side holster and waited in the pine trees at the side of the road. As the trees behind were illuminated by the motorbikes headlight, Hercules took a breath.

***

Wolf flew round the corner in hot pursuit, he spotted the Land Rover in the road, early enough to slam on the rear brake, but as he slowed a shot rang out and his front tyre exploded, sending him sprawling over the bars as the bike twisted beneath him and he collided with the stationary vehicle. For the third time that day, the Wolf took a short nap.

***

Hercules was climbing into the car when the shot was fired, like every time he'd been shot, initially it felt like being hit with a cricket bat. This time it hit him in the shoulder, spinning him round. The burning searing pain came later, followed by a dull ache that lasted months even with good care. For now he took the hit, adrenaline flooded his bloodstream and he reoriented himself, dragging his shocked body into the car. The bullet had gone through, but there was tissue damage and it was pissing blood.

Wrapping a shirt round the shoulder and strapping his belt around it under his arm, he applied pressure, it was better, but he was still leaking and needed medical attention soon. Right now, he needed to get up this mountain, away from the pursuers and back to his daughter. Hercules put the automatic car in drive and pushed onwards.

53

The Bell's were discussing their worst bRosiezard experiences when they took a sharp bend and saw a long-haired biker with a pistol waving at them.

"Mary?"

"Fuck that, drive on!"

Bolt floored it and swerved round the dazed and bloodied mad-man, who was left waving furiously in their mirrors.

***

Wolf took a breath; he couldn't commandeer private vehicles. With clear starry sky above, It would be a cold wait for company assistance to come out. He put the gun away and contacted control, requesting a 4x4 vehicle and bike pick-up.

Wolf cleaned himself up, started a small fire at the roadside and drank some hot coffee from his thermos. Caffeine was probably a bad idea, his head was thumping from at least one concussion, but he refused to mess with the pills the younger agents munched down. Wolf was feeling his age. It had been one of those days where you really earn your money.

The phone beeped:

Vehicle ETA 90min. New orders with vehicle.

"*New orders, why so cryptic? They were called control for a reason.*" Wolf drank more coffee, rested and watched the flames, enjoying the warmth on his face.

54

They had been on the move all day, almost continuously climbing as they navigated the rising terrain. The night was getting cold as the trail grew steeper, the mountains towering in front of them. Layla was warm despite the night as she tried to keep up with Rory. The moon, was almost full and everything was illuminated. After the long ride and following hike, her legs were unsurprisingly tired and she could feel her calves tightening, glutes and quads starting to suffer. The rucksack was growing heavier with every kilometer yet there was still so much ahead of them; this was relentless, she focused on engaging her core and breathing, which as they gained altitude wasn't easy either. They reached another crest, ahead the high peaks seemed to retreat as she saw a long snaking downhill across a wide valley and onto more ascent. While her legs relished the descent for a change, for every metre lost, Layla knew there would be a metre to regain on the path ahead.

Rumi looked at her quizzically, she could go all day and night with glee.

At the back, Bear was moving well for such a big guy, even with his big backpack on he was easily keeping up - glad to be off the horse. Rory paused and took a drink of water and scanned the path ahead and behind. It was becoming more sparsely wooded in the valley ahead, which left them open to being spotted on a clear night. They would be hidden as the track took turns and followed the topography of the mountain, but Rory was getting nervous.

"How you doing, Layla? Bear?"

Both nodded and drank some water.

"Make sure you're eating. They have to be closing in again now. We need to be ready for anything from this moment. If we are engaged and are separated at any point, we will meet at the lake where we will stop for a rest. It's a good few more hours tough hike from here. There are various routes up, we're taking the easy one, it's marked the whole way. It's not as direct as some of the climbs but we will move faster and safer. Bear, I want you to cover our rear from off the track. It will be slower going for you, but if anyone is following you'll see them. Layla and I will push on, we'll stop and prepare some food at the lake, I know a cave where we will be safe to rest and let you catch up. We'll be exposed for a while now, I think I would feel safer knowing that our six was covered."

"No problem, got your backs."

Bear nudged Chance with his elbow as she drank more water, spilling it on her chin, she gave him a good humoured shove, as he handed her some dried fruit and nuts.

"Focus guys. After the cave and first lake, we climb further and pass through a short, narrow gorge, beyond that there is a flat plateau with small turquoise lake, that's where we're most vulnerable and need to take precautions. If we make it to the higher ridges beyond, we have the cover of the craggy terrain and the option of resting for a while, whilst having a visual on any hunters approaching from the rear. We could even potentially make a stand at the gorge if necessary, it all depends what's coming at us. Right onwards and upwards."

Chance gave Bear a grimace and a smile and they pressed on as Bear, took out his field glasses and made his way diagonally off the track, picking his way over rocks, round shrubs and through small clusters of pine trees. After a few seconds Layla looked behind them; she couldn't see Bear anymore, he'd disappeared into the night like a ghost, she rubbed Rumi's ears for mutual reassurance.

"Stay close girl."

The guns stayed in her backpack, but Layla took her bow in hand and slipped an arrow from her quiver, her Dad's words in her head once more.

Hope for the best, be ready for anything... Chance looked at the mountain ahead and wondered how much trouble Hercules was getting in without her.

55

Ascending the other side of the mountain range, Layla's father had forged on in the Land Rover. Focusing on the white lines flashing past and trying to stay conscious. The driver's seat and his clothes were covered in his blood and the adrenaline was starting to wear off. He needed to stop the bleeding. Hercules pulled into a lay-by and parked behind some trees. Checking the boot for a medical kit - he wasn't disappointed. *Nice one Doc*. He laid out gauze, alcohol and tape. Then picked up a sachet of white powder and poured it over the small entry and larger exit wounds. On contact the powder fizzed and bubbled. Hercules has forgotten how much it hurt, the pain knifed through his shoulder like an icy dagger. Another sachet was emptied as the fizzing pain progressed into his shoulder like an icicle being slowly pushed through the burning muscle. Hercules thought back to previous times he'd been shot in the field. Once in the upper leg, once in the butt. The science worked but the treatment was excruciating, most people passed out... which as he reached for the gauze and the world started spinning, is exactly what happened to Hercules.

***

Still an hour from Soldeu and in need of a comfort break, the Bell's pulled into a rest stop to answer the call of nature and put the kettle on, possibly with the intention of stopping there for the night rather than venture into town. There was only one other car in the lay-by and they had their lights on so were probably about to leave.

Mary went into the back and put the kettle on and found another pack of biscuits in the cupboard.

"No more biscuits Mary, got to look after my waistline now we're on the run. Might not be on skis next time."

Mary opened the packet, ate a biscuit and put them on the side.

"You don't have to eat the whole packet tonight." Mary smiled.

They shared a look that said, they both knew they'd be finished by morning.

"Has that car gone? I'll go for a nature wee rather than use the tank."

Martin Bolt leaned out the van and took a look. It was still there, lights on inside and out and a door open. But, Bolt hadn't seen any movement or heard anything.

"Still there."

"I'm going anyway, I'm busting."

When Mary came back from the trees, Bolt was already halfway to the black Land Rover. Mary jogged to catch up and they arrived together to see a man face down on the floor his white t-shirt soaked in blood. Mary went immediately into care mode and checked for a pulse.

"He's alive."

Bolt was looking around nervously at the motorhome, as Mary rolled Hercules over.

"He's very handsome."

"What?" Bolt appeared at her shoulder, she had his attention. "Well, yes, I guess he is."

At that moment Hercules groaned into consciousness and tried to sit up, falling back. Bolt caught him and lowered him back to the ground.

"Take a minute Thor, you've lost a lot of blood. We can call an ambulance but we can't stick around to answer questions I'm afraid."

"No time, hunters are coming, you're in danger. My daughter, Soldeu." Hercules struggled to assemble the words before he passed out again.

Mary and Bolt were astonished. How could this guy know the hunters were after them? Why had he come to warn them and how had he got shot? There was no time for answers. Bolt checked the car and found a gun, large holdall bag and the medical kit. He took them to the van and then parked next to the Land Rover.

They manhandled Hercules into the back and onto the bed. Mary stayed in the back with their new companion and started dressing his wounds. Bolt grabbed his tea and the biscuits, climbed into the front and started the engine. Abandoning the lay-by and car they headed up the mountain towards Soldeu.

56

Bear had found good cover behind a ridge and was working his way up adjacent to the path, he stopped for some water. Scanning the stunning vista of forested mountain stretching below illuminated with lunar highlights, Bear wondered how he'd found himself back in the mountains, riding horses, in another combat situation.

Last time was Jordan, it was supposed to have been *the* last time. Bear had been sent to take out a target - he later discovered was the Prime Minister of Jordan; who after funding and support from foreign nations had grown in power and popularity. No longer compliant with the requests of the UK and US governments and their allies in the area, he had to be removed from the board.

Bear didn't follow politics, he was a weapon and did the jobs he was ordered to do. His focus was and had always been, get in, get out, be the best.

Disguised in tribal dress, head and face covered but for the eyes. Despite his artillery, Bear had made it early to the location. Through field glasses he watched from a rocky outcrop on a cliff, he was positioned high above a valley through which the target should pass in a convoy. There should be two military land rovers and a Humvee, the target would be in the Humvee.

Next to Bear on one side was a shoulder mounted RPG with four grenades loaded. he'd be glad to ditch the heavy weaponry having humped it in. On his other side, barrel resting on its folding legs was a high powered rifle with impressive looking sight.

There was no need for camouflage, the mission was clear. Take out the convoy and make sure any witnesses see a local rebel doing it... then escape through the mountains to the RV point, 50 clicks away in Israel, evading any pursuers. It seemed excessively far, but the bosses wanted complete deniability on this as usual.

Bear broke from an almost meditative state as his ears picked up a faint rumble and in the distance he picked out a dust cloud moving along the road. As it closed Bear knew something was wrong. The dense dust kicked up by the snaking vehicles was too long before dispersing, there were more than three vehicles. Bear called it in on a secure line.

"Control, this is Ghost, be advised, I have new intel, target approaching in a large convoy, insufficient munitions to neutralise all vehicles. Request air support."

"Received. Air support request denied; we can't have any birds in the air, orders are to proceed with mission, eliminate primary target and proceed to rendezvous."

Bear couldn't believe it, they were hanging him out to dry, this was suicide. Orders were orders. The approaching convoy consisted of three sand-coloured Humvee's, one at the front, one in the middle and one at the back. Between each of them were open back long-wheel base military land rover's with machine guns mounted on the bed manned by soldiers dressed in green.

Bear shouldered the rocket launcher and followed his target in the sight.

***

In the valley below, the Prime Minister of Jordan was on his way to a meeting with leaders of neighbouring Syria. The target was practising his speech, denigrating the latest actions of the oil grabbing West and their methods of economic control. His head of security, Hammed was looking out the windscreen while nodding along in approval - when the land rover in front of them exploded.

Bear fired a second grenade and the vehicle and machine gunner behind was neutralised in a ball of fire. The lead Humvee sped forward looking for cover ahead, the primary target vehicle squeezed passed the burning land rover and followed, while the rear Humvee reversed away from the wreckage blocking its pathway. Bear fired again, the grenade exploded underneath the lead Humvee, it flipped and rolled twice, settling on it's roof.

The target was bustled out of the other vehicle by Hammed and pushed towards the cliff face opposite Bear, who patiently watched his prey sprint for cover behind some boulders. Shaken soldiers from the upside-down vehicle helped each other do the same. The Prime Minister's driver just made it clear as heat and force of the Humvee blowing up behind him sent him sprawling off his feet and scrambling after the others.

Bear had taken out their heavy artillery and all but one Humvee, but he was out of grenades. Switching to the rifle he started locating the various targets hiding in the boulders, their assault rifles out of range, their cover insufficient. He counted eight spread among the rocks.

Systematically Bear worked through the targets from easiest shot to hardest, as their colleagues dropped one after the other, Bear knew they would panic and run.

Three head shots and two shots through the heart later the soldiers from the lead vehicle were all dead. He couldn't get a clean shot on the last three.

***

Hammed radioed in to the other Humvee, not interested in excuses.

"Find a fucking way, we're being picked off here.

"Stay low Sir, we're safe here, back up is coming."

Despite Hammed's calm words, the Prime Minister was terrified, his security detail were dropping like flies.

Bear, saw the other Humvee reappear in the valley, it was moving fast as it launched high off the raised roadside skidding on the rough rocky ground. Bumping along the edge of the dusty road, picking its way between the boulders and a scattering of small olive trees, the approaching Humvee would be impervious to his rifle rounds, he had to execute this mission before it arrived. Bear aimed at the boulder next to the driver and squeezed.

***

It was the last straw when another shot rang out; metres from him, his driver screamed and collapsed to the floor holding his leg - the boulder next to him disintegrating into a puff of dust and razor sharp shrapnel slicing through his knee. Writhing on the floor he was only screaming momentarily as a bullet hit him between the eyes and he lay still.

The Prime Minister ran, breaking cover, Hammed's fingers just missing his jacket collar. Bear's target made it four metres before he fired two rifle rounds which destroyed the right ventricle and aorta. The target dropped to the floor like an abandoned marionette, strings of life permanently severed.

***

On the cliff-top above Bear had already folded the rifle away and despite knowing he was fucked, was running for his life. The remaining Humvee and soldiers in the armoured vehicle were hot on his heels. They would find a track out of the valley, join his exit route and use the off-road vehicle to it's full abilities to catch him. He needed to slow them down.

At the top of the steep farm track the trees stopped and a kilometer of plateau opened ahead before the track disappeared into sparse woodland again. Bear put a shoulder to one of the smaller trees and gave it an almighty shove, it moved. Putting his feet on a larger tree, legs like hydraulic pistons he pushed again, forcing the gap to grow an inch at a time, with a crack, the ground and roots gave way and the tree fell across the pathway.
Bear picked himself up and ran. This was going to have to be a fast kilometer.

The Humvee made it up the steep slope and arrived at the tree. A soldier jumped out and scanned the trees weapon ready, he took position at the back corner of the Humvee, covering the sides and rear, the plateau ahead clear. Another soldier unreeled the winch cable and attached it to the trunk.

The soldier covering the woods died first, head jolting unnaturally, body limp. The winch man heard the first shot whistle past, but his head snapped sideways before his comrades body hit the ground. he was unceremoniously dragged back down the hill as the Humvee reversed quickly, pulling the tree and his corpse out of the snipers sight.

***

Bear was running again, he knew the Humvee and remaining pursuers would cross that plateau in minutes. Once he passed a final lonely mountain village ahead - barely waterproof shacks with sheep-pens, he knew the rough track narrowed to a goat path, beyond a wooded basin and then disappeared up into the higher peaks and Israel beyond. Bear pushed harder, legs and lungs burning, expecting to hear a vehicle or gunshot from behind. If he could make the woodland cover, the pursuers would abandon the vehicle and he may have a chance.

At the far edge of the village, the sound of a vehicle approached fast. Bear leaned against a wooden gate in the fenced farmland and accepted defeat. Another open stretch ahead of him, the villagers had cleared the trees. That wasn't on his intel.

Bear exhaled deeply. On the other side of the fence, answering with an exhalation of its own, a large black horse in a dusty paddock shook its mane as it moved towards him from behind an almond tree.

Bear didn't ride, but there was no way he could cross the open ground fast enough on foot. Sliding the wooden pole across he entered the paddock and speaking softly approached the horse.

"I need your help boy, don't be afraid."

Hiding his own fear Bear swung up smoothly on the horse and held tightly to the mane. The horse calmly walked through the opening in the fence and stood still on the track. From it's back, Bear could sce the Humvee roaring towards him.

"Go horse... Yeehaa... Go!"

The horse watched the approaching vehicle inquisitively.

Bear gave the horse a big kick and nearly fell over its backside when it responded. Galloping away from the Humvee, it raced down a slope and across the plateau towards the wooded trail beyond. Bear floated above the horse, holding the mane and squeezing with his legs. They had almost made it to the cover of the woods and elevation ahead, when a hail of bullets ripped through the air from the Humvee now stopped halfway across the plateau, soldiers firing wildly at their escaping assassin.

Bear assessed the damage as his mount pushed further up the goat path into the wilderness, well and truely spooked. The horse was unharmed, but Bear had taken a bullet low in the side, just above the hip, it had come out the other side, but he was leaking. The main issue was the round that had entered his back and remained there, somewhere near his shoulder blade by the feel of it. Bear persuaded the horse on and forced himself to somehow stay conscious. The horse seemed to know where it was heading.

Bear made it to the RV to be welcomed with an empty landing area and radio silence. It took a further fourteen hour ride to collapse near a friendly base where he was eventually found near dead on the roadside. No witnesses ever saw the horse, some thought he had imagined it. Bear preferred to believe it returned home, its mission complete.

57

I wonder what happened to that horse.

Bear snapped back to the moment, there was movement on the path a mile back, clear in starlight, the guy was moving fast. Faster than Chance and Rory. Bear put the water away, thought about unpacking his rifle, but took out his pistol instead. Leaving his pack on the ridge, Bear moved silently back down the hill.

The speed at which he covered the ground was unbelievable. "*Watch your footing soldier, you're not as nimble as you used to be.*" He warned himself as he made his way down the rocky ridge, leaping from boulder to boulder, running through the brush before disappearing down a steep bank and into a copse of Ash and Fir trees below.

From the trees he watched the hunter silently, there was something familiar about the way he moved, the build and the neat beard... Jerry's. This guy had bought him breakfast, Bear let him pass and then followed him comfortably and without a sound.

***

Hawk had been flying up the mountain, a go-pill from his standard issue kit had helped him find a good pace and hold it. He was ready, switched on and looking to finish this mission, get paid and get home. Ahead the winding turns opened into a wider grass floored pass with high walls, the path climbed less steeply for a few miles before disappearing into the towering cliffs ahead. Hawk paused to re-hydrate and check his rifle and the horizon.

Through the sight he scanned the valley bathed in the moonlight, looking for movement. Nothing, more nothing - they must be moving fast. Something caught his eye... approaching the cliffs ahead. His scope snapped back, a dog... and a blonde girl.

The kids weren't supposed to be here. Where was everyone else? Unless this was just a night-hiker with a dog, unlikely. They were nine hundred yards away, he adjusted the sight. It was definitely the Chance girl and her dog. The shot was in range and his orders were clear - he could always double check. Hawk called into control.

"Steve, are the kids off the kill order?"

"That's a negative and that comes from above the Director of Hunter Division, it went to the top. That's not important right now... I was just about to call you.

Andy, I'm really sorry, I have bad news. I don't know how to tell you this... it's Sarah. I'm sorry Andy, your daughter passed away half an hour ago. Anna, told me she passed peacefully in her sleep. I'm so, so sorry Andy. I'll go down there myself as soon as my shift finishes."

"Thanks Steve, over and out."

Andrew Hawkins slumped to his knees. Sarah was gone. She had barely experienced life, stuck in a hospital bed since she was a toddler, he'd barely left the Forces, had joined the hunters at Sixty-five and then everything changed.

Tears running down his face, head racing with amphetamines and grief, Hawk un-holstered his pistol, put it in his mouth and closed his eyes. Soon it would all be over and they would be together.

***

"You don't want to do that fella." Appearing phantom-like from the trees, gun in hand, held calmly at his side, Bear had heard the whole thing.

Hawk removed the gun.

"What the fuck d'you know. I've got nothing left to live for, my daughter is... gone. My reason for living, fighting, for killing, hoping and now, for dying." Hawks eyes were manic.

"What about revenge?" Bear waited.

"... Revenge? On who? She was sick."

"But why was she sick and who kept her that way? The company of course, they play dirty, keep loved one's sick, entrap a family member or just kill them - all to control employees. It's not a new tactic for the company. You need to talk to Raptor."

"I killed your friend, why would you want to stop me?"

"Three reasons I didn't execute you - I was about to put two in the back of your head when you asked about clemency for the kids rather than blindly following orders, so you're not a monster. That empathy saved your life.

You followed orders and killed my friend; but Tom took a risk and broke the law, then ran rather than face the consequences. He didn't deserve to die, but that wasn't your call. I've followed orders before, so I have to forgive that.

Second, I am truly sorry about your daughter, there's a bigger common enemy 'Hawk'right. I'm going to need your help to take them down and keep my friends alive. What do you say, can you save dying for another day?"

"Yeah, for revenge, I guess I can. You really think the company had something to do with Sarah being ill?"

"Can't hurt to find out. Either way, you are no longer a threat...right?"

"Not to you. But, if the company had anything to do with my daughter's death, I will do what I can to take them down and help your friends escape. I have nothing to return for - there's nothing left to lose. What was the third reason?"

"You bought me breakfast when we bumped into each in outside the hospital. You're not a bad guy, you're just doing bad things. I been there and I didn't have the excuse of a sick child. I just knew no better."

"That morning seems like a life time ago. Mike, right? I am sorry about your friend, I read his file and I didn't want to pull that trigger. This is the last gun I want to use, then I'll be with Sarah."

"Do you think that's what Sarah would want? There's another child on this mountain running for her life, Layla hasn't done anything to deserve this and the hunters will keep coming for her whether you're alive or dead. I think Sarah would want her father to help, not quit. This time you can save lives."

Hawk took a moment and holstered his weapon, he knew Mike was right.

"Okay. Let's keep the rest of them alive and make life a misery for the Company."

"Thank you Hawk, call me Bear."

58

It had been ninety-minutes since Bear had gone. Chance missed him already, she felt safer when he was around. Like with Dad, but without all the rules and control. She still felt safe with Rory, but right now she almost resented the robot, as he marched on relentlessly.

Rumi still thought they were playing a wonderful game, but even she was now sitting and resting any time they stopped. Layla had found a rhythm and was just about keeping up with Rory's rapid ascent; he clearly loved the mountains and with the added danger, was ascending quickly between rocks and trees. Scanning the massive expanse of terrain, then waving her on to and then moving to the next spot.

At steep sections they were scrambling with both hands, the bow back on her pack. Layla was mentally and physically exhausted; but felt like she could keep going. The pain in her calves and thighs had eased into an all over ache, her back and neck were tired from looking up, but it was almost comforting knowing they had come so far and she still felt strong. The pack now seemed like part of her and her lungs were getting used to the altitude. They had gone from almost sea level to over 2000m already, but she was adapting.

Rumi learned fast and would lie down, silent and motionless whenever her person stopped. Layla felt like any hunter within a mile would be able to hear her heavy breathing and screaming legs as she scaled a section of large step-like boulders. It went on forever.

As if a final torture to the mammoth day, they scrambled up a steep scree slope, the loose shale slipping beneath each footstep making progress painfully slow.

When Rory finally waved her through a narrow pass with high walls, and pointed behind a huge fallen boulder the size of a house, Layla could have kissed him and given the cave an immediate five-star review. Legs shaking, she lay down immediately on her back, spent. Rumi lay down next to her, head in her lap. Eventually Chance groaned, rolled over and struggled with her pack.

"*Sort your shit then rest.*" Hercules words muttered from his daughter's lips.

Rory helped her off with her pack.

"Well done Chance, that was a hell of a yomp. Your parents would have been proud of that effort. I'm knackered. Get your foil blanket out and wrap up, you've created the heat, might as well keep it in as long as possible. Drink some water, have a nibble and shut your eyes for a bit. We're safe here. I'll get some tea and food sorted."

Layla drank some water and went outside for a wee, legs still shaking. Returning to Rumi, she lay back down and wondered how Coco and Royal were getting on. She realised on her torturous yet zen hike, she hadn't really thought much about her

Mother, Father, Aaron, the horses, or anything but the next few steps on the mountain path. Now she was exhausted and before the water on the stove was warm, Layla was fast asleep.

***

When Layla woke, it was cold, she must have been asleep for an hour and it was quiet. Something was wrong, she sat up.

Rumi was standing statue still, pointing at the cave entrance, hair bristling. Rory was nowhere to be seen, but there was hot tea steaming away and some sort of food bubbling on a small stove. Rory had been busy.

There was an open pack of beef jerky on the ground nearby, but Rumi wasn't interested in food. A low growl starting to roll in her throat.

"Easy girl, everything's okay." Was she talking to herself or Rumi. Her short elm bow - ideal for shooting from horseback - was already in her hand and with a swift movement, an arrow flashed up to the string. Moving silently towards the entrance, Rumi crept forward with her. Rumi quietly growling, she smelled someone she didn't know. The bowstring was at Layla's ear; she was scared. The lethal potential energy ready to be released, transferred to the arrow and deadly kinetic energy. Why her Dads scientific explanations came back at this time, she wasn't sure.

Rumi's growl got lower and turned into a bark. Layla was sure of something, Rumi wasn't happy and Rumi was an excellent judge of situations, as some boys had found out to their dismay. Chance decided; whoever came around that corner was getting an arrow in the leg.

"Chance, you awake? We have guests." It was Rory. Was she awake? Layla lowered the bow and quivered the arrow.

"Yes, I'm awake."

"Thought I heard some barking. Bear's back and he has company. They're coming in, just answering the call of nature first."

Bear walked into the cave, his big pack on his back, collected with Hawk en-route. To Layla, the man with him looked a good looking rugby player - dressed as a soldier. Past the weaponry, he didn't look at all dangerous. Strong and tough, but not dangerous. If anything, he looked sad. He couldn't be a prisoner as he'd been allowed to keep his weapons.

"How's the legs Chancer? What a day, brutal last shale slope." Bear grinned.

"My legs are pretty tired, but I'm okay; you don't look like you even broke a sweat."

"Everyone's tired, even Rumi." He nodded at the sleeping dog, who sensing all was okay, was curled up by Layla's bag already dreaming about tomorrow.

"I was very impressed with you today, the rest of us had years of training or was a Vizsla, you're a chip off the parental block. Super-stamina."

Rory looked up from the food and opened his mouth, but then looked back at the stove.

"So, enough about me... who is this guy? Rumi wasn't keen, I nearly shot Uncle Rory in the leg."

This time Rory looked up and spoke.

"What with the guns I made you, ironic?"

"No, just an arrow."

"Think it's my boy that took the arrow."

Everyone laughed but the new guy.

"Chance, this is Andrew Hawkins. Hawk's joining us for dinner, there's a lot to discuss, let's sit down. I'm starving."

"Hawk or Andy."

Layla shook the offered hand. Too tired and hungry to push for further information.

"I'm Chance."

Hawk took some food rations out and added them to the meagre supplies. Bear grinned, he hated travelling light when it came to food. But when it's life or death, speed is essential and hungry is temporary - whereas death is always permanent.

"Looks like we're joining Hawk for dinner."

Rory dished up and put some more dehydrated rations in the pan and added more water.

They ate in almost silence, Rumi was the loudest and finished first too, returning to her spot. When everyone had had seconds and Bear thirds. They sipped their tea from enamel mugs, warming their hands.

Eventually, Hawk broke the silence.

"We have a lot to discuss, I guess I should start by telling Chance who I am. I'm a hunter. The hunter who has been tracking you and your friends. This all started, when Tom Kind did a brave but foolish thing, or more importantly when he got caught and ran."

"You killed Kind!"

Layla was on her feet, hands in tight fists and eyes wide with fury. Rumi was on her feet and at Layla's side in a second, heckles up.

"I'm sorry about your friend Chance, but I was just doing my job. Following orders"

"That's what the fucking Nazis said." Layla looked at Bear.

"How have you not pulled his fucking arms off? You loved Tom, he was your best friend. How can you sit there and be okay with this?"

"I'm not okay with it Chance, I'm still sad about my friend. But I'm being practical, Tom took risks and made choices knowing the possible consequences and his action has endangered so many others by proxy. Including you. Besides, Hawk's retired."

"Retired? He's a hunter, they don't get to retire."

"I retired, so did your parents." Rory spoke. "We are all capable of change."

"My Mother didn't get to retire did she? The Company poisoned her. What makes you so special Hawk?"

"They have nothing on me anymore, my daughter was sick and after many years, died today. Your friend Bear believes the Company has something to do with it. I've heard rumours of blackmail. But murdering children."

"I guarantee it. They killed my Mother and wouldn't hesitate to kill me."

"That's not entirely accurate, the kill order on you and the boy were unusually delayed initially and then later when I tried to circumvent the kill order on you, the Director of Hunter Division supported the application, but was over-ruled by the board. Cobra's file was also locked at first, you've made it a long way kid, maybe you have a guardian angel."

"That's true, I heard the transmission." Bear shrugged. Layla soften and asked,

"Okay, so if you've switched sides, what can you tell us about who else is hunting us?"

"Not good news, but I'll tell you what I know... I'm the rear guard; there's a team coming in by helicopter at first light and two more hunters closing in on your Father from the other side of the mountains. He blew up a building in Barcelona apparently."

"Good. Sounds like Dad's having fun." Layla smiled and tried not to worry, Hercules could take care of himself and was on his way.

"So, what's the plan?"

"We retreat and try to out run them while Hawk leads them away, or we rest here and prepare to defend our position. If we get caught between them on the mountain were dead." Rory answered. Bear nodded in agreement and asked,

"So do we run or do we fight?"

"You fight, you'll die, they're bringing a helicopter... if I were you I'd run before dawn. I'll keep heading up at first light and report my progress. They'll track my position." Hawk offered little doubt.

"Okay, let's rest a few hours, then we run down." Rory decided.

Layla looked pale, but lay down in agreement and shut her eyes.

“Don’t worry Chance, we’ll get away. We have an opportunity to disappear now we have Hawk. Trust me.” Bear ruffled her hair. Layla opened her eyes.

“I trust you Bear, hasta manana.”

59

After too many hours in the saddle, the riders and their string of steeds arrived in darkness at a farmhouse, exhausted. Alex and Aaron watered and fed the horses at their friend's yard and took them to the field. Coco and Royal were corralled nearby, not yet fully-integrated with the others.

Alex had taken the key from under the flower pot and let them into the house, Aaron headed up to the bathroom and Alex went into the kitchen. Putting the kettle on, she spooned loose leaves into a pot and then slumped into a kitchen chair, she was ready for a cup of tea.

She had almost succumbed to hope; for so many years they had kept a low profile away from cameras and police drones. No holidays, no city breaks, just the quiet country life of farming, the mountains and horses. It was wonderful in a way, but was a beautiful prison in others. They had come to settle into their family world; as Aaron got older and broadened his horizons, her fear had silently grown. What if he moved to a city, they couldn't even visit. Now the past had caught up with them, Rory could no longer hide and if he was a fugitive, then they all were.

Aaron was taking first shower, their friends were away in Rome on another city break, they wouldn't mind.

Alex poured two cups of tea through a silver strainer and found a packet of chocolate biscuits in the snack cupboard. After four hobnobs, Aaron's tea was cold, she threw it in the sink, took the cosy off the teapot, topped up her cup and put the kettle back on. The shower was still going; *he wasn't even out yet.*

Alex caught her reflection in a cabinet door and considered how long she might need in the shower to feel human again.

"AARON, don't use all the hot water." No response. Alex sighed and climbed the stairs to the bathroom door. "Aaron, you nearly done? There's tea downstairs." Alex waited a moment and banged on the door. *Nothing.*

"Son, I hope you're not in someone else's shower wanking over that Chance girl."

That would have got a response. She tried the door and it opened. The window was open, through the glass door she could see the shower was empty, she turned it off and dried her hand on a fresh fluffy towel as she looked out the window into the night.

"Crazy son of a...n Irishman. He's gone after the girl."

Alex, took a moment; turned the shower back on, stripped off and stepped into the hot cascade. The water held her like a calming blanket, cleansing her body and clearing her mind, as she processed her racing thoughts. Aaron was a young man now, he had made his choice. He would certainly be more use in the field than her and she could hardly go chasing after him through the countryside. Aaron knew the mountains, he would be fine, he'd find Rory on the route to Soldeu and they'd look after each other. But, then what?

Alex massaged shampoo into her hair and washed the long ride out before conditioning. After the shower she shut the window and towelled herself off before borrowing some Almond oil and moisturising. After she had brushed her teeth with a finger and toothpaste, dried and brushed her hair through - Alex felt like a new woman.

She went into the bedroom and borrowed some clothes, changed and threw some bits in a small bag, before grabbing a ski jacket and bobble hat from the back of the wardrobe. Catching her reflection in the mirror, she gave herself a reassuring nod, it was going to be okay. It had to be.

Ready to face whatever came next she took a breath, there was no race against those on foot in the mountains, she might as well look and feel human, who knew when she might get the opportunity again.

Downstairs, Alex found the keys to Sally's horsebox on the hook as always. Washed up and left a note that simply said,

"Sally,

Popped in for post-ride shower, had to borrow the van and some clothes. I will explain when I can. What's ours is yours - House and horses.

Love you all. A xxx"

What's ours is yours, they always said that. Sally had been a great friend. Never pushing for answers, she'd certainly have some questions this time.

Alex locked up and loaded Layla's horses in Sally's van: She'd made a promise, she could hardly leave them behind. Alex punched Soldeu, Andorra into the navigation system, selected a car park they had used before when they'd gone climbing and drove out the yard, wondering if she'd ever see that farmhouse, her horses or Sally again. She assumed Hercules and Marcus would find them not there and head to Soldeu too. Alex had to worry about her family, trust her gut and react to the situation. She may not be good with a gun or her fists but she was a fighter and she was smart.

Alex looked in the rear-view mirror - Pretty lady going to ride ponies in the snow, definitely not the wife of an ex-hunter turned hunted, trekking over the mountains with the most wanted or Mother to a love-sick puppy, running off into the night to be a hero. Just a pretty lady going to ride ponies.

60

Aaron wasn't running through the night. After climbing out the window, he had fueled his friend's motocross bike, borrowed a helmet and pushed for half a kilometre before daring to start it. The surrounding night so silent, he was sure his mother would hear the bike and give chase like he was an errant kid.

He had basic rations - his Dad had most the food, he put on extra layers, a fleece and a light-weight windproof jacket. His rifle, ammunition, a jet-lighter, knife, medical kit, water, purification tablets and a foil blanket. It was going to get cold. He could only get so far on the bike, and there were trained killers out there, but he couldn't leave his Dad... or Chance on their own. Aaron wasn't sure what he felt about Layla, but he hadn't felt it before, she was different and he just knew had to help her. They had a good head start but with the bike, then taking the shorter, steeper route on foot and free-climbing the relatively easy cliff face at first light, hopefully he'd catch them before the gorge and steep trail; it wasn't going to be easy. *Things that matter never are.* Time to catch his old man. It was going to be a long night.

61

It had been less than ninety minutes when a four-wheel drive van pulled up next to the lone Wolf's fire. He warmed and flexed his hands, standing up, bristling, heckles raised. So, who the fuck had the company sent with orders for his mission? This could get ugly.

The driver's door opened to the sound of country music and a pair of cowboy boots stepped out. Wolf rounded the back of the van.

"Howdy, Wolfman, long-time you old dog."

"Coyote? It's been years. What the fuck are you doing here? Thought you were retired."

"They sent me back to the USA to ride a desk and advise on the sixty-five bill when it passed there. I still do private work here and there. I was sort of on holiday in Valencia when I got a call to come join some big hunt that's causing the brass problems. Got to Barcelona this afternoon and they told me I was your delivery boy and to assist you where I could.

Actually what they said, is - You're the only one we can send to help he probably won't kill. What's happening Wolf? Not going to kill me are you?"

Coyote laughed his loud American laugh - Wolf had actually missed that laugh. Coyote laughed a lot, like he didn't have a care in the world, a confident bellow, that resonated and mocked the world and its worries, as if to say - Yes, it's gone to shit, it's burning down, but fuck it, might as well go with a grin.

Wolf wasn't sure whether he really didn't have a worry in the world or it was the only way the crazy bastard knew how to operate in this business. Maybe it was a luxury of the mentality ill being completely ruthless and carefree in their job. Wolf didn't throw the term psychopath around, but Coyote always seemed to be a little too keen to kill. Hot-dogging his skills as the yanks called it, or tidying up loose ends that weren't a threat, maybe he was a psychopath, but maybe Wolf was too, he wasn't a shrink. He was a hunter and professionally, Coyote was up there with the best.

Wolf had never seen a faster draw and despite mocking him at first for antiquated weaponry, it was amazing what Coyote could do with twelve bullets in less than a second. They all had coping mechanisms, his were coffee and prostitutes - dressing up like a mad cowboy was okay by Wolf, as long as you got the job done and Coyote certainly did that.

Enough of that. He sounded like the in-house therapist. All he knew was it was fun hunting with Coyote and he could trust him to have his back. Things were finally shaping up.

The two men shared a brief hug, unusual for either, but in this case completely natural. Coyote was of a smaller build than Wolf, a couple of years older, but clearly hadn't stopped the fitness regime. His curly blonde hair still reached his shoulders, he couldn't see in the light but assumed the unavoidable greys were less visible than in his dark hair, one thing was for sure... the white Stetson must have been replaced many times because it looked new like every time he'd seen him.

To most he looked like a rugged Marlboro-man. To the more observant; the slightly punch-worn face, scars on the eyebrows and knuckles and the dangerous glint in his grey-blue eyes, were all indications that this was not a man to fuck with and Coyote wasn't even wearing his six-shooters yet.

"Fuck me, it's been almost a decade you crazy cowboy. I missed you man, you were the only fucker I ever worked with that made it enjoyable. So what we got in the back?"

"Two Honda's and kit. Usual, med kits, crappy food rations and teabags. Decent arsenal, couple of hammocks, bivvi-bags and a kettle - oh yeah, I also picked up a French press and some coffee, can't hunt without our morning brew man."

"Everything we need. You Coyote, are a diamond. Let ride"

"Regulators... mount up."

62

Hercules felt warm, but constricted as he opened his eyes and looked around. He was tightly wrapped in a blanket, only one arm free. A beautiful lady with a kind face was looking at him. In her day she must have been absolutely stunning, a fresh cut was healing on her cheek. She looked relieved.

"Hello young man, how are you feeling?"

"Okay, I think? I can't move."

"Sorry about that lovely, duct tape, just in case. I've patched you up, you'll be fine if you rest. You'll feel awful for a while, you need to keep drinking water, you lost a lot of blood. We didn't take you to a hospital, you said we couldn't. We're parked in the camper in a car park in Soldeu. What's your name?"

"Layla... I have to get to my daughter. My name is Cornelius, my friends call me Hercules."

"Hercules. We need some answers, how did you know the sixty-five hunters were after us and closing in? Why did you come to warn us?"

"What? Head foggy, Hercules tried to understand. "No, they're after me, my daughter and my friends... You're running too?" The lady nodded.

"I'm Mary, this is Martin."

"Mary, it's not just sixty-fivers they chase. Anyone they can manipulate into signing up, if they run, they will chase. Anyone they can't control, they will hunt. I worked for them once, I've seen what they can do."

Hercules opened up to Mary and told her the whole story. Martin sat in the front, listening.

When Hercules had finished, Mary, wiped away a tear and cut the duct tape. Martin came into the back and introduced himself.

"So what's your story Mary and Martin?"

"I'll put the kettle on... but like you said, sixty-fivers caught in the system."

"I need to get to Layla."

Mary reassured him.

"Don't worry young man, we'll get you to your daughter, but first you to need to rest, eat something and re-hydrate, we'll need you in better shape if we're going to war."

"We, war? What are you suggesting Mary? We should get the hell out of here."

"Well technically we're in Andorra now, so they would have to apply for permission to use lethal force. That usually takes twelve hours to process. So we're safe, the others are technically in France and will still be green-lit for shoot on sight." Hercules offered.

"So we're safe right here for a few hours, but we're going to go towards danger out of choice, on a suicide mission." Bolt didn't like this idea of walking into the lion's den.

"There's a car park higher up the mountain, it's still Andorra, you'll be safe, but I can get on to the trails from there and find them, alone."

Bolt looked at Mary, he knew there was no point arguing with her on this, besides it seemed there was a new path for them to follow, *as long as they were together*. He climbed into the driver's seat, popped a biscuit between his teeth and started the engine.

"Well navigator, where's this car park then?"

"You, rest." She directed at Hercules, who nodded and lay back.

"And you...." She climbed into the passenger seat and kissed Bolt on the cheek as she passed. "I love you."

"Love you too crazy lady. Til death do us part." Bolt grinned, Mary rolled her eyes.

63

Coyote and Wolf made it up to Soldeau later that night and considered stopping in the camper-park in town, but they had a location on the group on the other side of the mountain thanks to "Golden Hawk" the company, moral soldier. His location and updates were always regular.

Wolf could guarantee the Cobra would be attempting to re-join his daughter and Raptor. No point hunting a whole resort if you know where they're going. They put the truck floodlights on and continued higher up the mountain. The SatMap showed a parking area that gave access to trails down the other side of the mountain, if they took the high ground first, with Hawk below stopping a retreat, it didn't matter where the others were, they would hold ground and cut them off. They could even wait for the Fox team if needed.

Coyote made coffee and they ate some of the bland food rations, before they headed out into the darkness with their long guns and side-arms a few hours before dawn.

***

Their eyes adjusted quickly to the light or lack thereof. It was a clear night, cool, but with no wind, the stars and almost full moon made it relatively easy to move quickly downhill. After a ninety-minute jog, Wolf chose the spot; off the path and out of sight, among a little crop of rocks and small pines. Their position was above a plateau with a small turquoise lake in the middle, they could see the long trail snaking down to and around the edge of the lake and then disappearing into a gorge in the distance. From there they could wait until their targets were in the open with no cover and would have clear shots from less than 800m. They set up and waited, glad to be still warm from the run, Coyote took a swig from a flask of coffee and offered it to Wolf.

"Thanks mate, I'll have swig, but then no more caffeine for me until after, I want to keep a steady hand. These guys are ex-professionals and even though we have all the cards, I want to make sure. We know the two guys and the girl are down there. Cobra is slippery and is out there somewhere with a bullet in him, injured snakes are dangerous."

"Well, we're dug in now, nobody will have seen us coming down in the dark, when he shows up, he'll be a sitting duck. This will be a turkey shoot man. What's that Hawk guys location?"

"Golden boy is over twelve miles away; according to his reports he was trailing them approximately a mile behind. On this terrain, depending on rests, they should be here before midday."

"I don't know what that is in kilometres, but noon sounds perfect hombre. You good to take a watch and I'll grab some zee's."

"Wake you in ninety."

Coyote pulled his hat over his eyes and with the gift few have but soldiers, was asleep with minutes. Snoring very slightly. That was new, he used to sleep silently. Wolf mused, they were both getting old, he was getting up most nights to take a piss these days.

If he wasn't doing this, what would he do, sit on a boat, fish, drink and get fat. Get a dog and a lodge in the mountains, or a villa by the beach. Listen to music, learn the guitar? Awesome for a few months of distraction but then what? Travel, see the world? *Been there, seen it, it's dark...* but then, the parts of the world he'd seen were usually in some form of conflict, or his role there shrouded in violence. Maybe there was another world out there for him. But, retirement - reading novels, watching screens and golf... fuck that. That was for the normals, not the warriors. Retirement was coming, one way or another. Maybe the private sector would be interested in someone with his experience and training. Even then he'd soon be forced into a chair. He had already turned the Director down once when offered a managers role, his own office would still be just a desk with the Company.

Scanning the valley below and trail above he could see no sign of movement, he kept watching and pondering his future, glad of the camouflage bivvy bag keeping him warm.

64

Aaron was cold, he kept moving, pushing his aerobic limit. Jogging the little flats and downs, walking fast uphill, but not so fast he would build up lactic acid. He had to pace this right if he was to make it to the plateau in time to liaise with the others. From there he could see the path up the mountain, if they weren't visible above, he could make his way round the blue lake, through the narrow gorge. Layla would leave a sign if they'd passed already, if not and they were below he could jog down to meet them. Other alternatives he pushed to the back of his mind and broke back into a jog.

It had been colder on the motorbike, the clear night sky sucking away the warmth of the day, as the cool air rushed past him cooling his body, hands and feet freezing by the time he ran out of fuel. He pictured himself relaxing on a boat in the sunshine with Layla; or riding along a sandy beach at the waters edge, salty spray kicking up from the horses hooves. Layla's golden hair flowing in the wind, reflecting the light, tanned face and perfect white teeth grinning as they galloped into a warm setting sun.

Now, despite the cool air, he was warm again, under a blanket of brilliant stars and a fat moon, he felt good. The heavy rifle felt part of him after all the trips with Dad. Moving efficiently up the mountain path, steady breathing, making sure of his footing. Heading for the climb.

The first landmark was The Tower; one of various popular climbing routes here. This was an easy climb if you're tied in, no overhangs, just an eighty metre wall, his Mum had even climbed it with them a few years back. Without equipment it would be risky at day and dangerous to attempt it at night. While Aaron could climb, he would not consider himself a climber. By his estimates he should be at the Tower around 4am, he could rest at the base and then start the climb at dawn. He hoped to be up the wall and onto the steep path by 7am, five hours hike from there and he'd be at the lake and back to Layla and the dinosaur. Aaron checked his pulse, assessed his breathing and slowed to a walk. Fueling the machine after catching his breath, he ate an energy bar and washed it down. It was going to be a big day.

***

It was 3.30am when he arrived at the base of The Tower, with three huge faces it offered options of various technicality for ascent. Aaron knew the route he'd take, the easy one. First he drank some water from his bottle, ate a protein bar and chewed on some beef jerky. His dad always made him carry it on hikes, partly because it was a high energy, lightweight food source, mainly because Rory loved it and they'd always eat both packs on the walk or drive back. Aaron hadn't really liked it when he was younger, but chewing away with his Dad, legs tired, but proud to have conquered another mountain together, he grew accustomed to the taste. Now, beef jerky, always brought back memories, usually of triumph over challenge. Aaron fished out another piece and chewed away,

"I'll save the rest for tomorrow Dad, we can share it with Layla."

Wrapping himself in the foil blanket to trap his hard-earned body heat, he shut his eyes, time for a power nap. He was too nervous to sleep properly, but just lying down for an hour or so, would give his body and mind a break.

***

As the night slowly began to lighten around him, Aaron stretched the aches out of his legs. It was spring, the days could be hot and sunny, but it was still the mountains, lying still had let the heat escape his body, but the foil blanket had helped delay it. His hands and feet were cold again, so he swung his arms in circles forcing the blood into the extremities like a centrifuge and did the same with his legs. Well before dawn broke fully, Aaron was on the wall. Bag and rifle slung over his back. This made it more awkward, but taking every movement carefully, he slowly made progress; the first part was relatively easy, a flat climb with easy hand and footholds. It was when he reached the top of this the challenge would begin, he would have to traverse a narrow lip and climb around the right-angled corner of the tower faces. In the past (with ropes) he had fallen here, once swinging in a long arch and injuring his shoulder on the wall. This time it wouldn't be bruises, it would be broken bones and probably a slow painful death. Aaron kept climbing.

The morning was breaking, lighting up the green carpets of dark trees and bright dewy grass below. Aaron wasn't looking at the view below him. Intensely focused instead on squeezing his cold fingers into a narrow crack above, keeping the toe of his clumsy hiking boot pressed into the lip below and reaching high around the corner with his right arm. Aaron located his anchor and hooked three fingers over a small unseen ledge in the wall. Taking a breath, he made sure his rifle was out of his way, released his left hand from the crack and allowed his body weight to swing him round the corner, he knew there was a comfortable ledge there, just beyond where you'd want it, you couldn't see it in the light or dark, but it was there, he'd taken this leap of faith before.

It was perfect, his right toe found security. The ledge Aaron was standing on was the widest point he'd stood on since he left the ground, right now he missed his tight climbing shoes, but he was past the first tricky section. A swig of water and a glance at the watch, he was doing well, but it was time to move. Face to the cliff, he'd edged along the slowly rising but narrowing ledge. The slick walls gave no option upwards with his kit and with almost no finger holds he had to keep his body close to the wall. Moving slowly, pressing his finger tips into the smooth rock, searching for anything rougher than sandpaper to find some friction and lessen the seemingly growing weight of his pack, which felt like it was going to drag him off the wall and onto the rocks far below.

Taking care, Aaron reached another wall to his right that offered more holds, he worked his way up the less steep wall and then up a crack between the two walls. Eventually, sweating and shaking, he scrambled the last few metres over boulders, rolled over the top, removed his pack and lay on the flat ground breathing heavily.

"*Never again.*"

Looking at the dawning sky, Aaron offered a note of acknowledgment and appreciation to the universe that he wasn't man-jam at the bottom of the climb. There wasn't time for self-congratulation though, there was a long way to go. Aaron drank some more water, he was getting low, but there were streams above he could fill up from in an emergency.

Getting to his feet, he set the pack comfortably and started at a fast walk. He had to get to the gorge at the plateau, he had made a promise, he had a date.

65

Running through the night, Layla and Rumi were in the woods. The smooth path they were on cut through woodland at the tip of a narrow lake that hugged the mountain, caught between her giant wrinkles. The trees around them and canopy overhead kept them hidden, but also made it dark. Layla was trusting Rumi, who was towing Layla by the lead and being patient with the pace.

Once past the flat ground near the lake, the path through the trees began to climb. Legs stiff from the previous day, it wasn't long before the lactic acid was building up and Layla was breathing heavily as her body tried to repay the oxygen debt.

"Easy Rumi, let's walk for a bit... when we get to that big tree, we'll jog for a bit. We have to keep going."

Layla couldn't let them go down the mountain for two reasons. Firstly, because unbeknownst to them, Aaron was meeting them at the gorge that led to the plateau with the small blue lake. What she now knew and Aaron didn't, was that there would be hunters waiting there with a clear shot who would have him on file and consider him a target. If she could get to Aaron (without a lot of fuss) before they saw him, then they could go back to the others and make their way down.

The second reason was Hercules, Hawk said he was on the other side of the mountain, if they retreated, he would follow and be caught between hunters and a helicopter.

Chance could have told the others; come clean, faced the music and had the conversation but, hey *shoulda, woulda, coulda.* Layla like to take a chance on resolving a problem herself and ask for forgiveness later, rather than enter a drama or discussion. So with Rumi tugging the lead she kept trudging upwards. After some hours, the path gradually became rockier. Unleashing Rumi, who bounded up the relentless boulder staircase ahead, Layla followed. The high steps draining her legs as she clawed her way upwards, the path wound steeply up the side of the valley as it narrowed into a visible gorge leaving the trees below. Layla knew she couldn't go beyond that gorge.

***

Eventually one tired step after another, they made it to level ground, the entrance to the short narrow gorge ahead. Layla had seen a photo of Aaron and his dad there. If you stood in the right place you could photograph the mountain up through the gorge from one side, or the expansive trees, pastureland and valley vista below from the other. Layla assumed that a rifle shot could also be taken through that gorge. So they ventured no further forwards, instructing Rumi to stay and guard her bag, Layla headed off the path with her bow and arrows slung.

It was a reasonably easy scramble, steep, with loose shale under foot but various hand holds in the rocky face and roots of stubborn mountain shrubs gave purchase. Cutting below the gorge and the plateau out of sight. Layla reached a wide crevice, the ground ahead washed away in a natural landslide. With a view over to the other side of the mountain, this would suffice. Now all she had to do was wait.

The morning was warming up into a nice day, so for the first time in a while Layla was both resting and comfortable. Chance looked out over the mountain below waiting for signs of movement. In the moment of calm, her mind wandered to her Mother and the veil of lies, wondering what she would say to Hercules when she saw the lord of secrets next. It would almost certainly start with,

"*Hypocritical asshole...*"

66

Rory had relieved himself and was on his way back in to start waking the others when he sensed something wasn't right in the dark cave. Something was missing. There should be the sound of more breathing... he flicked his torch on - no Layla, no dog. The other trained men were awake in moments.

Bear was on his feet and had slid a small case from his bag. It had a hard shell and was the size of a narrow briefcase. In less than sixty-seconds, he had removed three components and using a neat wrench, assembled an impressive looking rifle.

"Remington CSR, classic."

Hawk was impressed, the Concealed Sniper Rifle was a deadly weapon in the right hands and was easy to transport, the special 16" barrel was the longest piece, an upgrade from the 14" for extra range. Not many people outside special ops got their hands on them. With a ten round magazine of .338 Lapau Magnum shells, it was a great all round rifle.

Bear feeling rested, took control. Rory was happy to go with it, this was clearly a man who was no stranger to high pressure situations. Rory, until a few days ago just had a small farm and had enjoyed a simple family life for sixteen years. He threw his pack on. I'll bring up the rear, don't wait, get to Layla I'll catch up."

With that, three highly-trained, heavily-armed professionals, set off into the night after a girl and her dog.

The girl and dog were both waiting patiently, one for a boy and one for her owner. Rumi had done a lot of running and was quite content sleeping in the sun next to the bag. Layla was getting impatient and had finished her water.

***

Aaron, was running through woodlands, he'd been taking the direct route after the climb, making his way up to the crescent lake and filling his water bottle from a fast running stream and dropping in two iodine tablets. It was the opposite end of the almost symmetrical sickle shaped lake Layla had passed, he was fed up with pine trees. The needle carpet compressing and sliding backwards, it was like walking in snow, but the gentle path up to the lake wasn't an option, not enough time. So he pushed on, using the sticky trunks to pull himself forward and keep moving upwards. Soon the crescent lake was below and the woods ended. Grass, sky and sun-warmed stone lay in front of him. No more pine needles. Above the grassy area was a short rocky climb to the open plateau and blue lake, then he would be done with ascent until the others arrived. If they had somehow passed, Layla would leave something at the gorge as a sign. If not he would wait there until noon, his legs were ready for rest.

It was still late morning when Aaron stepped out onto the grass in the sunshine thinking he was alone. Someone had seen him. Someone, had a shot lined up, from 110 yards - they took it.

Fortunately for Aaron the marksman was an excellent shot. The arrow scared the shit out of him as it whistled and then thudded into the ground ten yards in front of him. The fletched tail of the arrow pointed to his right - there she was, with her blonde hair and big smile, bow in hand. She looked like a Marvel character.

Layla was waving, *something was wrong, she was alone.* Aaron made his way over, through shrubs, a scramble up some rocks and across some shale. They were about five metres apart, a deep chasm between them. The soft sides of the cliff unsuitable for climbing around.

"What are you doing here? Where are the others?"

"I'm fine thanks, nice to see you too. You're late." Layla couldn't help a smile at his bewildered exhausted face.

"Sorry are you okay? I was worried I wouldn't catch you guys, I've only stopped for an hour."

"I was teasing handsome. I'm knackered, but we have bigger problems. There are hunters covering the plateau. That's why I'm here. The gorge is not a picnic option."

"I could go and see if I have a shot, if they're looking at the gorge..."

"No, I didn't just run up a mountain in the night to stop you getting shot, so you could go and get shot. If you want to show off take the jump and give me a kiss."

Aaron looked down into the rocky crevasse and then at Layla and the run-up and landing, it was very risky, but it was probably do-able.

"I was joking Aaron. There have been developments, the others are talking of going back down, apparently there's more hunters on the way. Dad's up the mountain somewhere. We need to regroup and figure out a plan fast."

"Okay, go back down, I'll meet you at the tip of the crescent lake on your side and we'll go back to the others. You got water?"

"No, I'm out."

"Throw me your bottle."

Layla threw the bottle across the space, Aaron caught it deftly and threw his across. Layla caught it in one hand, blew him a kiss and laughed as he blushed, then she was gone scrambling across a landslide and behind some rocks.

This girl was badass. Moments later Aaron was back in the trees, an arrow in his hand, running through pine needles again, at least it was nice to be going downhill.

***

Bear reached the gorge first and was worried to find the dog and pack but no Chance.

"Hello girl, where's Chancer?"

Rumi just nuzzled his hand and continued to look at the bushes. Hawk wasn't far behind and set up cover position on the ground, he couldn't quite see through from there but anyone who entered the passage from the other side would be a sitting duck.

Rumi heard her coming first and then Bear saw her as she scrambled round a rock face hanging onto an impossibly thin branch.

There wasn't a moment of anger, he just hugged her tight. Rory rounded the corner with a red face, looking like he might explode. Layla wasn't sure if it was the climb or emotion. Once he'd taken a moment to catch his breath he spoke.

"Don't do that to me girl, Jesus. I've had time to think on this morning yomp, trying to figure out what would send you on a fool's errand into the mountains like that. So, tell me Chance... where's my idiot son?"

Layla explained. Rory, girl and dog, headed down, while Hawk and Bear put a new plan into action.

67

Bear just about followed Layla's route to the crevasse, the soft ground and thin vegetation less inclined to hold his mass. He took his rifle off the pack and launched the bag as far as he could. It landed a few metres on the other side and rolled to a stop. Layla was right, about five metres. He checked the edge was solid for take-off, walked back to the edge of the flat grassy area and sprinted.

In an explosion of power, rifle in hand, he moved like a charging bull, sprung like a cat and landed on the other side comfortably. Leaving his pack at the edge of the woods, he made his way carefully to the top of the rocky crop to see if he could find the shot Aaron had sensibly walked away from. Finding some flat cover behind a rock and thorn bushes, he became another rock on the mountain and started hunting.

***

Just over a kilometre away as the crow, or more rapidly, bullet flies, Coyote was getting restless.

"If his tracker has moved to the gorge, where the fuck are they? They haven't come this way. I should move and get a visual on the other side of that ridge in case they've gone off-track to avoid being in the open."

Wolf paused. Something wasn't right, Hawk was clearly almost within scope sight. The targets had either got past him or got past them.

"Go, check it out, I'll get on the radio."

Coyote grabbed his gear and moved. It was what Bear had been waiting for, the movement was easy to see and he found his target, the man ran towards the path and the ridge ahead. Bear held his target, slowed his breathing, exhaled gently and squeezed. Coyote heard the shot taken from over a kilometre away.

Wolf didn't, he was dead before the sound could reach his ears, or ear as it was now with half his head missing.

Bear made the smart choice, removing the static sniper. Coyote on his feet continued his run as predicted, not what Wolf would have done from a shooting position had the roles been reversed. Bear switched targets, the Cowboy rounded a bend and was out of his sight, another shot rang out that signalled Hawk had taken position in the plateau. A minute later two pistol shots indicated the threat had retreated. Rory would have heard all four shots and known it was safe to head back up the mountain... again.

Hawk had heard Bear's shot and walked confidently through the passage at the signal. While he wasn't in threat of being shot as he was a friendly, he'd rather they didn't see him fighting for the other side. Up the mountain the Cowboy in the white hat ran, not fast enough, Hawk lined up the shot and aimed centre mass. Coyote was just entering a zag as the bullet flew, it missed centre mass but tore through the shoulder spraying blood. Coyote rounded a bend and disappeared, all that was left in sight was a slightly blood-spattered Stetson.

Bear collected his bag and made his way over the crest into the open plateau and up to the snipers nest. A quick check of the hunter's pockets presented cash and some car keys, he took both, along with a comprehensive looking medical kit from the dead mans pack. Bear humped his rucksack and rifle over to the track, set his scope on the mountain track above to where the Cowboy had retreated and waited for the others.

Throwing his smart device to one side, Hawk held his position at the gorge, he had a better range of the terrain and wanted to impress on the kids and Raptor that the danger wasn't over yet. The other teams and drones could be here any moment. In the past there had been worry that armed drones and operators would replace hunters, but drones could be hacked and were easily shot down when close enough to engage a target, some kill-ready and recon drones were still used by agents. Hawk preferred the anonymity of the lone, silent approach, until the shot they never hear coming. In his experience drones spooked people and made the chase more frantic and prey more unpredictable. At the same time, if they get hunters, a helicopter and a drone out here they would out manoeuvre them before they reached Andorra. Bear was a kilometre above him, from there the hike to the top was around four hours. These kids need to move.

***

Rory, Layla and Aaron, were moving fast considering the fatigue in their bodies, fear and adrenaline will do that, for a while. Rumi was the only one still having fun. Rory hadn't bothered with an argument at the lake, Aaron had arrived first, the steep downhill through the woods was fast as he almost skated over the needles; a narrow, flat path ran around the lake linking the path to the climbing area and the track the others were on. Rory had spotted him from a distance and whistled him up to join them, while he and Layla drank some water and caught their breath.

"Eurgh! This water is rank." Layla spat hers on the ground. Rory took a sip.

"Iodine, it's to purify natural water sources so you don't get sick. Could be a dead sheep up stream. Aaron?"

"Yes. I'm grateful I guess." Layla took a few more sips and shrugged, better than no water, but the lake below looked deliciously refreshing in the heat of the day.

***

Aaron arrived and handed Layla her arrow.

"I think you dropped this Maid Marian. Sorry, Dad, I can explain."

"I'm sure you think you can and later you'll have your chance. For now, let's move. The others have taken the plateau, but Hawk is convinced more are very close. We need to shift."

"Anybody remember what it was like going for a stroll?" Layla grimaced.

"Hopefully there will be time for walks in the park later, today we've got a mountain to climb."

"So we are going up. Okay. Who's Hawk?" Aaron was confused.

"I'll explain on the way let's move."

They set off, Layla had Rumi back on the lead giving her a little tow, it was just the assistance she needed to maintain the pace. The gentlemen behind thinking they would let Layla set the pace as the slowest member soon found themselves having to work very hard to keep up.

"You must have put in quite the effort to get up here son... were you worried about me?"

"Yes, I thought you might run out of jerky and start telling Chance your Dad jokes. Sorry, I lied."

"It's not me you need to worry about it's your mother on that one son, no doubt she's on her way to Andorra already with Hercules, Marcus and the horses. I was hoping you two were out of this mess. Still a few hours ago we were retreating, now we're less than five hours hike from Andorra."

Layla heard the five hours bit and wasn't sure whether to be gutted or grateful, so she just kept moving her legs and refusing to be beaten by this mountain, determined it would run out of metres before she ran out of steps. Knowing the path helped and the gorge seemed to come faster than earlier in the day.

***

Hawk was stretched out on the ground, focused on the path ahead, still no movement. Their footsteps and heavy breathing were easy to hear as they approached and with a final sweep, he was on his feet, pack and rifle on his back.

Layla drank more iodine water and Aaron laughed at her wrinkled face, squished with distaste. He had been drinking it for years, as a boy he'd ignored his father and filled up with the sweet fresh water of a fast stream and not added the metallic tasting tablets. What happened later needs no further expansion or illustration than the fact he had always used and carried iodine since, as well as a spare pair of pants. He passed round some jerky to help with the taste of the water.

Hawk wasn't letting them rest though.

"Let's move, Bear is up ahead. We need to get out of the plateau before more hunters arrive. Bear took one out and there's one injured retreating up the mountain. Our immediate problem is there's a helo inbound and if we're caught in the open we're dead. Double-time to Bear then up the track to the tree cover."

Layla looked across the plateau, past the brilliant azure lake, to where the path then got steep and zig-zagged through a barren rocky section, before reaching pine and spruce above. To Layla, it seemed a very long way, it looked like something a hobbit might look at and think - *Well, that's far enough, it's a good enough view from here.*

Beyond the woods, Aaron had promised her the path became less steep and smoother, before reaching more towering peaks, delightful. Layla un-clipped Rumi's lead and gave her ears a stroke.

"How you doing super-dog, even you must be getting tired now."

68

Driving up the Andorra mountain road with the two horses, Alex tried to formulate a plan. It would have been easier for them all to have stolen Sally's horsebox and driven to Andorra, but that had never crossed her mind until Aaron had run off.

It had taken her less than four hours to get into Andorra even with the loaded van. Within another hour she was parked up with a few other vans and campers at the top car park, from here they'd previously walked down to those lovely lakes and horrible Tower climb. The walk back was pretty gruelling too as she remembered. She wasn't about to go running off in the middle of the night, *if you're not part of the solution, then you're part of the problem.* Alex lay down on the bed and tried to sleep, disturbed by intrusive thoughts and the arrival of other vehicles through the night.

At the first sign of dawn Alex, abandoned her restless pursuit and made a cup of tea from Sally's stash of Earl Grey. She drank it in the cool morning light at the back of the van, while talking to the horses. Royal nuzzled her shoulder, his long neck and head stretching over the back doors, stamping his feet in a suggestion of freedom from this box.

They could wait here, this was where they were meeting, plans had changed but this was the spot. It was very unlikely they had made it here on foot before her. Hercules could be on his way, already scouring the mountain for Layla, or waiting with a rifle somewhere nearby. Or... Alex pushed that thought away.

She couldn't just sit here; she knew which path to take. Finishing her tea, she got on her boots, helmet and jacket and brought out the horses. Their bridles were on, so it was just a case of throwing the saddles on, doing up the girth and tying a lead rope from Royal to Coco. While the latter was the bigger horse, faster in the gallop, higher in the jump and all-round decent competition horse, she was a little highly strung too. The former had experience and a calmness that came with age, Royal was the better lead horse. Alex undid their head collars, managed to get her foot up into Royal's high stirrup and mounted.

***

Hercules was coming back around from a long sleep, helped by some Valium Mary had put in his water. It was the first time she'd spiked anyone - she'd done worse. It was for his own good, he needed to rest not charge into the night three pints' low on blood. If he got caught he could lead them back to them... if Bolt didn't drive off as soon as he turned the first bend in the path.

In the drivers seat, Martin was still sleeping, tired from all the driving and chaos. Mary was awake early, making herself a cup of mint tea about to open a book when the lady rode past on a horse.

"Oh horses." It was softly and only to herself, but Hercules heard from his waking sleep.

"Horses. Layla. I need..."

"To find Layla. It's okay Hercules. Don't worry, you are in Andorra, in the car-park where you are meeting them. Are you feeling any better?"

Hercules had to admit he was, he felt slightly groggy and hungover, but well rested and certainly better than he last remembered. He sat up slowly, restraints removed and checked his shoulder; it was neatly bandaged and mainly white, it didn't look like it had bled for some time, the stitches must be good. It ached and he felt rough, but he was certainly now fit enough to get out there and find his daughter.

On his feet, in a clean white shirt from Martin, drinking tea and eating some toast forced upon him, Hercules gathered his gear. Bolt had thoughtfully transferred it from the Land Rover after they moved Hercules.

"There's a sandwich in your backpack in case you get hungry, nothing fancy, just cheese and ham." He gave Mary a big hug.

"Thank you Mary, for everything; I won't wake him, but thank Bolt too, I don't know what I'd have done without you two."

"Thank him yourself when you get back with Layla, we'll be here until the clock runs down, we've got seven hours."

"Mary. If it looks dangerous, you run." Mary nodded an affirmation.

69

Apart from a white horsebox, there were just a few four-wheel drive cars and camper vans up there. One truck did stand out - a mean looking 4x4 van, high top, black with tints. It had purpose and it wasn't vacation. The hunters were here already. Hercules jogged to the end of the car-park where he could see a large wooden trail map, glancing at his route, he then stashed his rifle and pack. Secreted under a lightweight jacket were his side-arms, holstered at the hips. With his injured shoulder, the rifle was useless, he had one working hand and it was his left, not his dominant hand. He wasn't here to bring the fight, he was here to find Layla and run, he hoped to pass for just another hiker.

As he made his way down the path at a fast jog, Hercules was on high alert. It was gravel and stones, steep, with sharp hairpin turns, that seemed to be infinite. Eventually he rounded a corner and looked down the ridge, still a long way below he could see it flatten out into a gentler gradient, with open grassland spreading to the forest of pine and spruce beyond. Hercules kept moving, not seeing any sign of human life ahead until he was almost halfway down the hairpins. In the distance a pair of horses with a single rider, traversed the last hairpin and galloped across the grassy pasture beyond and covering the distance in no time. The horses in full graceful flow and slim rider with blonde hair streaming behind, seemed somehow familiar and reminded him of Layla, on her horses galloping across fields and soaring over jumps, back when life was more simple. Hercules rode too and enjoyed it, but they were Layla's horses.

***

The horses were enjoying being out of the box and in the mountain air. Alex had taken it slow on the steeper downhill, horses don't go well on the descent, but they had a blast across some open flatland. As the wind blew though her hair and the animal underneath her opened up into full flow she almost forgot her worries. It wasn't until she got nearer the woods and was pulling up she noticed the man emerging from the trees onto the path ahead.

"Howdy ma'am, beautiful day for a ride." The cowboy smiled.

Coyote had seen her across the plain after she emerged from the cover of the mountain path, nothing sexier than a pretty lady on a horse. Reining in after the gallop, she was even more beautiful than his imagination had created. He had for a moment considered stealing a horse, *they used to hang a man for stealing a horse.* Robbing a lady wasn't in this cowboy's nature, he considered himself a gentleman.

It wasn't until he got closer Alex noticed the rifle, kit bag and bloody stain showing through the jacket on his right shoulder. She smiled down at the cowboy as she passed.

"Hola caballero, un dia bonito."

Coyote grinned, the pretty lady knew a caballero when she saw one. He continued on past the lady and her mounts, preferring to make it higher ground under his own steam. He wasn't sure if he could shoot the rifle accurately from a great distance, but he'd taken a morphine ampule and an adrenaline shot, so if he could find the right cover in the higher ground ahead, from there he could pick off any tails while they were crossing the open grass with relative ease - if not without pain. If anyone got close he had his six-shooters at his hips, the left hand would suffice.

It would be nice to take some kill bonus money back for the mattress on top of the agreed basic. The hunters closing in would mop it up, but he didn't want them to take all the spoils. Later he would get up to the van and then to a medic and back to his office in America. Fuck this young man's game. The last thing Wolf had been talking about was getting a dog for his retirement, now the mean old bastard was gone. Coyote was going back to his desk, in a few years he'd be able to retire and buy his ranch, get a dog and horses and enjoy the peaceful life. These Europeans were crazy, too many old grudges, men in dark suits and hidden agendas. Actually, that all sounded pretty familiar, but home was home. *Fuck dying in France.*

70

It was early evening when Kiri bumped along the track into the Jungle refugee camp in Calais. Rosie had slept for hours and woke with a nudge.

"We're back Rose."

They passed the Afghan Flag, no evidence of the event that had occurred there just thirty hours previously. The tickets for the ferry crossing home to Mo were booked, but they had agreed they had a job to do first.

Parking the van in the Kurdish meeting tent again, they knocked on Raf's tent and the Kurdish leader emerged with a smile.

"Rosie, Kiri, I am very sorry about Kind. A very bad thing - I make tea..."

The English reputation for tea being the solution to all problems was well known here. On this rare occasion the ladies had to refuse.

"Thank you Raf, but we don't have time today. I have something for you. Tom would want your community to have this."

Rosie handed Raf a wad of cash, it was ten thousand euros. In various pockets, Kiri and Rosie had more wads of notes secreted, Kind's getaway fund.

Raf was amazed and thanked them repeatedly for the gift to his community, he promised to help many Kurdish families with the kind gift.

"Kind would want you to have it, he trusted you Raf, he believed you were a good man, we do too."

Rosie and Kiri split up, they had a lot of people to see. Amir in the showers received a gift and Rosie received a huge bear hug in return, as they both shed tears for their lost friend.

Kiri found Naseer and his group at their shelters, the kitchen now finished. Naseer ran and hugged Kiri, he had clearly been crying. News travelled fast in the Jungle and by now everyone in the camp had heard that Kind had been executed for smuggling a young boy to the UK.

"Kiri. I don't want to believe truth, I am so sad Kind has gone... you want coffee?"

Kiri gave Nass a big squeeze.

"No coffee today thanks Nass. I can't believe he's really gone. I have a gift for the group from Kind."

Kiri pressed the notes into Naseer's hand, his eyes widening. There was enough money there to pay smugglers for three people crossing to the UK. Or to feed dozens of his brothers and sisters here for months.

"What I do with it?"

"It's a gift, you were a good friend to Kind, you knew him well. Do whatever you think Kind would have wanted."

"I will help many people in the Jungle, like Kind did."

"He'd like that, I have to go now, more people to see."

Navigating the Jungle maze, Rosie gave gifts to the ladies at the women's and children's centre, saw Manny in the Sudanese area; the two Mohamed's, one a community leader for the Iranians, the other Iraqi.

Kiri went to the Afghan zone, Eritrean area and then little Syria. Waiting for Rosie at the van, she smoked a spliff and tried to process the last days events.

"Let me help you with that. " Rosie took a long drag.

"Deliveries made Santa?"

"All done Rose, let's go home."

"Hell yes."

They finished the joint in silence, then left the Jungle. A last stop at the warehouse, another package entrusted to Leon to fund the kitchen and wood-yard. Winter was coming.

In the setting September sun, Rosie, Kiri and Cherry traversed Calais, drove through the docks and onto the ferry, easy when you have the right papers.

Standing at the rail, smoking a roll-up and looking out at the dark English Channel, Rosie thought about Mo's future. The fallout from his illegal passage and the potential chaos that seemed to follow him everywhere. *He better be a good boy.*

Along with her British passport, Rosie had some more papers hidden in her jacket. One last package, for Mo. He had a new life to start and Kind would have been more than happy to help him start it.

71

It was getting dark when Gorilla turned his truck into the underground garage and flashed his pass at the machine and parked.

It may have looked like an office from the outside. Inside, in addition to a floor of offices, desks and a basic kitchen, there were two other floors. One with a high-tech communications and tracking centre with various glass war-rooms surrounding the main pit. On the other floor was an armoury and bunk-room with showers and medical unit. The access from the elevator connecting only their floors and the secure car-park in the basement. Agents of Solution sixty-five could use their out-post for secure communications, equipment, transport, rest or whatever else was required by the company. They may be in Europe, but it was still British run and everything was for the good of the company. Everyone answered to London.

Gorilla sat at a computer terminal with a coffee from the canteen and made his report from the comfort of an ergonomic chair in air-conditioned office. His ears were still ringing from the explosion. Control instructed him (as was protocol) to get checked out by medical while waiting for the Fox team to arrive.

The Doctor while beautiful, was also stern despite her sexy accent.

"We 'ave wules for a weason monsieur Gorille. You 'ave 'ad a sewious concussion. You 'ave to west for some hours before wesuming active duty. Wait for ze helicopter, sleep."

"I miss the good old days, when they'd stick a needle in you and have you on your way." Gorilla winked.

"C'est la vie." The Doctor shrugged and indicated he should roll over and drop his pants, before giving him a shot with a cocktail of vitamins and other drugs, known only among hunters as the "Deadpool" shot due to its regenerative powers.

The Doctor then cleaned up a few superficial cuts sustained from flying debris. Apart from his head, Gorilla was good to go - his company enforced therapist would suggest that was nothing new. The Doctor handed him a clipboard and pen.

"Sign here. A little west and you are weady. Bon chance."

***

Killing some time, Gorilla reviewed files. He knew the information on Cobra and Raptor, the Ghost's file was barren, an exemplary early Military service, followed by redacted files that were more black blocks than text. *Useless*.

The updated report had little new information on Vipers demise. Clean shot from an easy distance. The shooter was likely the ex-Olympic medal winner, Mary Bolt. Biathlon. Partner, Martin Bolt also an ex-Olympic skier, less success, but still an exceptional athlete and an educated man. All indicators showed they were headed out of France, to Spain or Andorra. They fully expected the later, partly because behaviour patterns clearly predicted the couple would return to their environment of expertise in the mountains and because of Andorra's stoic refusal to be forced into Solution sixty-five. Partly due to their financial independence, secured by questionable banking practices as a tax haven.

The Bell's would be located, monitored during their cooling off period and then engaged when the legalities were sorted or they left Andorra. Gorilla would be flown in by helicopter to engage Raptors group on foot. They were waiting on the arrival of the Fox team from their base; three ladies he knew only by fierce reputation.

Gorilla did a kit check in the armoury and headed to the bunk-room for some sleep. After his "Deadpool" shot he'd feel a million dollars by take-off. These boosters weren't great for you over time, but on occasion you've got to do what the job requires. Gorilla closed his eyes and dreamed of nothing.

***

Gorilla was on the bird, enjoying the blue sky morning and feeling good when they cat-walked the helipad towards him.

They were about as terrifying as three women could be. Unapproachable, beautiful beyond description and tooled-up to the hilt. As they strode from the elevator to the helicopter draped in weapons, there was no need for an anthem. They created their own atmosphere.

Not one of them ducked as they strode under the whirring helicopter blades. Arctic Fox led, dressed in white with long blonde hair, she was everything you'd expect an ex-Finnish special-forces, silver-medal Olympic cross-country skier to be. Tall, slim, athletic and beautiful. Icy blue eyes and porcelain skin, if looks could kill that face would be a weapon in itself.

To her left a red-haired women followed, medium height and more muscular. Red Fox had a very different back ground. An Irish revolutionary in the quashed New Troubles, Red was a sniper, expert in explosives, hand to hand combat, counter-intelligence and technology. Fierce green eyes danced in a pale, freckled face that had broken a hundred Irish hearts.

On the right of the trio, was Bengal Fox. Equally attractive, shorter and built more like a ballet dancer than a fighter, she was the deadliest of them all. Gorilla noticed the handles of two samurai swords on her back, he had only heard rumours, it seemed they were all true. It was going to be a good day; he could feel it.

"Morning ladies, looks like you've got all the gear. Gorilla, nice of you to join me... I've never been part of a foursome, must be my lucky day."

Arctic fox looked Gorilla up and down as she strapped herself in.

"I doubt if you know how to please one woman. Be silent, we've had one long flight today already." The Fin's words cut him down.

"You are joining us, preferably quietly." Bengal foxes blade was at his neck before he had even seen her hand move.

"Sure thing ladies, just here for the ride." The blade was sheathed and she sat.

"Honestly, I like strong women."

"No, you don't. But, we'll tell you the plan and you'll do as you're told." The red-head sat down and strapped herself in as they took off. "So, Gorilla, are you going to be any use or are you as stupid as you look?"

Despite the late morning sun, Gorilla's morning was turning cloudy.

72

After another fast ascent, Layla's group had reached Bear. They took on water and kept moving upwards, keen to reach the cover of the woods ahead.

Rory resumed the lead, Layla, Rumi and Aaron close. The two professionals followed, regularly scanning ahead with scope or field-glasses. Waiting to hear the sound of a chopper.

"So, Hawk. Who we up against here?" Bear asked marching on as if he'd only just set off, the sweat soaked shirt and glistening brow the only betrayal of effort.

"You took out Wolf, he was an old pro, excellent tracker, great with a rifle, if he'd got anyone in his sights he wouldn't have missed."

"I remember Wolf, didn't know him well, but he wasn't our biggest advocate. Ruthless. What about the one you missed?" Rory winked. They had passed the bloodied hat already.

"I *hit* Coyote; the American. I don't know much, been state-side for a long time. Dresses like a cowboy. Legend has it he's insanely fast with a pistol."

"Okay, who else might be on their way?"

"That's the bad news. Gorilla is en route, he's dangerous and they've called in Fox Team. Three very nasty ladies. Never been in the field with them, but they are summoned to wipe the board.

Relentless and ruthless. They don't fail. To get to you they will neutralise anyone whose hand you've ever shaken, any baby you ever kissed and they'll smile while doing it. They rarely work in Europe, mainly high-level jobs in the East. They have deadly hand to hand skills and weapons training in everything that can kill and the funds and access to technology and transport local hunters don't have. Basically, if they get here before we reach safety, we're done."

"What if we did take them out?" Bear pressed.

Until today, he hadn't killed for years, but, it was done now and he had people he cared about to protect. Promises he'd made and people who were trying to kill him. It was time to fight again.

"They won't quit unless you get to Africa or out to international waters. Even if you killed enough hunters to stop them sending more. They would open a private bounty on your heads and then you have to deal with every amateur on the database doing their work for them. The company like to deal with things in house, quietly and efficiently, but, they don't mind getting their hands dirty if necessary as we know.

I called in my last position as the gorge at the blue lake, told them I was pinned there and you were at Wolf's last known location, I left my tracker for them to follow. From now on the other hunters can't track me, but we're blind too. Soon they will know Wolf has been terminated and figure out I'm not down there."

They had made it to the canopy cover of the trees finally and stopped to rest for a moment.

"Good to have you with us Hawk. I guess people can change." Chance said sharing some jerky.

The respite didn't last long though as a few minutes they heard the sound of a helicopter in the distance and pressed further into the woods.

They saw three Parachutes, the Foxes they guessed dropping close together down somewhere near the blue lake. The helicopters machine-gun manned by Gorilla, covering their descent before wheeling away out of sight.

"They went for the bait; but we will have to move fast to get across the grasslands on the other side of this woodland. There's cover on the hairpin track to the top, but we need to make it before this hunter reaches the edge of the trees and can get a clear shot at us as we cross the open plain." Rory swept his hands up. "Come on, last stretch, let's go people."

As they somehow got to their feet and kept moving, they heard the helicopter again, a parachute floated down and they caught a glimpse of its owner landing lightly on the edge of the woods not far behind them. This was a problem, once it was reported they weren't below at the lake, he would assume they were ahead and this hunter would pursue them. It would be easy make the shot from the cover of the trees as they were exposed on the open field ahead, desperately close to the safety of the mountain path.

"You guys keep going. I'll deal with this guy quietly; we don't want to give away our position." Hawk shook Rory's hand.

"I can help with that if you want." Bear offered.

"No, go with the kids, get them to Andorra. Get Layla back to her father. I'll hold them off as long as I can... and catch up. They won't expect a rear-guard."

Layla, Aaron and Rumi were already moving forward through the woodland. Rory and Bear hesitated, Rory nodded and left. Bear looked him in the eyes while shaking Hawk's hand.

"Thank you Andy, find peace."

"And vengeance." Hawk replied.

Hawk took off his heavy pack, lay down his rifle and drew his Bowie knife before quietly heading back down the path towards the edge of the woods. Holster unclipped, side-arm loaded, safety off.

***

Gorilla was kneeling at the edge of the woodlands, rifle resting on a rock, attention on the track below to where his quarry would be flushed by Fox Team. He was pissed off, dumped up the hill away from the action. Those bitches would clean up below and take the bonuses. Gorilla knew he was out ranked by reputation alone, so he waited.

***

Knife in his right hand, Hawk was only a metre behind when Gorilla sensed something and spun round. Though silent, Hawk was ready for this, a killer's senses are keen. As his opponent turned and defended himself instinctively, Hawk also went into autopilot.

The butt of Gorilla's rifle came at his face as he moved in for the kill, Hawk bobbed left and threw a jab into Gorilla's nose, who staggered backwards...

Hawk waited for an opening. He almost ducked under the second brutal swing of rifle as he bobbed low and right; the momentum of the rifle leaving the soft underbelly vulnerable, Hawk threw an uppercut into Gorilla's solar plexus. This time the blow wasn't a fist, but his knife. It moved efficiently through the soft tissue, as Hawk plunged the blade of the knife up behind the rib cage and through the left lung, the tip just missing the heart but catching the Vena Cava - the main artery leaving the heart.

As his chest cavity and lung began to fill with blood, Gorilla knew he was dead.

The rifle had glanced off Hawk's temple, it was a decent blow, but he knew Gorilla was done. Slightly stunned, blood running down his face, he staggered against the rocks, staying on his feet he tried to regain his composure.

Gorilla had been stabbed before, several times in fact. But he knew this was different. Alongside the heat and searing pain deep inside and the sticky, warm flow from his torso, he could feel life draining out of him and he was rapidly drowning in his own blood. In a last act of defiance, in fury at having being cheated out of life by a rat; he tore the knife from his body and falling to his knees, plunged the knife deep into Hawks thigh.

Eyes stinging with blood and vision blurry, Hawk saw the movement and drew his side arm, but his dizzy reactions were too slow. Before his finger pulled the trigger he felt his own knife pierce into his muscle - roaring in pain, teeth gritted and eyes wide open; he looked down at the pain and anger filled eyes that met his own world of fury, then he pulled the trigger.

That gunshot did a few things. The most immediate effect was that Gorilla's brains were obviously blown out the back of his head brightly decorating the rocks and forest floor. His eyes closed and his pain and anger stopped, forever.

The next consequence, was that the slightly bewildered Fox Team (having found a smart device at the gorge and located the agent 'Wolf' but found no sign of the targets or 'Hawk') now realised the fight was at higher ground and made a rapid ascent. No response from the chimp up the mountain, they assumed he was compromised and sent out a drone, controlled from a screen on Red's wrist.

***

Up ahead the shot echoed through the wood. Bear and Rory knew that a silent execution had not been possible. They were running out of time, hunters were closing in and Hawk was likely not joining them.

***

Alex almost fell off Royal as he fully reared and whinnied at the loud crack, spinning instinctively and looking for danger as Coco was swung along behind. Tied together they didn't know which way to go, Alex reined Royal in and led them in a tight circle until, seeing and hearing no further danger they listened to Alex's calming voice and grew still.

***

Layla heard the gun-shot and the horse, it sounded a bit like Royal, but horses are horses, right. It couldn't be. *Unless it was Dad.* Could he be meeting them with the horses, she would be as relieved to see him as the ponies.

Rumi pulled harder, leaving Aaron in their wake. They almost skidded round a corner when Layla saw the horses and female rider in the distance ahead. It wasn't Dad, her heart sank.

Rumi sped up. As they got closer and the light through the trees gave the silhouettes colour and definition, she was sure. *They were her ponies*. It was Alex. Layla dropped the lead, Rumi ran and greeted the horses and then returned to Layla. She had collapsed to the floor, leaning against a tree in relief at seeing familiar faces and no longer having to walk.

Alex trotted over, Layla heaved herself to her feet and hugged her horses.

"Coco, Royal, I thought I might never see you again. I've got so much to tell you." Layla buried her face in Coco's neck and held back tears of exhaustion and fear, before taking a deep breath and asking the question. "Alex...where's Dad?"

"Layla, why are you alone? Where's Rory? Aaron ran after you..." At that moment Aaron skidded round the corner, ran towards them and stopped.

"Oh shit..."

"Oh shit indeed, you hormone-filled clown, we'll be having words."

"The others are coming but we have to move, we're in danger. Alex, where's my Dad?"

"I heard the gun-shot. Sorry love, after Aaron left, I had to go. Don't worry, your Dad will get to the meet, he will get back to you."

Alex dismounted and hugged the two teenagers tightly.

Bear followed by a weary Rory rounded the corner. Rory overtook Bear as he ran to his wife, held and kissed her and embraced his family again. Bear gave Layla a hug, she looked at him and the horses and for the first time in a while, a glimmer of hope sparked a new energy.

"Did you see anyone on your way down love?"

"Yes, a cowboy. He pretended not to be injured and I pretended not to notice."

"How bad was the injury and where was he?"

"Shoulder, definitely not fatal, he was moving well and seemed okay, so probably just a flesh wound. We passed just before I came into the woods."

"Shit, he'll be able to hold-out, set up at higher ground on the hairpins and pick us off when we leave the cover of the woods. There's cover, to the right behind the boulders at the bottom of the track, but we'd never make it. We can't go back as there's three uninjured, terrifying women behind us. We have to push on to the edge of the woods. I have a plan but nobody will like it." They pushed on as Rory explained what he saw as their only option.

***

Up the mountain, upon hearing the gun-shot below, Coyote had done exactly as Rory predicted and was settled behind some rocks rifle aimed at the treeline below. It wasn't a tough shot with a good shoulder, picking off people walking or even running in the open would normally be child's play. The drugs helped and he was surprisingly content waiting completely motionless, almost invisible on the sun-warmed mountain.

***

Alex was not happy.

“You can’t ask her to do that Rory.”

“It’s okay Alex, he’s right. I’m the lightest, the best rider, she’s my horse, I’m our best chance.”

“Wait, so you’re going to ride out into the open alone and hope that me, Bear or Dad can spot some movement and take the shot before a trained killer shoots you. Mum’s right, I don’t like it, either.”

“Well, to be honest I’m relying more on them than you, but I trust you guys, the guy is hurt and Coco is really fast. You’ll have to hold Royal, he won’t like being left behind.”

“He won’t be, I’m coming with you. I’m not much heavier, I’m a better rider and Royal is plenty fast enough too. Besides two moving targets are harder than one.” Aaron had decided. His parents nearly protested, but knew their days of telling him what to do were at an end. He was his own man.

“I don’t know about better rider, but you can try and keep up.”

Rory and Bear set up near the edge of the woodland with their rifles. The kids mounted light, leaving all their kit including saddles, only her bow and quiver of arrows slung on her back, speed was essential. They headed back along the path for a run up.

“Okay stud, let’s see who the better rider is.”

Layla grinned to lighten the mood. Aaron smiled back at her. With long, blonde hair and elfin face, bow and arrows slung across her back, she looked like a classic heroine protagonist, ready to ride into battle; she was awesome and he would follow her anywhere.

Alex gave a wave and Aaron gave Royal a kick, the older horse launched forward. Coco followed. Faster and lighter and thinking there was a race on, she quickly passed Royal and hit full gallop, Layla and the horse moving as one. Royal and Aaron gave chase and the four runners burst out the woods.

73

High above them hidden in the mountain, Coyote saw the horses and followed their movement. Same horses, different riders. It was the young female target, with the young male target. Then it clicked, the hot-mum from the file - she was the rider that morning, he'd been distracted by a pretty face... and a bullet hole in his shoulder.

The girl was faster, she wasn't just on a faster horse, she was the better rider, smoothly switching left and right as they zagged across the open plain at full gallop. Off the path, the lead horse leaped a patch of boulders and a fallen tree trunk. The second horse and rider following close behind.

Coyote lined up his shot, preparing to take out the slower target first, then the girl at a closer range. The cowboy imagined himself on a quiet open-range, he pulled the rifle tight into his shoulder ignoring its complaint, zeroed in on the boy's chest and exhaled.

***

Layla was flying, she had never gone so fast, weaving forward, trying to avoid obstacles and jumping the unavoidable, she prayed there were no rabbit holes and urged Coco on, waiting for a shot to ring out, terrified at any moment it would all be over. The horse felt the electrifying fear and grew wings.

Royal and Aaron kept up for a bit, clearing the fallen tree less ably than Coco, after a few hundred metres they were left chasing behind. Older horse, heavier rider and not as in tune with each other, Aaron felt the target on his chest grow as he wondered what the hell he was doing. Galloping towards a mountain like the charge of the light brigade, forward to an almost certain death. Not for war, glory or orders. This was for the survival of those he loved. It had to bc, he was out here because he loved his parents and... he loved her. Aaron gave Royal another kick and a sharp swerve or two, ready to die for love.

***

Bear and Rory were still scouring the mountain searching in vain for movement or a barrel or scope flash in the sun. Alex was holding her breath and watching from behind a tree as the horse carrying her son got slower and slower.

***

From above it all, Hercules saw the riders burst from the trees into the open as he ran down the hairpins. Two riders this time and the girl on the fast one seemed familiar... that was his girl. That was Layla on Coco. Hercules sped up. Skidding around a corner, he saw the sniper ahead on the ground, lying behind some rocky cover off the path, horses and riders in range.

The gravel under his feet gave him away as he slid to a stop and instinctively drew his weapon with his right hand, pain shot through his arm as he lifted and aimed in what felt like agonisingly slow motion.

Coyote was about to squeeze the trigger when he heard the crunch of feet behind him. Abandoning the rifle, he rolled left over his good side and instinctively drew his pistol with his right hand, pain flooding through his shoulder.

They had each other dead to rights.

"Whoa there gladiator, nobody needs to die today... or at least not both of us."

"You were just about to shoot my daughter, I'm ready to die, but I'm listening."

"Old school. Fastest draw. We're both shot up, so we can use our lefts to make it fair and interesting."

Hercules liked this, he was almost as fast with his left as his right, more importantly, he'd never come across a faster draw than him, even with their dominant hand against his weaker one. This cowboy was going to lose and he would live and see his daughter.

"Deal cowboy, we'll go western, twelve paces backwards, draw and shoot."

Very slowly they lowered their weapons and then holstered them. Coyote stood and walked towards the man, standing face to face a few feet between them, they looked each other in the eye, Hercules nodded and they took a step backwards, eyes never moving.

Coyote couldn't believe his luck, a duel. This guy was determined and would take a bullet to protect his kid. Coyote wanted a kill shot to drop him before he could get a shot off. Right between the eyes.

74

Chance and Aaron made the cover of the boulders and were off the horses in a second, holding them close - all four breathing heavily. No shots had rung out, no bullets had whizzed past.

Rory and Bear had spotted movement above and could see the unmanned rifle pointing skywards, but had no visual of the shoot-out about to take place. Rory made the call.

"We've missed him. He would have had a clear shot, but didn't take it. He must have moved on the kids position, maybe he wants hostages... we need to move."

The two men charged across the open ground. Bear extending his lead sprinting towards Chance, despite the extra bag, his rifle and rucksack and Coco's saddle, somehow looking small slung over his left forearm. Out of his bag and in his right hand was a Glock 15 semi-automatic pistol.

Behind Bear, Rumi towed Alex, next to them Rory, laden with Aaron's kit and saddle ground out another burst of pure grit. All fitness and energy reserves had been used hours ago. It was all determination and instinct now.

***

Aaron was holding the horses when Layla told him to stay and started climbing the boulders. A little annoyed at the command which sounded a lot like when she spoke to Rumi, with love but an order. But, he was holding two horses and she was very pretty, so he did as he was told and watched as she ascended the rock-face easily.

***

Layla didn't know why she needed to climb, something told her to get to high ground. Maybe they were being flanked. Either way she trusted her instincts and after a short climb and further scramble over huge boulders, she reached the top of the largest of the giant marbles and took cover behind a small round rock seemingly balanced on top. There was movement near the path up to her left, beyond the pile of boulders, someone was talking.

75

Hercules and Coyote had taken ten steps backwards each, eyes still locked. Coyote was poised. They were taking their eleventh step when they both heard a quiet whistling sound.

Hercules recognised the sound, Coyote should have known it, to a real cowboy the sound of an arrow would be familiar.

Instead he was genuinely surprised as Layla's arrow hit him in the chest and pierced his heart killing him almost instantly. Coyote's lifeless body fell on its back, his mortally permanent look of surprise, only matched but that of Hercules, who turned to see his daughter standing atop a boulder, bow in hand, forty metres away.

"Hey Dad... bring my arrow."

Layla waved and disappeared behind the boulders leaving him wondering if it was a dream until he turned back to the cowboy on the ground. Hercules ran down the path so fast that he almost ran into Coco and Royal as he turned the last corner.

Rory was there, Alex and Rumi, Aaron and Bear...then she appeared from above. Lightly climbing down, before sitting and jumping off the last three metres into Aaron's outstretched arms. Aaron caught her, lowered Layla to the ground and kissed her.

Layla looked different; older, leaner and harder. Hercules had clearly missed something.

"I *stayed...*Where did you go?" Aaron asked.

"*Good boy*. I had to save my Dad." Layla laughed and ran to her father hugging him fiercely.

"Thank you my love, I don't know what to say..."

"I'm sure you had him Dad, but I wasn't taking the chance."

"We'll have to talk about this later, it's a big deal..." Hercules shed a tear as he handed her the arrow he'd retrieved and cleaned. Not from the pain in his shoulder, but from a mixture of pride, relief and sorrow.

"I know, but it was a considered and rational decision Dad, I'd do it again."

That's what scares me. Finally, he could keep her safe again, or maybe from the looks of it they would keep each other safe. Either way they were together.

Layla squeezed her Dad again, tighter than she had for years and only let go when she finally looked at his grimacing face.

"Have you been shot? I knew you'd get into trouble without me. Where's Marcus?"

"Marcus is with Doc getting a boat. Yes, I may have found myself some mischief. I'm okay, some new friends patched me up. It certainly hasn't been boring. You?"

"We've just been for a walk."

Everyone laughed and hugged for a brief moment, before Rory moved them on.

"We still have hunters on our tail and more ahead if we make it to Andorra, we need to move."

Behind Rory, Layla and Aaron exhausted, rode the horses. Alex had the freshest legs. Even Rumi had given up towing and was walking alongside her new friend following the ponies. After they had stayed in the woods, Layla had run away on the horse, Rumi wanted to follow but the lady had held her close and said soothing words. Now, Layla's big person was back and everyone was happy. So Rumi was happy, ignorantly, blissfully happy.

Hercules joined Bear at the rear. A handshake and nod enough for now to communicate Hercules gratitude at Bear's kept promise. Bear smiled and shrugged, they marched on, steep hairpin after hairpin, Bear giving a grateful Hercules a little assistance with a hand in the lower back, pushing him onwards. The day's exertion after losing so much blood was starting to take its toll and from the patch of scarlet on his shoulder he'd probably opened some stitches.

Rory was like a machine, pushing the pace, he knew how close they were to safety and how much faster their fresh-legged, highly-trained pursuers would be, it was crunch time.

76

As the rabbits ran for safety, the Foxes called in to control, the missing hunter Andrew "Hawk" Hawkins was now suspected dead, a hostage or possibly a threat. The misleading information following the death of his daughter had allowed the targets to escape and cost the Company more hunters.

Fox team were moving fast but with care; Red Fox, furious at the lack of professionalism in Europe, was taking measures to find intelligence and ensure they knew what was waiting up the mountain.

***

Hawk was waiting up the mountain, lying in the sun; he had made a tourniquet but was slowly bleeding out from the deep wound in his thigh. He didn't remove the blade, it was currently packing out the wound, instead pouring the fizzing white powder around the wound and screaming in pain. He forced himself to stay conscious.

There was no forward or back, this was the place. Despite being quite aware of this, he was at peace. Soon there would be no more hunting, killing or pain. Soon he would be with Sarah again. Hawk rolled onto his back and awkwardly extracted a mobile from his pocket, wiped the blood off the screen of the basic cell phone and called a number looking up at the bright blue sky.

"Andy, you okay, why you on my private number?"

"Hey Steve, I'm down. I'm not going to make it back this time. Did you hear any more about Sarah?"

"Sorry to hear that Andy, it's been a crazy ride man. Nothing concrete on Sarah, but I called the hospital again and asked to speak to nurse Anna. The young nurse on the phone, Gemma, said she'd left suddenly, promoted to run a ward in a hospital in Brighton."

"She'd been there longer than Sarah and was her prime-carer, that is strange."

"I did some digging through a personal friend in the Psychotherapy Department. There's definitely more than rumors that company operatives are being blackmailed or financially manipulated into service, talk of "no questions asked" black ops, secret experimental medical research and extreme tactics. It's like the bad old days, but on the quiet. There's evidence emerging from Registration Department of manipulation, illegal coercing of those in debt or legal trouble into signing up. The whole thing stinks, but the house is shaking. I'm sorry for how this has all ended Andy. I'm sorry about Sarah. I'm done here too. I'm out."

"Thanks Steve, confirms what I'm hearing this end. I'll be with Sarah soon. You stay safe, disappear. I've got to go now, think I'll have some company soon. Take care of yourself. Over and out."

Hawk lay on his side, uncomfortably at Gorillas rifle, trying not to move the knife still inefficiently plugging the hole in his leg.

***

Hawk already had company. He couldn't see or hear the drone high above, but it could see him, the heat signature camera would have spotted him in pitch black. The Fox team stopped behind a ridge, aware if they proceeded the sniper ahead would pick them off with ease.

"One body with decreasing temperature, could be that fool Gorilla. Threat with rifle covering the path. Six hundred yards, elevation sixteen degrees, edges of the woods, behind some rocks."

Bengal Fox called into control and they confirmed Gorilla's demise, his red light had officially been illuminated. Intelligence suggested agent Hawk had taken him out. Hawk's vitals were dropping and his location chip hadn't moved, but he should still be considered a threat.

Arctic Fox took a tangent route through trees, shrubs and boulders, five minutes later she crept to the edge of the ridge behind a spruce tree. Through the sight she could see the barrel aimed down the mountain, but not its owner. Arctic pressed her microphone.

"*Engage*."

Red let the drone drop fast, it headed straight for Hawk and then zipped away to his left, his attention following. Arctic saw the movement clearly in her scope, the rifle turned and the top of a head became visible, she exhaled and squeezed. The head snapped sideways with a spray of blood and the drone returned to confirm the lifeless body lay still on the ground.

"Target down, proceed."

They continued their chase, only stopping to photograph the two bodies and relay location to a clean-up team. Red sent the drone on ahead and they continued their run through the woods.

***

Hawk died instantly. Back at control, a red light came on and a long tone alerted a computer operative that another hunters heart had ceased to beat. The information was relayed upstairs. While the suits and others in the gossip pond were furious at his betrayal, Steve was sad. He and Hawk weren't close friends, they mainly communicated for work, but he was one of the good guys; the bosses were livid. They'd lost five agents now and still didn't have a confirmed location on the targets. Fox team needed to earn their exorbitant fee and clean up this mess.

A few hours later, it was the end of his shift. It was the end of more than that. Steve picked up some files and put them in addressed envelopes to various journalists, hopefully there was still at least one decent hack out there. Stuffing them inside his jacket he walked out the office into the warm afternoon. The sun on his face, he smiled, he wouldn't be back.

Dropping the letters in a post-box, he crossed the street and went into the cool Underground station, it was only four stops to his small apartment.

Steve didn't have a girlfriend, dog, cat or goldfish. There was no vinyl collection, the clothes in the wardrobe were few and inexpensive, there was kitchenware for one and not a single picture on the wall or photo in a frame. There was nothing to leave behind.

What Steve did have; was most of his savings in cash, a fake passport from a Belgium contact, a change of clothes, hair-dye and coloured contact lenses, all were ready in a black leather holdall. In a false bottom was a side-arm and ammunition. Taking the bag, he pulled a flat cap low over his eyes and left his apartment by the back window, shimmying down the drain pipe. Following a planned route though alleyways, a market and an underground car-park, he knew he'd lost any potential tail, human or technological. Keeping his head down he entered the crowded Underground again, making his way to Liverpool Street and then on to Cambridge.

***

Long before he hadn't turned up to work the following day, Steve had caught a ferry from Harwich and was on a lorry onwards out of Belgium with a friendly Icelandic driver called Eero. A soft red light painted the sky as he looked out the window, sun setting but still warm on on his face. He was a ghost, he could breathe. Glad to be off-grid, off the phones and away from the constant suffocating cloud of death that had now lifted, the unrealised burden jettisoned, the dark cloak cast away. 'Stefan' (as the new passport confirmed) had never visited Scandinavia, but it was somewhere he had always wanted to explore.

77

Rory and the rest of the group had somehow kept their exhausted bodies moving forwards, feet, backs and legs were screaming silently for rest. After what seemed like the longest day of her life, Layla could barely believe it was the top. The last hours had been a blur. The horses took the last rising hairpins and then the path flattened and they saw vehicles through the trees ahead.

Hercules collected his pack and rifle and made his way to the camper, while Alex and the youngsters loaded the horses. Relieved to see the Bell's van still there. Hercules grinned as Mary's worried face broke into a smile at the window following his knock.

"You look terrible Hercules, let me check you dressing. This must be Layla, come in everyone." Mary put on the kettle for fresh tea.

Before joining the others, Alex and Aaron watered and loaded the horses, hay nets gratefully received.

Hercules made the introductions as Bolt passed around some tea that was already in the pot and handed out sandwiches. They had been nervously busy while waiting for his return. As well as the food, Bolt had already been out and switched their number plates with another camper. Alex then borrowed a screwdriver and did the same with the horse box. Bear had no trouble finding the hunters blacked out van and opening it with the remote key, but apart from helping himself to their food rations, there was little else of use. He and Rory had decided the van and bikes would certainly be tracked and therefore no use. Rumi was already asleep on the passenger seat, Bolt facing backwards in the captain's chair stroking her ears.

"So what's the plan, we're safe in Andorra for an hour, but once they have our location it could be impossible to lose them. We need to get to Valencia to Doc, Marcus and the boat and get out into the Mediterranean." Rory was ready to move again.

"Aaron, Rory and I will take the horsebox." Alex wasn't asking. She was keeping her family close from now on.

"Layla and I will ride with the Bell's as long as you guys are in. I need to rest some more if that's okay."

"Of course. You should both rest. After everything your dad has told us, I'm looking forward to chatting with you Layla, but first you all need to recover."

"Bear can come with us too." Too tired to protest at her separation from Aaron, she at least wanted Bear with them.

"I've got another idea." Bear spoke up. "What if I take the van. I'll lead them away, then dump it, I can use one of the motorbikes in the back to catch you up. I'll be a lot faster than your vans so I could meet you at the docks in Valencia."

Layla wanted to complain, but was out of fight, her feet were throbbing, her legs were cramping and her back ached, so she ate her sandwich instead. Rory opened his mouth but closed it again. Hercules spoke.

"That's actually an excellent plan. They don't know we have transport. They'll assume we stole the hunter van. Risky though, they'll track the bike too, you'll need to dump the van fast and then make distance on the bike before they catch up to you. They'll catch up with tracking and drones, you will be a sitting duck."

"Not for the first time, it's a risk we'll have to take. I'll leave now on the road to Perpignan, I suggest you head for Valencia sharpish it will take you six hours, maybe more. Have you got any hot water bottles in here Mary?"

"Yes, always have a couple, gets chilly in the mountains."

"I'll need to borrow them, could you boil the kettle please, I'll need some cold water too."

"Only room temperature bottles sorry, but there are natural springs on the roadside down the mountain. Icy cold, I've got a big bottle you can fill."

Bolt located the large plastic bottle and Mary filled the hot water bottles.

Bear rearranged his pack a little and readied himself to leave.

"I'll see you there. Don't worry I have a plan." Bear ruffled Layla's already messy hair, she looked at him and forced an exhausted smile.

"You *better* be there... I trust you Bear, be safe." The harsh insincere adolescent instinct, softened into genuine sentiments. On this occasion the need to show she cared overpowering the need to protect herself from vulnerability.

Bear hoisted his pack, looked each of them in the eye and stepped out the door. They heard the van start and drive away.

"Right, let's move."

Rory and his family filed out the camper door giving weary hugs on the way. Minutes later the two vans left the car park. Within quarter of an hour everyone but the drivers were asleep as they wound down the mountain road under the cover of the tree canopy. Bolt in the lead, taking it easy as Alex followed with tired horses and her two snoring men.

***

In the car park far behind them, the whine of a drone could be heard as Fox Team searched in vain for their quarry, before calling into control for retrieval and relocation. Targets currently unknown.

They were quickly relieved to have some luck, informed that a company vehicle had been taken from the car park at the peak and was headed into France, the helicopter would be there within thirty-five minutes. They made it to the top car park in thirty and jumped onto their chopper as it kissed the ground minutes later and immediately took off, Fox team on board.

The sounds of helicopter blades faded quickly as it chased into the dusk after the tracked black van. Once again the mountain was silent.

78

Bear was driving again and he was enjoying it. In the past he had driven a lot of vehicles, he'd had training in defensive, evasive and aggressive driving methods. Bear could drive, anything, anywhere, but, it had been a while. Living a minimal, non-residential lifestyle. It had been some time since Bear had put the pedal to the metal. The first few miles were spent getting comfortable with the handling and weight of the vehicle and the braking efficiency. The height and load gave a slight over-steer and the mountain road wasn't easy.

As it got dark, Bear drove faster, taking the corners with a racing line. He would see any headlights of ascending vehicles coming up the mountain. The steep descent and sharp hairpin bends would also make his lights easy to spot by drone or helicopter and they could already be tracking him. He was concentrating on driving so hard that he passed the first pull-in spot, he glimpsed the trough with spring water flowing from a brass pipe too late and pushed on.

Further down the mountain, Bear was now in the zone - this wasn't his vehicle, he had zero interest in its longevity, just getting distance between the assassins and his friends on this suicide mission. Excuse given, he was absolutely ragging it.

The back tyres screeched as he slid around the hairpins, the front tyres screamed as he dropped gears for corner exits, inclines and short straights, he punched the gas, feathered the brakes, drifting round corners, rubber on the road tearing him forwards, motor roaring and brakes white hot. He hadn't seen a single other vehicle, it was his road.

Full of adrenaline, Bear hit the stereo and some country music came on, grinning but focused on the road, he was pushing the boundaries. The only way to know where the line is with a vehicle and truly know how far you can push it... is to cross that line.

As Bear came to a slight incline after a sharp bend he gave it a little too much, a rear wheel hit a small pot hole, the back of the heavy van lost traction and span towards the feeble barrier at the edge of the mountain road and a fatal drop below. Bear's reactions were instinctive, turning into the skid, he rectified it, accelerated, gave a little further steering correction... and came to a stop, facing back up the mountain.

Idiot. Stop fucking around - mission head. It had been a while since he'd been in the field. He left that life behind and some of the discipline that went with it.

It's okay Bear, you're human, it's been a while soldier. Time to focus. Time to get sharp again.

Taking a breath and turning off the stereo, he turned the van and drove on down the mountain. Still flying along at breakneck speed, but now fully focused. Spotting another water trough ahead he slowed and pulled in.

Submerging the bottle rather than waiting for the leisurely flow from the brass pipe. The bubbles escaped and the water replaced it, still painfully slowly. Bear looked up the mountain, no headlights were following; but beyond the engine of the van and the gurgling bottle relinquishing its air, he thought he heard the faint thunk of chopper blades. As the last bubble left, so did Bear, roaring down the mountain. He pressed on for another five minutes, upon seeing a forest access road, he swung off the tarmac and bumped along a track for a few hundred yards stopping among the pines on a dusty road.

Taking one of the bikes and giving the hydraulic brake line on the other a nick with his knife, he rode off on the forest track, came to a T junction and headed downwards. They'd be coming sooner or later but, he knew that. Bear just wanted to keep them distracted for as long as possible, he wasn't worried, alone in the mountains, this was his playground. They might think they were hunting, but Bear was of the same mind-set and he was deadly. These ladies may have killed a lot of aged civilians, maybe even been military elite in their countries during their careers... Bear was a ghost; sent to eliminate without trace, whether military elite kill teams, powerful politicians protected by the best of the best or billionaire businessmen kept safe by highly trained private security, Bear had never failed to have a clean and successful mission. He had been, the perfect soldier.

79

Fox team touched down lightly on the mountain road, from tracking they knew the van had stopped once, according to the map - possibly for water, which made sense, the group would need to re-hydrate after their long hike and collect water for future endeavours. There was an access road for fire-fighting and forest management, the mountains were webbed with them. The van was stationary further ahead and it appeared one company motorbike had been taken.

“Only one set of tracks, someone has decided to be the hare.” Arctic Fox read the ground like a book.

“We need to split up, I’ll take the drone and bike and find this cheeky wee fucker. You guys find out where the other targets have gone.” Red waited, Arctic gave the nod.

“Stay on comms.”

“Affirmative.”

Bengal and Arctic Fox returned to the chopper and reported, requesting further intelligence.

***

Red Fox rode into the night, tracking the stolen bike and keeping an eye on the screen indicating heat signatures beyond, high above, the drone tracked it’s operator. Red could ride, since a kid on her Uncle’s farm she’d ridden bikes and quads. She was gaining on her quarry as she flew down a long straight slope and the bike approached a sharp left turn. Changing down gears and using the back brake to kill the speed. The back brake did nothing.

"Shite... Feck!" Red overcooked the corner and shot off the track having to pick her way through the trees and sliding the bike to a stop in the undergrowth. Once back on the track she checked the lines and found a leak.

"Okay, playing dirty are we, you'll have to do better than that." Red gunned the bike and continued her pursuit, relying on her gears to control her speed.

***

After an hour of descent, Bear stopped the bike. The trees finished and ahead pastures led to farms and cottages. Hiding the bike in the woods, he took his gear and headed back up the mountain, this time a little way off the track. His legs complaining at being asked to do more ascent, but it was a familiar ache and his body automatically doing what was asked of it despite the challenge gave him hope, maybe he was still who he needed to be, who he used to be, a killer.

Bear found a small opening in the woods not far from the track surrounded by thick bushes, it was perfect, he took off his pack, removed the hot and cold water bottles and stripped off and lay naked on his clothes. The cool night breeze drifted down the mountains through the trees. Bear was a silent tree in the dark woods, there were no birds, just the whispering trees and creaking boughs, murmuring in his ear.

"*You've changed.*" They whispered to his conscience. Bear had changed, but he had friends to protect and whoever was

coming, was coming to kill him. He heard a new sound - a motorbike, it stopped. Bear poured the hot water over the clothes and disappeared into the bushes gun strapped to his leg, cold water and knife in his hand.
It was a few hundred metres from the location of the bike when the drone spotted a heat signature hiding not far off the track ahead. Red left the bike and sent the drone closer to have a look. Sure enough the clear outline of a human lay prone and warm on the forest floor near a clearing. Red brought the drone to a high altitude hover, took position approaching from the rear and started to close in on the target.

Bear knew they had the drone from what Hawk had told him. Lying under a broad fallen Oak in the silence of the forest, he listened to the insect-like whine of rotor blades, this was his green light, he moved fast. Bear poured the icy mountain water over himself and disappeared into the woods and began the stalk.

***

Red checked the drone once more, the yellow, orange and red shadow of arms, legs and body hadn't moved. She moved in for the kill, lowering her own infra-red glasses, silently closing, Red Fox stepped from behind a Beech tree and put two bullets in the ready-brek glow in front of her. Removing her glasses she was allowed the briefest moment of realisation, a rare final gift of knowing you've fucked up and it's game over.

Bear had moved like a wraith and was behind Red before she pulled the trigger. As she realised her mistake, a huge arm went round her throat and lifted her clear off the ground, the other wrapped both arms pinning them to her body, trapping Red in a cold, wet, suffocating embrace. Her chin raised, his forearm was crushing her larynx, exposing her throat as she struggled to breathe, legs kicking. With lack of oxygen to the brain, Reds vision was blurry, this was it, she knew she was dying. The legs stopped kicking, then the struggling stopped altogether, next one eye closed and the last thing Red saw was Bear's knife coming towards her throat, then Red went to black.

80

Bear was cold and wet; he collected his pack, quickly dried off with a micro-towel and dressed in fresh clothes. He ate a protein bar and an energy gel he'd found on the woman. Throwing her weapons and ammo into the woods, he headed back to the bike. Bear wasn't the most technical guy, computers weren't in his life, so he left the drone hovering above it's operator, like a buzzard eyeing carrion.

***

When the red light blinked and the call came in they couldn't believe it. Over a decade of Ops, with an almost perfect record - the Fox team while originally a quartet, had lost Cape Fox in their early days. The following period was hard for the team, emotional walls were built, professional lines drawn, but the future years and missions had brought them closer again.

When the company relayed the zero heart rate report on Red, it was both incomprehensible and almost impossible for Bengal and Arctic Fox to process. The idea their sister was dead was unthinkable. There had to be an error. Mistake or not, protocol was crystal clear. The priority was always the target. Satellites showed two vehicles leaving the car park shortly after the company van and heading to Spain, proactive tracking was underway. Fox team, or it's remnants returned to base to refuel and conclude a record loss for agents in a day for the company. The board would not be happy. This band of renegades were decimating company resources and threatening to expose their weaknesses. If the public heard that their agents and the Company were this vulnerable they would have a tidal wave of people removing their chips and making a run for it.

***

Jumping back on the motorbike, Bear kept running. He knew it was tracked, but if it kept them away from Layla and the others and they kept sending cannon fodder, then it seemed like a better plan than walking. He rode down through the country dirt tracks, woods turning to open pastures and scattered hillside farms until he crossed a tarmac road and gambled on a right turn towards a faint glow in the distance.

Mountains left behind, he found a self-service petrol station in a village and filled up, paying with some euros he had in his pack. Riding late into the night until he was nearly out of fuel, Bear abandoned the bike near a town called Marines outside Valencia. He walked into town, found a local park and got a few hours sleep on a bench. Finally feeling anonymous again.

81

It was cold and she was shivering when Red came to and realised she was still alive, Bear was long gone, she was both furious with herself and somewhat confused at why she she'd been spared - the guy was clearly a professional. Weaponless, Red returned to the bike and headed back up to the main road the drone following. It would be a while until she rendezvoused with the others, but the radio update and consequential berating from the Arctic queen could wait until she was on the road. She wouldn't have to wait long for contact.

***

Three long minutes after they had watched their friends heart rate stop, Bengal and Arctic Fox were informed to return to the control room. Red was alive. Five minutes after her heart restarted, she was moving. They would be rendezvousing asap. The board was relieved, but wanted results and fast.

***

Red pressed the intercom for the radio, listened and replied.

"Honestly, I'm fine. Confirm see you at RV in twenty minutes. I'll explain."

82

Many miles behind them all, a clean-up team had already landed on the mountains and collected the bodies of the fallen agents, Gorilla, Coyote, Wolf and Hawk. They were located easily with their chips, then moved and loaded into a helicopter by the lake. The crew exchanged looks but didn't voice their surprise aloud, they were used to collecting runners not agents, the job was the same.

Dave had worked alone in the fading light, collecting weapons, shells and any trace of their presence. In truth he would have rather been using his scuba skills on the coast than in the mountains, but at least he was left alone. He preferred it that way, he could ponder the complexities of life, the job and his place in the oncoming collapse of society.

Dave was a failed journalist; he liked his conspiracies a little too much and the industry and his editors didn't want to share uncomfortable truths and soon lost patience. He had applied for this job to find out more about The Company for a book he was supposed to be writing. With travel, health benefits and significantly better money than writing, he'd extended his research a few years and decided when he eventually published, it would be a trilogy.

***

Mountain clean, the chopper took off. Dave looked out the window and mulled over this unexpected plot twist.

Unknown to the deceased agents on board; in death the company would give them the same respect as all those they had tracked and killed in their long careers. Dave's quiet snooping had slowly gathered proof that the bodies they collected would be taken to the company morgue, after the standard coroner's report, their viable organs would be removed, cataloged and shipped on ice to the firm's cryogenics lab in Switzerland before being sold to the highest bidder, often via Turkey or China. In a time when science would soon be able to offer the wealthiest a life span of one hundred and fifty years, all that was needed was a good stock of parts. After sixty-five years the rate of cell deterioration rapidly increased and organs became less viable for transplant.

Dave knew, they couldn't have everyone living to one hundred and fifty years old, that was for the very few. With environmental complexities, food, water and fuel issues, the solution was fewer people. Aside from proving that the model of less elderly and sick worked for the economy, the pandemics had barely scratched the surface of the healthy population. A different approach was needed, an offer they can't refuse, the solution was money, the solution was: Solution Sixty-five.

Death was a business and the profits didn't end at the final heartbeat. The mean cost to society to support a non-working citizen aged from sixty-five to death was £67,358. The average value of the organs of a healthy sixty-five year old was on average well over £1 million (a younger heart was worth that alone) at sixty-five the heart was generally at the end of its best life, but could be reused as a budget option. The liver, kidneys, skin and eyes, if healthy were worth eight hundred thousand pounds. The company insisted on head shots for a reason, they'd ask for strangulation if the science allowed brain transplants.

For a £65,000 investment per unit, it was a good return and with the younger organs of criminals and political refugees who ran, they had a sufficient supply of livers for the excessive drinkers, enjoying the fruits of their investments, numbing their existence... or struggling with life. Dave had done the research, kidneys went to those sick with cancer from the increased electromagnetic waves surrounding them, the teeth; to the daughters of the wealthy, theirs destroyed by anorexia in a desperate attempt to achieve the unachievable perfect look as plastered on every screen brainwashing the youth. Skin at £10 per square centimetre, was increasing year on year with the increased UV light as the planet warmed. The company was stockpiling.

It was all in the small print, the very small print. But who reads the small print and the short passage could easily be missed:

*I agree to donate my organs to the Solution Saviours life-changer programme. Solution Saviours can use my eyes to allow another to see or my heart to allow another to love for longer.

Even if they had read it, while ending their lives early for the good of society and family, they would not question it. The company had the models, the influx in capital would lead to a financial boom and excess in consumerism, they had fingers in pies and if their friends got rich that was always good business. The model predicted as the years passed; a lack of older role models in society would take effect. The "Grandparent generation" a period in life when people can finally release themselves from the child-student-parent-worker roles and mellow into the calm, loving, grandparent role, sharing their experience, that wisdom and understanding would be lost in a generation.

The successful investors of the solution would spend money on cars, bigger houses and on their kids, the kids would follow their lead and the cycle would continue. Without the calming influence and universal understanding of the grandparent generation, a focus on wants, not needs, would take over.

Dave had processed the data, the ensuing excess would lead to total collapse in society. The only available role model would be the system, the only guiding star their lies. A complete and unfounded faith in Orwellian double-speak, where the truth was no longer fact based but a fallacy built on misconceptions.

Dave had spoken to experts in psychology, for good mental and physical health, people needed to have some long-term respect for their bodies; a plan to rest, to survive, to say enough work, enough parties, enough abuse. It can't all be endless excess, we have to pace ourselves if we want to make old age, eventually we have to sit with ourselves and say stop. If we remove that need to survive physically and financially past the aged of sixty-five, the model predicts it creates a society of chaos, greed and vanity.

The remaining competitive, aggressive, arrogant, horny and scared younger generations, would implode at first in the excess of easy life. Drugs, alcohol, sex, technology and fashion. Too late they would realise they knew nothing; having had it on a plate, due to and despite a comprehensive access to an infinite amount of knowledge, they had squandered the opportunity to learn in deference to watching a cute cat video or someone fall off a log into a river, safe in their ignorant belief the knowledge would always be there at their fingertips. One day the lights will go off, the WiFi will die and we will reset, they won't allow us infinite knowledge and un-monitored global communication, it would make us too dangerous... like the knowledge of the grandparent generation - that it all comes down to love and adventures... and a life working is a life wasted.

***

"Dave, you awake man? Beer?" The chopper had landed.

"Yeah, lets get unloaded and logged and go for a pint."

One thing was for sure, there was something fucked up going on, Dave had never picked up a single agent before, let alone four. Something was happening and after a cold beer he wanted to get back to the flat fast and to do some digging.

83

The two vans wound their way down the mountain and refuelled in Llieda. Rory figured if they headed into the country roads from there, they could lose any tail but satellite, which thankfully due to its nature was delayed and impeded by tree cover - so long as they kept moving, they should be fine. It would take many hours to make their way to Valencia, but until then they should be safe.

Hercules slept, waking once briefly, only to have soup immediately forced on him by Mary. He consumed it hungrily and then collapsed back. Mary looked worried.

"He'll be fine, don't worry." Layla had a few hours sleep but woke with cramps in her calves. Mary gave her a mix of orange juice, water and a pinch of salt.

"Electrolytes lovely. You had quite the workout, your body needs...well, everything. Don't worry, me and Bolt are good at recovery."

"That's lucky, I think we might need it. I feel like I'm in a relay race, but I keep handing myself the baton and screaming at me to run."

"From what I've heard from your dad and the others, you have had a hell of a time sweetheart. Give yourself a minute, it's not a relay, it's a marathon, but you've been forced into a sprint start. Now the pace has slowed, breathe, rest, recover. You are capable of more than you can possibly imagine. Now, finish your soup, hydrate and try to sleep."

"I don't know if I can sleep Mary. Something happen out there, I... I *killed* a hunter on the mountain. Now, every time I close my eyes, I see my arrow burying itself in his chest, his eyes wide in shock frozen in death. He was trying to kill Dad, I had no choice... but I still took a human life Mary. I never thought I would say those words."

Tears ran down Layla's cheeks. Mary put an arm around her.

"I'm so sorry you had to make that decision honey. None of this is your fault. I understand how you feel. In the Alps I killed a hunter, I had only ever shot targets before. I still feel sick about it, but I had to choose between someone I love and someone who was being paid to kill us. I haven't made peace with myself, but we have to accept that the rules have changed. The world we used to live in has gone, our moral freedoms and simple decisions with it. We are in a survival, kill or be killed situation, we have to evolve. Every choice matters and if we try and exist in a moral world that no longer exists for us, we will lose. It's a lot Layla, you're young, but you seem to be a fighter and a protector, trust your instincts, they've kept you and yours alive so far."

Layla finished her soup and lay back.

"Thank you Mary, it's really nice to have a... you here." Layla drifted back into sleep next to her dad.

***

"How you doing pilot? Need a change?"

Martin stayed focused in the road and sat-nav and reached for a biscuit.

"I'm good love, I'll have some coffee from the thermos, but it sounds like you're doing important work back there. If you can rest, I think this could just be the beginning... besides I've got Rumi."

Rumi was now stretched across from the passenger seat, head in his lap as he steered with one hand and stroked her with the other. Mary passed him a coffee and kissed him on the cheek.

"How are you doing with all these Alpha's around, I noticed you've let them call the shots, not like you love."

"Too many chiefs... besides, they're protecting and making decisions their children's lives depend on. That's a lot of responsibility. I'm just on a terrifying adventure with the love of my life. Their plans have been good so far, we both knew if we ran, it would probably end in a hail of bullets. Whether we're alone or helping Hercules, we're almost certainly screwed. Might as well have some company, what's the worst that can happen? You rest darling. I've got the driving for now."

"Then I'll close my eyes, love you Bolt, next adventure."

"Love you too Mary, next adventure."

84

Bear woke up cold and stiff, it had been a tough couple of days for an out of shape veteran. As he stretched and sat up an early morning runner passed. Bear smiled and nodded. Both in respect to the gentleman's commitment on this fresh morning and his defined legs, there wasn't an ounce of fat and the rope like muscles lay over each other, flexing but each refusing to give quarter. The jogger continued a short distance and stopped. He pressed his watch, turned and walked back towards Bear and the bench.

Bear guarded himself for the usual barrage of questions.

"Who are you, where are you from, why are you here in my town sleeping rough, how long are you staying?"

The runner reached the bench and sat down.

"Hola hombre, como estas? Cuando comiste?"

Food!

"Buenos dias senor, que ha sido un tiempo."

It had been a while.

"Venga, ven conmigo para desayuno, hace fresca hoy."

Breakfast.

"Siempre digo si al desayuno cabellero, muchismo gracias."

Why not.

"De nada, me gustar una historia interesante y creo tu tienes muchos. Vamos."

Nice guy.

Bear grabbed his bag and followed the runner, never turn down breakfast in exchange for a story. Besides, disappearing for a few hours could be a good idea.

"Como es tu llama, senor?"

"Senor no, soy Anton, tengo una tienda de deportes en Marines, cerca una cafe, vamos."

"Venga, soy Bear, encontado."

"Igualmente."

85

Doc and Marcus pulled into an anonymous industrial area on the outskirts of Valencia and stopped in front of a garage door; painted white like the identical ones either side and behind them, in long rows. 132 was painted on the top right corner of this door. Doc unlocked the garage and drove the Mini in. Shutting it behind him and turning on the lights.

Marcus could now see that the units either side and behind were also connected to this one. There was a basic workshop, kitchen, medical room, sleeping quarters with two beds and various storage. It was compact, but it was perfect. There was even a Ducati motorbike leaning in the corner.

Marcus took it all in as he followed Doc to the kitchen, Doc put on the kettle, then went to the workshop and turned a few knobs on some sort of radio.

"What is this place Doc?"

"Well Marcus, you know how in dirty business you sometimes need a Go-bag. Passports, Money, Weapons... in very dirty business you need a Go-pad. It's completely anonymous and is near my exit strategy, Valencia Marina. We can prep for our exit, we've done well to make it this far, but I don't think it's over yet.

We have a boat at the Marina ready to sail, but we will be safer here while the others catch up. Hercules has a transmitter, he just pushes the button and we will know they are on their way to the boat and can track their progress. Now, tea or coffee... and do you need gun."

Doc pressed a button and the wall behind the workbench spun to reveal a moderate but well organised array of weapons.

"I'd love a coffee... I've never even held a gun before."

Doc handed him a pistol. It was small but heavy.

"This is a Walther PDP 9mm. Very easy to use."

Marcus inspected the knarly looking black pistol with ergonomic handle. Doc took it back.

"Hold it like this and look down the barrel to aim. It's loaded."

Doc pressed the cartridge release, it slid it out and he snapped it back home with a click. Safety, here - then it's just point and squeeze. Easy stuff. The key if we do get into some trouble is don't hesitate. I promise you, they won't."

Doc handed him two spare cartridges pre-loaded. Marcus put the cartridges in his pockets and tried the gun in his waistband, it didn't feel natural, but then what did right now. Doc made coffee, found an unopened tin of biscuits and talked about sailing, he was excited to finally fully retire and put his escape plan into action. Marcus hadn't sailed before, he had been seasick on the ferry once, but having come this far he was beginning to feel like he could survive just about anything.

86

Bolt had been driving for hours, he was ready for a comfort break and the fuel was staring to get low. Having left the main road once down the mountains, they had stuck to the back roads since. GPS set to avoid highways, Bolt would take a wrong turn once in a while, drive for a distance and allow the GPS to find another route variant to follow.

Martin had been trying not too listen, but it was hard not to hear as Mary and Layla were chatting over tea and biscuits. Rumi had abandoned the passenger seat for a spot next to Chance, her chin resting on Layla's feet.

"It's not just that he kept secrets about Mum and I'm pissed off about that. It's also that I don't understand why we are going on a boat and leaving you guys and the horses behind to go with this Doc guy. We have the vehicles to keep moving through Spain and cross to Africa by ferry later. We can help keep each other stay safe and have more options should we need to split up later, if they find us, there's nowhere to run on a boat."

"I can't speak for your father, but if he trusts this Doc character, it must be with good reason. As for the horses, sometimes we have to make sacrifices and say goodbyes. They would be well taken care of by your friends and have a good life, yes, you would miss them, but you have to survive. As far as looking after each other - I do think we have a better chance now if we stay together, but I'm also scared what happens if we do and they catch us. I don't blame Alex for wanting to get her family home safe. You should talk to your dad, he seems like a reasonable man."

"Yeah, sometimes. Do you really believe after the last few days and with Rory's connections to the company, they will just be allowed to go back to their lives? I don't think the company is that forgiving."

"Well Layla, I certainly agree with that. I think every last one of us and everyone involved is still in very close and mortal danger. Our next choices could be crucial. And, don't worry about the boy; he's come back for you once already, I saw how he looked at you. I can't see him walking away now, your godfather either."

Layla was still too tired, sore and scared to smile, but that did make her feel a little warmer inside - he had, hadn't he, despite his parents, Aaron had came back for her, she would have to remember to thank him.

"I have a idea Mary, but Dad's going to hate it."

"How do you know, what's your plan?" Mary asked already fearing the answer.

"Because, I hate it and it's my plan..."

In the front Bolt knew he'd heard those words before. Saying nothing, he listened to Layla's idea.

***

Hercules woke with a start. Sitting up with enough speed to make him dizzy and lay back with a groan. Rubbing his eyes he tried to clear the fog from his brain, he was damp from sweat and aching. He had that annoying feeling that something had to be done, but he was still groggy and felt like he had been asleep too long. He sat up again and swung his legs off the bed.

"You're alive then." Chance leaned over and gave him a squeeze. "You smell."

"You smell too, but I love you." Hercules squeezed her back and gave her a kiss on the cheek, Layla scrunched up her face, pretending not to like it.

"You've been out a while young man, the bullet wound and exertion really took it out of you. You had a bit of a temperature but the fever broke. Take a couple of paracetamol now and two more in four hours."

Hercules took the pills emptying a glass of water.

"Thanks Mary, you're an angel."

"Careful now pretty boy, that's my angel." Martin grinned from the front seat.

"How's the driving going Bolt? We in stealth mode?" Herc asked.

"Absolutely, still using the GPS trick that worked in the Alps, if it weren't for that we'd be completely lost, it's been a very illogical route. We need fuel soon and I'm sure the guys behind will too."

"Next petrol station we'll stop and refuel, I have cash. We should get some food and speak to the others too. While we may be off radar now, they will track us sooner or later when we break cover. We need some camouflage and I need to alert Doc."

***

They pulled into the service station, the horse box behind following them in and parking at the pump adjacent. As Bolt filled up, Rory did the same; faces hidden under baseball caps. Mary and Alex, wearing wide brimmed hats bought supplies from the shop and pretended not to know each other, before paying for fuel and groceries, both with cash. Alex also had a couple of tins of black paint and brushes in her basket. Ten minutes later they were a few miles up the road in a picnic area, squeezed into the Bell's van.

"Right, first things first...who's hungry?" Mary asked. There was a general murmur of agreement. "Okay then, outside everyone, it's dark, but it's not raining, you can have your meeting alfresco, while I prepare the food and make tea and coffee. Everyone out."

"Shall I help with the food?" Alex asked.

"No, you are going to be needed in that meeting, you have important decisions to make, not food. Martin can help me if necessary."

They filed off the bus, Hercules and Bolt the last to leave.

"Gentlemen..."

They turned and looked at Mary,

"No big decisions without me, but in principle, I agree with Layla." Bolt stroked the cut on her perfect cheek with his thumb and kissed her on the lips.

Layla has a plan.

Hercules realised his fever may have broken, but he may have some heat still to deal with, he stepped into the fresh air and pressed the small blue stone in his ring; before speaking briefly to

Aaron, who nodded and climbed up onto the roof of the RV, Hercules passed the a pot of paint and a brush and Aaron got to work changing the roof from white to black.

87

In the go-pad near Valencia, Doc and Marcus were eating oven-cooked, frozen veg and lasagne, that they both had to admit wasn't too bad. A beeping sound alerted them and Doc checked a screen in the workshop area.

"They're not too far now, a few hours depending on their route. They're way off the beaten path, must be trying to avoid detection."

"When do we leave?"

"When they're near the Marina. We'll catch them and guide them in."

"In the Mini?"

"No, the Ducati will be better for the last burst. Do you ride?"

"No, not something I've done, but it can't be worse than racing a train."

"Don't worry, I got you, Doc's an old pro, you just have to hold on sunshine."

"Bring it on."

"That's the spirit lad."

88

The co-pilot ducked as he loaded Red's Honda into the chopper to be returned to the engineers at HQ. Arctic and Bengal Fox both walked tall under the blades spinning above their heads. Red had braced herself for a dressing-down from her team leader, but after they thought they had lost her, Arctic Fox was the first to embrace her sister.

"Good to have you back, you had us worried for a moment there."

"Don't do that to us Red." Bengal's eyes glistened.

They boarded the chopper and it was down to business, past errors were left exactly there.

"Where are we headed?" Red was keen to put the pressure on while the group was without one very clever, but merciful soldier.

"All signs for the main group point to Valencia, but we don't have a current location or confirmation that's their goal. Tech is on it, satellites picked up two vans leaving the car park in Andorra shortly after the company van. They are trying to track them now, they are also searching gas station cameras, they have to refuel.

The target you... met, was tracked to the abandoned motorbike near Marines, we have been ordered to focus on the main group, other players are in the field to tie up that loose end."

"Alright then ladies, let's go!"

"We were just waiting for you Red... and getting some food."

Bengal Fox threw her a cling-wrapped, fully-loaded baguette and passed a thermos of coffee. Red refuelled as the chopper took off; they would take position near Valencia ready to move at the first information.

89

Hercules joined the others who were seated at some picnic benches next to the van, he stood and was about to say something, when Layla spoke.

"Dad, sit with us." Chance gestured to the bench opposite her and Hercules sat down heavily. "This has all happened so fast, we are all exhausted, but I was speaking with Mary and I think we all need to take a minute to discuss our plans as a group, rather than constantly reacting. So if anyone has anything to say, this is the time. I certainly have questions..." Layla paused. "The current plan is to get a boat from Valencia, who, how many, what about the horses? Rory, Alex, what's your plan? Bolt what happens to you and Mary if you stay or leave us, what's more dangerous?"

Hercules had waited, allowed Layla to finish and paused to permit Rory or Bolt to speak, but Rory was looking at Alex and Bolt was looking at him.

"The reason for the yacht, is given a head start we can disappear at sea. Doc is a trusted friend and a genius, he has an exit strategy, if he says he can get us out he can, I trust him. He will be ready and will join us when we need him. Trust me."

"And the horses? Also how do we get a head start when as soon as we hit the city the cameras will spot the vehicles or our faces."

"Alex said she could take care of the horses back home in France..."

"About that, we have been talking as a family and I don't think we will be going home. We've kicked over some rocks and to be honest, we always knew this day could come, that's why we were ready. At this point, there is no going back, home might not even be there. We used to burn out houses on orders. We're with you guys now." Rory squeezed Alex's hand. From the RV roof, Aaron smiled at Layla who for the first time in a long time managed a tired smile in return.

"What if some of us went on the boat and some of us went overland with the horses?" Bolt spoke up. Layla knew he'd been listening, but he'd done a good job of pretending not to. "We have been lucky to get away so far on land, but if they thought we had escaped into the vast sea, they would give up the hunt. We really could disappear on land, with the vans and horses. We could make our way towards Gibraltar and try and cross to Africa. That's where Mary and I were heading, we were going to pick up kite-surfing gear in Cadiz and board to freedom if necessary. Just a backpack and each other."

"You guys are so romantic, I love it." Layla smiled, Bolt grinned sheepishly.

"Morocco works for us; the horses, Layla and Rumi are welcome to join us." Alex looked Hercules in the eye with sadness and it dawned on him. He was the bait, he had to go on the boat, meet with Doc and Marcus and maybe Bear if he was still alive. They needed to draw them away from these guys and hopefully manage to escape themselves. That meant doing it again. Leaving

Layla. Hercules looked at his daughter, a smart, strong young woman who had saved his life once already and made it worth living everyday, she was making this group stronger just by being there. It was time to let go.

"This is what you want, to stay on the land and cross to Morocco? You know horses can't kite-surf."

"I can't give up on them yet, we'll find a way. I don't want you to go, but you can't abandon Bear, Marcus and your friend and for us to get away they have to think we're out in the Mediterranean or..." Layla wiped a tear.

Rory stood and moved round the picnic table stretching his legs; Alex slid along the bench and Hercules got up and sat next to Layla holding her tight.

"You've got this Chancer, I'm so proud of you. You can do anything... and thank you, for saving my life."

"I'll be fine. You better look after yourself now... and Bear, please. I love you dad."

"Love you too. I guess I'll see you all in Morocco." Hercules forced a smile.

"For the record, I'm cool with the Morocco plan." Aaron jumped down from the roof to collect the second can of paint from the table. Layla gave him a shove on the shoulder.

"Duh... also, thanks for coming back Aaron, I'm glad you're here."

“Me too. Thanks for not letting me get shot - Mum would have killed me.” They all laughed.

Mary leaned out the van.

"You can help carry this now gentlemen..."

Hercules and Aaron collected the trays of food and Rory carried the tea.

"Did I miss any big decisions?" Mary asked.

Hercules looked worried. Bolt didn't.

"No my love, just a few more companions for our journey to Morocco."

"Lovely, we're going with Layla's plan then."

Mary smiled as they all tucked into chicken and salad baguettes and tea and coffee. Aaron finished his sandwich quickly, climbed onto the horsebox roof, crudely painting it black from white. Paint dripped down the sides, but there wasn't time to make it look pretty, just to disguise it from aerial view.

"So, when do we steal you a motorbike Hercules?" Mary asked. Hercules looked at Mary, then Layla, who shrugged.

"To be honest, a motorbike is a good idea, we'll find one near Valencia and make contact with Doc." Hercules relaxed a little, she'd be fine... but would he.

They finished their food, Layla collected their mobile devices (some switched-off for weeks) and gave them to Hercules.

Hercules and Rory embraced, Alex being pulled in and squeezed by both. Aaron received a firm handshake and a clap on the shoulder.

"Good luck young man, try not to let her do anything crazy."

They got back in their vehicles and under a cloud of uncertainty headed towards Valencia. On board Hercules pressed and held the blue stone again switching off the transmitter. Five minutes later he turned it on again. This was repeated six times. Then remained on.

90

Marcus ate a cornetto, Doc moved to the workstation and opened a notebook, checking the codex:

Six at five minute intervals - Change of plans. Coming into rendezvous hot.

"Looks like we could be up for some more excitement Marcus. Hercules reckons they're coming in hot and he's changed the plan. No surprise he memorised that code. He's always messing with my carefully laid plans. Guess we meet as planned and follow his lead."

Marcus took a second cornetto from the freezer, no point wasting food.

"Well you know what they say Doc - If you want to make God smile, make plans."

"Good man, now, you're getting it."

91

Bear followed Anton to a cafe, the sign above read “La Telaraña” and was decorated with a silver spider web. Next door was a running shop, “Sigue Corriendo”.

Anton paused, raised the shutters and turned on the lights, in the window as a centre piece was a very cool Harley Davidson. Inside Bear could see rows of trainers and racks of sports gear.

"Buen moto."

“Gracias, ella es mi amor.”

They went next door and Anton ordered a coffee and a cheese and ham croissant, Bear nodded and Anton ordered the same.

"Mismo de siempre para mi, otra croissant de mismo y una cafe invitado." The tall, heavily tattooed chap behind the bar nodded silently.

“Bear, please allow me to practice my English.” It was precise, accented but well spoken. They took a table by the fire, Bear closest warming his body from the night, the runner shielding himself from the heat and still sweating from his run.

"You speak well."

"I ran in my youth, I learned English on the European circuit. French and Italian, some German too. Later I did international meets, got close to the Olympics but never quite made the qualifications. Lack of discipline, too young, too many distractions and injuries. It is what it is. What about you Bear, where are you from, where you going?"

"Ex-forces, some time between accommodation in the UK, then a road trip. Next, Valencia, just looking for a change of scene, England is bleak, I needed some sun. Funds are low so been hitching and hiking my way, sleeping where I have to, mornings are fresh, but it's not like London."

Anton nodded sympathetically.

"I'll get a shower and open the shop; take your time, finish your breakfast and order more food or coffee on me. Come to the shop when you're ready, I'll make some calls and see if any of my suppliers are headed to Valencia, we might get you a ride to the city in a van. Welcome to get a shower while we wait, but for now relax."

"Perfecto, gracias Anton."

"De nada, hombre. Anywhere in the city in particular?"

"Not really, I'm happy to explore on foot, maybe the beaches near the Marina. I fancy a swim."

Bear ordered a second coffee and a pastry filled with some sort of sweet cream and enjoyed the fire.

***

Anton went next door to shower at the back of his shop, first he made a phone call.

"Scorpion, it's Spider, you saw that notice I forwarded from the agency about the target near Marines, picked him up this morning, I've got him in The Web."

"Shit Spider, that's a payday. What's the plan?"

"He's a big bastard, ex-forces, I'm not going to handle him on my own. Can you get over here in the van. Get some stock from the lock-up, you're going to be the delivery driver, we'll take him to his friends. I'll follow on the bikes with the lads."

"Why don't we just take him at your place, hand him over and get paid Spider?"

"Because Scorpion, I'd bet our bikes that this guy is on his way to meet the others and while he is a payday. The group together is retirement money. I'll call the Lizard boys for back up this could be a huge score. If he's meeting the others at the Marina, so are we. If we have to make him talk, we will."

Spider made a few more calls, he did not contact the agency, while he could request assistance, he would make more cash with a straight hand-over than giving information in exchange for money and letting the company strike.

Spider headed into the back, stripping off to reveal a torso covered in a variety of tattoos, including various webs and spiders. He went for a quick cold shower, dried and treated himself to new underwear. The running shop was a perfect front for laundering money from the lads activities distributing narcotics. The occasional job for the suits kept him out of legal trouble and in business, sports gear... and clean pants. This job could let him finally retire from the game altogether if it worked out. He pulled on fresh running leggings and a thin merino base layer with a roll neck, ideal for under the motorbike gear, which he pulled on next. He had a feeling today would be active, hopefully the brothers and Scorpion could keep up. *Good lads but not the sharpest.*

"Okay, even that monster must be out by now."

***

Bear had enjoyed the pastry and it was so good to drink decent coffee that when the barman brought over a third mug and a different, twisted pastry - this time with chocolate cream inside, he couldn't see the harm.

"Este es mi favorito, invitados de la casa senor." The gruff looking waiter actually smiled.

Rude not too.

"Gracias amigo, porque no." Bear smiled and allowed himself another long hot hit of caffeine and ingested more sugar until felt a little sick and his hands were trembling. It would pass. He lay back by the fire and shut his eyes. Just five minutes...

***

When Scorpion arrived and pulled up outside in a white van, it took the barman, Spider and Scorpion to carry Bear to the van and squeeze him through the side door into the small space left in the back. They cuffed each hand to rings on the panels either side, wings spread, his back to the bulk head. His long, heavy legs were shoved into the cramped space, his pack unceremoniously thrown on top of him and the door slid shut. The barman returned to his post as if it was just another Tuesday. Spider pulled on his jacket and helmet and climbed onto the Harley.

Inside the van, blocking the view from the back window was a clothes rail with various items hanging, behind that a pallet of shoe-boxes strapped to the floor, taking most of the space, you could look down the sides but it would pass a quick inspection.

"The pallet of weird sizes that you got that deal on boss, just chucked the whole pallet on in case any one wonders why we're heavy and has a nose about."

Spider nodded. Two other Harley's came into sight and stopped at the end of the road, he pointed to the van and snapped his visor down. He hated wearing a helmet but it wasn't worth the hassle with the Guadia Civil.

Scorpion jumped in the van and headed towards Valencia. Spider rolled past the other bikers and signalled to follow, they slid in behind him. They didn't need instructions, just follow the boss and do what needs to been done if shit goes down.

In the back of the van, Bear was finally getting some sleep. Deep sleep.

92

Less than twenty kilometers from Bear, Mary pulled into a lay-by, there were two motorcycles in the car-park at the bar they had just passed.

"Bike Herc."

"Already?" Layla, took a breath.

Hercules pulled her close and told her once more all the things she already knew and had heard her whole life. You are loved. You are awesome, just be you.

"I love you Dad, see you in Morocco... don't get killed. Me and Rumi would miss you."

"Stay safe love. Good luck everyone, follow me and remember at the tunnel you guys split, the clock starts. I'll hit the Marina with Doc and Marcus as fast as possible and then I'll turn on your phones. You guys get into the countryside and find somewhere to lay low, use the back roads and mountains to cross the south of Spain, stay hidden."

Hercules gave Layla one more confident smile and a nod and shut the door, their mobiles safely in his dry-bag. He spoke to Rory in the van behind briefly, shook hands through the window and headed into the bushes and towards the bar.

The vans continued towards Valencia; within ten minutes a white BMW motorbike caught them on a straight clear road, it came alongside, gave a tidy wheelie, pulled neatly into the lead and dropped the front wheel.

With no helmet to steal, Hercules grin was clear to see. He got the expected eye-roll from Layla as he passed the window. Rory gave a more generous fist pump out the window. Then it was onto the mission. The convoy continued.

93

Dave was back in his flat after the strange job in Andorra. He had gone online and first checked his bank balance, which was as it should be. They always paid fast. Then he checked his usual networks for any whispers and theories.

There was a press-release covering a hunter execution in Calais. Tom Kind, some activist. Unofficial reports of a man killed with a rifle last week in the Alps, shot from a distance, a company operative apparently. In the bar after his job, there had been talk of another collection higher up the mountain, apparently an American hunter.

There were few details and many wild theories, but nothing solid to go on. To release the information he had on the organ stockpiling, he needed to join forces with other stories exposing the practices of the company. Otherwise he would just be eliminated before it got traction. He needed something bigger, he needed something viral. This could be the story. The myth was broken, someone was evading and taking out the hunters, making them beatable and mortal. This could change everything, not only would the truth come out, people would revolt, they certainly would stop signing up to give away their organs and many more people would run - the company would be unable to stop their numbers. Who were these hunter-killers on the run?

***

Later that day Dave checked his anonymous postal box. Inside was a beige envelope. Sometimes journalist friends passed him on the "crazy" stories or information their editors wouldn't consider. The envelope, was heavy. Dave slid out a file. On the front in black letters it simply said:

"THOMAS KIND"

"Eliminated - Calais" in red ink below.

Kind, Calais. This was the link he needed. He pulled more files out the manila envelope.

Rory "Raptor" Beaufort. There was an old photo and personnel file from the company hunter department. He pulled more files out.

Mike "Bear" Higgins, Marcus Drummond, Cobra, Doc, Layla Chance, Aaron and Alex Beaufort.

This was not a runaway killer, but a group and it was a thick envelope. The dates didn't work for the Alp's victim, but maybe that was a false lead or just a lucky runner.

Dave bought some groceries and returned to the flat, where after making a bacon and egg sandwich and pot of tea, he started reading the files and taking notes.

94

There had been enough ketamine in the coffee Bear drank to put a horse to sleep for over an hour and relaxed for two more. Maybe it was the sugar in the pastries or the caffeine consumed with the K, or just the fact that Bear was an absolute machine. Whatever it was, in the back of the van, he was coming round.

Bear was groggy, his mouth was dry, his head was pounding and the world was spinning. His knees were under his chin, there was something pressing on his face and his arms and his chest ached.

Bear shook it off and forced his eyes open - it wasn't too bright at least. He shrugged his rucksack off his face and chest and it fell to the floor next to him. In the front Scorpion was singing along to some Spanish pop song on the radio. He heard nothing and kept an eye on the three bikes behind and the traffic ahead. It was getting busier on the roads.

Bear took in his surroundings, in front of him was a pallet of shoe-boxes, clear wrapped, with one strap over the top, securing it to the bed. On top was a box of Brooks running shoes, it struck him as strange, because they were in Bear's size - 49 and he loved Brooks. He tried to focus, he needed air, he needed space. With his back on the bulk head and his feet on the pallet he shoved the shoes toward the back door, the boxes on top crushed beneath the strap and inch by inch the pallet slid.

Bear was now able to move a little and he was pissed off. His shoulders and chest ached from his crucifixion and the cuffs had cut into his wrists, small dried trickles of blood ran to the elbows, around the wrists was still sticky.

Bear braced himself for the pain, put the cuffs under tension and raised his body before dropping and ripping his arms towards him. The bindings gave with less force than Bear expected, the screws holding the heavy steel rings ripped out of the side of the van and swung from Bears arms at the end of the cuffs. Bear had thought the links in the cuffs might break, but this would do. Bear took the Brooks trainers out the box and stuffed them in his pack, catching sight of the company medical kit he'd collected from the dead sniper. Inside was a pill-box, fully stocked. Bear recognised the yellow go-pills from his forces days. He popped two in his mouth and swallowed the contents of his water bottle, that should help clear whatever they'd slipped him.

Thanks for the trip Anton, time to get the hell out of here. Bear released the ratchet strap on the pallet and reached around the boxes with a long arm, his finger tips finding the handle of the back door and gently releasing the catch, before donning his pack and hammering a big fist on the bulk-head.

***

Spider's first indication that something wasn't right, was an erratic swerve from the van as Scorpion heard a banging from the back and naturally turned to look, despite the bulk head blocking his view. He turned off the radio and listened.

Spider's second indication something was wrong, was the back doors opening and an almost-full pallet of merchandise rolling out towards him, on his left was a fast moving car, on his inside an RV and a horsebox, no escape. The tumbling shoe-boxes filled his path, the pallet exploded into splinters and his bike went down. At that moment he was glad of the helmet.

Scorpion, slammed on the brakes seeing the scene behind as a traffic jam began in the chaos. The brothers, quickly pulled into the hard shoulder ahead and waited.

***

Bear burst out of the van, cuffs and rings swinging, eyes wild, sprinting towards Spider who had pulled off the helmet and winded was sucking in air, grateful his underwear was still clean. Shaken from his spill, he was too slow, Bear swung a right hammer-blow, knocking Spider out cold, before he could reach his gun.

Bear forced on the helmet on, wrestled the heavy Harley back on it's boots and shot down the road towards the van; his gun drawn and pointed at the wide mouthed Scorpion as he staggered from the van. Bear eyed the Lizard brothers as he passed. They didn't move. As he looked into the remaining mirror he could see that without their leader, there was no pursuit.

The brothers turned their bikes around in a wide circle and headed to Spider who was coming round, a swollen jaw and blood running from a nasty gash on his forehead where the square plate on Bears new bracelets caught him. Scorpion reversed back to them and they helped Spider into the van.

"Follow him, don't let him get away, if we can't follow him to the others - one dead runner is still a good payday."

The brothers, Gecko and Iguana nodded and shot off after Bear, guns un-clipped in chest-holsters, safety off. The van made it's pursuit behind. The boys weren't bright but they were fast and they could shoot.

***

"Shit, did you see that Dad?" Aaron asked.

"Yeah, was that biker okay? Something fell out that van back there. There was no hard shoulder - I had nowhere to go."

"I think he'll be okay; we weren't going fast and the van and other cars stopped. Stick with Layla."

A few minutes later, the Harley Davidson, a little bit battered, roared past them up the road.

"Yeah, he was fine Dad, see."

Moments later, two more bikers shot past.

***

The brothers moved into the fast lane and over took a long, double-line of lorries as they curved up a hill in fast pursuit. The morning roads were getting busy as empty lorries passed the slower fully-loaded trucks. When they passed the queue to clear straight road ahead of the lorry convoy, Bear was gone. The brothers looked at each other, where did Spiders chopper go? They pressed on, this guy must be really pushing it.

***

Behind them, Bear had slowed down and slipped between the trucks, riding between the commercial traffic in the two slow lanes. Lorries close either side, he carefully rode the white line, as he dropped back between them and his pursuers flew past. Bear slipped out the back of the convoy, leaving his hiding place sandwiched between the high vehicles. He nodded at the confused drivers as he overtook them again and began his stalk.

***

After a few minutes racing through traffic, they still hadn't caught him. The brothers slowed, they had missed something.

***

Bear was between some trucks again, hiding the sound and sight of his ride by staying on the tailgate of the enormous beast in front, hoping the driver didn't brake suddenly. Ahead around the bend, Bear spotted the two bikes dropping back in search of him as expected.

By the time they saw Bear tucked tightly behind a lorry adjacent to them, gun ready, it was too late. Bear easily shot out their front wheels and they both went down hard, sliding to the edge of the road, the bikes tumbling and depositing pieces across the carriageway behind. He pulled out from the lorries, slowed a little and let the goliaths pass, opening the face visor he breathed some fresh air in and enjoyed some clear tarmac ahead of now him. He needed to get to the Marina and find the others.

***

"Bloody hell, what's going on today?" Rory looked at Aaron as they passed two shaken looking bikers and their wrecks.

"Strange."

***

On the BMW at the front of the convoy Hercules noticed they were catching the erratic Harley again and looked across as they over took. Visor up, the biker seemed somehow familiar...

***

Behind, Mary was driving with Layla and Rumi in the passenger seat. Layla was looking out the window as they passed.

***

"There he is again Dad." Aaron said in the horsebox.

***

As the convoy passed him, Bear did a double-take, that was Hercules on a BMW without a helmet, hair blowing in the wind. Layla's face passed in the window of the camper and behind was the horsebox.

Not recognizing him in the helmet, he tore it off, threw it bouncing to the side of the road and gunned the engine. The back doors of the van were open at the top he could see Royal and Coco looking out. Heads inquisitive to the world.

***

Scorpion screeched into the side of the road and the brothers jumped into the back of the van, which immediately sped off. The boss was furious.

"Fucking find this guy." Spiders web was unraveling fast.

***

Hercules heard and saw the Harley appearing again in his mirror, this time the biker had no helmet and was grinning and waving to the two vans behind.

He nearly fell off his bike when Bear pulled alongside and moved in close.

"Hola Hercules."

"Good to see you Bear. Trouble?" Hercules yelled.

"A little, what's the plan? Think I've got still got company."

"I'm leading the hunters away on a boat, the rest are going overland, we meet in Morocco."

"Do you need my help man?"

"Yes Bear, look out for my daughter, while I do what I have to do."

Bear nodded and they bumped fists.

"Looks like my company is here." The white van was catching the convoy fast.

"Let's do this."

Hercules pulled to hard-shoulder on the inside of the RV and pulled out his gun, nodding to Rory as Bear pulled away.

***

Layla and the Bell's in the camper and Aaron and his parents in the horsebox watched the stocky guy on the big bike drop back after the chaos, as Hercules and the two vans overtook the slowing bike and Rumi barked at the rider.

A moment later he returned once more. Without a helmet and waving and smiling, Bear rode alongside the convoy. Layla and the others could hardly believe their eyes. Bear was back.

Bear and Hercules communicated and then moments later; Layla watched as all hell broke loose.

***

The mercenaries raced through the traffic, four furious men, their bikes and hope of a fortune battered.

“There he is boss, up the road ahead of those vans.” Spider and the brothers readied their weapons as Scorpion chased the Harley, catching fast - until a white van cut them up.

"Stupid horse cunt, nearly killed us!" Scorpion slammed on the brakes, the horsebox moved back in and they pressed on, the Harley in their sights. As they closed the gap, Hercules followed them on the BMW as they rounded a bend, windows down and weapons up, ready to mow down Bear.

Hercules appeared alongside them, shot out the two right tyres and watched with satisfaction as the driver lost control and screeched off the road and into a barrier with a crunch.

Bear dropped back to the convoy, nodded to Hercules, waved to Layla and then pulled alongside the back end of the horsebox. Crouching on the saddle, throttling on and adjusting the handlebars, he found the right balance, let go of the bars and stood up. Hopping onto the back of the horsebox as it passed Bear climbed over the doors, letting the motorbike ghost-ride and eventually fall to the ground and slide into a tree. Destroyed.

Well, that was exciting, no more go-pills.

95

A mile or so further up the road a sporty looking motorbike appeared from behind, approaching fast. The bike he had been waiting for, it had two passengers. Hercules sighed, it was nearly time, they must be close to the tunnel, tollbooths and then shortly after, the Marina. He dropped back to level with the RV, glancing over his shoulder at Rory and his family with a thumbs up. Then he looked up at Layla's face in the window of the camper. She looked fierce and unwavering. They smiled briefly.

Doc and Marcus pulled alongside on the Ducati, Hercules pointed for them to follow, gunned the engine and with a final look at his daughter, shot away into the tunnel.

The vans took a right and headed inland away from the coast.

***

A few miles behind, Spider called the suits, at least info could get him some money. He gave a last know location of the target "Bear". The money would be in his account by morning should the tip-off prove correct.

***

One minute later Fox team's helicopter was in the air.

96

Hercules, pulled into a toll booth and Doc came alongside.

"Cover is blown, not getting away clean."

"It was always a slim chance, the escape plan was for one or two people to sneak away undetected, this was always going to be messy son. So, I assume we're the bait."

"Bait?" Marcus didn't like the sound of that, the gun in his waistband poking him uncomfortably in the thigh.

"Afraid so, you got a radio? The clock is about to start."

Doc handed him a radio and took off his helmet and indicated for Marcus to do the same.

"We're going live then?"

"Yes." Hercules turned to a open channel. "Layla, Bolt, Rory do you read me? We are on our way to the boat. Stay there and be ready to sail at any moment. I repeat, stay on the boat."

There was of course no response. He repeated the message, handed Doc the radio, paid the toll and smiled at the camera overhead. Doc gunned the engine and flew through the gates, he knew his escape route well. Marcus even more terrified now without a helmet, did his best to hang on as the wind and world swept past, Hercules did his best to keep up.

97

At hunter headquarters screens flashed and alarms sounded. Facial recognition hit confirmed. They had an exact location and live tracking, as well as a radio broadcast. Two motorbikes with three targets were headed toward the coast to meet the rest of their group. The helicopter carrying Fox team zeroed in, closing fast.

Spider would get a payday which might replace his Harley and allow his extra curricular activities to continue, but there would be no retirement and the company would investigate his mission and it's timeline. If he had cost them time, or the opportunity to intervene, there would be consequences.

***

In the back of the horsebox, Bear spoke calmly to the horses, Coco was a little perturbed at a surprise visitor having intruded into their space. Royal recognised his over-sized jockey immediately and nuzzled Bear fondly, happy to have his neck stroked and some company on this journey.

After giving his travel buddies some attention to make sure they were all friends. Bear turned on his old phone, recorded and sent a short video then checked behind the van before throwing the phone into the passing trees. He was tall enough he could look out the back of the box with the horses, together they watched the city disappear behind them.

***

It was quiet in the back of the camper, Layla and Rumi curled up together.

"Well, shall we check on Bear?" Mary slowed and indicated right, letting the horsebox pass on her left.

Despite fears for her father, Chance couldn't help but smile as she looked through the windscreen at her two beautiful horses and Bear's face smiling back at her.

98

Flying towards the Marina were Doc and Hercules, Marcus hanging on and trying to lean into the rapid turns with Doc as they weaved between cars. They were less than six kilometers from the coast when they entered a long tunnel. Marcus was almost starting to enjoy it. That ended when the tunnel did.

It was impossible to turn back when the helicopter dropped sideways into view and seemed to fill the exit of the tunnel. Blades spinning, side-door open and an angry looking redhead at a machine-gun that was pointing right at them.

This is it.

Might as well go out with a fight thought Marcus, he drew his Walther from his waistband and fired two wild shots at the helicopter, which wheeled away.

"Yeah, motherfuckers!"

Doc grinned, the lad was getting brave. He and Hercules ignored the helicopter and accelerated. No way the hunters would risk civilians casualties with that sort of weaponry, it was fear tactics, but, they were now in real and present danger, time to ditch the tail.

Doc nodded to Hercules to follow him and at the next roundabout rather than taking a lane, he flew between two cars, bisected the roads and took off a grassy mound through some bushes. Hercules had to assume this was the plan and followed, disappearing into the foliage of trees and tall grasses. The helicopter had lost them, it gained altitude and began to circle, scouring the ground for the bikes.

Doc landed heavily with Marcus bouncing around, snaking the back end they held it as he accelerated forward. Hercules landed lightly behind and followed Doc into the tree cover. They were in the Barranc de Carraixet - as Doc knew. Hercules felt like he had disappeared from civilisation into a stretch of jungle, bushes and branches whipping past, following Doc's dust trail, skidding along a stony riverbed hidden underneath a canopy of branches, tall bamboo fencing them in. In the rainy season, it was a canal for the water run off, now pretty dry, it would lead them to the sea. After which, it was only a few kilometers of sand between them and their escape to the open ocean.

A few hundred meters before the beach Marcus tapped Doc firmly on the shoulder and they came to a stop. Hercules pulled up.

"Que pasa?"

"We're close now right?" Marcus asked.

"Yes, nearly at the beach and then just sand to the port, the boat is waiting lad. I promise we're nearly there."

"What if, instead of riding two motorbikes along the beach, we stripped to shorts and t-shirts and just walked or jogged there like tourists. Let's blend in."

"He's got a point Doc, they're looking for bikes, let's take a minute."

The last kilometers were taken at a leisurely pace as the three men walked along the beach. They looked like tourists. Hercules in his khaki trousers with rolled up legs and shirt off, folded, a pistol concealed within. The dry-bag over one shoulder, covered his bandage and held his documents, another pistol, ammo, boots, cash and the mobile phones.

Doc, wearing a black t-shirt, had cut off his denim trouser legs with a penknife, ditched the motorbike jacket and boots and walked barefoot, toes in the sand on the edge of the shore. Soon he would be barefoot on his boat, out on the water, wind in his grey hair.

Marcus carried his trainers, his grubby white shirt and tired looking hoody both open from neck to waist, tracksuit bottoms pulled up to the knees. The tie-cord barely resisting the heavy gun trying to pull his trousers down. It would be nice to get on a boat and chill. Marcus enjoyed the feel of the fine white sand mixing with seawater, massaging and cooling his tired feet.

Children laughed and played, families ate and drank, gorgeous women tanned and adolescents played music. Ignorant to what Marcus had been through in the past few days. *If he just sat down on the beach now, could he become one of them again?*

***

It all seemed too easy as the three tourists climbed onto the sail boat in the marina, after a few checks Doc started her up. Hercules turned the mobile phones on while Marcus untied her lines. They slipped between her neighbours and within minutes they were leaving the marina along with various other pleasure craft. It was painfully slow as they turned right and Doc pushed the two-knot speed limit.

Following the long wharf wall, they passed the rest of the huge marina where the expensive yachts were moored. They crossed a wide mouth, access for the cruise-liners to pass. After a few wide freight entrances, the vast shipping container park and the area for motorboats they were finally nearly past the port, sand stretched ahead to their starboard as their vessel moved to blend in with the other yachts heading south along the Spanish coast.

Hercules was below deck checking some scuba gear and spear guns and stashing their side-arms and ammo in the waterproof go-bag. Hopefully they wouldn't need them for a while. From the cabin he could see Marcus now standing behind the wheel, bare feet and torso.

Marcus had a smile on his face, sun warming his chest, steering the boat, this was easy. When slowly motoring it is easy, when the sails were up, in good wind it would take Doc's considerable skill to handle with only these amateurs to help. Doc had left Marcus on a compass heading and instructions to stay below four knots and had moved to the back of the boat. After tidying the lines and fenders, he was looking fondly at the port and city behind, he would miss Valencia, she was a beautiful city.

"*A new adventure.*" Doc smiled.

99

Bengal fox had taken the North port and had a shot as she watched them approach the marina along the beach. She was told to hold and let them locate the boat, the chopper was nearby, waiting for a clean shot, clear of sunbathing civilians. Arctic fox had taken the South port.

Having been told to stand down at the tunnel when she had the targets in her cross-hairs, Red was eager to take out this whole group once an for all. Intercepted radio broadcasts had told them these were the last three fugitives to join the rest of the targets on a boat. Rather than search all the boats, they would watch and wait until Doc, Marcus or Cobra were spotted on board a vessel, then once at sea they would engage.

***

Arctic fox got the call that the targets had been spotted and then was updated they were headed south. She watched the boat motor round the marina from a powerful sight, mounted on an impressive rifle. She watched Doc show Marcus the ropes and tidy his lines. From her sight, she saw Doc smile.

"Red, you a go?"

"Affirmative."

Arctic Fox exhaled and squeezed the trigger. The bullet left the dock from a stack of shipping containers and entered Docs chest nine hundred metres away driving him backwards onto the deck.

"*Crack.*"

Hercules head snapped up.

"Doc, no!" Marcus screamed.

"Marcus get down here now." Hercules yelled grabbing the go-bag.

Above deck, Marcus had heard the shot and turned in time to see Doc fly backwards and crumple on the deck. He ran to the back of the boat to see Doc limp on the deck, blood pouring from his chest. Marcus froze as he realised the danger he was now in.

"MARCUS MOVE! Get down here now."

Marcus moved. As he bent and grabbed Doc, a shot whistled over his head. Crouching low he dragged Doc to cover and they tumbled backwards into the cabin.

Hercules lifted Doc onto a bench and lay him down, blood pouring on the cabin floor. He pulled Marcus to his feet.

"What the fuck was that?" Marcus asked. "Is he?"

"Sniper. Marcus, I'm sorry man, they're on us. Doc is gone. Are we headed towards the beach or the sea?"

"We're headed out to sea now."

"Then I'm afraid it's over, they will simply wait and take us out with a rocket from the helicopter. It's been a pleasure Marcus, sorry fella."

Hercules squeezed Docs hand. "Lo siento amigo, you were one in a million."

Doc squeezed Hercules hand and coughed weakly.

"Wrong on three accounts lad. I'm one in five billion, I'm alive and it's not over yet."

"Shit Doc, I thought you were dead for sure." Marcus squeezed his other hand.

"I am dead Marcus, just not yet. There's an airlock escape hatch in the back cabin, big enough for two. Take the scuba gear and disappear when this boat does. it's been a journey gentlemen."

Hercules put the scuba gear on Marcus' back first then his own, tears on both their faces. They pulled the masks on. Herc picked up the go-bag and held Doc's hand firmly, before handing Marcus his adjustable fins and grabbing a pair himself.

"Remember when you beat that train Doc? That was awesome."

"What about when you shot up that helicopter lad? You're awesome Marcus, be afraid of nothing."

The sound of helicopter blades thunking approached, getting louder until it reached a hover and machine gun fire raked the cabin.

Hercules and Marcus ran for the cabin, lifted the double bed and dove into the airlock below. Pressing a green button. The panel above sealed and the box filled with water. Marcus tried to stay calm as the water rose around him, attempting to breathe normally through the uncomfortable mouthpiece. Within seconds a door in front of them fell open and they swam downwards, pulling on their fins.

Above them, bleeding and wheezing, Doc had pulled the cushions off one of the benches and managed to remove a shoulder-mounted, rocket-propelled grenade from the storage. The cabin door was still open, slumped on the floor, his back against a bench he sat ready, aiming, he just needed the helicopter to move into his window. Machine gun fire peppered his boat again and he coughed up more blood. He was feeling weak now, the bullet had gone through his lung and probably caught an artery on the way. He didn’t have long either way.

Doc heaved himself up on the kitchen counter and steadied himself, RPG on his shoulder.

"It’s five steps Doc, five more steps in this life, then you can go. Left leg, right leg, just five more steps." He coughed up more blood and spat on the floor. The first step his legs nearly gave way, but with the next his foot was on the first stair, his left hand pulling on the rail, feet finding the second and third stairs. Doc stepped up into the sunshine and span to face the chopper to his right. Dropping to one knee he fired.

The pilot saw the movement on deck but hadn’t expected to see an RPG, he pulled up just in time and the grenade exploded harmlessly as Red fired the machine gun raking the boat again, Doc collapsed back into the cabin. It was done.

***

When Red switched to missiles and finally ended it; Hercules and Marcus were well away and headed towards the beach where they could hide in the twenty kilometer stretch of Parc Natural that lined the coast. Underwater they heard and felt the explosion; paused, surfaced briefly and looking back acknowledged their friend, the smoke twisted upwards above the blue sea, bright sunlight dancing on the water.

Everyone within a mile heard and felt the explosion. Doc had a few toys on the boat, so when Red fired, Doc and the boat were engulfed in an instant, the fireball visible from the beach over a kilometer away. The remains of the boat sinking like a stone.

100

It was done. Red and the chopper hovered for five minutes, waiting in vain for unlikely survivors to surface, then flew away and collected the rest of the team.

Arctic Fox reported back to HQ from the helicopter.

"Confirm. No one left the boat. All passengers on the escape vessel were neutralised. The three targets we tracked led us to those hiding on the yacht. We took out the boat at sea... completely destroyed, yes. Absolutely no chance of survivors, it was a fireball, what was left was on the seabed in seconds. The ten target files are considered closed... yes, the adolescents too."

The Fox team took a team moment, fist-bumps and smiles. This would be their biggest payout ever. They could retire. They wouldn't, but they would certainly be upgrading their lives when they got home. They were seriously wealthy and their reputation was now unquestionable, they could relax on private jobs for celebrities, the elite, sheikhs and princes. Easy money.

101

At the Sixty-five building in London, news that it was over reached the ear of the Director of Hunter Division. Ten manila folders were placed on her desk.

"All ten files closed Ma'am."

"Understood, thank you Angela, *I'll* dispatch a clean-up team. That will be all."

The Director stood at her large wooden desk in front of a huge leather chair and looked at the top file and smiled briefly.

"*Doc*" she placed it to the side. She didn't need to read that file, after all their years at the Company, she knew Doc well and had kept a close eye, even if it had been many years since they'd had contact.

The files of Bear, Marcus and the Bell's she placed in a pile next to it. Raptor, his wife Alex and son Aaron she placed on top of those with a sad look and a sigh, then she took a deep breath and opened the next file.

Cornelius "Hercules" Chance - "Cobra"

With a flash of happy memories, the Director couldn't help but smile as she saw the faded photo of Hercules and then the latest images, still handsome. Her eyes glistened and her lungs stuttered as she exhaled. Through the building tears she saw the name on the last file on her desk.

"Layla Chance"

She didn't even open it. That was enough, the dam broke and the tears ran freely, pouring down her cheeks, sobs racking her body.

"I tried my child, I tried."

Sofia, the Director of Solution Sixty-five's Hunter Department and biological Mother to Layla Chance; collapsed back in the leather chair and wept. While she feared this the likely outcome, the sudden grief for a child she had already given up once, was crushing and despite her icy nature, the tears flowed.

Down such dark and twisted paths our choices can lead us. She would have stayed in that hospital bed had she known the outcome of the ultimatum,

"Join us or die."

102

Layla, was in a remote Spanish lay-by, off a country road, running down the RV steps to the horsebox as Bear clambered out the back.

"Your horses are lovely, but I may smell a bit Chancer." Bear laughed as Layla gave him a huge hug.

"I'm so happy you're here Bear, you have to tell me everything. Dad has... gone."

"Plenty of time to catch up. Let's hit the road. Don't worry, I have a feeling we'll all be together again soon. Trust your father, he's a survivor."

***

Hercules and Marcus ditched the scuba gear and swam the last few hundred metres. They dumped the fins in the surf as they made their way to the shore. Mountains in the far distance, beyond vast green plateaus rising to hillside pasture land. Hercules knew the topography and was only too aware they couldn't head back towards the city and they couldn't wander the twenty plus kilometers of beach southwards. Both too risky. The only option was through the kilometers of Parc Natural and its paddy fields and snakes.

Marcus was a little shell-shocked in his wet joggers and bare feet, but he was now used the chaos and felt like he had switched back on autopilot, the idea of chilling on a boat long gone, he was in survival mode.

103

In his flat, Dave was just putting the finishing touches to a volatile article, the files - proof in hand. Characters and circumstances now set, the human story to go with the more gruesome evidence of organ harvesting and speculations for a society where only the elite would have the privilege of old age.

What would happen once he released it? No more job, whether it brought The Company down or not and for sure a target on his back, he would have to disappear. Dave checked his bank account again.

The video of the boat explosion went viral fast, caught on phones from the beach and other vessels. The Company released a statement that they had successfully eliminated a group of dangerous criminals on the run, but wouldn't comment further.

Conspiracies spread as a posthumous video message appeared, sent from Bear. He talked about Tom Kind and the chaos his actions had triggered. Outlining their journey from Calais, Bear accused the company of targeting children and finally reported the group were headed to a boat in Valencia. This had been added to an online thread via @PeterParkRuns. It was all rumour and speculation.

Dave held the keys to the story, the identities and the truth.

It was the final puzzle piece, an end to Dave's story. Somewhere two horses ran wild, the rest all tragically died, even the dog. It was perfect for his piece, not the ending he'd have chosen, but a conclusion. In his small flat, Dave took a cold beer from the fridge and drank half of it down. One way or another today was going to be a payday.

"What about tomorrow?"

Dave sat at the desk, drinking his beer and looking out the window at the city and the people scurrying along below with their busy lives.

Taking another beer from the fridge, Dave called a number and waited patiently on hold; until after repeating himself many times he was eventually put through to someone of a high enough pay-grade.

***

In a large office at Sixty-five headquarters in the Hunter division. On an empty wooden desk in front of a huge leather chair, a phone rang.

The Director, Sofia picked up the phone and listened to a clean-up agent spill his guts.

"Yes, I am able to sanction that purchase of information. We would need all files and information gathered, no back-ups with lawyers or in-case-of-death clauses. All copies, and you are aware of our policy should you choose to double-cross us, David... Very good. On my desk by eight o'clock tonight...

Yes, I am well aware of the time, I have your personnel file and address. I expect you to gather everything you have, walk out of your door and bring it to me immediately...

Excellent, you will continue to work for us, where we can keep an eye on you. After you bring me the information, I have a salvage operation for you, in Valencia. Off the books, you seem to be good at gathering delicate information. You report directly and only to me now David...

I'm glad we understand each other, you have seventy-four minutes."

The dircctor hung up and sunk into the chair once more. Hopefully that was a PR disaster crushed. The board would not be happy with the number of agents lost, it was a huge cost to the department and company. If they weren't terrified of Sofia´s skills and what she knew, she would have been lucky to keep her job, instead she played for greater stakes as always.

104

As a camper and horse van slowly made their way though the dark, sparse Spanish hills, traversing narrow tracks of dust and stone; despite having half a tank of fuel, the horsebox started to splutter...

The END... of the beginning.

Other titles by the author

Little steps around the world
Published 2012
ISBN 978-0-9563617-9-0
A biographical family backpacking adventure. Following the experiences and adventures of a budget trip around the world with a three-year old child, through Africa, Asia and beyond.

Mud, Sweat and Tear gas
Published 2016
ISBN 978-1-909345-15-7
A biographical account from one of the many volunteers who helped refugees in the camp known as the Calais Jungle. Sharing interactions with and the stories of the humans stranded on a refuse dump just thirty miles from the United Kingdom.

Printed in Great Britain
by Amazon

45517598R00249